## ALSO BY S. CRAIG ZAHLER

*A Congregation of Jackals*

*Wraiths of the Broken Land*

*Corpus Chrome, Inc.*

# MEAN
# BUSINESS
## on
# NORTH
# GANSON
# STREET

# MEAN BUSINESS
## on
# NORTH
# GANSON
# STREET

S. CRAIG ZAHLER

THOMAS DUNNE BOOKS ❧ ST. MARTIN'S PRESS NEW YORK

THOMAS DUNNE BOOKS.
An imprint of St. Martin's Press.

MEAN BUSINESS ON NORTH GANSON STREET. Copyright © 2014 by Steven Craig Zahler. All rights reserved. Printed in the United States of America. For information, address St. Martin's Press, 175 Fifth Avenue, New York, N.Y. 10010.

www.thomasdunnebooks.com
www.stmartins.com

Designed by Steven Seighman

The Library of Congress Cataloging-in-Publication Data is available upon request.

ISBN 978-1-250-05220-9 (hardcover)
ISBN 978-1-4668-5351-5 (e-book)

St. Martin's Press books may be purchased for educational, business, or promotional use. For information on bulk purchases, please contact Macmillan Corporate and Premium Sales Department at 1-800-221-7945, extension 5442, or write special-markets@macmillan.com.

First Edition: October 2014

10  9  8  7  6  5  4  3  2  1

I wish to thank the following people—

my manager, Dallas Sonnier, for his friendship, his cackle,
and his tireless efforts on my behalf;

my father, C. Gary Zahler, for cultivating my palate,
decades of encouragement, and the initial;

my queen, Pam Christenson, for being an incredible source of joy in my life;

my mother, Linda Cooke Zahler, and my sister, Jody Zahler;

my valued supporters, Jeff Herriott, Graham Winick, Fred Raskin, Jeff
Wagner, Marty Rytkonen, William M. Miller, David Lau, Julien Thuan,
and Lydia Wills;

&

Jennifer Barnes at Raw Dog Screaming Press and Don D'Auria for
publishing my earlier novels.

# MEAN
# BUSINESS
## on
# NORTH
# GANSON
# STREET

# I

# Something Stuck
# in the Drain

The dead pigeon flew through the night, slapped Doggie in the face, and bounced to the ground, where its cold talons clicked across the pavement as it rolled east. Eyes that resembled red oysters looked to the far end of the alley.

Four men who were dressed in well-tailored suits returned the vagrant's gaze, watching him through the steam of their exhalations. At the front of the group stood a big black fellow, the one who had kicked the pigeon as if it were a soccer ball.

"Leave me the fuck alone," Doggie said from his seat atop a fine piece of cardboard.

Light flashed in the foremost individual's eyes, and steam rose from the wide nostrils of his broad nose, which resembled that of a bull. At his left shoulder stood a very slender Asian man whose pockmarked face looked as if it did not have the muscles that were required to produce a smile.

"Where's Sebastian?" asked the kicker, his left foot producing another feathered corpse.

Doggie pressed his back to the alley terminus. "I don't know anybody named Sebastian."

"Bullshit."

The big black fellow kicked the pigeon. Doggie shielded his face, and a talon tore across his right palm. Dislodged feathers zigzagged through the air like needles stitching fabric.

"Everybody in Victory knows Sebastian."

An idea navigated the damp and angry contents of the vagrant's skull and arrived at the thinking part. "Are you guys cops?"

Nobody answered the inquiry.

"Here's another one."

The big black fellow looked at the speaker, a doughy redheaded guy who had sad green eyes and wrinkled clothing. In front of his right loafer lay a splayed bird that resembled a martyr.

"Good one," said the kicker.

"I try."

Over the years, Doggie had noticed a lot of dead pigeons on the streets of Victory.

The big black fellow pulled gloves onto his huge hands, leaned over, and seized the dead bird by its head. "Hungry?" he asked, eyeing the vagrant.

"Fuck you, nigger."

Guns materialized in the hands of the two men who stood behind the pock-marked Asian as the big black fellow walked toward Doggie, carrying the pigeon corpse. Beyond the far end of the alley lay a dark, silent street.

"White bums have the worst attitudes," the redhead remarked as he inspected a hangnail. "I've always preferred the black ones."

"Me too," agreed the pockmarked Asian. "Why d'you think?"

"Well . . . a black guy who's homeless accepts being homeless. He can point to his history and say, 'This country stole my people from the motherland, shackled us, and forced us to work. Now I'm free, and I refuse to work. This country owes me—for the slave days and those shitty bus seats and a thousand other injustices—and I'm collecting for life.'"

"Restitution?"

"Exactly. Restitution. But a white guy who's homeless—it's different. There's no restitution. His parents thought he was going to college and so did he. Grad school, maybe. So he sits on the street, getting drunk, crapping his pants, thinking, 'How'd I get stuck with all these niggers?'"

The big black fellow stopped directly in front of Doggie. Suspended in the air was the dead pigeon, its belly swollen by the gases of putrefaction. Crooked feathers pointed in all directions.

"Where's Sebastian?" The kicker pivoted his wrist, and the corpse swung like a pendulum. "Tell me or it's Thanksgivin' Part Two."

Doggie did not like blacks, and they did not like him. Whenever possible, he isolated himself from his dark-skinned peers by flopping in the fringes of Victory, where he could alter his chemistry and beg for money in peace.

"Where?" The big black fellow's eyes were small and merciless.

Doggie had no friends, but he did have one acquaintance, a man who gave him liquor to deliver packages, spy on people, and act as a lookout. The name of this generous enabler was Sebastian Ramirez, and the vagrant had no intention of saying anything about this good hombre to some nigger in a jacket.

"I don't know who—"

A kneecap slammed Doggie's sternum, and he shouted. The bird filled his mouth.

"Liar," said the big black fellow.

The derelict tasted dirt and feathers as a beak scraped across his hard palate. Ineffectually, he slapped his assailant's huge hands.

The big black fellow soon withdrew the pigeon.

Blood filled Doggie's mouth and stole down his chin in a thin crimson line that resembled a serpent's tongue. Frightened and sick, he eyed his persecutor.

"Next time it goes in deeper."

"You should believe him," remarked the redhead.

The pockmarked Asian and the fourth man watched the event with what appeared to be a passing interest.

Doggie spat blood. "He ain't here."

"Where'd he go?"

The derelict could not risk alienating Sebastian, even if it meant sucking on the head of a dead bird. "Fuck you, nigger."

"He's back on that again," remarked the redhead.

A shrug curved the shoulders of the pockmarked Asian.

Frowning, the big black fellow slammed a knee into Doggie's sternum and leaned his weight forward. The derelict yelled, and was again silenced by pigeon. A salty bead that was the bird's left eyeball slid across his tongue, and as the pressure on his chest increased, a rib that had been broken by a bunch of cackling black teenagers snapped for the third time in as many years. He tried to shriek, but could only gargle feathers.

Yawning, the redhead looked at the pockmarked Asian. "What kind of gravy goes with turkey?"

"Giblet."

"I think he's about to make some."

"Not on my shoes," said the big black fellow, withdrawing the bird.

Doggie turned his head and heaved a bilious load of candy popcorn onto the asphalt.

The redhead glanced at his Asian peer. "Always wondered who ate that stuff."

"Mystery solved."

"Next time the bird goes all the way," warned the big black fellow. "Where's Sebastian?"

Doggie spat sour tastes from his mouth and wiped detritus from his beard. "He went to—"

Lightning flashed.

The redhead spun ninety degrees and fell to the ground, clutching his left shoulder as a gunshot echoed. The pockmarked Asian dragged his wounded peer behind a metal garbage bin while the big black fellow and the fourth guy slammed their backs against the opposite wall, pointing firearms.

Silence expanded throughout the alley.

Crawling toward a recessed doorway, Doggie shouted, "There're four of them! Cops! Two of them are hiding behind the—"

White fire boomed. A bullet perforated the derelict's larynx, and his skull slammed against old bricks. Bitter cold invaded his rent neck, and a heartbeat later, the pavement smacked his face. Gunshots crackled all around him, growing fainter and fainter until the exchange sounded like a deck of cards being shuffled for a game of poker.

"Wonder if he realizes how many black guys are in Hell?" asked someone in an alley that was now far, far away.

Doggie imagined cackling blacks who had horns, red eyes, sharp teeth, baggy pants, and big radios. This version of Hell was in his mind as his heart stopped.

"He looked like an atheist."

A shotgun thundered, and the big black fellow who kicked pigeons yelled.

# II

# Oblivious to Oblivion

It was December, but the hot sun that hung in the sky over western Arizona did not heed the calendar. Squinting, W. Robert Fellburn eyed the police precinct and applied the flask of liquor in his right hand to his lips. The fellow then eliminated the warm remainder, dropped the vessel, and ambled across the pavement, dragging his shadow over faded parking lot lines.

His palm landed upon the glass of a revolving door, and there, he saw a forty-seven-year-old businessman who had puffy eyes, thinning blond hair, and a wrinkled navy suit, which was dark around the armpits. Staring at his unhappy reflection, Robert arranged the errant wisps atop his head and straightened his tie. These things were done out of habit, thoughtlessly, as if he were a self-cleaning oven.

A beautiful woman appeared in his mind, and Robert pushed against his sad, pale face.

The revolving door spun, ushering the businessman into the reception area of the police precinct, where a smell that was either disinfectant or lemonade filled his nostrils. Moving his marionette legs, he proceeded across the linoleum toward the front desk, which was attended by a young Hispanic man who wore a police uniform and a mustache that looked like an eyebrow.

"Are you drunk?"

"No," lied Robert. "I was told to come in and talk to . . ." He looked at the name that he had written upon his left shirt cuff with a permanent black marker. "Detective Jules Bettinger."

"What's your name?"

"W. Robert Fellburn."

"Wait there."

"Okay."

The receptionist dialed a number, spoke quietly into the receiver, returned the phone to its cradle, looked up, and stabbed the air with an index finger. "There."

Robert stared at the digit.

"Look where I'm pointing."

The businessman traced the invisible line that led from the Hispanic fellow's finger to a nearby trash basket.

"I don't understand."

"Pick it up and take it with you."

"Why?"

"In case your breakfast decides to do some sightseeing."

Rather than contradict the rude appraisal of his condition, Robert walked over and claimed the receptacle. The Hispanic fellow then motioned to the hallway that ran along the front of the building, and the businessman began his journey across the linoleum, carrying the basket. In his mind, he saw the beautiful woman's face. Her eyes slowed time.

"Mr. Fellburn?"

The businessman looked up. Standing in the open doorway that led to the precinct's central pool of desks was a lean black man in an olive suit who was about two inches under six feet. The fellow had a receded hairline, sleepy eyes, and extremely dark skin that swallowed the light.

"You're Bettinger?"

"Detective Bettinger." The policeman motioned through the portal. "This way."

"Do I have to carry this?" Robert lifted the bucket.

"It's for the best."

Together, the duo walked down the middle alley of the central pool, between desks, officers, clerks, steaming coffees, and computer monitors. Two men played chess with pieces that were styled in a canine motif, and for some unknown reason, the sight of the crowned dogs greatly disturbed Robert.

A desk corner slammed into his hip, knocking him sideways.

"Stay focused," remarked Bettinger.

The businessman nodded his head.

Ahead of them was a faux wood wall that had eight brown doors, all of which were adorned with teal plaques. The detective motioned to the far right and followed his charge into the indicated room.

Morning sunshine bathed the office, poking Robert's brain like children's fingers.

Bettinger closed the door. "Have a seat."

The businessman sat on a small couch, rested the trash basket beside his six-hundred-dollar loafers, and looked up. "They said you're the one I'm supposed to talk to. You do the missing persons."

The detective seated himself behind the table, plucking a pencil from a ceramic cup that had an illustration of a smiling sun. "What's her name?"

"Traci Johnson."

The graphite fang moved four times. "That's with an *i* or a *y*?"

"An *i*."

Bettinger struck a line, dotted it, and continued writing.

Robert remembered how Traci had drawn a circle above the letter *i* whenever she signed her name, as if she were a sixth grader. It was an endearing affectation.

"When did you last see her?"

The businessman grew anxious. "They said I didn't have to wait forty-eight hours."

"There's no rule."

"Night before last. Around midnight."

Bettinger wrote, *Saturday the eighth. Midnight.*

"You don't put that in a computer or something?"

"A clerk does that later."

"Oh."

"Traci's black?" asked the detective.

"African American. Yes."

"How young?"

Robert looked at Bettinger's dark, square face, which was an inscrutable mask. "Pardon me?"

"How young?"

"Twenty-two," admitted the businessman.

"How would you describe your relationship with this woman?"

Filling Robert's mind was Traci's bare, caramel body, prone upon a bed of maroon silk, her lush buttocks, thighs, and breasts warmly illuminated by an array of candles that smelled like the Orient. Light glinted in the woman's magnetic eyes and upon the many perfect surfaces of the diamond that adorned her left hand.

"We're engaged."

"She lives with you?"

"Most of the time."

"Did you notice anything unusual on Saturday?"

Robert's heart raced as he recalled the evening. "She was scared—her brother was in trouble and . . . and she needed help. Didn't want to ask me, but . . ." His throat became dry and narrow.

"What's his name?"

"Larry."

Bettinger wrote this down. "What kind of trouble was Larry in?"

"He owed some people money—a lot of it. He had a gambling problem."

"Was this the first time Traci asked you to help out her brother?"

"No." Robert looked at his hands. "It happened before."

"How many times?"

"Three, I think." The businessman expelled a tremulous sigh. "She thought he'd stopped gambling after that last time—he promised—he swore that he had—but . . . well . . . he hadn't."

Bettinger returned his pencil to the coffee mug.

Robert was confused. "Don't you need to write?"

"How much?"

"Excuse me?"

"How much money did you give her on Saturday?"

"Seventy-five." The businessman cleared his throat. "Thousand."

"And the other times, the amounts were smaller—two to five thousand."

This was not said as a question, but still, Robert nodded an affirmation. A terrible feeling expanded in his stomach, spreading throughout his guts. He thought of his ex-wife, his two children, and the house that all of them had contentedly shared before he had met Traci at the VIP party last March.

"The guys her brother owed were in the Mafia," said the businessman. "She told me that . . . that they'd kill him—maybe come after her—slash her face if—"

"Want anything from the vending machine?" Bettinger asked as he rose from his desk. "I'm partial to cinnamon cakes, but I've been told—"

"Hey! This is serious!"

"It isn't. Yell again and our conversation is over."

"I'm—I'm sorry." Robert's voice was small and distant. "She's my fiancée."

"After I get my cakes, I'll pull some binders for you to look through. See if you can identify her."

"What kind of binders?"

"Prostitutes."

The businessman flung his head at the trash basket, and the frothy contents of his guts splattered the bottom of the receptacle. Convulsions that resembled orgasms wrung out his digestive tract.

"Thanks for containing that," remarked Bettinger. "Wanna come back another day?"

Dripping into the basket, Robert offered no reply.

"Let me educate you, Mr. Fellburn," said the detective. "Traci's probably skipped town by now. She has money that you gave her—willingly—which isn't the kind of thing that compels a national manhunt. And if we do happen to get her, it'll go to court, where you'll have to explain to a judge—maybe a jury—how you were driven around like a fancy golf cart by a black hooker half your age."

Robert was appalled by the thought of further embarrassing his ex-wife and children.

"Traci's beautiful?"

Inside the trash basket, the businessman nodded his head.

"And that's the glossy—a rich white middle-aged predator and some pretty young black girl. I don't think seventy-five nuggets and a diamond ring are worth going on stage for that kind of theater."

Robert raised his head and wiped his mouth as Bettinger walked across the office.

"You really thought you were going to marry Traci with an *i*?"

The businessman cleared his throat. "We're very different people . . . but it could happen. Stuff like that happens all the time."

"Not honestly."

A ponderous silence filled the room, and the detective opened the door. "We're done?"

Robert nodded his pathetic head.

"Take the bucket." Bettinger motioned outside. "And don't be such a god-damn idiot."

Ruined, the businessman rose from the couch, walked through the door, and crossed the central pool, a forty-seven-year-old bachelor who had lost his family, his money, and his dignity not because of a beautiful young whore, but because of his own weaknesses—his ingratitude, his lust, and his incredible capacity for self-deception. Robert imagined himself standing before a priest, looking into Traci Johnson's eyes, exchanging vows, and in an instant, he knew that he was a deluded and ridiculous fool, no different from the chess piece that he had seen on the policeman's desk—the dog that wore a crown on its head and thought it was a king.

It was a good thing that the businessman knew how to end his humiliation.

Resolved, he approached the front desk, slammed the trash basket over the receptionist's skull, and seized the fellow's semiautomatic pistol. A warning cry sounded within the receptacle as the officer toppled backward, blinded by puke.

W. Robert Fellburn swallowed the steel cylinder, thumbed the safety, and squeezed the trigger until his shame covered the ceiling in gray and red clumps.

# III

# A Singular-Choice Question

Bettinger watched two grimacing members of a cleaning service mount a ladder and apply brushes to the suicide's final remark. The young officer who had received a vomit crown and matching epaulets had departed early, shaken by his experience while the lobotomized corpse was taken to a place that had steel doors, an astringent smell, and digital thermometers that displayed low temperatures in both Celsius and Fahrenheit scales.

The detective opened the package that he had moments ago retrieved from the vending machine. Footfalls garnered his attention, and a man cleared his throat.

"The inspector wants to see you."

"I'll never eat these goddamn cakes."

"I think you'll have some time. The way the inspector said your name, maybe a great big heap of it."

Bettinger faced Big Tom, whose nickname referred to his impressive belly rather than his altitude, which was that of a Chinese woman. At that moment, the detective realized how much the senior clerk's head resembled an onion.

"The inspector's upset?" inquired Bettinger, more curious than concerned.

"Right after he summoned you, there was a thunderclap." The clerk motioned to a window. "But the skies look pretty clear."

Together, the two men retreated up the hall and entered the central pool, where a dozen officers glanced at Bettinger. As he secreted the cinnamon cakes in his jacket, a heaviness pressed down upon his shoulders.

"Maybe you'll have time to make pastries from scratch," remarked Big Tom. "Knead your own dough. Monitor the oven. Harvest sugar cane."

"I tried to help the guy." Bettinger attempted to sound sincere. "Honest."

"Don't be offended if I remove you from my list of emergency contacts."

A few more strides brought them to Big Tom's desk, where the porcine fellow heaved his rump into a plastic chair. Bettinger continued to the door nearby, closed his right fist, and knocked directly below a plaque that read INSPECTOR KERRY LADELL.

"Bettinger?"

"Yeah."

"Get in here." The tone of the imperative did not engender positive extrapolations.

The detective took a breath, twisted the doorknob, and pushed, revealing an office that had more pine and oak than a forest. Sitting behind the desk in a brown leather chair was Inspector Ladell, long and saturnine, his lips pursed beneath his silver mustache and baleful eyes.

"What the fuck did you say to Robert Fellburn?"

The words flew at Bettinger like bullets, eliciting glances from the central pool. "Should I close the door?"

"Answer my fucking question."

The detective shut the door.

"Don't sit."

"It's that kind of conversation?"

"Fellburn came in here for help, walked into your office, walked out, killed himself."

"Fellburn got squeezed by a black pro half his age. I illuminated the situation and offered some advice."

"Was it, 'Kill yourself'?"

"I told him to forget the money and move on."

"He moved." Inspector Ladell glanced up at the ceiling.

Bettinger sat in the chair that had been forbidden to him. "Why're you coming at me like this? He was an idiot."

"You know John Carlyle?"

The detective's stomach sank. "The mayor?"

"Not the second baseman who struck out forty-one times during his brief stint in the majors back in 1932."

Bettinger knew that this crummy conversation was about to get a whole lot worse.

Inspector Ladell popped a mint into his mouth. "Here's a singular-choice question for you. Guess who was married to Mayor Carlyle's sister up until a couple of months ago?" The boss sucked his confection. "Choice A. The man who came in here for help, walked into your office, walked out, killed himself."

"Fuck."

"That's the right word. 'Fuck.'" Inspector Ladell nodded. "Maybe if you'd said something nice to him, we wouldn't be using all this profanity."

"What does this mean?"

"Nothing good." The boss gave the mint a tour of his mouth. "Most politicians don't want to be associated with infidelity or suicide or hookers, and this Fellburn casserole's got all three ingredients."

"There's stink."

"When the mayor found out about it, he called the police commissioner directly." Inspector Ladell clicked the mint against a tooth as if he were cocking a gun. "Please take a moment to imagine the nature of this call."

Bettinger's extrapolation was instantaneous. "Where am I?"

"Did you see these?" the boss asked as he opened a catalogue and set it upon the edge of his desk. A finger poked a glossy photograph in which a woman who was far too pretty to be a police officer modeled a bulletproof vest. "A good one saves lives," the fellow remarked, turning pages until he reached a dog-eared photograph of a hunk who held a sleek assault rifle in his well-manicured hands. "And guns that don't jam are helpful when people are trying to kill you."

Inspector Ladell closed the catalogue, leaned over, and dropped it in a garbage pail.

"Because of you," he continued, "we lost all of that gear—shit I've been lobbying for since the time when black presidents were science fiction. And incredibly enough, that's not even the worst part. Commissioner Jeffrey is now no longer certain that the mayor will approve our new benefits package."

"Christ's uncle," remarked Bettinger.

Inspector Ladell reclined in his leather seat. "The commissioner and I talked. He believes that the mayor would appreciate us getting rid of a certain detective." The boss crushed the mint with his teeth and swallowed the shards. "Want another singular-choice question?"

No words came out of Bettinger's mouth.

"Is there any chance that you might just disappear somewhere?"

"As in teleport?"

Inspector Ladell nodded. "Something like that."

"Never learned how."

"Anything you can overdose on? Some medication your wife takes?"

"No. She's very healthy."

"That's unfortunate."

Bettinger needed a solid answer. "Does all this mean I'm fired?"

"I called around. Said I had a bloodhound that does really good work, a top-notch sleuth that shit on a priceless rug and can't stay in the house anymore." Inspector Ladell opened a drawer. "You know anything about Missouri?"

Chills tingled the nape of the fifty-year-old detective. He hated cold weather and thought that people who chose to live in it were aliens. Reluctantly, Bettinger pushed the conversation forward. "It's a place, right?"

"Achieved statehood a while back. Has a city in the northeast part called Victory. Heard of it?"

"Has anybody?"

"Part of the rustbelt. Had a future back when Asians were Orientals." The boss hitched his shoulder, and a manila file slid across his desk, stopped, and overhung the precipice like a diving board. "When you flush a toilet in Missouri, that's where it goes."

Bettinger opened the folder and scanned the cover sheet, which told him that Victory had an alarming number of abductions, murders, and rapes. The city looked like a hunk of third-world flotsam that had somehow drifted into the middle of America.

"They want you," stated Inspector Ladell. "They're reorganizing and need a detective. If you transfer, we'll pull the suspension."

"I'm suspended?"

"Didn't I tell you?" A shrug curved Inspector Ladell's shoulders. "At this stage, I need to hurt you or the department, and I won't even pretend there's a dilemma. You're an asshole. But I'm trying to give you something because you're talented. Go to Victory. Finish your itinerary. In four years, you can retire, come back here, and throw eggs at the mayor's house."

"Five years." Bettinger looked at a photo of a ghetto that resembled Nagasaki after the bomb, peopled by the black survivors of a concentration camp.

"You might be able to swing a transfer at some point, though I doubt it—they're desperate for badges up there."

The detective thought about his wife and children. Rubbing his temples, he looked at his boss, who had tented his long fingers.

"This is garbage."

"It is," replied Inspector Ladell. "And you earned it."

# IV

# Smudged

The detective carried a box that contained clothing and forensics books through the revolving door and into the parking lot. Walking toward his dark green sedan, he noticed a discarded whiskey flask.

"Bettinger."

The detective turned around and saw the anxious and wrinkled face of Silverberg, a man who had saved his life once and whose life he had saved twice.

"It's not right," stated the Jewish fellow. "If a civilian wants to blow his brains out, let him. I approve. So would Darwin."

Bettinger shrugged and continued toward his car, accompanied by his peer.

"Where're you going?"

"Home."

"Call if you want to get a drink. Or go to the range. Or drink at the range."

Bettinger unlocked the passenger door of his sedan and set down the box.

"You okay?" inquired Silverberg.

"Fine." The distracted detective shut the door, rounded the vehicle, and reached the driver's side.

"You still have a marker with my name on it."

"We're even."

"We aren't. Anything. Anytime. Anyplace. You can call it in."

Bettinger nodded, flung the door, and sat upon the warm upholstery. As he slotted his key, he glanced at Silverberg, who was one of the few friends that he had in the precinct. "Take care."

"Anything. Anytime. Anyplace."

The detective shut the door, jerked the gear, and departed from the parking lot of the building in which he had worked for the last eighteen years.

Suddenly, Bettinger was home. He could not recall the trip nor any navigational details like stopping or turning, but when he looked through his windshield, he saw that he had somehow arrived.

The sedan slowly drifted up the driveway toward the beige, four-bedroom house where the detective and his wife had lived since the birth of their first child. Its façade grew until it was all that he could see.

Both of the kids were still at school, and Bettinger knew that he should speak with his wife before they returned. He killed the engine, and the quietude that followed was like a headache.

Suddenly, the detective was walking toward his house, holding his keys, but not the box of possessions that he had taken from his office. Three stone steps altered his altitude, and soon he was on the landing, where he slotted metal and snapped bolts. He then entered his air-conditioned living room, discarding the circular shadow that the sun had stuck between his feet.

"Jules?"

"It's me."

Soft footfalls sounded in the den, and Bettinger turned around. Approaching him was his wife, Alyssa Bright, a black woman who had a caramel complexion, deep dimples, big eyes, a small nose, and hair that was a dandelion array of medium-length twists. Her ripped jeans were discolored by royal blue paint as were the fingertips on her left hand, her Sierra University T-shirt, and her sharp chin, which she had evidently rubbed while inspecting her art.

"Is everything okay?" asked the woman, glancing at the clock on the wall.

"I was suspended for some stupid bullshit, and the only way I can dodge a termination is by relocating to Missouri."

Alyssa was stunned.

A moment later, she padded across the room and took her husband's hands. "Is this definite?"

"Yeah. Name of the city is Victory." Bettinger snorted. "Think of the worst slum you've ever been to, shit on it for forty years, and you'll have an idea."

Alyssa pondered the thousand-pound lumps of information that her husband had just heaved onto the living room floor. "I spent some time in Missouri when I was a kid," she remarked without any fondness.

The detective looked into his wife's eyes. "We'll do whatever you want and think is best for the kids."

"Thanks for saying that." Alyssa squeezed his hands. "Is there a decent city near Victory? Someplace safe where we could live?"

"Stonesburg. Eighty-two miles away."

"A highway connects it to Victory?"

"Yeah."

"Speed limit?"

"Varies, but mostly sixty-five."

"So you'd have a ninety-minute commute each way?"

"About that."

Alyssa rubbed her chin exactly where she had earlier applied the dollop of blue paint. "Let's go online and look at Stonesburg."

"If you want to."

"I'm portable. Karen doesn't like her new school, and Gordon could use some better friends." The woman motioned to the study. "We need to see what our options are."

Certain that he had married the loveliest and most pragmatic woman in existence, Bettinger set a kiss upon his wife's mouth and slung an arm around her shoulders, which were five inches below his own.

The couple entered the study.

Alyssa flicked a switch, and a standing lamp threw light on a desk that had a computer. "You're a total baby when it comes to the cold," she said to her husband, "and you'll have to wear layers. Lots of them. Long johns and undershirts. Gloves and sweaters." She turned on the central processing unit. "Socks. Earmuffs."

"I hate it already."

The computer began to whirr, and to Bettinger, it sounded like a blizzard.

# V

# Decapitated Signs

A thin slice of nighttime remained. It was the hour of newspaper delivery guys, people who worked the late shift, and tacit weirdos. Wearing a blue parka, brown corduroy pants, and gloves, Bettinger backed a yellow hatchback out of a two-car garage in Stonesburg, Missouri. His green sedan had died after six days of cold weather (which seemed like a prophecy), and since most of the family money was tied up in bonds and the Arizona house, the detective had been forced to buy himself a cheap replacement. This lack of available funds had also impacted the quality of their new home, which was small and the color of salmon. Bettinger did not relish the idea of signing a deed of ownership in Missouri, but if the place down south sold, the family would move into a better house, and he would buy a car that did not resemble a condiment.

Clenching his jaw so that his teeth did not chatter, the detective ratcheted the heater to its maximum setting, passed the edge of the frozen grass, cut the wheel, and drove along dark suburban streets until he arrived at the interstate, which he employed. The lavender night sky glowered as he sped north.

Bettinger surveyed the local radio stations and learned some stuff about Jesus Christ, who seemed to have an especially wrathful disposition in Missouri. A preacher spoke of omnipotence, and the detective cut him off mid-sentence so that he could drive through the cold without being browbeaten. The stereo that came with the car accepted only audiocassettes, and he needed to purchase a few for his daily commute. (Gordon seemed to think that tapes—like records—were making a comeback, but Karen had been completely oblivious of the format.)

Bettinger drove north. The few cars that he saw on the road were being driven by hunched creatures that had no faces.

An hour passed.

Golden light was shining on the hem of the eastern horizon when the detective saw a bent and gunshot sign that read EXIT 58: VICTORY. He nudged his car toward the off-ramp and looked out beyond the safety rail. There lay a vast gray metropolis that resembled a capsized sewer.

Something growled deep within Bettinger's guts.

The lane veered sharply, and he dialed the wheel counterclockwise, matching the deviation. Loose stones rattled in his wake.

Ahead of the detective and down a steep decline stood a yawning mouth that was an underpass. The hatchback's headlights stabbed into the darkened enclosure, and a moment later, the vehicle was swallowed.

Muscles tightened along Bettinger's shoulders as he drove through the passage. Standing at the far end of the tunnel was a silhouetted figure who had an unnaturally long right arm. The detective slowed down, and it soon became clear to him that the asymmetrical fellow was holding a baseball bat.

Stopping the car, Bettinger glanced in his rearview mirror and saw a second man—a black fellow in an overcoat who stood seventy feet behind the hatchback. A metal pipe slid out of his right sleeve and clanked against the stone.

The trolls approached the purring vehicle. Red taillights and white high beams turned their eyes into glowing gems.

"Step out your car," said the fellow with the baseball bat.

Bettinger withdrew his gun from the holster that lay on the passenger seat and then rolled down his window. "I'm a policeman."

"No cop drives a vehicle like that," remarked the troll who carried the pipe. "It's ridiculous."

"I've got some proof I can give you." Bettinger displayed his semiautomatic. "Nine pieces."

The trolls paused.

"They're kinda hard to see," the detective added, "but I'm pretty sure you'll feel them."

"Don't," said the one who carried the baseball bat. "We just messin' wit you."

"Drop your weapons and step aside."

The trolls bolted into the shadows.

"Don't be here the next time I am." Bettinger's imperative echoed throughout the tunnel like the voice of a deity.

"We remember that car for sure," replied one of the trolls.

The detective rested his gun upon the passenger seat and accelerated. Cold poured through the open window, burning his skin as he traversed the remainder of the tunnel.

Bettinger cleared the enclosure and continued underneath the lavender sky until he arrived at a red light, where he stopped, rolled up the window, and looked for signs.

Affixed to a pole on the right side of the road was a wooden plank that read WELCOME TO VICTORY. Human excrement had been smeared across the greeting.

"Classy."

A glance at the bent sign on the opposite corner told him that he had come to a street named "Fuck Y'all"—a road that he did not at all recall from his map. The light turned green, and he accelerated, continuing down the decline. Scores of dilapidated charcoal-hued tenements drifted past, as did several nameless streets.

Lost, the detective parked the hatchback alongside the curb, reached into his glove compartment, and retrieved the wrinkled map of Victory that he and Alyssa had found online. The document had been printed on paper rather than papyrus, confounding their expectations.

Something moved in the corner of his eye.

Seizing his gun, Bettinger looked south. A big man in a hooded parka that shadowed his face was emerging from the front door of a nearby tenement building.

The detective rolled down his window and eyed the stranger. "Good morning."

"Is it?"

Bettinger pointed at a signpost that had been decapitated. "What street is that?"

"You lost or somethin'?"

"I'm trying to get to Darren Avenue."

A shrug curved the shoulders of the hooded wraith. "So?"

"Is that Darren Avenue?"

Somebody yelled something, and the stranger ducked his head as if a bullet were on its way. "Be considerate!" he shouted across the street. "People tryin' to sleep!"

Bettinger looked over. On the distant stoop stood a curved elderly person who wore kitchen mittens and no less than three bathrobes. The oldster scooped up a hideous cat (which clawed the layers of fabric to no avail) and yelled back, "I was just lookin' for my little—"

"Shut up, all of you!" advised an unseen third person. "Or I'll come down and make you quiet!"

The unwilling feline was carried into a dark opening, and the detective returned his attention to the hooded wraith.

A pale hand that was covered with lesions gestured at the hatchback. "You get that for sweet sixteen?"

"My Bar Mitzvah."

A steamy chuckle emerged from the hood, and a moment later, the wraith pointed at the intersection. "That's Leonora. Darren's the one after. At least that's how it was back when."

"Thanks."

Bettinger rolled up the window, shifted gears, and continued his tour of the decrepit fringe area, avoiding most of the dead pigeons that lay in the road. A fifteen-minute drive across Darren brought him to the major four-lane street, which some ironic ghoul had named Summer Drive.

Oriented, the detective drove north. The road was nearly empty, but what traffic there was consisted of run-down vehicles that resembled barges and flashy cars that looked like toys. As he progressed deeper into Victory, abandoned buildings were replaced by inhabited ones that were covered with iron. A billboard on the east side of Summer Drive had an advertisement in which a smiling white woman talked into her cell phone, oblivious of the spray-painted genitalia that threatened her anatomy. The hatchback had transcended the wasteland of the outer fringe and entered a region of sustained poverty.

Bettinger glanced at the map and a street sign, confirming his location, and then snapped the turn signal. Spinning the wheel counterclockwise, he drove his car onto Fifty-sixth Street.

The hatchback passed by Lonnie's Pawnshop, Checks Cashed, a grocery store named Big Shop, a somber place that looked like a funeral parlor, Baptist Bingo, and Claude's Hash House. Standing at the end of the block on the north side was a tall concrete building with an American flag and an etched sign that read POLICE PRECINCT OF GREATER VICTORY. This edifice was bright and clean.

Bettinger thought that it resembled a pillbox from World War II.

Dialing the wheel, he entered the parking lot and slotted the small car into a big space. A glance at the dashboard clock told him that he was twenty minutes early, a fact that did not surprise him since he had given himself plenty of extra time to reach his destination.

The detective killed the ignition, clipped the holster to his belt, and tucked the gun in its home. Bracing himself, the man from the southwest exited the hatchback. The cold cut through his clothes and attacked his skin.

Cursing the feeble sun, Bettinger shut the door, turned the lock, and walked toward the precinct entrance, which was made of mirrored glass like the kind that was used to cover the eyes of motorcycle cops.

He reached for the handle, and his reflection swung away from him, revealing two middle-aged men who were on their way out of the building. One was a doughy redhead in blue who had his left arm in a sling, and the other was a gaunt, pockmarked Asian in a charcoal suit.

The white fellow pointed at the hatchback as he walked outside. "Visitor parking's in the rear."

"I've got a badge."

A subtle look passed between the pair that the detective could not read. These guys knew each other well.

"Jules Bettinger," the man from Arizona said as he extended his hand. "I've been reassigned here."

"Bet you're happy about that." The redhead clasped the proffered append-age and gave it a pump. "I'm Perry."

Bettinger traded the fair-skinned hand for the one that belonged to the Asian.

"Huan."

"Nice to meet you."

The pockmarked fellow shrugged. His eyes were remote.

A few tacit nods were offered, and as the duo walked into the parking lot, Bettinger continued toward the mirrored entrance. In the reflection, he saw Perry point at the yellow hatchback.

"You still might want to park this in the rear."

"Or near a precipice," suggested Huan.

Flinging the door, Bettinger walked into the precinct. Steam continued to emerge from his face.

"May I help you?" inquired a young black woman who sat at a big desk in the middle of the receiving room, wearing a white hat, an orange parka, and a pair of mittens. Standing beside the lone interior door was an armed officer who was dressed in a woolen overcoat and scarf.

"Is the heat broken?" inquired the detective.

"No. May I help you?"

Exhaling a plume of steam, Bettinger approached the receptionist. The sen-try took very little notice of his progress.

"I'm Detective Jules Bettinger. I was reassigned to this precinct."

"Inspector Zwolinski isn't here yet, but you can wait right there—" The young woman motioned to a cold steel chair as if it were a thing upon which a human being could sit.

"I'll stand."

The receptionist wrinkled her face.

"Is the heat on?" asked Bettinger.

"A little."

"Why only a little?"

"The inspector told me to set it to forty-five."

The detective was confused. "Fahrenheit?"

"He doesn't think a police precinct should be a comfortable place." The young woman rubbed her mittens. "Really keeps people moving during winter."

The frozen sentry flapped his arms like a penguin.

Bettinger thought of Arizona.

"My name's Sharon," announced the receptionist. "What should I call you?"

The detective knew that his mind needed to be clear when he worked, not clogged with pointless anecdotes about somebody's boyfriend or pet hamster.

" 'Detective Bettinger' gets my attention."

A cartoonish frown wrinkled Sharon's face. "Okay."

The detective thrust his gloved hands inside his pockets and proceeded to a one-way window that admitted a view of the parking lot, Baptist Bingo, and the building that looked like a funeral parlor. Steam rose from his mouth, fogging the glass.

"Detective Bettinger?" inquired the receptionist, overenunciating every syllable in his name. "Would you like a coffee?"

A dark and shivering reflection nodded. "Yes, please."

Sharon rose, circumvented the desk, and disappeared inside the inner door. Her disembodied voice inquired, "Want any milk? Sweetener?"

"No, thank you."

A moment later, the receptionist returned, carrying a cup that generated more steam than did a witch's cauldron. "You have the darkest skin I've ever seen," she remarked as she extended the coffee. "Dark as this."

Bettinger accepted the beverage, which smelled flavorful and radiated warmth.

"It's like . . . outer space," Sharon added as she returned to her desk, "without the stars."

# VI

# Inspector Zwolinski

Bettinger watched Victory through the front window as he drank his coffee. At three minutes before nine, a blue town car that looked like an aircraft carrier pulled into the lot and engulfed two parking spaces. The driver's side opened, and a huge, broad-shouldered white fellow whose arms were as thick as a soccer player's thighs snatched a checkered blazer from the passenger seat and climbed outside. A hard elbow slammed the door, and the sound flew across Fifty-sixth Street and returned, echoing off of the funeral parlor. Striding toward the precinct, the man scratched his hair, which was a thick silver pelt, and wiped sweat off of a lumpy surface that housed a couple of eyes, a bunch of freckles, and a nose that looked like a root vegetable.

Bettinger suspected that the titan ate raw bricks.

"That's the inspector," said Sharon.

Upon hearing this information, the sentry stopped flapping his arms.

Inspector Zwolinski flicked his free hand, and the door fled as if it were both living and afraid. Entering the precinct, the big fellow appraised Bettinger. "When they said you were black, they weren't kiddin'."

"It's nice to—"

"You're almost purple." The inspector hurtled like a meteor toward the inner door. "Follow."

Bettinger followed.

Zwolinski tossed a candy bar onto the front desk, where it slid until it bumped against a big white phone. "That garbage will rot your teeth."

Sharon smiled as she reached for the treat. "Thank you."

"I warned you."

The sentry opened the door. "Good morning."

"Not today."

"You'll get him next time."

Bettinger noticed marks on Zwolinski's big hands as he followed him into the next room. There, buzzing fluorescent lights hung on long cords, illuminating a large and white open space where clerks and officers worked, typing, murmuring, and sifting data at mismatched desks. A narrow window sat atop each wall, framing a piece of lavender sky.

"I box before work," the inspector explained as he led the detective through the central pool. "Mondays, Tuesdays, Thursdays. Fridays if there's a worthwhile opponent."

"You favor a left uppercut."

Striding inexorably toward the far wall, Zwolinski grinned. "Lookin' for clues already."

"I haven't found an off switch."

"I like what's fallin' out of your mouth."

Bettinger surveyed the gathering, which was a variegated group of just over twenty people. Everybody was working.

"Watch your step."

The pair walked onto a dais that supported a very large desk and a cast-iron watercooler that looked like it belonged in a silent movie.

"Ever since I put that up here, people drink less." Using a curled index finger, the inspector picked up a steel chair and set it in front of his desk. "Saves time on both ends—comin' in, goin' out."

Zwolinski landed in a wooden chair, and Bettinger flattened his buttocks against the proffered square of cold metal.

"Take off that jacket if you want."

"No, thank you." The detective's reply was visible.

"How do you like Missouri?" The inspector flashed a palm that could stop a truck. "Don't go into detail—you've already got nine cases."

"Feel free to proceed to your next question."

"Okay." Zwolinski clapped his huge hands. "There's somethin' you need to understand—somethin' that sets the parameters and defines how we operate here."

Bettinger nodded.

"Most cities in this country have one law enforcement officer for every five hundred civilians," continued the inspector. "That's the average . . . though a big, rich city like New York is closer to one cop for every two hundred and fifty civilians." He gestured around the room. "We've got twenty-four guys with badges, includin' you and whoever's got a day off.

"Accordin' to the most recent census, the population of Victory is twenty-six thousand. So we're a little below what's considered the lowest acceptable ratio in this country—one cop for every thousand people."

The detective had seen this sobering statistic in the file that he had received from his previous boss.

"Looks like you knew that," remarked Zwolinski. "But that isn't quite accurate either, since there's an estimated six to ten thousand people who live in the abandoned areas—includin' the sewers—who aren't in that tally."

The detective imagined life inside of a Victory sewer.

"So," the inspector continued, "that gives each officer in this precinct about fourteen hundred people, though that's not even the bad part.

"About seventy percent of the males in Victory aged eighteen to forty-five have criminal records. And it's a good bet that the ones who live in the abandoned areas and sewers elevate that number to eighty percent—

"That's an eight followed by a zero."

Bettinger grimaced.

"So here's some ugly math." Zwolinski cracked his knuckles. "Each officer in this precinct is responsible for a minimum of seven hundred criminals, four to five hundred of whom have committed violent acts."

The detective wondered if his family should be more than eighty-two miles away from Victory.

"That's the overview," the inspector said, "and you need to keep that in mind when decidin' which cases to throw your time into. Savin' the lives of innocent people is more important than stoppin' gangs from shootin' each other. Stoppin' gangs from shootin' each other is more important than jailin' a drug dealer. Jailin' a drug dealer is more important than catchin' a car thief. Don't swat flies when there's a goddamn hornet in the room."

"Understood." Bettinger was heartened by the idea of having a boss who was a sensible policeman rather than a bureaucrat.

"There are three things that close cases: work, luck, and bad-guy stupidity. You can only control the first thing, and lots of times, it isn't enough. And since you'll always—always—have more cases than you can handle, your most important decision becomes which cases you go after."

"I can prioritize," responded the detective.

"Your partner's wayward." The inspector pointed across the room. "The big black guy with the bandages."

Bettinger looked in the indicated direction. Sitting at a warped desk was a very large, well-built black fellow who had an olive green suit, a nose like a bull, and white gauze on his face and neck. His small eyes were focused on a computer that had survived the nineties.

"His name's Dominic Williams."

Bettinger faced his boss. "Wayward?"

"He broke some laws and got some bad press, so I reprimanded him and his partner—turned 'em into corporals. I think—I hope—Dominic's a fly and not a hornet. You know the difference?"

"A fly pinches a bag of weed after a bust. A hornet plants evidence, leans on civilians for money, and shoots people he doesn't like."

"Right." Zwolinski scratched his silver pelt. "You don't seem like an ass-hole."

"Give me time."

"You're with him now. Don't let him get away with anythin'—even fly stuff."

"I'll be strict."

"Go over these." The inspector pointed at a stack of folders that was a five-inch edifice. "Start with the case on top—a murder that turned into multiple acts of necrophilia."

The detective leaned over and claimed the documents. "Whoever did that isn't going back to his wife for missionary twice a week."

"Right." Zwolinski gestured at the floor. "Get to work."

# VII

# Thanks for the Epilogue

Carrying files that weighed more than a lunch, Bettinger walked toward Dominic Williams. The seated officers whom he passed were so engrossed in their work that they did not even seem to notice his shadow drift across their desks. Soon, the detective arrived at his destination, where he tucked the collection of documents under his left arm, removed his gloves, and extended his right hand.

"Jules Bettinger."

Dominic glanced at the proffered appendage as if it might spit venom. "You a real bloodhound or IA?"

"The earlier."

"Sounds like you went to college." This remark was not a compliment.

"And graduate school."

"You look like a fuckin' eclipse."

The detective lowered his hand and dropped his files upon the big fellow's desk. "What've you got on Elaine James?"

"Who?"

"Murder victim found in a shop on Ganson Street. Sodomized postmortem. Repeatedly."

"White chick?"

"Yeah."

Dominic's brow wrinkled, and the bandages on his face migrated toward its center. His thought process appeared to involve a lot of muscles.

"Got anything other than her skin color?" inquired Bettinger.

The big fellow shrugged.

"Seen the body?"

"Yeah." Dominic pointed at the file.

"Just the pictures?"

"There're a bunch of 'em."

"Let's go to the morgue."

"Go ahead. I'm on this here—" The big fellow slapped his computer, which displayed the mug shots of two young white thugs.

Bettinger fingered the Elaine James file. "This is our priority."

"'Our'? We're engaged?"

"Inspector Zwolinski partnered us. And to be clear about things, you're a corporal, and I'm a detective."

Fury flashed in Dominic's small eyes, and Bettinger half expected him to launch a fist.

A moment later, the big fellow calmed himself and shook his head. "Nigga is provocative."

"You know where the morgue is?"

"I know where the fuckin' morgue is. I've worked Victory for—"

"Shut off your computer and let's go."

Bettinger slid his hands back into his gloves, picked up the Elaine James file, and walked toward the exit, followed by his new partner.

The big fellow settled in the driver's seat of his silver luxury car while the detective closed the passenger door. Purring, the vehicle glided through the lot.

"I won't even bother," Dominic remarked as they passed by the little yellow hatchback.

The silver car sped east on Fifty-sixth and turned south on Princess Drive, a wide road that paralleled Summer but was in far worse condition. Neither man said anything during the course of the twenty-minute ride. Soon, the vehicle landed in the parking lot of the John the Baptist Hospital of Greater Victory, which was a large mint green building. A three-minute walk brought the policemen to a lobby of the same color, a place that was inhabited by overweight attendants, groaning oldsters, and the smell of urine. The pair proceeded to a bank of elevators, and as Dominic stabbed a cracked button with an index finger, Bettinger notice the nine bullet holes that were in the ceiling directly above the registry desk.

A bell chimed, and an old Hispanic woman in a hospital gown ambled out of the lift, rolling a metal stand from which depended two bags of rose-hued fluid. The big fellow walked past her, as did the detective, who looked back and saw the patient's exposed spine.

Dominic fingered the button for the sixth floor, and the door closed, squeaking across old grooves. The elevator then launched itself into the air.

Bettinger clasped a rail, steadying himself. "Morgue's on six?"

"Nope. Just wanna see my grandma."

"You don't seem like the type."

"Who'd visit his grandma?"

"Who'd have one that wanted him to visit."

"Asshole."

"Morgue's on six?"

The big fellow nodded his head, and the bell chimed.

Together, the policemen exited the elevator and walked down a badly lighted vanilla corridor that had a wrinkled floor. Bettinger stumbled on a warped piece of linoleum and quickly regained his balance.

Curvature appeared on Dominic's chin. "Mind the floor."

"Thanks for the epilogue."

The pair passed through three lighted patches and stopped outside a closed wooden door, which had a placard that read MEREDITH WONG. No letters followed the woman's name, and Bettinger unhappily surmised that the person who handled corpses in a city with a terrifying murder rate was a coroner and not a medical examiner.

"What?" inquired a hostile female.

The big fellow flung the door and strode inside, followed by his partner.

Perched on a stool behind a tall table was Meredith Wong, a plump Asian woman who wore a smock and a frown. "Make an appointment like everybody else," she said as a guy in a rubber monster suit chased a blond girl across the screen of a black-and-white television.

"You don't look busy," said Dominic, pointing at the movie.

"I'm on my break."

"Take it later."

"Get the hell out of my office."

Bettinger interposed and extended a hand toward the coroner. "I'm Detective—"

"Make an appointment."

"We're on official business, and we need to see the body of a murder victim."

"I'm watching a monster chase a girl through the Bayou, and I need to see if she gets eaten."

Bettinger swallowed his irritation and framed a polite response. "What time should we come back?"

Meredith Wong appraised the rubber monster's abilities. "An hour."

As the policemen left the room, the blonde screamed, and the coroner cackled.

Bettinger walked across the hospital lobby toward a vending machine that looked like it had been attacked by a jaguar. He stopped and peered into its guts, which were empty, except for some fiber bars. Stomach growling, the detective glanced at the big fellow, who was in the far corner on a vinyl couch, thumbing a text message into his cell phone.

"Is that diner any good?"

"What?" inquired Dominic, without looking up.

"Is that diner any good? Claude's?"

"Disgustin'."

"Where do you eat around here?"

"Claude's."

"Even though it's bad?"

"They've got two dishes that won't kill you."

"Which ones?"

The big fellow shrugged.

Pulling on gloves, Bettinger walked toward the exit. "Let's go."

"Let me finish this."

"Now, Corporal. We need to be back for our appointment with Wong."

Dominic continued to type as he unstuck himself from the couch. "'Bettinger' has two *t*'s, right?"

"Yeah."

"'Fuckface' is one word or two?"

The policemen exited the hospital, entered the silver car, shared eighteen minutes of rolling silence, and landed in front of Claude's Hash House. Striding toward the squat red diner, Bettinger looked through its front window and saw a rotating cake display, six hunched customers, and a lot of empty seats. A bell jingled as he opened the door.

"Table for two?" inquired a cheerful, six-foot-tall blond woman who looked like a marathon runner.

"We're not sitting together," replied the detective.

Dominic strode past his partner toward the rear of the diner. "I'll be at my usual."

The waitress led Bettinger to a corner booth, where he sat on cracked plaid upholstery and received a menu.

"I'm Chris," said the woman. "Would you like something to drink?"

"Coffee, please. And what's the best thing on the menu?"

"Fried shrimp. Or the smothered pork chops with red-eye gravy, though lots of people like the snoot."

"Snoot?"

Chris tapped her nose. "Pig snout—it's deep-fried. Comes on a toasted bun with some barbecue sauce."

There was a gurgling event inside of Bettinger's guts. "When you fry a snout it becomes a snoot?"

The woman wrinkled her face. "I'm from Michigan."

"I'll take the pork chops."

"Side of snoot?"

"Snootless."

Chris flashed an easy grin and vanished into the kitchen.

Three minutes later, the food arrived. Its near-instantaneous delivery caused Bettinger to suspect that the cook was a guy with a microwave, but when he examined the steaming pile, it looked and smelled delicious. His subsequent oral investigation proved to be disappointing (the flavors were dull, and the pork was threaded with gristle), but the food was edible.

As the detective neared the bone of his third and final chop, the black luxury car that he had earlier seen outside of the precinct pulled into the lot and spread its wings, yielding the redheaded cop named Perry and his pockmarked Asian contemporary, Huan. The pair entered the diner, walked directly to the back, and sat across from Dominic, who drank a chocolate milkshake.

Something flashed outside the diner, and Bettinger returned his attention to the window. A gray luxury car had landed in the lot, and its driver was approaching the door. The fellow was a silver-haired white man who had a nose like a scavenger's beak, black sunglasses, and a navy blue suit. As he passed by the waitress, the detective was able to estimate his height, which was no more than three inches over five feet.

Quick strides carried the diminutive man to the back of the diner, where Dominic slid into the bench, opening up a seat. The new arrival claimed the space, tilted his head forward, and began a quiet conversation. Nobody was smiling.

Bettinger sipped his coffee, watching a meeting that he suspected had been arranged by his partner's text messages. Almost every statement made by Dominic or Perry or Huan was followed by a look at the diminutive fellow, and it was clear that he was someone to whom they deferred.

A glance at the clock on the wall told the detective that he and his partner needed to return to the hospital for their meeting with the coroner. After paying the bill, he rose from his bench and strode toward the back of the diner.

"Corporal Williams."

The diminutive fellow climbed out of the booth, opening up a passageway for Dominic, who then slid his bumper across the plaid. Bettinger nodded his head at Perry and Huan.

"Don't tug that 'Corporal' line too hard," the doughy redhead advised, "or you'll pull in a great white."

"A black one," added the pockmarked Asian.

The small man slid a steak knife into his coffee and stirred. His face was pink and bone white, discolored by vitiligo, and his eyes were hidden behind his sunglasses.

"Out of spoons?" inquired Bettinger.

No response issued from the mottled man. Metal clinked against porcelain as he stirred the black beverage.

Bettinger turned around and strode across the diner, followed by Dominic. Outside, they proceeded toward the silver vehicle.

The detective eyed the big fellow's reflection. "Was that little guy your previous partner?"

Dominic shrugged.

"Your memory isn't so good."

# VIII

# Some Pairs

Flickering fluorescent lights illuminated the nude corpse of Elaine James, which lay on a plank that Meredith Wong had seconds ago withdrawn from the morgue wall.

Bettinger surveyed the victim. Her pale body was covered with abrasions and iridescent bruises (especially around her neck), and all of the flesh had been rubbed off of her knees, exposing her off-white patellae. Sitting in the middle of her gasping face was a crushed nose that was the color of an eggplant.

The twenty-seven-year-old woman had died in agony.

Dominic looked up from his cell phone. "Her implants are still goin' strong."

"Why's she in minus?" asked the detective.

The coroner was confused by the policeman's question.

"Why is she in negative temperature?" clarified Bettinger. "Frozen?"

"Nobody's claimed her yet." The woman pointed at a chart on the wall. "She gets two weeks before cremation. Standard procedure."

"We need to—" Something snagged the detective's attention. "What's that under her tongue?"

Dominic and Meredith Wong looked at the corpse's open mouth, and Bettinger switched on his penlight. The beam shone past smashed teeth and upon the bottom tip of her tongue, illuminating a tattoo of four inverted teardrops.

"Hold on." The coroner walked over to a sink, filled a paper cup with warm water, and returned to the body. Then she brought the beverage to the dead woman's mouth.

"Wait," cautioned Bettinger. "You don't want to crack—"

Meredith Wong upended the cup, and the corpse hissed, fog billowing from its mouth and nostrils. The coroner then donned a latex glove, seized the tongue, and pulled. Frozen blood crackled.

The detective leaned closer, shining his penlight. Tattooed to the underside of Elaine James's tongue was a hairy phallus that squirted four teardrop-shaped bullets.

Meredith Wong contemplated the penis as if she were a math professor. "Hmmm. Didn't see this."

Bettinger looked at Dominic. "You've seen a mark like this before?"

"No."

The detective was not convinced that the big fellow was telling the truth. "Any idea what it might mean?"

"Dick was her favorite flavor?"

"Be polite," said Bettinger. "And take a picture of it with that phone you're so excited about."

"Whatever."

The detective returned his attention to the coroner. "We'll need to do an autopsy."

"Because she has a tattoo?" asked Meredith Wong, annoyed.

"Because she was murdered." Bettinger let his words settle inside the woman's head. "We need to get evidence before you incinerate her."

"I already swabbed semen from her vagina and rectum, and the cause of death is known." The coroner pointed to the iridescent, bluish-black indentation that encircled the corpse's neck. "She asphyxiated."

The detective was surprised that the woman knew such a big word. "You've performed forensic autopsies?"

"Of course I have. Who else would?"

Bettinger thought, *A qualified medical examiner,* but did not voice his inflammatory response. "When can you have the body ready for autopsy?"

"Tomorrow morning."

"What time?"

"Ten thirty."

Dominic looked over. "There aren't any movies?"

"Muzzle that." Bettinger returned his attention to Meredith Wong. "We'll be here at ten thirty."

"Make it eleven."


Bettinger scanned the Elaine James file as the elevator carried him and his partner toward the lobby. Locating the address, he said, "We're going to six twenty-four Ganson Street."

"That's where they found the body?"

"So you were a detective."

"You got any idea where that is? Ganson Street?"

"My driver does."

The elevator chimed like a bell in a boxing match, and the policemen entered the lobby, where an elderly black man kicked the vending machine in a futile attempt to free one of the fiber bars.

Dominic pulled a few quarters from his pocket and gave them to the oldster, who was too angry to thank him.

# IX

# A Big, Educated Maybe

The silver car sped west on Fifty-sixth Street. Twenty minutes later, it carried its two silent inhabitants from the edge of the lower-middle-class area into a dilapidated region that resembled the one through which Bettinger had driven earlier that morning. Poverty surrounded the policemen, and overhead, the sun hid behind dirty clouds.

"What's this part called?"

"The Toilet."

The detective saw an abandoned building that was covered with so much graffiti that its original color was now a fable. "This whole area's like this?"

"Gets worse up north."

"That's possible?"

"Very."

"What's that part called?"

"Shitopia."

On the far corner, Bettinger noticed a dead cat that had been nailed by its head to a telephone pole. "Christ's uncle."

"You gonna object to some music?" inquired Dominic.

"You listen to that shit that glorifies violence, criminality, and misogyny?"

"Rap?"

"That's what I described."

The silence that followed this reply was an obvious affirmation. Gordon played rap music at home, claiming that he enjoyed it "for the beats," but Bettinger would not suffer it at work as well.

Ten quiet blocks later, the big fellow broke the silence. "So we just listen to each other breathe?"

"We can discuss the case."

Dominic ignored the suggestion, tapping the wheel with his fingers as if he were experiencing some kind of rap music withdrawal.

Bettinger asked, "What do you think about that tattoo on Elaine James's tongue?"

"Dick."

"And?"

"And nothin'." There was a defensive edge to Dominic's voice, as if he did not want to look stupid.

"What do you think she did for a living?"

"What'd the file say?"

"She's been collecting unemployment for three years."

"Glad to see taxes payin' for things like fake tits and dick tattoos on white girls." The big fellow guided the car away from a pothole. "America."

"That obviously wasn't her only income. Her apartment's in a decent area—relatively speaking—and she had fifteen nuggets in her safe."

Dominic raised an eyebrow. "Fifteen grand?"

"Yeah."

"So what do you think?"

"I think she made a living with her hide and just collected because she could."

"She had the equipment."

"And that tattoo . . . it's her only one, it's vulgar, and it's in a painful place. Not the kind of ink a girl usually gets the first time."

"She probably just wanted a little dick to wiggle."

"Seems like something she might've been forced to get," posited Bettinger. "Maybe something a pimp makes all of his girls get—like a cattle brand. A label that says, 'This property belongs to me,' or maybe, 'This girl is under my protection.'"

Dominic spun the wheel clockwise, guiding the car onto a riven street that ran north. "That's a big bucket of 'maybes' you got."

"Educated ones."

"Like you, Detective." The words were not said with any affinity. "A big, educated maybe."

"Turning maybes into yesses is what I do."

"Mr. Humble."

"Modesty's a form of dishonesty I don't subscribe to."

Applying the brakes and cutting the wheel, Dominic turned onto a dirt road where the pavement was kept in heaps. The silver car rattled, and a moment later, the big fellow flung the vehicle around a bent sign, which read GAN-SON STREET. Tires ground gravel into grit and pounded that into dust as the automobile rumbled north.

"Shitopia," announced Dominic.

Bettinger scanned the area. The sidewalks and streets were deserted, and the tenement windows were nothing but black openings, wholly bereft of glass. Vandals had not even bothered to put their initials on these buildings.

The detective's theory was confirmed by what he saw. "Elaine James—blond, white, pretty, with engineered cleavage and fifteen nuggets in her safe—isn't working out here." He tapped his index finger against the window. "This is where her abductor brought her."

"Then why're we botherin'?"

"Same reason we're doing the autopsy."

"What's that?"

"Looking for crumbs—things that were missed."

"'Cause everyone out here's so incompetent?"

"We don't have anything solid right now—just a handful of maybes. Going to the crime scene and requesting an autopsy are standard procedures."

The silver luxury car rolled past a street that was blocked off by an overturned pickup truck, which had been torn open like a zebra on the plain.

Dominic motioned to the wreck. "The procedures are different out here."

"They're not different anywhere—that's why they're called 'standard.'"

Snorting derisively, the big fellow flashed his hand.

Bettinger saw a building that had some of an address, and he surmised that the crime scene was on the opposite side of the street and a little to the north. A few moments later, the silver car entered a strip of abandoned shops and landed outside a red market that was adorned with police tape, which had been cut up and turned into celebratory festoons. The big fellow killed the engine, pocketed his keys, and withdrew his gun (which was a semiautomatic with an extended clip), while beside him, the detective armed himself.

Brandishing weaponry, the policemen stepped onto Ganson Street.

Harsh wind seared Bettinger's face and eyes. Although it was still midday, the temperature seemed to have dropped fifteen degrees since he was last outside.

The policemen surveyed the hundreds of black windows that yawned on either side of the street, any one of which might conceal a crook. Nothing was visible beyond these openings but shadows and ruin.

The detective and the big fellow hastened directly to the store that contained the crime scene. Pressing their shoulders to the façade, they examined the entrance.

The door was ajar.

Bettinger leaned forward and looked through the opening.

Nothing stirred within the dark interior.

The policemen exchanged a nod and attached tactical lights to their weapons.

"Police!" shouted Dominic, loud enough to make his partner's ears ring. "If anybody's in there, let us know right fuckin' now!"

The words echoed and died.

Nobody responded.

Bettinger flashed four fingers at the big fellow, who nodded in response.

"We'll count to ten," said the detective. "One." He let the number echo inside of the store. "Two." Again, he paused. "Three," he said, raising his firearm. "Four."

Dominic slammed an elbow into the door. "Police!"

"Don't move!" shouted Bettinger, pointing his gun inside. Nothing stirred within the darkness, excepting the dust that swirled like a specter around the beam of his tactical light. A smell like a homeless man's armpit climbed into his nostrils.

"We're coming in," announced the detective. "If you're hiding, come out. If you're a rat or dog, learn English."

Bettinger strode into the market, breathing through his mouth and scanning the aisles, while behind him, Dominic straddled the entryway. Although the detective did not have a high estimation of his partner, it was clear that the guy could shoot things.

Bettinger walked across rotten floorboards toward a battered front counter that had six off-white lumps, each of which was decorated with a series of gray lines and squares. He soon recognized that these masses were moldering newspaper deliveries.

"There's a guy watchin' us from down the block," reported Dominic.

Bettinger glanced at his partner, who stood silhouetted in the doorway. "Doing anything?"

"Just watchin'."

The detective circumvented the counter and entered the far aisle, where his tactical beam illuminated something that knotted his stomach. Lying on the floor fifteen feet away from him was a severed human head. Tangled brown hair covered most of its face.

Bettinger turned to Dominic and called out, "Where's the civilian?"

"Stayin' put."

"Let me know if the situation changes."

"Like if he gets a bazooka?"

"Like that."

Pointing his tactical light at the severed head, Bettinger walked up the aisle. Floorboards groaned beneath his boots, and as he drew nearer, he saw that something was wrong with the blood that surrounded the bodiless specimen.

It was the color of ketchup.

The detective stopped and looked over his shoulder.

Nobody was there.

Facing forward, he swept his tactical light across the ground between his boots and the severed head, and in that space, he saw an open newspaper. Unlike the sodden periodicals on the front counter, this one was still white.

Bettinger kneeled beside the newspaper and swept it clear, revealing a shallow hole that contained the sharp, stainless-steel teeth of a bear trap.

"Christ's uncle."

"See anything?" inquired Dominic.

Bettinger shone his tactical beam up the aisle, illuminating a dirty rubber mask and a brown wig. Suddenly, the setup was clear: The fake head was there to lure some hapless police investigator into the bear trap.

"They don't like cops here, do they?" asked the detective.

"Somebody leave a message or somethin'?"

"Something."

The detective doubted that a necrophile would return to a crime scene to set up what was essentially a very nasty prank. Most likely, this bit of stainless-steel ugliness had been arranged by some civilian who just hated policemen.

Bettinger claimed an unopened can from the shelf and threw it into the hole. Steel teeth flashed, and the tin ruptured, spilling coffee grounds.

"The fuck was that?" asked Dominic.

"A bear trap."

"Man . . . haven't seen that in a while." The big fellow's remark sounded nostalgic.

Looking at the device that could have removed his foot, Bettinger knew for the first time how much the people of Victory hated the system and its servants.

Dominic leaned outside. "We saw your bitch-ass bear trap, nigga!"

"Why're you yelling that?" asked the detective.

"He's runnin' off."

"Is that a strategy?" Bettinger was incredulous. "This thing could've taken off my foot, and you—"

"He ain't the one that set it—the nigga who hangs out never is. But you missin' the point. He bolted. He's gone."

Suddenly, the detective understood. "No more traps?"

"The big, educated maybe just got himself a yes."

# X

# Insectile Witness

Bettinger stepped over the frozen puddle of ketchup and walked to the back of the store. Outside the office, he swept his light in every direction, divining rotten boxes, moldering floorboards, and rusty shelves, inspecting everything until he was satisfied that there were no more nasty surprises awaiting him.

The detective seized the doorknob with a gloved hand and twisted it around. Metal squeaked, and the latch clicked. Gently, he nudged the office door forward a fraction of an inch.

Bettinger retreated to a near aisle and picked up a can of coffee, which he then threw. The projectile clanked against the wood, knocking the door wide open.

"Police!"

Employing the tactical light, the detective scanned the office. The room appeared to be uninhabited.

Bettinger strode inside and pointed his weapon at the concrete floor, illuminating a pair of reddish-brown stains. Atop the dried blood were hundreds of pale flecks that had once been the victim's knees.

"You still alive?" inquired a distant voice that belonged to Dominic.

"I'm at the scene."

"Keep a eye out for big black footprints. And also a handkerchief with initials."

Bettinger would have paid fifty dollars for a working lightbulb and ten times as much money for a new partner.

The detective withdrew a knife, thumbed the blade until it clicked into place, and kneeled beside the stains. There, he closely examined the yellow pieces of detritus, which were from the victim's hypodermis, and the narrow white shards, which were bone splinters. The human debris yielded no new data.

Bettinger stood up, stepped back, and circled the evidence. All of the bloodstains and smears were perfectly parallel, indicating that Elaine James had not struggled during the sex acts that had occurred on the floor of this office. It seemed possible that she had been murdered in some other location and brought here afterward for the acts of necrophilia.

Although the detective loved his twelve-year-old daughter as much as he loved his son (and oftentimes, far more), investigations such as this one made him doubt the wisdom of bringing a woman into the world of hideous men.

"Find anythin'?" The acoustics of the market turned Dominic's voice into something that came out of a child's walkie-talkie.

"Looking."

The detective panned the tactical light along the dark seam that joined the floor to the wall. Something flashed, and he stilled his hand, illuminating a crevice.

Two antennae twitched.

It was then that Bettinger beheld the largest cockroach that he had ever seen, which was remarkable since he had thrice visited Florida with his wife and kids. Slowly, he approached the creature, which boldly held its ground.

"You see what happened here?"

Antennae waggled like the eyebrows of a sage who answered every question that he was asked with a question that made no sense.

Bettinger turned away from the bug and began a slow and systematic inspection of the floor, looking for anything that had not been visible in the shabby (and incomplete) crime scene photos. The cold sneaked under his parka during this tiny activity, and soon, he was shivering.

A glance at the crevice confirmed that the cockroach was still interested.

"I'm gettin' hungry," Dominic announced to his partner, the bug, and the entire block.

Bettinger was two strides away from the end of his floor inspection when he saw something. Kneeling, he looked at the anomaly, which was a collection of intersecting scratches. These radiated from a central point that was a little bit deeper, but still quite superficial. No more than two feet away from this asterisk was a second, very similar mark. A glance to his right showed him one more collection of scratches.

Bettinger stood up, stepped back, and looked at the evidence. Together, the three asterisks formed a perfect equilateral triangle.

The realization of what he was looking at hit him a moment before the pang of revulsion.

"A goddamn tripod."

Disgusted, the detective finished his inspection of the office and returned it to its owner, the cockroach.

"Nigga made a movie?" Dominic posited as he drove his silver luxury car south on Ganson Street. "Like a snuff movie?"

"I don't think she was killed in that office."

"He filmed it when she was dead?" The big fellow turned onto the dirt street where the pavement was kept in piles. "Sounds pretty fuckin' boring."

"I might use an adjective other than 'boring.'"

"'Adjective.'" Dominic repeated the word as if it might put warts on his tongue.

"If we don't get anything from the autopsy, we'll interview prostitutes—try and find another who's got the same tattoo or who knows something about it."

"I was doin' other stuff before you started this here. I got important things t—"

"Now you're doing this," interrupted Bettinger.

Dominic tightened his fists on the wheel. His bandages rippled, but he said nothing.

The car proceeded south.

Soon, the policemen exited Shitopia and entered the Toilet, where the twilight sun painted cracked streets and broken civilians the color of urine. Although it was past four o'clock in the afternoon, most of these people looked like they were just waking up.

# XI

# Disregarding Mauve
# and White

Wearing jeans and a sweater and weighed down by a warm dinner, Bettinger entered the study that was located in the rear of his Stonesburg home. He traversed the small room in two strides and sat in front of his computer, surrounded by mauve, the unfortunate color that the previous (evidently blind) residents had chosen to paint the walls.

Turning on the CPU, Bettinger began his second investigation of the day. This one did not require the assistance of his partner.

He typed the words "Dominic," "Williams," "Police," and "Missouri" into a slot and fingered the Enter key. Over twenty million hunks of ether matched this search criteria. Subsequently, he refined his data, adding quotation marks and the words "Victory" and "Detective." Again, he fingered the Enter key.

The top line of the screen declared, *3,842 search results.*

Bettinger looked at the first listing, which read, "Brutality Charges Against Two Victory Police . . ."

He stabbed the ellipses with a tiny arrow and clicked a button. A wheel spun and was replaced by a digital article that resembled a real newspaper (including artificial folds and tears, which were silly).

The headline stated, "Brutality Charges Against Two Victory Police Detectives Are Dropped in Sebastian Ramirez Case. Suspect Remains in Critical Condition." Photographs of Dominic Williams and the short, aquiline fellow with vitiligo were directly below this headline. Beside these images was a grainy picture of a bandaged Hispanic man, the machine that kept him alive, and two unhappy females. The article was from November.

Somebody knocked on the door. The height of the concussion and its volume told Bettinger that it was Alyssa.

"Yes?"

"Can I come in?"

The detective shut off the monitor. "Sure."

The woman strode into the room, tightening the belt of the green robe that she wore over her pajamas. "Pretty late for your first day."

"I need to get oriented."

"Okay." Alyssa was curious by nature, but rarely pried. "Karen's upset."

"I saw that at dinner. She'll talk when she's ready to talk."

"I'm concerned."

Bettinger was the parent who dealt with Karen when she was troubled, and Alyssa was the one who handled Gordon. For many years, these had been the assignments.

"I'll talk to her in a few minutes."

Relief shone upon the painter's face, as if her husband had already fixed the problem. "Thank you."

"Of course."

"And if you get to bed before midnight, I'll be open for business."

"Expect a customer."

Curvature appeared on Alyssa's chin.


Eight minutes later, the detective stood outside his daughter's room and knocked upon her flimsy door.

A small throat was cleared. "Yes?"

"Do you want to talk?"

Bettinger heard a sniffle rather than a reply. Karen cried far less often than did most girls her age, and the sound was significant.

"May I come in?"

Silence followed his inquiry.

"Karen?"

"I don't want to talk about it."

"You don't have to. But you need to pay your rent."

Again, the girl sniffled. "What?"

"I usually get a hug when I come home from work. Sometimes, after dinner or when I'm helping you with a project. I didn't get one today and you owe me."

Karen cleared her throat. "Okay."

Bettinger gripped the doorknob, which rocked in its housing, but did not turn. "Want me to pick the lock?" he inquired. "I've got tools."

"I'll get it."

Footfalls approached, and a button clicked. As the little walker retreated, the detective nudged the door open.

Karen sat at the head of her bed, looking down at her folded legs, which were covered by a wool blanket. The girl's lean torso was lost inside her father's sweatshirt, one of several hand-me-downs that she preferred to her pajamas.

Bettinger entered, shut the door, and padded across the carpet to Karen, whose large eyes were red and dripping. A lump materialized in the detective's stomach as he sat beside his daughter.

Bettinger opened his arms. "Time to pay up."

Karen leaned into her father, mashing her face against his chest. Two small limbs encircled his back.

Today was the beginning of the girl's second week in Stonesburg Junior High, and Bettinger knew that whatever was upsetting her had occurred in that place. It was a reputable public school, but its racial demographic looked like something that had been washed in bleach.

"If you're not ready to talk about it, that's okay," the detective said as his daughter's tears warmed his sweater. "I just need to ask you two things. Did anybody hurt you?"

The wet mush that pressed against his chest slid left and right, and his apprehensions diminished.

"Did anybody threaten to hurt you?"

Again, the girl shook her head.

"Okay." The detective patted his daughter's narrow back and placed a kiss upon the perfect part that lay directly between her pigtails. More than likely, her unhappiness was caused by some hurtful words and could be discussed whenever she was ready to have a conversation. "Do you want me to tuck you in?"

Karen clutched her father like a little wrestler, and for a moment, Bettinger feared that she might smother herself.

"It was just boys talking." The girl sniffled. "That's all."

Bettinger did not know what this meant. "Were they calling you names? Things like that?"

"No." Karen released her father and sat upright, wiping her eyes. "I don't know why I'm crying. They weren't even talking to me."

"What were they saying?"

"I can't." The girl shook her head back and forth. "I can't say it."

"What kinds of things?"

Karen stared at the blanket that covered her folded legs. "Dirty."

"Sexual?" This was a word that Bettinger could not recall using in front of his daughter, who was twelve.

Karen nodded her head. "They were talking about that stuff at lunch. They were sitting behind me and—and—and talking real loud about the kinds of things that black girls do."

Fury paralyzed the detective, and for a moment, he imagined himself slapping the faces of little blond rednecks. Relocating his anger to a back alley, he took his daughter's hands and cleared his throat. "Can you sit somewhere else at lunch? Away from these boys?"

"Yeah. It's not assigned seats."

"Then sit somewhere else. And if they follow you around—talking like that—let me know." Again, Bettinger imagined violence.

"Okay."

The detective hugged his daughter, trying not to think of Elaine James's corpse. "Should I shoot them?"

"Not yet."

# XII

# Reading Her Insides

"Bettinger!" The name rebounded throughout the white pillbox and landed inside of an uncommonly dark ear.

Breathing steam and wearing a parka over his blazer, the detective from Arizona rose from his desk, traversed the precinct, and carried a steel chair across the dais to the inspector's desk.

Zwolinski pointed a thick finger at Dominic, who sat on the far side of the enclosure. "Corporal Williams doesn't look delighted."

"He isn't." Bettinger winced when his buttocks struck cold metal.

"Keep him that way."

"I'll do my best."

"Is the Elaine James case worth a big chunk of police time?"

"It is."

"Where are you?"

"We've got an autopsy at eleven, and we're talking to hookers, since she was one."

Thick hands rubbed a purple bruise that the inspector had earned earlier that morning in a boxing match. "The file said she was a parasite."

"She collected checks, but that was just gravy. The woman has a condominium."

"Any ideas on the necrophile?"

"No. But he manufactures his own evidence."

Zwolinski's eyebrows climbed toward his silver pelt. "How so?"

"There was a camera at the scene."

"I like what's fallin' out of your mouth."

The boss dismissed the detective, gesturing with a hand that had knocked two teeth out of another man's face earlier that morning.

———

Light glared on the stainless-steel blades of the enterotome that cut across the corpse's esophagus and duodenum. A moment later, Meredith Wong extracted a purplish-red sack from between the severed pipes, placed it in a kidney-shaped pan, and claimed a scalpel.

Bettinger monitored the autopsy, flanked by Dominic, who typed text messages with thumbs that seemed too large for grammar.

Meredith Wong punctured the stomach wall, inserted the bottom blade of the enterotome into the incision, and cut across tissue that squeaked like rubber. A terrible smell like cheese and excrement spilled from the opening, and the detective pulled on a doctor's mask. Grimacing, the big fellow withdrew to the far wall.

The coroner slowly exposed the inside of the stomach, which looked like a dirty diaper.

"What's that?" inquired Bettinger, pointing at something that resembled an embryo.

Employing toothed forceps, Meredith Wong secured the item and raised it from the mire. Close inspection revealed it to be a dark brown cashew.

"Are there more?" inquired the detective.

The coroner searched the inside of the stomach. "There's this," she said as she pulled out another object. Gripped by the teeth of the forceps was a crinkled chili pepper.

"Looks like Szechuan."

The Asian woman eyed the black man.

"My wife's favorite."

"Wife?" Dominic looked up from his phone. "There's a woman who didn't laugh or shoot when you proposed?"

Bettinger inspected the cashew and the chili pepper. "How long would these stay in her stomach before descending? Two hours?"

"Peppers and nuts are hard to digest," Meredith Wong said, "especially when they're not chewed enough, so it's—"

"She was a swallower," remarked Dominic.

"Muzzle that." The detective returned his attention to the coroner. "What's the longest it might've been—between her last meal and the time of death? Three hours?"

"Could be that long. Probably less."

Bettinger faced his partner. "Pull up a list of every Chinese restaurant that's three miles or less from the subject's apartment. And put the Szechuan places on top."

Big thumbs clicked tiny keys, and a moment later, Dominic lifted his gaze. "There a difference between Szechuan with a *z* and Sichuan with a *i*?"

"It's like Hanukkah and Chanukah." The detective enunciated the latter word with a guttural inflection.

"Don't get Jewish." The big fellow saw something on his cell phone. "There's only one Sichuan near her apartment—Sichuan Dragon."

"That's where we're having lunch."

"I prefer sushi."

The remainder of the autopsy was fruitless, and shortly after twelve, both policemen exited the hospital and returned to the silver car. Ten minutes later, they were on Summer Drive, driving toward the Chinese restaurant.

The two-way console on the dashboard squawked, garnering Bettinger's attention.

Dominic flicked his hand dismissively. "Don't pick it up."

"It's a police radio."

"Those calls ain't for guys like us."

Bettinger plucked the receiver from the two-way unit and thumbed the talk bar. "Detective Bettinger and Corporal Williams. Copy."

The device emitted a series of hisses and crackles.

"Where are you?" asked a sexless voice. "Over."

"We're busy," replied Dominic.

Bettinger thumbed the talk bar. "We're on Summer and Twentieth. Over."

"Proceed to five forty-three Point Street, apartment sixteen ten. There's a civil disturbance. Do you copy?"

"We copy. What's the nature of the disturbance? Over."

"Domestic violence. Over."

"Who lives at this address? Over."

"It's unclear who lives there. Over."

"We're on our way. Over and out."

Bettinger clipped the receiver to the console.

Dominic seized the two-way unit, tore it from the dashboard, and tossed it into the rear of the car.

"Five forty-three Point Street," said the detective.

"I fuckin' heard."

"Apartment sixteen ten."

Unable to look at his passenger, the bandaged, bull-nosed corporal tightened his fists upon the wheel. "You tryin' to get me to take a swing at you? Turn my demotion into a suspension?"

"Who knows why I do anything?"

"Well I ain't gonna throw no fists at you."

Bettinger was not sure if the man was implying some subtler form of retaliation, but he let the comment sail.

# XIII

# Crabhead

The vehicle sped west, and gradually, the surrounding parks, retail stores, and brownstones were replaced by rows of tall tenement buildings. Peopling the bleak sidewalks of this area were a few shambling oldsters and some pale skinheads who wore big jackets over their Hitler tattoos. On the corner of Tenth and Charles, a white teenager whose pierced face looked like a shrapnel museum eyeballed the black policemen, walked to the edge of the road, and scratched his underarms, chattering like a monkey. His contemporaries on the far side of the street applauded his wit.

Dominic drove past the idiot, turned onto a narrow road, and parked alongside the curb. Together, the pair exited the car and walked west.

Five youths on skateboards zoomed around the front courtyard of a gray project building that wore the number 543. The top two stories of the twenty-story structure were illuminated by sunlight, but most of it was in shadow.

"Cops," announced a light-skinned black kid who wore a gold sweat suit and had elaborately braided hair.

Two of the youths rocketed away.

Bettinger and Dominic entered the courtyard, and the remaining skateboarders kept their distance. Far-off shouts continued to announce the presence of law enforcers.

The detective gauged the building as he walked across the concrete. Its front door was a combination of bulletproof glass and iron bars, and the intercom panel looked like it had been struck by a meteor.

Pausing, Bettinger eyed the light-skinned black kid. "You seem knowledgeable."

The youth shook his elaborate braids as he skated. "I ain't."

"Come here."

"I didn't do nothin'."

"Ever heard of a place called school?" asked Dominic.

"Never."

"Well you s'posed to be in it right now—learnin' how to be better than this."

"I learn plenty right here." The kid zoomed around the policemen. "The courtyard's educational."

"What's your name?" asked Bettinger, monitoring the satellite.

"Let me go ask my momma."

The light-skinned skateboarder veered away from his inquisitors.

"If you make me come get you," Dominic warned, "you ain't gonna be talkin' clever."

The youth skidded to a halt. "Why you need my name? I didn't do nothin'."

Bettinger thought that the kid's ornate braids had a crustaceous appearance. "We'll call you Crabhead until you give us something better."

"The fuck you will, nigga."

Dominic launched himself at the youth, seized his left wrist, and twisted it around until the kid dropped to his knees.

"Don't talk that way to policemen!"

"Okay! I won't—I w—"

"Not fuckin' ever."

"I hear you, nigga, I hear you!" The youth's bravado was gone. Suddenly, he was a skinny kid at the mercy of a big adult who could break his limbs and toss him in a place where people studied geometry. "Now—now—now let go. Please."

Dominic released the kid and kicked his skateboard across the courtyard. "Stand up."

The youth rose to his feet, shaking his sore arm as if it were a damp noodle. "My name's Dwayne."

"It's Crabhead."

Bettinger joined the duo and gestured to the building. "We need to get to apartment sixteen ten."

"Okay." The youth nodded his head. "I'll take you there."

The three of them walked toward the entrance.

Rubbing his arm, Crabhead eyed his jettisoned skateboard, which was lying on its back beside a far-off bench. "Can I grab it so nobody'll take it?"

"Nobody'll take it." Dominic pointed at a white teenager who stood near the bench. "Watch Crabhead's board. If it gets taken, you and me'll have a discussion."

"A'ight," said the skinny fellow whose bereft gums indicated that he had an addiction to crystal meth. "I'll watch."

Crabhead slotted a key into a lock that was surrounded by iron bars, twisted his hand, and leaned forward, but the door did not move. Clenching his jaw, he slammed a shoulder into the reinforced barrier. Hinges groaned, and reluctantly, the door swung wide.

"Gets stuck in winter."

Led by the young guide, the policemen entered the building. Very little sunlight penetrated the bluish-gray lobby, which had an uninhabited security booth and the incomplete remains of a dozen plastic chairs, the limbs of which were still bolted to the floor. Three fluorescent bulbs flickered like wartime telegraphs as Crabhead brought his guests to the elevator bank.

Dominic raised an eyebrow. "These shits work?"

"Go up to twelve." The youth hammered a steel button with his fist. "We can ride up there and walk the rest."

Gears groaned within the shaft, and the big fellow withdrew his cell phone.

"That the Phantom Sleek?" asked Crabhead.

"Yeah." Dominic's thumbs became insects.

"Got sixty-four for videos and shit?"

"Yeah."

The exoskeleton nodded. "Gotta get one of those."

Bettinger wondered if Crabhead even knew the name of the state capital.

Something clanked within the shaft, and the door opened, revealing two bearded white guys whose jittery red eyes were shaded by baseball caps. The smell of marijuana wafted from the pair as they walked into the lobby.

Crabhead led the policemen into the pale green lift and fingered the eroded button that sat above the one for the eleventh floor.

Something clanked, and the door closed. The elevator shuddered, lifting off like a rocket.

"You know who lives in apartment sixteen ten?" asked Bettinger.

"Nah." The crustacean shimmied. "Ain't hardly been up there."

A metallic screech echoed inside the shaft, and the elevator lurched to a stop. The door groaned, sliding into the wall.

Crabhead exited, followed by Dominic (who was still typing on his cell phone) and Bettinger. The magenta hallway in which they stood looked like an infection and smelled like a combination of fungus and old sex.

Yawning, the youth brought the policemen to the emergency exit and slapped the push bar, revealing a dimly lighted stairwell. Heavy footfalls echoed on another level.

Bettinger and Crabhead walked onto the landing, followed by Dominic, who was pocketing his cell phone. As the trio climbed toward the next level, the detective noted myriad graffiti tags and a vivid illustration of a black horse astride a white woman, whose bulging eyes, ecstatic hair, and curled toes indicated that she was in an orgasmic situation.

"Nigga's talented," observed the youth.

Bettinger was not sure if Crabhead was referring to the artist or the stallion.

The group passed doors that were numbered 14 and 15 and continued up the stairwell. Something heavy thudded, shaking the walls.

Bettinger crossed the landing, flung the door, and looked up the hallway, which was empty. Returning his attention to the youth, he said, "Go back down."

"I wanna watch."

"Go."

A woman yelled.

Dominic grabbed Crabhead's left shoulder, spun him around, and shoved him toward the stairs. "Scamper."

# XIV

# You Earned This

The policemen hastened up the hallway, which was infected with the same viral magenta that had overtaken the twelfth floor.

A woman yelled "You earned this!" and a child that was either a girl or a prepubescent boy shrieked.

Bettinger and Dominic hammered fists directly below the number 1610 and shouted, "Police!"

"Get away from that kid!" yelled the detective.

"Open up right fuckin' now!" added the big fellow.

"Don't interfere with my family!" The woman inside the apartment had a wheeze and a twang, and Bettinger surmised that she was an obese redneck. "I know you ain't real cops anyways."

A child began to sob.

"Ma'am," Bettinger said, "you need to open thi—"

"Leave me alone—this ain't your business."

"It is our business," declared the detective. "Come to the door or we'll force our way in."

The woman whispered something, and suddenly, the child stopped crying.

Dominic pounded the door. "Five seconds or we break this down."

"I'm comin'."

Footfalls echoed within the apartment. The policemen raised their badges, and several neighbors poked their heads into the hallway so that they could better view the tableau. One white oldster appeared to be eating gumdrops.

A shadow darkened the space underneath the door, and the peephole turned black. Inside the apartment, the woman muttered, "Oh shit."

Bettinger pocketed his badge. "Open the door."

"Sorry about the noise. I'll keep it down in here." The woman sounded anxious.

"Let us in or this conversation happens at the station."

A bolt snapped, and a chain rattled. Latches clicked, and the door swung inward. Standing in a pink hallway was a morbidly obese white female who wore a tight baby blue nightgown that revealed more bare skin than was possessed by two nude women of average size.

Bettinger looked deeper into the apartment, but did not see the child. "Where's the kid?"

"In the bathroom."

"Take us there."

The woman led the police up the hallway, which smelled like a sour combination of flatulence and cheddar cheese. Soon, they reached a closed door.

"His name?"

"Peter."

The detective knocked on the door. "Peter?"

"What?" The boy's voice was dim and wet.

"Are you okay?"

"Yes."

Bettinger faced the woman. "Your name?"

"Liz."

"Liz what?"

The woman ruminated for a moment. "Smith."

"Get your driver's license and put—"

"I don't have one."

"Then your birth certificate or social security card."

"I don't have those either."

"Get something with your name on it—a credit card or a bill—anything—and put on some clothes."

"I'm dressed." Liz tugged at her nightgown, disturbing breasts that resembled the eyes of an alcoholic. "Lots of women wear this around the house."

"Yours needs an addition," said Dominic.

"I'm not ashamed of how God made me."

"Don't let Him take all the credit."

"Muzzle that." Bettinger waved his hand and eyed Liz. "Please, Miss Smith. Find some identification and put on a robe."

The woman turned around, paused, and looked over her shoulder. "My last name's Waleski."

"Okay."

"Used to be Smith."

"Of course it was." Bettinger's reply was hard.

Dominic followed the pale wall that was Liz's back into a garbage-strewn living room.

Alone in the hallway, the detective turned to the bathroom door and knocked. "Peter?"

The boy offered no response.

"I'm a policeman, and I need to talk to you. I'm going to come in, okay?"

No reply issued from the bathroom.

Bettinger gently opened the door. Sitting inside a teal bathtub and obscured by a mildewed shower curtain was a small, blurry boy.

"Peter?"

A pale oval that was the child's face stretched across the fabric.

"My name's Detective Bettinger—you can call me Jules—and I need to talk to you." The detective entered the teal room, which smelled strongly of feces. "It's important that you tell the truth when I ask you things. Do you understand?"

The blurry oval shook. "I didn't do anything."

"I know. I want to talk about what your mother did."

"Go away."

"I need to make sure you're okay."

Bettinger reached for the shower curtain, and Peter slapped his hand.

"It's against the law to hit a police officer."

"I don't have to listen to niggers."

The detective recalled the skinheads who had been lingering on the nearby street corner and extrapolated the boy's destiny.

"Peter, I need to look at you and make sure you're all right. If you hit me again, you'll get in trouble."

The blurry oval was silent.

Bettinger pulled the curtain back, revealing a fearful blond six-year-old boy who wore red shorts and purple bruises. Lumps of feces sat on his face and chest.

"Dominic!" the detective shouted through the doorway. "Call for an ambulance!"

"On it."

Bettinger snatched a washcloth from the wall, turned on the faucet, and dampened the fabric. Kneeling beside the bathtub, he wiped the brown matter from the boy's lips and chin.

"I forgot to flush," admitted Peter.

The detective folded the washcloth over and continued to clean the boy. "That's why your mother made you eat it? Because you didn't flush?"

Peter nodded his head. His lower lip trembled, and tears shone in his eyes.

Bettinger wiped ochre-brown excrement from the boy's chest and threw the soiled cloth across the room. "You didn't do anything wrong, Peter. Your mom was bad—what she did was wrong. Do you understand that?"

Peter started to cry. A shadow darkened the bathroom, and Bettinger turned his head. In the doorway stood Liz Waleski, holding an envelope and wearing a red robe that looked like a tent.

"Get out," barked the detective.

The woman retreated.

Bettinger followed her into the pink hallway, shut the door, and looked at Dominic. "She doesn't see the kid again."

"Peter's lying." Liz began to shake. "Whatever he said, he's lying."

"The kid doesn't need to hear this," remarked the detective.

The big fellow shoved the woman up the hallway. "Make like an avalanche."

Bettinger followed the duo into a room that was more mess than kitchen. "How long for the ambulance?"

"They said fifteen."

The detective withdrew his cell phone. "I'm gonna call child services and I—"

"No!" screamed Liz. "You can't do—"

"Quiet." Dominic motioned to the bright pieces of hard cereal that covered the floor. "Yell again and it's breakfast."

The woman clenched her jaw. Fury and fear were at war within her mean head.

The big fellow looked at his partner. "What'd she do to the kid?"

"Beat him. Made him eat his own shit because he didn't flush the toilet."

Dominic's face darkened.

"My son's lying!" protested Liz. "He—he makes things up all the time. You can't—"

"He has bruises all over him," Bettinger said, "and a mouth full of excrement . . . some of which is still underneath your fingernails."

The woman looked at her dirty hands.

Dominic sighed as he walked toward the far side of the kitchen. "It's hard raisin' a kid these days. 'Specially for a single parent like you."

Liz wiped her sparkling eyes. "It is."

"Real difficult." The bandaged, bull-nosed corporal lowered the blinds and tore a paper towel from a roll. "A real challenge." Using the white sheet, he picked up a butter knife by its rounded blade.

Bettinger's stomach sank. "Corporal."

Dominic extended the weapon. "Hold this."

Liz clasped the handle.

Shouting "Drop the knife!" the big fellow threw a fist into the woman's throat.

Liz slammed against the wall, gasped, and dropped onto her buttocks. An open hand slapped her face, knocking her over.

Bettinger grabbed Dominic's right arm. "Enough."

The big fellow shoved his partner away and turned back to the prone child-abuser.

"Stop," said the detective, interposing himself between his partner and the woman. "Go downstairs and wait for the ambulance." He set his feet in a fighting stance and knotted his fists.

The bandages on Dominic's face rippled, evincing some type of thought process.

"Go downstairs," repeated Bettinger.

The big fellow growled like a tiger, shook his head, and left the kitchen.

Liz picked a piece of bloody cereal from her face and started to sob.

"Shut up," said the detective.


The paramedics gave Peter two dosages of activated charcoal, put him in the ambulance, and took him to the John the Baptist Hospital of Greater Victory, where he would have his stomach pumped and then meet the agent from Child Protective Services who would see to his housing needs.

Bettinger carried bagged evidence into the magenta hallway and shut the door. Several wide-eyed oldsters stood nearby, discussing the events.

"The police department wants to thank all of the people who reported this crime."

A delighted oldster who looked like he had just witnessed the resurrection of vaudeville swallowed a gumdrop. "You're welcome."

"Because of you, Peter Waleski is going to a safe place." Bettinger said this with conviction, even though he had doubts about the foster care system in a place like Victory. Once the child had been relocated, he would visit him and make an appraisal.

The detective descended the stairs, strode across the lobby, and entered the courtyard. As he walked toward the silver car, he waved at Crabhead, who was currently zooming across the concrete on his skateboard.

The youth nodded in reply.

Bettinger climbed into the silver car, closed the door, and looked at Dominic. The big fellow's thoughts were on Jupiter.

"Sichuan Dragon," the detective said as he stretched his seat belt and slotted the buckle.

Dominic twisted the ignition, shifted gears, and dialed the wheel. Purring, the luxury car floated away from the curb.

Neither man spoke as they passed through the projects and entered the central downtown area. There, the big fellow avoided a dead pigeon and then skirted its niece and nephew on the next block.

"Zwolinski's gonna hear 'bout that?" asked Dominic. His voice was distant and subdued.

"Crabhead seemed fine."

"Crabhead?"

"His arm seemed okay—the one you twisted."

"I ain't talkin' 'bout that."

Bettinger continued to play dumb. "Then what're you talking about?"

"What I did to that woman." Dominic sighed through his nose. "Is Zwolinski gonna hear 'bout that?"

"Of course he is."

"Of course he is," repeated the big fellow, who looked as if he had just bitten into something that was filled with bugs.

"She came at you with a knife. Tried to stab you."

Surprised, Dominic glanced over. "Is that what you saw?"

"Yellow." Bettinger pointed at the traffic light.

The big fellow stomped the gas, accelerating through the intersection. "She came at me with a knife? Tried to stab me?"

"That's what happened." The detective shrugged. "You had no choice."

The big fellow grinned, nodding his head. "Sichuan's on me."

"No thanks." Bettinger reached into the backseat of the car, grabbed the two-way radio, and set it on the dashboard. "And this stays up front."

"You're somethin'."

"I've been called worse."

# XV

# Sichuanese Bones

A quiet ding indicated the arrival of a text message. Driving the vehicle with some small fraction of his attention, Dominic withdrew his cell phone and read the display. Concern shone upon his bandaged face, and a moment later, he pocketed the device. A second ding emerged from his jacket as he turned off of Twentieth Street, and a third one sounded as he accelerated through an area that had six pawnshops.

"You're popular," remarked Bettinger.

"Ex-wife's pissed about somethin'."

The detective suspected that this reply was a lie, since the big fellow rarely offered any information about himself and was not the kind of guy who would tolerate a nag.

"When'd you split?"

"Two years ago."

"Amicable?"

"Nobody got knifed."

Dominic dialed the wheel clockwise, and the red façade of Sichuan Dragon scrolled across the windshield. Surrounding the restaurant was a large parking lot, which had five crummy cars and a hundred empty spaces. The delivery bicycles that sat near the front door looked like they had carried egg rolls to Antarctica.

"Kids?" asked Bettinger.

"No. You?"

"Boy and a girl."

"Lucky."

Dominic slotted the silver vehicle near the entrance, and again, his phone dinged.

Bettinger pointed at the restaurant. "I'll be inside."

"A'ight."

Carrying the Elaine James file, the detective exited the car, closed the door, and walked into the Sichuan restaurant, which was a green and red place that smelled like sesame oil, garlic, and fish tanks.

A balding Asian man who wore a faded tuxedo and chin hair approached the new arrival. "One?"

"Two. Something by the front window."

"Your car won't get stolen."

"I'd like something by the front window."

"Right this way, sir."

Bettinger pocketed his gloves and followed the fellow across the carpet to a table that was covered by a red cloth. There, he sat upon a shiny cushion that hissed.

"I'd like tea."

The host nodded and departed.

Bettinger looked through the window at Dominic, who was in the silver car, talking on his cell phone. Even from a distance, it was clear that he was discussing something far more important than an alimony check.

A white cup materialized beside the detective's left elbow, placed there by the waiter, who was, in fact, the host transformed.

"Hot," warned the Asian fellow as he tilted his teapot. Amber fluid arced into the porcelain vessel.

"Thanks."

The waiter set menus upon the table and turned one of them over, revealing the crinkled pink notice that adorned its back cover. "The lunch special stops at three."

A glance at the gilded wall clock told Bettinger that only two minutes sat between him and the deadline. "I'll wait for my associate."

"Then no lunch special."

"We're extravagant."

"Cash only."

The waiter departed, and the detective opened the menu. Underneath the rugose lamination were photographs of shining, vibrant delicacies that could not possibly exist in Victory, Missouri. Sipping tea, he perused fabrications until his partner entered the restaurant and sat on the opposite side of the table. The big fellow's troubles were remarkably well concealed.

"How's that angry ex-wife of yours?" asked the thing that lived inside of Bettinger's mouth.

Dominic claimed the other menu. "She's whatever."

"Did she hang up on you?"

"Huh?" The big fellow looked over, wiping condensation from his nose.

"First time I looked outside, you were talking on the phone. Next time I looked, you were dialing a new number. So I figured—"

"Stop figuring."

Something deadly shone in Dominic's eyes, and Bettinger put his needles away.

Decided upon what he would order, the detective folded his menu and reached for the Elaine James file.

"Don't show that 'til our food's on the table." The big fellow took the folder and set it on an empty chair, which he then slid under the table. "You didn't tell them we were cops, did you?"

"I didn't." Bettinger tilted his head. "Why?"

"If he's got any kind of operation goin'—gamblin', immigrants, hookers— he'll tell the cook to give us the shits. Discourage us from comin' back."

The detective's eyes flashed with disbelief. "They poison policemen in Victory?"

"Not everywhere. Claude's welcomes cops."

"Their food tastes law-abiding."

The waiter returned to the table and surveyed his customers. "Would you like to start off with some chicken wings?"

Bettinger laughed for the first time since the previous night, when he had bumped his elbow on the nightstand during a vigorous carnal engagement with Alyssa. "I'd like the dandan noodles, the wontons with chili oil, and the braised snow pea shoots."

Dominic closed his menu. "Spare ribs."

"Half order or full order? Half is five ribs."

"I want twenty."

"Two orders," the waiter said as he scratched an ideogram that looked like a map.

"Twenty ribs." The big fellow wanted no mistakes.

"You get two orders of fried rice with that."

"You ever see any stray dogs 'round here?"

"Sometimes."

"Give it to them."

"Okay."

"For real. And bring some ginger ales with my ribs."

"How many?"

"Three."

The waiter departed, and ten minutes later, the food landed upon the table. Dominic seized a dripping, odiferous rib as the Asian departed.

"Excuse me," said Bettinger.

The waiter paused.

"Is the manager in?"

The Asian fellow adjusted his flap of silver hair and turned around, transformed into his own superior. "Want to complain about the service?"

"No complaints. And the food smells great." The detective set his badge upon the corner of the table, where it turned into a chunk of sunlight.

"You're policemen?"

Bettinger nodded his head, and Dominic ripped sinew from a rib.

"I follow the laws," stated the manager.

"We're not investigating you or this establishment. I'm Detective Bettinger and this is Corporal Williams."

"Harold Zhang."

"We're looking for information." The detective reached into the manila file and withdrew a photograph that showed Elaine James as a teenager, sitting on the hood of a blue sports car while holding a cigarette and talking to some friends. "This woman was murdered, and her last meal might've been here."

Bettinger gave the picture to Harold Zhang, who treated it like a flower petal.

The detective dropped a wonton inside of his mouth, and across the table, the big fellow sank his incisors into a rib. Chewing, the policemen watched the face of the balding manager who was his own staff.

"She comes here," announced Harold Zhang. "Though she looks different." The fellow cupped the air in front of his chest.

"That's her." Bettinger swallowed a pulverized wonton and reclaimed the photograph.

Dominic slurped ginger ale. "She's like a band with two smash hits."

"She's dead?"

"Yeah." The detective withdrew a mechanical pencil, thumbed the eraser, and opened his notepad. "When did you last see her?"

"Last week."

"Do you know what day?"

"Monday or Tuesday." Harold Zhang adjusted his flap of silver hair and ruminated. "Tuesday I think."

"That fits. Was she with anybody?"

"No."

Bettinger was disappointed by the response. "Are you sure?"

"She always came alone. Ordered everything very, very spicy—hotter than most Chinese people can eat."

Dominic set a fleshless rib upon a spare plate and cracked open a second hissing can of ginger ale. "Sounds like she wanted a colonic that went top to bottom."

Bettinger wrote, *Spicy food = Day off?* and returned his attention to Harold Zhang. "Did she eat here or take out?"

"Ate here. Just before closing."

"When do you close?" asked the detective.

"Ten. Earlier if it's empty."

Bettinger considered the partially digested contents of the victim's stomach and wrote, *Death occurred between 11:30 P.M. and 2 A.M.* upon his notepad. "Anything different about her that night? How she looked or behaved? Anything she said?"

"I don't think so."

"Did anybody talk to her?"

"Just me." Harold Zhang pointed at the far corner of the restaurant. "She sat over there—where she usually did—ate her usual, and paid. She always tipped a lot." His last remark had a wistful timbre.

Dominic set a fourth fleshless rib upon his spare plate, completing a square of bones.

"What was she wearing?" asked Bettinger.

"Baggy clothes—like she was a jogger. Gray or blue."

"Sneakers?"

"I think so."

"Did she walk here?"

"I never saw a car."

The big fellow started to construct the second floor of his bone edifice.

"You know which way she went when she left?"

"East." Harold Zhang shook his head. "You don't want to go the other way at night."

"Okay." Bettinger withdrew a business card and gave it to the manager. "If you remember something else—or hear anything—call."

"I will."

"Thanks for your help."

"It's my duty." Harold Zhang pocketed the card. "I hope you find the guy."

"We will."

"This city," the manager lamented as he departed.

The policemen focused on their food, and ten minutes later, Dominic completed his five-story bone condominium.

Bettinger motioned east. "Let's take a stroll."

The big fellow drained the remainder of his third ginger ale and set a twenty atop the one that his partner had already yielded. "To eighty-four Margaret Drive?"

"So you can read."

Together, the policemen left the table, watered urinal cakes, washed their hands, crossed the restaurant, and walked outside.

# XVI

# Sidewalk Rambling

The cold attacked. Bettinger shoved his covered hands into his jacket as he entered the parking lot, flanking Dominic, whose mind was again on Jupiter. Shivering, the detective marveled at the existence of sprawling cities in places that were cold enough to murder improperly clothed Homo sapiens. The businessman who had shot himself in Arizona was probably a direct descendant of the idiot who had settled Alaska.

Surrounded by air that was seventeen degrees (and lethal), Bettinger considered the Caribbean and then returned his mind to the case. "Has it rained or snowed since Tuesday?"

"No."

"Then there's a chance of finding something along the way."

Dominic snorted.

"Keep an eye out for signs of a struggle." The detective gestured at their concrete surroundings. "Scuffs, scratches, blood. A watch, earrings. Something that could fall out of a purse or a pocket."

"Like a gun with a name tag?"

"Find that and you can play rap all day."

The policemen reached the sidewalk and turned east. Parked in the middle of the road at the far end of the block was a long black car that had tinted windows. Sonic thuds resonated inside the vehicle like exploding depth charges.

Keeping an eye on the suspect automobile, Bettinger scanned the immediate area for evidence. "How far's her apartment?"

"Ten, eleven blocks."

The black car shuddered, awakening, and rolled forward, turning a pigeon carcass into feathered pulp.

"There are a lot of dead birds in Victory," remarked the detective.

"You're pretty observant."

Fifty feet remained between the creeping automobile and the policemen. Depth charges thudded at forty-two beats per minute.

"How come?" asked Bettinger.

"How come what?"

"How come there're so many dead pigeons everywhere?"

The music stopped, and its absence was a warning that the detective felt on his nape. Silent as a shark, the car continued its slow approach.

Dominic threw a hard look at the vehicle and rested a palm on the handle of his gun. Tires screeched, and the long, four-wheeled organism shot past the policemen.

Bettinger gleaned the car's license plate number and wrote it down in his notepad.

"That ain't nothin' but some niggas with nothin' to do."

"Probably," the detective agreed, "but there's no harm in running the plate."

"You can get those here for ten dollars."

"License plates?"

"Yeah." Dominic led his partner across the street. "I once busted a nigga who had more than three hundred in his crib—he took the metal from construction sites and junkyards and had his grandma paint on the numbers."

"Did you make that bust with Tackley?"

Prior to that moment, neither policeman had uttered the name of Dominic's former partner, the short man with vitiligo who stirred his coffee with a knife.

"I forget."

The duo reached the end of the block, and the big fellow motioned south, redirecting their ramble onto a street of high walls, iron gates, and tall apartment buildings. Bettinger circumvented an open manhole and returned to the sidewalk, stepping over a dead pigeon that was wedged against the curb. Rigid talons extruded from its feathers like the legs of a cancan dancer.

"Any idea what's killing these things?"

"Birds can go anyplace they want, right?" Dominic gestured at the sky. "Flap their wings, and these niggas is in Hawaii, enjoyin' the sun, or maybe over in Paris, shittin' on ridiculous hats. So it figures that the ones who stay in Victory are damaged."

"Psychologically?"

"I'm thinkin' somethin' with their radar or whatever. Either way, it's been like this for years. Niggas just droppin'."

Something occurred to the detective regarding the Elaine James case. "Who's the best clerk in the pillbox?"

"Ain't like you got a lot of choices."

"Of them?"

"Irene."

Bettinger recalled a stuffy, middle-aged white woman whose orange perm resembled a planetoid. "The one with the hair?"

"She's in there."

"She's reliable?"

"You got any idea what these people get paid?"

Passing a concrete playground, the detective stripped off a glove and withdrew his cell phone, which was an old device that looked like a calculator.

"Arizona didn't pay too good," remarked the big fellow.

"Disposable technology isn't where I put my money."

"I seen your automobile."

"In a city like this, I'd classify a car as 'disposable technology.'"

"So then you must live in a mansion."

Bettinger thumbed the preset number for the front desk and brought the receiver to his ear.

The receptionist answered on the second ring. "Police Precinct of Greater Victory."

"Hello, Sharon. This is Detective Bettinger."

"Hello, Detective Bettinger." The woman spoke with a formal flourish.

"Please connect me to Irene."

"She likes to be called Miss Bell."

"I'll respect her wishes."

"Hold."

The connection clicked over to a doo-wop track that featured a falsetto singer whose keening voice was almost a bird noise. Listening to the high-pitched tale of love gone awry, Bettinger followed Dominic onto Margaret Drive. A verse spilled into a chorus, and as the vocalist repeated the refrain, "Put your love in my lunchbox," the detective noticed a broken streetlamp and stopped walking.

"Williams."

The big fellow looked at his partner.

Bettinger said, "We should—"

"Miss Bell speaking."

"Hello, Miss Bell. This is Detective Bettinger. We met earlier."

"Yes. I remember. Good afternoon." The woman sounded like a robot the day before it received the chip that contained its personality.

"Good afternoon. Are you familiar with the Elaine James case?"

"Mrs. Linder built that file. Shall I transfer you?"

"I'd rather you assisted me, if you don't mind."

A keyboard rattled like a machine gun. "Murdered. Raped postmortem." A vacuum of silence followed these proclamations.

"I'm looking for cold cases that might be connected to this one."

"Mrs. Linder found no viable matches. Necrophilia is very rare—even in Victory."

Bettinger constructed a careful question that he hoped would not offend the clerk. "Is it possible that we have an unsolved murder case where the act of necrophilia occurred but was not identified?"

There was a click on the line, and the detective wondered if the robot had ended communications.

"It's . . . possible," said Miss Bell, her voice betraying a glimmer of humanity.

"Then I'd like files on every woman who died in Victory during the last eighteen months—accidental deaths, natural causes, murder victims—all of them. Put the last six months on top, and put prostitutes on the very top. Please."

"The information that you have requested will be on your desk by five o'clock today." The robot had returned. "I shall also send digital files to your e-mail account."

"Thank you very much, Miss Bell."

"Have a good afternoon."

"You too."

Bettinger cut the connection and pocketed his phone. Gloving his frozen right hand, he examined the overhead streetlamp. Bits of sheer plastic that looked like baby teeth sat in the broken fixture, as did a bird's nest and a few rocks.

The detective swept an arm in an arc that included the sidewalk, the street, and the parking lot of a two-story teal building. "It would've been dark in this area when she was coming home."

"As dark as you."

"Clever."

Bettinger entered the parking lot, eyeballing the teal building, which had a sign that read CHRIST THE SAVIOR COMMUNITY CENTER. A pale oval drifted behind one of the windows, paused at an altitude of six feet, and was joined by three smaller dots that barely crested the bottom edge of the glass. Silent and still, the children and their monitor observed the trespasser.

The detective withdrew his badge and angled it until he saw its bright reflection upon the windowpane.

Suddenly, the watchers vanished.

"Ain't eager to help."

Dominic entered the parking lot, and together, the policemen searched the area. The dumb gray canvas yielded nothing of value.

"We ain't turnin' up much," the big fellow remarked as he and his partner returned to the sidewalk.

The pair continued south and soon arrived at a well-maintained redbrick high-rise that wore a bright number 84 on its chest. Bettinger proceeded directly to the security gate, where he stopped, scanned the intercom, and fingered the button for the superintendent. Nearby, Dominic leaned against an iron pole that looked like a spear.

Static crackled. "Yes? Who is it?" The voice that emerged from the grill sounded like it belonged to an old man.

Again, Bettinger fingered the talk button. "It's the police. We'd like to see apartment five twelve."

There was a moment of silence, followed by two squirts of static. "A policeman was already here. He looked around and did his business."

The detective recalled the name of the officer who had done the inspection. "Officer Langford?"

"My wife thought he looked like some actor."

"We'd like to inspect the apartment again."

This request was followed by a long silence. "Why?"

"We just want to double-check."

The speaker spit static, and the oldster coughed. "He didn't do it right the first time?"

"We just want to double-check."

"Um . . ."

A woman whispered something. Wet crackles erupted from the grill and were replaced by silence.

The detective leaned on the talk button. "Sir? May we see room five twelve?"

"Someone's in there."

"Who?"

"Mexicans. A family."

The policemen exchanged a glance, and Bettinger thumbed the talk button. "You rented it?"

"People want to live in this building. We . . . we didn't know."

"Nobody told us or the owners that we couldn't," defended the super's wife.

The grill spat static.

Bettinger exhaled steam and fingered the button. "What did you do with Elaine James's possessions?"

"Donated them to charity," said the old fellow. "There wasn't much."

"Thanks for your time."

"That other officer should've told us—we didn't know you'd be back."

"Thanks for your time."

"Okay. Bye."

Static crackled.

The detective looked at his partner. "Officer Langford's young?"

"Shavin' is a seasonal event for him."

"Christ's uncle."

Bettinger faced the intercom, scanned the numbers, and thumbed the button for apartment 512.

Static crackled, and an excited little muchacho inquired, *"¿Quién es?"*

The frustrated detective turned away from the iron gate and began his journey back to Sichuan Dragon.

"Where to now?" asked the big fellow, trailing his partner.

"The pillbox."

"Not Bermuda?"

Bettinger hoped that Miss Bell's files would contain something useful, because the cold winds of Victory had just frozen the case.

# XVII

# Her Opportunities

"Congratulations." Happy for the first time that day, Bettinger kissed Alyssa on the mouth and hugged her. "A show in Chicago," he said into her wild curls. "Wow."

"I really didn't expect to hear back from him." The woman withdrew from her husband and took a glass of grapefruit juice from the refrigerator. "I squeezed some before."

The sight of the beverage conjured a salivary premonition in the detective's mouth. "What's the name of the gallery?"

"David Rubinstein Gallery of Chicago."

"Sounds rich."

"He is. And so's his clientele."

"I'll dust off my yarmulke."

"Too bad they're worn on the back of the head."

Alyssa eyed her husband's balding scalp.

"Hey." Bettinger slid a palm across his head until he reached the silver-and-black growth that began on the far side of the North Pole. "I'm sensitive."

"You aren't."

The woman drank some of the grapefruit juice, puckered her face, and gave the glass to her husband, who received it happily. His eyes stung and his throat burned as he swallowed the astringent beverage.

"This's the bitterest one yet," said the detective.

"It sure is."

Bettinger returned the glass to Alyssa. "Almost impossible to drink."

"I know. Right?"

Both of them liked challenging grapefruit juice.

"What pieces are you going to show?"

"*The Breathing Cargo.*"

Disbelief shone upon the detective's face. "Really?"

"Uh-huh."

The series depicted white aristocrats dining, playing croquet, and lounging atop piles of black bodies in the cargo holds of slave ships. Unlike most of Alyssa's paintings, which were subtle and impressionistic acrylics that had nothing to do with race, the *Breathing Cargo* pieces were highly detailed and politically aggressive.

"You know how much I like that series." There was an implication in the detective's remark.

"Rubinstein thinks they'll really get people's attention."

"They'll do that."

Alyssa drank the rest of the juice, revealing the host of little citric leeches that clung to the inside of the glass. "You don't think they'll sell?"

"I don't want to say that." Bettinger flashed his palms. "I don't know the art world in Chicago, and those pieces are terrific."

"But . . ."

"They're provocative. They make people feel guilty or angry, maybe both, and are better suited for a museum than a banker's condo, where they'll sit on some wall beside a seventy-two-inch plasma screen and pictures of a blond woman who flashes the same exact smile in every photo."

Alyssa grinned. "I look forward to meeting some museum curators who share your opinion."

"You will." There was no doubt in Bettinger's voice—his belief in his wife's art was absolute. "Rubinstein doesn't think they're too dark?"

The painter poured more grapefruit juice. "He's not sure, but even if they don't sell, they'll establish me with his clientele."

"To whom he'll offer more palatable works by the very same artist?"

"That's the plan." Alyssa grimaced as she swallowed the astringent fluid.

"It lets these people be 'edgy' without actually going to the edge."

"Exactly." The painter extended the glass to her husband. "You can have the rest."

"Not sure I'll survive."

"There are worse ways to go."

Bettinger drank the searing remainder of juice. "It's almost sulfuric."

"Right?"

A door closed in an adjacent room, and the detective faced the hallway. "Gordon."

"Yeah?"

"Dinner's at seven thirty."

"Okay."

"If you're late, you're doing dishes for a week."

"Relax, officer."

"Come here."

The lean, sleepy-eyed fifteen-year-old inhabited the doorway and plucked a white bud from his right ear. "Yeah?" His voice was sullen.

"Have you ever cooked dinner for our family?"

"Nah."

"Do you think it's easy?"

Gordon contemplated some smartass remark, gauging whether or not he should risk further irritating his father. Decided, he shook his head. "I know it's not easy."

"Don't make me threaten you with chores like you're ten years old. Respect and appreciate that your mother does a lot of work so that we can eat good, healthy food."

"I do appreciate it—she cooks good." It seemed like Gordon's rebellion was over.

"And tell her congratulations."

Confusion wrinkled the adolescent's brow. "She's pregnant?"

Alyssa chuckled. Although she was a youthful and very feminine forty-six-year-old woman, her laughter sounded like it originated in the chest of a white oldster who had pleurisy.

"Your mom's paintings are going on display in a prestigious Chicago gallery."

"Really?" Gordon's face brightened. "That's platinum." He pulled out his second earbud, walked across the linoleum, and hugged his mother. "Seems like they got better taste up here than in Arizona. More intellectual."

Alyssa squeezed her son's hand. "Thanks."

"Platinum."

Bettinger set his empty glass in the sink. "You'll have to watch your sister while your mother and I are at the opening."

"Fine." Gordon thumbed the buds back into his ears. "You're takin' Mom to a fancy dinner up there?"

"Of course."

"You'll go in a limo? Get her champagne and a hot tub?"

A couple of rheumy snickers were produced by the old man who lived inside of Alyssa's chest.

"I'll treat her right," said Bettinger. "Don't worry."

"Do it like it's New Year's for the year 3000." The adolescent activated his audio player and departed.

Ruminating, the detective rinsed his glass and set it in the washer. "He's got some definite ideas about women."

"Good ones."

"Daddy," said Karen, walking into the kitchen with a magnetic chessboard in her little hands. "You're about to get annihilated."

"Do you see where my bishop is?"

The girl looked at the array of white pieces. "Oh . . . I didn't."

"But your chess trash talk is really coming along."

"Can I get a do-over?"

"After you tell your mother congratulations."

"She's gonna have a baby?"

"Even better."

Flavorful and aromatic food was swept from plates into mouths, where it was squeezed by peristalsis toward gastric chambers. Karen and Gordon departed from the table, thanking their mother, and as Bettinger began the dishes, Alyssa relaxed in a nearby chair, cradling a glass of white wine.

Television voices and dim music crept into the kitchen area, and soon, the couple exchanged a meaningful glance.

The woman led her husband into the master bedroom and locked the door. Quietly, they removed clothes that smelled like cilantro and slid their bodies underneath a blanket. Gentle fingertips explored soft flesh, and Bettinger's phallus solidified until a warm ache throbbed in its core. Alyssa straddled her husband, and together, they found a slow, deep rhythm.

The feces-spattered boy and Elaine James's autopsied corpse did not impede the detective's ability to ejaculate hot fluid only a moment after his wife had climaxed. Compartmentalization was something that he had learned long ago.

Modesty soon returned to the shuddering animals, and they raised the covers over their bodies, grinning idiotically at each other. Heartbeats slowed, and ten luxurious Caribbean minutes passed before either of them spoke.

"I've always wanted to sleep with a celebrity," announced Bettinger.

"'Celebrity'?" Alyssa shifted her head on the pillow so that she faced her husband. "It's just one show."

The detective ran a hand down the small of his wife's back. "It's more than that."

"Well . . . I don't want to get too excited."

"You should get excited—this is big."

"We'll see."

"Don't hedge," said Bettinger. "A good thing is happening for you—for your career as an artist—right now. Enjoy it."

"But if it doesn't go well . . ."

"It will go well."

"But if it doesn't? It's conceivable that it won't."

"If it doesn't go well, you'll have other opportunities. And you'll also have the experience of enjoying the uphill portion of the ride rather than just worrying about it."

The painter considered her husband's advice. "I suppose you're right."

"Of course I am."

"You're a pretty optimistic pessimist."

"That's not the only thing I am." The detective raised an eyebrow.

"Already?"

"I told you I have a thing for celebrities." Bettinger placed Alyssa's hands upon his phallus, which was stiff. "And this doesn't lie."


Shortly after his wife had fallen asleep, the detective donned jeans and a sweatshirt, finished the dishes, and entered the mauve study, where he put a cup of coffee beside the stack of files that Miss Bell had earlier that day left on his desk at the pillbox. He yawned, reclining in a padded chair as he examined the cover sheet. Seventy-nine Victory women had become dirt during the last eighteen months, and over half of these deaths were suspected or confirmed murders.

"Christ's uncle."

The detective scanned the remainder of the document. Amongst the forty-three probable homicide victims were sixteen convicted prostitutes whose files were already at the top of the stack.

Bettinger sipped his coffee and opened the uppermost folder, which contained autopsy photographs of a woman who had no head.

# XVIII

# They Were Numbered

"I never understood why they call it toasted," said Officer Dave Stanley, poking the tines of his plastic fork into a breaded ravioli. "It's deep-fried."

"The appearance is toasted," replied a short, gray-haired Italian American who possessed fifty-four years, a dyed mustache, and the wheel of the parked patrol car.

"But why not just 'fried ravioli'?"

"That's a little obvious."

"Less syllables."

"True . . . but you don't just call a thing what it is." Gianetto opened his takeout bag and extracted an open-faced meat and cheese sandwich that wore more paprika than did nine hundred deviled eggs.

Dave Stanley bit into his ravioli, and a flood of warm and salty ricotta filled his mouth. "They make it good here."

"When it's fresh from the kitchen, it's a seven."

The young officer had anticipated this comment: Gianetto rated everything that he cared about on a scale that went from zero to ten. Food, movies, actresses, cars, the nine books that he had read in college, and a pantheon of classic rock albums had all received numerical classifications, as had less obvious things like cities, countries, his wife's dresses, dog breeds, and supermarkets. The only things that had ever received tens were Italy and Rottweilers.

Gianetto bit into his open-faced sandwich, and the sound was like the destruction of a rainforest. "Six," he said as he chewed.

"It's gone down."

"Half a point." Inspecting the paprika-covered comestible, Gianetto shook his head. "It goes below a six, and we're getting from Angelo's."

Dave Stanley ate another toasted ravioli. "Sounds like you've got it all figured out."

"I don't rate things for fun."

The two-way squawked.

"Shit," said the policemen.

The young officer thrust his plastic fork into a ravioli, plucked the receiver from the dashboard, and thumbed the talk bar. "Car nine. Officers Gianetto and Stanley. Over."

"We have reports of shots fired on Worth and Leonora," said the sexless voice that belonged to the entity in dispatch. "Proceed to the area."

"Copy." Dave Stanley clipped the receiver to the console.

"This call's a zero." Gianetto swallowed chewed food and took a new bite at the exact same time. "They should report when there aren't any shots—then we'd know something was wrong."

Unsure if this recommendation was a joke, the young officer replied with a shrug and a nod.

The corporal swallowed the tip of his sandwich, turned on the headlights, and shifted gears, coaxing the patrol car away from the curb outside of Paolo's Real Italian. "The middle was a six point five."

It took Dave Stanley a moment to realize that his partner was again talking about the open-faced sandwich. "Glad to hear it."

"It was the olives," Gianetto said as he turned onto Summer Drive.

The patrol car rolled south on the main road, slowing down but not stopping at the intersections. All of the prostitutes whom they passed received low ratings.

"I'm a faithful husband," the corporal remarked, "but I remember a time when the girls out here used to be tempting. Now it's just a bunch of threes and fours. And up in the Toilet, it's mostly twos."

"Maybe your standards have changed . . . ?"

"Definitely not."

Dave Stanley bit into a toasted ravioli that had burst in the deep fryer and contained nothing but air. "Jip."

"An empty?"

"Yeah."

"You can return that if you want. Get an extra the next time you order—I've done it before."

"Nah."

The patrol car passed a gaunt prostitute who had red hair, platform heels, and a blue vinyl raincoat.

Gianetto remained silent.

Dave Stanley looked at his partner. "No rating for that one?"

"It was a man."

The young officer turned around in his seat and eyed the diminishing figure. "You sure?"

"One thousand percent."

"You have a good eye," said Dave Stanley, resettling.

"My vision's good—'specially for a guy my age—but it's my mind that does the work." Gianetto ruminated for a moment. "Remember graph paper?"

"Sort of . . ." Dave Stanley was twenty-five years old and had never seen graph paper. "Maybe."

"It's this paper they used to make—maybe still do, I don't know—that's divided into squares for accounting, maps, charts, drawings—really anything can go on there. And everything you put on it is cut up into little squares, broken down into pieces in the exact same way. And that's what I do when I rate things—I put them on paper like that, but in here—" The corporal tapped his forehead, leaving behind a paprika fingerprint.

"Okay." Dave Stanley was uncertain if his partner was a genius or an idiot.

"We're almost there."

Gianetto drank the remainder of his soda and tossed the empty can into the night, where it clanked against the concrete. "You should only do that with stuff bums can recycle."

"That's thoughtful."

"Keep 'em busy." The corporal burped.

"Should we put on our vests?"

"This call's a zero." Gianetto patted his belly, which overhung his belt like the jowls of an Englishman. "Not sure one would fit me right now anyways."

As the cruiser rolled south, the policemen surveyed the night. Lying upon a street corner was a brindled mongrel that twitched as it froze to death.

"Poor guy," said Dave Stanley.

"There're worse ways to go." Gianetto spun the wheel counterclockwise, looked to the right, and then turned in that direction. "AIDS. Starvation. Cancer. Drowning. Concentration camp."

"I think concentration camp's the worst."

"It's a nine point five." The corporal flung the car onto a dark, narrow road. "This is Leonora."

"How can you remember all these streets?"

Gianetto tapped his forehead. "The graph paper."

A dark shape slid into the middle of the road.

The corporal jammed the brakes, and tires screeched. A distance of forty feet separated the stopped patrol car and the brown cargo van that now blocked off the street.

Gianetto honked.

The other automobile did not move.

"Can you see who's in there?" asked Dave Stanley.

The corporal thumbed the lever for the high beams. Light glared in the policemen's eyes, reflected by something in the van's passenger window.

Wincing, Gianetto killed the brights.

"One of those sun reflectors?" suggested Dave Stanley.

"Let's get official." The corporal turned the dreary block into a red-and-blue disco.

Leaning over, the young officer picked up the PA microphone and held it to his mouth. "Move that vehicle right now!"

The order echoed up and down the street, but elicited no response.

Dave Stanley surveyed the brownstones on either side of the patrol car, and when he turned around, his jaw slackened. A cargo van was blocking off the other end of the street. Red and blue lights colored the exhaust that rose from its tailpipe and flashed dimly upon its black surface. The second vehicle was as inscrutable as the first.

"We're boxed in," said the young officer.

"Something happens to me," Gianetto said, "tell my wife I thought she was an eight."

"Not a ten?"

"No way she would believe that." The corporal snorted. "She's really a five and a half."

"I'll say eight."

Dave Stanley thought of the precinct receptionist, Sharon, whom he had been dating for the major part of a year, but could not think of anything that he wanted to tell her.

Gianetto grabbed the PA microphone and thumbed the talk bar. "Clear those vehicles from—"

The brown van's side door slid open, revealing an opaque square. Something clicked within the darkness.

"Down!" yelled the corporal.

The policemen prostrated themselves.

White fire boomed. The windshield bulged and became a thousand spider webs. A second shotgun blast thundered, and the milky glass burst. Scintillating shards rained upon the backs of the huddled policemen.

Cold air swept into the vehicle, and Dave Stanley began to shake. Outside, a gun was cocked.

Gianetto thrust his revolver over the dashboard and squeezed the trigger, blindly returning fire. "Call for backup!" he yelled to his partner. "Tell them—"

Something smacked against the corporal's skull and landed beside him.

"The fuck was that?" Gianetto asked, rubbing his head.

Dave Stanley looked over. Next to the gas pedal was a hand grenade.

Emptying his bladder, the young officer opened the door, stumbled outside, and yelled, "Grenade!" The pavement slammed into his chest, and he looked over his shoulder.

Gianetto bolted through the other door, but was jerked back into the vehicle by his seat belt, which had caught upon his holster.

"Fuck!" yelled the corporal.

Dave Stanley covered his head.

Sunlight appeared at midnight, accompanied by thunder. Shrapnel tore into the prone officer's boots, legs, buttocks, arms, and back. It felt as if his entire body had just been dropped into a deep fryer.

The concussion echoed.

Ears ringing, Dave Stanley slid a hand across the hot pavement. The exertion agitated the bits of shrapnel that were buried in his scapula, but he persevered, fighting through his agonies. His fingertips landed upon his holster, and he mouthed the word "Motherfucker." His gun was missing.

Dave Stanley looked over his shoulder. Smoke that glowed blue and red swirled around the police vehicle, and three feet from its muffler lay the missing firearm. The weapon appeared to be intact.

Gritting his teeth, the young officer rose to his hands and knees and crawled. Shrapnel poked muscles and bones as he proceeded, gasping and trembling, toward the gun. A glance into the patrol car revealed the dead and armless thing that had tried to grab an active hand grenade during its final living moment. Surmounting its charred collar was a mass that looked like a rotten pomegranate.

Tears filled Dave Stanley's eyes, and the world glared red and blue.

"That one's still goin'," somebody said from within the brown cargo van.

Dave Stanley reached for his weapon.

A shotgun boomed.

Buckshot pierced the young officer's head, and he collapsed to the pavement. Ice-cold pellets sat in the very center of his skull.

"Get his badge," said a hoarse voice.

Footfalls sounded, grew louder, and stopped.

Immobile and near death, Dave Stanley felt a hand tear the badge from his chest.

"This asshole pissed himself."

"You get his badge?"

"I got it."

"Okay. Now pull down his pants and cut off his dick."

# XIX

# Executed

Bettinger reclined in his chair, yawned, and glanced at the clock on the wall. If he went to bed right now, he would get four hours of sleep before he had to wake up for work.

"Junk."

The detective looked at the two folders that lay on the right side of his desk, isolated from the tall majority. Both cases had gone cold many months earlier, but it seemed possible that either or both of these slain prostitutes had been killed by whoever had murdered Elaine James. Tomorrow, Bettinger would visit the locations in which the women had been discovered—an abandoned apartment building and a sewer access tunnel.

A plaintive gurgle sounded within his stomach, telling him to eat before he relaxed the overworked gray mechanism that sat in his brainpan. Irked by the demands of his body, the detective fitted oversized rubber bands around the documents and opened his file cabinet.

Something buzzed.

Bettinger looked to the far corner of the desk, where lay his cell phone. The alarm was set for two thirty (which was not for another twenty minutes), and its remonstrations confused him. Picking up the device, he looked at its display and saw the name "Williams, Dominic."

The detective unfolded the cell phone and placed the receiver to his ear. "What happened?"

"Two cops got it."

"Dead?"

"Executed."

Wide awake, Bettinger reopened his notepad and coerced graphite from his mechanical pencil. "Where?"

"Worth and Leonora."

"I'm on my way."

The line went dead.

Bettinger wrote the address and scribbled a vague explanation on the next page, which he tore off and placed on the nightstand for Alyssa to discover in the morning. After a scalding ninety-second shower, he dressed himself in a brown suit and backed his yellow car out of the garage, unsure whether he was continuing his second day of work or beginning a third.

Negligible traffic and heavy acceleration allowed him to collapse the sixty-five-minute drive up the interstate to a mere three quarters of an hour. Throughout the duration of the high-speed ride, the word "executed" sat beside him like a spectral passenger.

Bettinger snagged the off-ramp and entered the tunnel, startling the trolls, who were smoking something that had an impressive diameter. As he zoomed past the duo, they waved puffy limbs.

Nine careening minutes brought him to Leonora, a street with which he was already familiar, and soon, he descried the red-and-blue disco. There, he landed beside four patrol cars, yanked the stick, and zipped up his parka.

The detective exited his hatchback and strode toward the neon tape, behind which stood Inspector Zwolinski and nine officers, two of whom were female. Dominic was not amongst those gathered.

"Bettinger."

"Inspector." The detective ducked underneath the line and approached his superior. "What happened?"

"There were reports of shots fired in the area. Gianetto and Stanley went to investigate." The inspector pointed at a patrol car that looked like it had blasphemed in the Middle East on a holy day.

"Christ."

"My guess is that the people responsible for this are the same ones who cut off their dicks."

Bettinger wondered exactly when he had died and gone to Hell. "This sort of thing ever happen before?"

"Not even here."

The detective was momentarily at a loss for words.

"Goddamn fucking animals," said a stocky female officer as she wiped tears from her eyes.

Standing beside the woman was Langford, the handsome young recruit who was often mistaken for an actor, although currently he looked like a man who had just expelled a lot of vegetables through his mouth.

"Thought you lived in Stonesburg," said Zwolinski.

"I do."

"That hatchback's got wings?"

"Detachable." Bettinger gestured at the sundered patrol car. "Has the scene been documented?"

"The guys're on their way."

"May I look?"

"Just eyeballs."

The detective walked toward the rear of the blasted cruiser, the lights of which were somehow still functioning. Exhaling a plume of steam that shone alternately red and blue, he circled to the passenger side of the car and saw the prone body of Dave Stanley. The young man's face looked like offal, and a swatch of pale skin glowed where his pants had been yanked down. A nub of crimson ice sat below his pubic hair.

Bettinger leaned forward, closely inspecting the wound. One thick line of blood ran from the emasculating amputation, down the victim's scrotum, and to the pavement, telling the detective that the officer was either dead or unconscious when his phallus had been removed. Upon his notepad, he wrote, *Stanley. Shotgun blast, close range. Penectomy after.*

Bettinger turned away and approached the vehicle, wherein sat something that had once been a human being. The smells of burnt hair and charcoal filled the detective's head as he reached the open door, looked through, and descried the posthumous excavation that had occurred between the dead corporal's legs. Embedded in the body and throughout the interior of the car were numerous pieces of shrapnel.

Upon the notepad, Bettinger wrote, *Gianetto. U.S. Military Hand Grenade. Penectomy postmortem.*

Heavy footfalls sounded behind the detective, precipitating the arrival of the inspector.

"I get why crooks kill cops," said Zwolinski. "In a way, it's surprisin' that it doesn't happen more often. But why in the hell would they do that—" A thick finger pointed at the officer's groin. "This wasn't some lone psychopath who did all this, so there's got to be some logic—some reason."

"Intimidation."

The inspector ruminated for a moment. "Like that sick psychological shit they do in wars?"

"Yeah." An idea came to the detective. "Did you see their badges?"

"No." Zwolinski turned his head, filled his lungs, and shouted, "Langford, Peters, Johnson!"

Aided by the three summoned officers, the inspector and the detective searched the crime scene for ten minutes. The dead men's badges were not recovered during this operation.

Zwolinski dismissed the trio and eyed Bettinger. "So what does this mean? Somebody executed 'em, took their dicks and badges?"

"Not sure. The killers might've wanted trophies—like antlers on a wall—or maybe they wanna be able to prove that they did this."

"To who?"

"Us."

The inspector did not look happy. "Why?"

"Maybe we'll get that stuff in the mail and some advice about how to do our jobs."

Zwolinski's face turned into the ugly mask that his boxing competitors saw a moment before they were knocked to the canvas. Too angry for words, he turned away and strode toward the yellow tape.

Bettinger focused his attention on the environs, which the lights of the blasted car allowed him to observe. Standing beside a black sedan at the far end of the street were four men, wreathed in steam that flashed red and blue. The detective soon identified the members of the quartet as Dominic, Huan, Perry, and the small, mottled fellow, Tackley. Quiet conversation floated between their heads.

Bettinger walked toward the gathering.

As he circumvented the wreck, he and his partner made eye contact, and the dark opening below the big fellow's nose turned into a thin line. The pockmarked Asian lighted a cigarette, and the mottled man drank from a silver thermos that looked like an antiaircraft shell.

Stretching his arms, the redhead eyed the newcomer. "Since when does the night move horizontal?"

"I think it's dark matter," said Huan, dragging on his cigarette.

"Aren't the scientists looking for that?"

"Furiously."

"Looks like I picked the wrong day to soak my petri dishes."

"There's always a risk."

Bettinger came within smelling range of the quartet. "Any of you have any idea what this is about?"

Perry motioned to the crime scene. "That?"

"That."

"Somebody doesn't like cops."

Huan exhaled thick tobacco smoke. "I concur."

"Should we let the inspector know?" the redhead asked the man from Arizona.

"I think he has that part already."

"Then maybe the press?" Perry raised his eyebrows, which resembled pale caterpillars. "They love it when we give them scoops."

"Extra." Huan's cigarette glowed. "Extra."

Tackley sipped coffee from his stainless-steel thermos, and it was unclear if he was frowning or grinning.

"In other places I worked, a cop getting killed didn't inspire jokes," said Bettinger, trying to keep the frustration out of his voice.

"Where'd you work?" asked Perry. "I bet it was someplace nice, where everybody's real smart and knows the answer to everything."

Huan exhaled smoke. "New Geniusville?"

"Tell us," implored the redhead. "Where'd you solve mysteries?"

Too tired to maintain the prickly circumlocution, Bettinger gestured at the blasted cruiser. "So you don't have any idea who might've done this?"

"Someone who doesn't like cops." Perry shook his head and looked at Huan. "He forgot already."

"Any specific ideas?" pressed the man from Arizona.

"Someone who knows how to operate a hand grenade."

Huan's cigarette glowed. "All the steps."

"I got an idea," said Perry. "Put out an APB for a guy holding a pin."

Bettinger turned away from the group, saying, "Corporal Williams," as he departed.

"I think he's irked," remarked Perry. "Though it's hard to tell."

"Impossible at night."

The big fellow joined his partner, and together, they approached the crime scene. Thick parkas and wool hats covered a white guy and black woman who were near the patrol car, unloading photographic gear from a hand truck.

"You know them?" asked Bettinger.

"The forensic techs."

"What're their names?"

Dominic shrugged. "They're married."

The detective watched the technicians photograph the blasted cruiser. Artificial daylight illuminated the empty sockets of the thing that had been Gianetto, and when the black woman repositioned her bulb, a hunk of metal and three teeth glared inside of the corpse's mouth.

"This doesn't concern you?" Bettinger asked Dominic. "Cops getting executed?"

"Of course it does. I called you, remember?"

"I'd bet an inch of bills that Zwolinski told you to make that call."

"Whatever."

The detective glanced over his shoulder. Eighty feet away, Huan and Perry listened to the quiet things that crept out of Tackley's mouth.

"Your pals don't seem real helpful."

Dominic gestured at the corpses. "Did you even know who these guys were?"

"I met Gianetto, but didn't know him."

"And Dave Stanley?"

"Never met him."

"Right."

The big fellow nodded his bandaged head and folded his arms. He seemed to believe that he had reached the end of a conversation.

"Two cops were executed and mutilated," said the detective. "This is a threat to all of us, and it's not the time for you and your pals to withhold data and play secret clubhouse."

"You're livin' in a illustration," the big fellow proclaimed, "so let me give you a photograph."

"Please do."

"You're a cop by the standards of wherever it is you came from—Arizona, right? Someplace warm and easy and far away, where people drink iced tea all day. Me—I'm from Victory, I'm a product of this place. I been a cop here nineteen years, and each of them is like a decade anyplace else.

"So I understand this city good, and I knew these two guys—Gianetto made a speech at my wedding. But you . . . you're a Arizona cop on a field trip. You're a fuckin' tourist. You think you know, but you don't have any idea how this all works. I humor you with this Elaine James shit, but this right here's somethin' different."

"What is it?"

Dominic shrugged.

"Got anything to do with that guy you and Tackley put in ICU?" Bettinger recalled the name. "Sebastian Ramirez?"

"No." Anger shone in the big fellow's eyes. "You investigatin' me and my partner?"

"Your former partner. And yes."

An open hand thudded against Bettinger's chest, shaking the buildings and knocking him backwards. The detective set his feet, hardened his fists, and leaned into the forward fighting stance that was second nature to him after years of studying martial arts. In his peripheral vision, he saw a dozen turning heads, including the lumpy one that belonged to Inspector Zwolinski.

Dominic appraised his opponent and spat on the concrete. Blue steam poured from his nostrils as he walked away from the crime scene, toward Huan, Perry, and Tackley.

Bettinger wrote *Sebastian* upon his notepad. Dominic's reaction had all but confirmed a connection between the brutalized Hispanic and the executions.

Underlining the name, the detective appraised the quartet of law enforcers who stood in the shadows beside the black sedan. All four men were displaying their backs.

# XX

# Residents of Victory

The cordoned-off area was mapped and captured by the forensic technicians, and afterward, Bettinger (and other law enforcers) began a door-to-door survey of the buildings on Leonora Street. For twenty minutes, the detective tried to engage tenants who were either unresponsive or hostile.

Again, he pressed a buzzer.

"Ring that bell again, and I'll get my fuckin' bat!" threatened a woman through her closed front door. "The metal!"

"I'm a police officer," Bettinger said, "and I need to speak to you about the shooting that occurred earlier th—"

"I didn't see nothin'."

"May I come in and get an official—"

"I ain't puttin' on clothes and makeup for this."

Talking to a policeman at half past four in the morning was an activity that the citizens of Victory welcomed no more than they would an impromptu proctological examination.

Bettinger left the irate woman, climbed the steps to the third floor, and approached the apartment there that faced the street. Its door was adorned with a picture of Jesus Christ and a plaque that read OUR SAVIOR.

Seeing no buzzer, the detective knocked. "Police."

Footfalls sounded within the apartment, and the light dimmed in the Lord's left eye, which was evidently a peephole. "May I see a badge?" inquired a tranquil male voice.

Bettinger flashed brass.

"One moment."

A chain rattled, and a bolt clacked. The door withdrew into a snug apartment, revealing a plump, bald, and shiny forty-year-old Caucasian fellow who wore a maroon robe and slippers that looked like sheep.

"Come on in." The resident gestured fluidly.

"Thank you," said Bettinger, walking inside. The cozy interior was illuminated by the Christmas lights that adorned a fake white pine tree, and the smells of apples and cinnamon saturated the air.

As the door closed, the detective extended his hand. "Detective Jules Bettinger."

"Organist Peter Kesell."

They shook hands.

"Come to take it away?" The shiny musician gestured at the Christmas tree.

"I'll let it go if you cooperate."

"Would you like something to drink?" Peter Kesell asked through a grin. "I made apple cider last night."

"Thank you, but I have a lot to do. I just—"

"Indulge yourself," the organist said as he disappeared into a dark portal. "It's Christmas." A switch clicked, and an overhead light illuminated a kitchen wall that was inhabited by no fewer than fifty crucified Christs. Soon, Peter Kesell returned, bearing a mug from which emerged steam and a stick of cinnamon.

"Thank you," Bettinger said as he accepted the beverage.

"Where're you from? New Mexico? Colorado?"

"Arizona." The detective sipped the cider, which had a delicious and particularly complex flavor. "You've done something remarkable here."

"Thank you." The shiny fellow glowed with pride.

Bettinger gestured at the window that faced Leonora. "Did you see or hear anything?"

"A gunshot woke me up. I heard some other shots and an explosion— though for obvious reasons, I stayed away from the windows . . ."

Drinking an apple, the detective nodded.

"When I thought it was over," Peter Kesell resumed, "I looked. There was a lot of smoke, but I'm pretty sure I saw a van driving away—one of those long ones."

"A cargo van?"

"Yes."

Bettinger returned the mug to his host and opened his notepad. "What color?"

"Brown or black. Maybe dark blue. I'm sorry . . . there was a lot of smoke."

"Any marks on the van?" the detective inquired as he distributed graphite between blue lines.

"Not that I saw."

"Which way did it go?"

"East. I . . . I would've come down and told you, but it's not a great idea to stand in the middle of the block and talk to the police around here."

"Don't worry about it. And thank you." Bettinger pocketed his notepad and proceeded toward the door.

"Wait—before you leave—"

The organist handed the mug back to the detective, who consumed the remainder, nodded his thanks, and hastened down the steps into the cold. Warmed by the cider, Bettinger located Zwolinski and told him what he had learned.

"That's halfway between nothin' and somethin'," remarked the inspector.

"It's better than bubble gum."

The inspector's flat nostrils twitched. "You just eat an apple?"

"The guy gave me cider."

"Nancy got an omelet." Zwolinski pointed at a female officer who had eggshells and yolks in her hair.

"Hurts less than a cinder block."

"How do you live with all that empathy?"

The inspector gave a description of the vehicle to the Missouri State Highway Patrol, and the detective joined the trio of shivering officers who were surveying the east side of the block. Near the intersection, Langford found a few bits of safety glass that may or may not have belonged to the black, brown, or dark blue cargo van that was almost certainly on its way to a junkyard, chop shop, or lake.

Zwolinski yawned when he inspected the handsome young recruit's evidence. "This stuff isn't even halfway between nothin' and somethin'."

The bodies were sent to the morgue, and eventually, the police ran out of things to do. Like ashes from a campfire, the weary law enforcers drifted from the scene.


Bettinger parked his yellow hatchback in the pillbox lot, reclined the driver's seat, and shut his eyes. Heated air blew through the vents, warming his face, and he relinquished consciousness.


A dollop of sunlight landed upon the detective's right eyelid, rousing him from a dream that smelled like allspice. He stretched his arms, sat upright, and glanced at the clock, which showed that the time was ten minutes after seven. The arrival of morning would make it hard—if not impossible—for him to fall asleep again, and thus, he decided to visit Sebastian Ramirez.

Twenty minutes later, Bettinger strode through the mint green lobby of the John the Baptist Hospital of Greater Victory and arrived at the front counter, where a receptionist rested her messy head inside a barbican of folded arms.

"Pardon me," said the detective.

"Mmm . . . yeah?" inquired a mouth within the fortress.

"Where's ICU?"

"Fourth floor."

"Good night."

"Night?"

Bettinger left the collapsed woman, boarded an elevator, and ascended to the fourth floor. There, he entered a gray hallway, which was supposed to be white, and looked for an employee.

A door opened, admitting a pale old man who had a gown and a walker. "I need my bedpan changed," the fellow told the detective. "The call button's still not working."

"I'll let the nurse know."

The oldster endeavored a three-point turn as if his walker were a motor vehicle. Returning to his room, he muttered the word "Bureaucrat."

Bettinger continued up the untenanted hallway, looking for an office or an employee as he progressed. A door opened at the far end, and through the portal walked a male white twentysomething in a mint green uniform who had light brown hair, a goatee, and a clipboard.

"Excuse me," said the detective, eyeing the fellow's name tag, which identified him as a doctor-in-training.

"Visitors aren't allowed right now."

Bettinger showed his badge.

A hardness fixed itself on the resident's face. "Yes?"

"What room is Sebastian Ramirez in?"

"He isn't."

"He left?" Bettinger had not seen any mention of this online, though the most recent article on Sebastian was two weeks old. "Did he recover?"

A mirthless chuckle emerged from the resident. "Are you kidding?"

"But he checked out?"

"'Vanished' is the word I'd use."

"When?"

"Yesterday."

Bettinger recalled the series of phone calls that Dominic had received while he was driving to Sichuan Dragon—the ones that he had pretended were from his ex-wife. "Lunchtime?"

"That's when we found out about it, though he told us to hold breakfast the night before, so it could've been earlier."

"You call the police?"

"We weren't obligated to."

Bettinger figured that Tackley and Dominic had learned about Sebastian's departure from someone who was more amenable than the individual with whom he currently spoke.

"I've got a lot to do," said the resident, impatiently. "On a good day, I'm doing three jobs. Today isn't good."

"Where is he now?"

"Home. Or possibly North Korea."

"Any reason you're acting like a porcupine?"

"It keeps me awake."

"You didn't seem to like my badge."

"Did I hurt your feelings?"

Bettinger decided to gentle his approach. "I'm new on the force—I transferred here from Arizona and just started this week—and I'm asking for your opinion. Politely. With a blue ribbon and chocolates that have ganache."

The resident gauged the detective's sincerity and seemed to be satisfied by what he saw. "I deal with bodies failing and falling apart all day. That's what I do. That's what happens in this hospital, especially in ICU. We try to help people get better—or at least feel better. But from what I've seen, the cops in Victory are on the opposite side, hanging out with cancer and car accidents."

"Sebastian is a previously convicted felon. He—"

"So he deserves what you guys did to him?" These words were sharp. "He's incontinent. He's in a wheelchair, and he's breathing out of one lung—and that's who he is for the rest of his life. Every single day. That's what the Victory police did to him—after he was in cuffs—and he's not the only one."

Bettinger did not doubt the veracity of these accusations.

The resident cleared his throat. "And why do you think he dropped the charges against you guys? Santa told him to?"

The detective caught the baseball. "You're saying somebody threatened him?"

"I'm not saying that." The fellow's blue eyes were hard. "That's what you said."

An ugly silence sat in the air.

"Unless you're officially holding me," the resident said, "I'm going back to work—where the bowel movements I deal with don't wear badges."

No reply emerged from the thing that lived in Bettinger's mouth.

# XXI

# Everybody Listens
# to Zwolinski

The detective entered the big white refrigerator that was the pillbox, sat at his desk, and stuck the black piece of tape that he had received from the receptionist onto his badge. A visual survey told him that most of the Victory policemen and women were present, including Huan and Perry, who drank coffee around a plant that had no leaves. The absence of Dominic and Tackley was unsurprising.

An aquatic quietude filled the enclosure, and every time a phone rang, the noise seemed shrill. Bettinger sifted data on Sebastian Ramirez, wondering if Alyssa and the kids would learn about the executions from a television anchorman or a newspaper or the Internet.

Nine o'clock brought Inspector Zwolinski. He was dressed in black and his knuckles were purple from the punishment that he had given a punching bag, which may or may not have been a living human being. The titan reached the dais and turned around, facing the clerks, officers, and investigators who peopled the moribund interior.

"Don't talk to the press." The inspector's words resonated throughout the pillbox, bolstered by the heavy cabinet that was his chest.

Everybody listened.

"If you're harassed by these jackals," Zwolinski continued, "redirect 'em to my secretary, and she'll step on 'em. I'm talkin' to two papers today—the *Victory Chronicle* and *The National*—and the rest can suck fumes from those.

"Boostin' paper sales and creatin' entertainment isn't my priority.

"This is some mean shit we're dealin' with right now."

A phone rang.

Irene Bell launched an arm and yanked the cord from the device.

"Every case that was top priority is now second priority. Anthony Gianetto liked to—"

Zwolinski's voice cut out.

His eyes shined.

A phone rang, and Langford threw the device in the trash.

The inspector slammed a purple fist into an open palm and cleared his throat. "Anthony Gianetto liked to rate things—like he was a movie critic or somethin'. Findin' the guys who did this to him and Dave Stanley deserves a ten from every single one of us.

"Anyone who gives a nine point nine or less will earn some time in the boxin' ring with me."

Bettinger knew that his boss was not bluffing.

"Every cop in here needs to be on the street before I take my mornin' shit—which is what I'll be doin' while I'm talkin' to the papers."

A clerk placed a massive thermos of coffee in Zwolinski's right hand. "I spoke to Dave Stanley's family. They want to do the service in Nebraska, so we're sendin' him there tomorrow. Every single one of you sends flowers and a card to his parents. Write at least seventy-five words about how great Dave Stanley was in that card.

"No fuckin' e-mails.

"If you put seventy-four words or less—or just forget to do it—you'll earn some time in the ring with me.

"Last night, I went to Gianetto's home. Spoke with his wife." A miserable look reshaped the lumps that comprised the inspector's face. "She wants the full service—with the honor guard—and that'll happen on Friday.

"Show up late to that, and we're in the ring until you lose some teeth."

Zwolinski let his threat settle.

"And when I see Mrs. Gianetto at the service, I don't want to give her platitudes. No 'We are doing our best' kind of garbage. I want to show her a picture of the killers, dead on the street or sittin' in jail, with their sleeves rolled up, waitin' for injections.

"Don't embarrass me.

"Don't embarrass us."

Zwolinski gulped coffee as if it were water. Exhaling steam and massaging his hard belly, he eyeballed the assemblage. "You've got about three minutes."

Chair legs squeaked across the linoleum, and bodies flew into the air.

Bettinger snatched a paper from an ancient printer and strode to the clogged portal, through which he and other quiet cops then entered the receiving area, nodding their heads respectfully at Sharon, who sat at the reception desk, wiping her red eyes with a ball of tissue. (Earlier that morning, the detective had learned that she and Dave Stanley had been dating.) A pile of candy bars sat beside the woman's big white phone, dumped there by Inspector Zwolinski.

Bettinger zipped up his parka, exited the pillbox, and proceeded toward his yellow hatchback. His cell phone buzzed, and he put the receiver to his ear.

"Yeah?"

"I'm workin' on somethin'," said Dominic. "I'll catch up with you later."

"Don't rush."

The detective sat inside his hatchback and shut the door. Upon the passenger seat, he placed the printout, which showed the home addresses for Sebastian Ramirez, the dealer's older sister Margarita, and a white woman named Melissa Spring who had visited him regularly in the hospital and was presumed to be his girlfriend.

Bettinger examined his map, determined the simplest route to the first location, and tossed his hatchback into the line of growling vehicles. Marked and unmarked cars rolled onto the street like a fleet of ships looking for war.

# XXII

# Dark Doorways

A yawn exploded on the detective's face.

As he drove south, he conjectured. The city had dropped its charges against Sebastian Ramirez while he was in his coma (for obvious reasons), and when the battered fellow had awakened, he contacted his lawyer and filed a brutality lawsuit against Dominic Williams, Edward Tackley, and the entire Police Department of Greater Victory. There was a lot of evidence against the detectives—fourteen witnesses and even some video—and a trial would almost certainly yield two convictions and the same number of expulsions. It was a surprise to everybody when, five weeks later, the lawsuit had been dropped.

Sebastian Ramirez had told the *Victory Chronicle* that he just wanted to put the incident behind him and move on with his life.

The indignant resident at the John the Baptist Hospital of Greater Victory did not believe that the brutalized man had naturally arrived at his epiphany, and Bettinger also entertained doubts. It was easy for him to imagine Dominic and Tackley threating their disabled adversary.

Bleak, untenanted blocks changed into more habitable ones as the detective rolled south on Summer Drive, and the hot air pouring out of the vents turned his knuckles into reptilian leather. Upon his notepad, he wrote, *Buy moisturizer.*

A red light stopped the hatchback at a corner where a young white couple admired the contents of their baby carriage. Their contented grins informed Bettinger that the infant was not yet frozen.

The green light glared, and the detective dialed the wheel clockwise, guiding his hatchback onto Fifth Street, which was lined with three- and four-story brownstones. Glancing at a building number, he determined that Sebastian Ramirez's home would be several blocks ahead and to the right.

Bettinger did not know for certain if the abused dealer was involved with the executions, but the fellow certainly had a grievance against the Victory police, and his disappearance from the hospital on the day of the event was a coincidence that should be investigated.

A huge yawn erupted from the detective's head. Moisture dampened his burning eyes, and the road turned into a watercolor painting.

"Christ's uncle."

Bettinger passed through an intersection and saw a four-story brownstone that wore ivy and the number 261. A moment later, he landed the hatchback beside the curb, near two very big white guys who were tossing a football back and forth.

The detective holstered his gun and exited his car. As he reached the sidewalk, the fullbacks exchanged a glance and drew apart.

"Heads up."

The football whistled past the back of Bettinger's skull and slapped the palms of the larger fellow, who had sunglasses and a rusty beard.

Ignoring the provocation, the detective climbed the steps to the front door of the brownstone, where he pressed and released the buzzer of the rear fifth-floor apartment.

No reply emerged from the panel.

The detective waited a moment and fingered the button a second time, holding it down for a longer period of time, but again, his solicitation elicited no response. Behind him, the football whistled through the air and snapped against the palms of its recipient.

Bettinger faced the near fullback. "Excuse me."

"Yeah?" The bearded fellow threw a tight pass to his distant contemporary, who caught the projectile and held it aloft like a wartime enemy's severed head.

"You know Sebastian Ramirez?"

"Of."

"Seen him around?"

The football slapped between the fellow's pink hands, and he waved at his peer, saying, "Go long." As the other fullback walked east, the hirsute man returned his attention to the detective. "He's in the hospital. Been there a while." He eyed his friend (who had stopped retreating) and shouted, "Longer!"

"Thanks." Bettinger descended the steps.

"You look pretty beat," stated the bearded fellow.

The detective paused.

"You're hurting?" The fullback-turned-quarterback catapulted the football into the sky. "That why you're looking for Sebastian?" The projectile arced through the cold and snapped between the distant receiver's hands.

"You know where Sebastian is?"

"The hospital—like I said." The football appeared between the fullback's hands like a magic trick. "You interested in something?"

"You're picking up the slack while he's away?"

"Not me." The bearded fellow threw another long pass. "But I might know a guy who knows someone."

Bettinger had more important things to do than chase a drug relay operation. "Maybe later."

"I'll be working on my bomb."

"Until Sebastian gets back?" the detective asked as he approached his little yellow car.

"I don't think a wheelchair can go up and down those steps." The football snapped between the fullback's hands. "Well . . . I guess maybe down."

"That's tough." Bettinger sat inside the hatchback.

"See you soon."

The detective closed the door, shifted gears, and pulled away from the curb.


A twenty-minute drive brought Bettinger to the baby blue apartment complex in which lived Sebastian's sister Margarita. There, he parked his car, walked to the outer door, and thumbed the woman's buzzer.

The only reply that the detective received was from the wind, which keened through a cracked transom window.

As he departed, he located Margarita's red sports utility vehicle in the parking lot. It had a couple of flyers underneath its wipers, which seemed to indicate that it had been sitting there for a while. These details were added to Bettinger's notepad, even though he rarely forgot anything.


The detective drove, fighting the gravity well that was sleep.

Soon, he neared the third address, where lived the young woman who was said to be Sebastian's girlfriend. The sheet on Melissa Spring did not say much other than that she was a brunette junior college graduate who had been arrested as a teenager for shoplifting and driving while intoxicated.

Bettinger landed in the parking lot of the rose-colored apartment building in which the woman lived, locked his car, and walked along a cracked stone path that divided two rectangles of dead grass. His stomach growled, clamoring for something more substantial than a protein bar or coffee.

"Be patient."

As he reached the entrance, the door swung open, and he seized its handle.

A short white woman who had spiky black hair, a pierced nose, and a puffy lime green jacket emerged, glaring at the detective.

"Police," said Bettinger, displaying his badge.

"Do you have a warrant?"

"Sure I do."

The detective walked past the woman and entered the lobby, which was decorated with frosted mirrors that might have been fashionable in the 1980s for a period of one week. Three plump cats slept in the corner near a radiator, and the detective envied their simple existence.

"This is a privately owned building," the woman proclaimed from the doorway. "You can't just come in here because you want to."

"It's amazing what I can't do." The detective fingered the elevator button.

"That badge doesn't make you omnipotent."

"Let me get a dictionary."

The elevator door opened, and Bettinger entered a sarcophagus of frosted mirrors, where he was soon joined by the irate woman.

"You don't have anything better to do?" asked the detective.

"You don't have permission to be here. I want to make sure you don't damage anything or anyone or plant any evidence."

"Should the police department expect another donation from you this holiday season?"

"My partner's father works for the city, so I know the kind of shit you guys pull."

Bettinger wondered to what extent the Victory police force actually deserved their terrible reputation. As his adversary withdrew her cell phone from her lime green jacket, he fingered the fourth-floor button.

"My wife thinks my left side's handsomer—though you're the director."

The door closed, and the elevator shuddered.

A digital image of the woman's black boots appeared on her cell phone, as did a movie camera icon. "I won't get in your way," she announced. It was obvious that she was a very accomplished tattler.

The elevator stopped and opened. Bettinger entered a light blue passageway, and the spiky-haired woman followed after him, keeping her distance.

A dozen strides brought the detective to a door that wore the number 705. There, he paused and looked at the director, who was fifteen feet away from him. "What's my line?"

No suggestions came from the woman.

Bettinger returned his attention to the door and rang the bell. Inside the apartment, something heavy thudded upon the floor.

"It's the police," announced the detective. "I'd l—"

"I didn't call the police." The voice belonged to a young woman who sounded distraught.

"Are you Melissa Spring?"

"Her roommate."

"When was the last time you saw Melissa?"

"Go away."

"I'm a detective, and I'd like to talk to you."

The woman inside the apartment said nothing more. After thirty seconds of silence, the spiky-haired tattler paused her cinematic endeavors.

"How do I know you're really a cop?" asked the resident.

Filming resumed.

"I have a badge and a very nice business card." Something occurred to Bettinger. "Who else might I be?"

No reply issued from the other side of the door.

"May I talk to you in private?" asked the detective.

"I don't know where she is, okay?" Something wet and fearful was lodged in the back of the woman's throat. "Go away."

"Somebody else already came by? Looking for her?"

A sniffle sounded inside the apartment.

"I'm going to hold up my badge and slide my card under the door to prove who I am."

"I can't talk to the police."

"Ma'am . . . whenever anybody says 'I can't talk to the police,' they should talk to the police. Immediately. I can get a warrant, but then things become official." Bettinger produced his badge. "Look outside."

The peephole glass darkened.

"You see it?"

"Yeah."

The detective wrote a message on the back of his business card and slid it under the door. "Look down."

The peephole filled with light.

Thirty seconds later, Bettinger asked, "You read it?"

"Yeah."

"Say it loudly."

"I won't open this door until that nosy idiot with the camera goes away."

The detective looked at the director and shrugged. "I'm not positive, but I think she means you."

The spiky-haired woman glared at him.

"As of this moment," Bettinger declared, "it's interfering with an investigation if you keep that on." He aimed an index finger directly at the cell phone.

"I know what it means." The tattler turned off the device and tucked it away. "You're pretty clever for a Victory cop."

"I'm imported."

"That explains it."

A smirk glimmered upon the woman's face as she entered the stairwell. Her heavy boots thudded down the concrete steps, and soon, the sound was silenced by the closing door.

The detective returned his attention to the apartment. "She's gone."

"Okay." A bolt clacked. "I'm telling you now I've got a gun."

"Do you intend to shoot me?"

"If you're not who you say you are." The woman on the far side of the door sniffled. "I've had a bad morning."

"What's your name?"

"Kimmy."

"Okay, Kimmy. I'm Detective Jules Bettinger. You may call the police department and verify who I am if you'd like."

"I believe you."

A chain rattled.

Bettinger displayed his empty hands. "If you shoot me, where should I expect it?"

"The heart."

"That'll be difficult."

"Why?"

"Mine's the size of a grape."

A bolt clacked, and retreating footfalls sounded within the apartment.

"It's unlocked," said the young woman. "Let yourself in."

# XXIII

# Kimmy's Likes and Dislikes

Bettinger entered a domain that had furry couches and mismatched rugs and smelled like a combination of berry air fresheners, incense, and marijuana. Beside a recliner chair that looked like a leopard stood Kimmy, a skinny, blond twentysomething who had busted lips, large dark eyes (one of which was swollen), and a red robe. A huge revolver dangled from her right hand, pointing at the middle of the corresponding foot. Although the young woman had two fingers curled around the trigger, the detective did not know if she had enough strength to successfully launch a bullet.

"Mind your toes."

Kimmy saw that the muzzle of her firearm was trained upon her bare right foot. Carefully, she scooted her toes to safety.

Bettinger asked, "Should I close this?"

"Go ahead."

The detective gently shut the door.

"Do the bottom lock."

Bettinger turned the bolt that was directly above the doorknob. "Do you want me to stay here while we talk?"

"You can sit."

"Cheetah or zebra?"

"Zebra."

The detective walked across a paisley rug and sat upon a furry white couch that had black stripes. A bong lay underneath the opposing recliner, but he did not remark upon it.

Bettinger gestured at Kimmy's busted lips and swollen eye. "Did your previous visitor do that to you?"

"Yeah."

"Can you tell me what happened?"

The young woman nodded.

"Okay. I'm going to take out a notepad and a pencil. Please refrain from shooting me in the heart."

"I won't shoot you."

The detective produced his notepad, set it on the sofa, and withdrew a mechanical pencil.

"I remember that kind," said Kimmy. "Had a class where we used them." The young woman ruminated for a moment and shook her head. "I can't remember what it was."

Bettinger did not gesture to the bong that lay underneath the recliner. "You can sit down if you'd like."

"I'm too wired." Kimmy leaned against the arm of the cheetah sofa, her gun carelessly threatening the life of a ratty stuffed animal that was either a moose or a bear. "So this morning," she began, "like five in the morning, somebody buzzes the door. Usually me and Melissa just ignore it when people buzz—it's mostly kids or bums—but this guy keeps ringing and ringing, and she wasn't here to get it."

"When did Melissa go away?"

"Monday."

"You know where?"

"No."

"Have any guesses?" asked Bettinger.

"She didn't say anything, she was just gone. She's gone a lot."

"Does she have a car?"

"No. Her boyfriend usually gets her."

"Sebastian Ramirez?"

"Yeah, though he's in the hospital now. Or I thought he was until what that guy said."

"What guy?"

"The one from this morning. Let me tell it." Kimmy pointed the hand that lacked a firearm at the intercom, which was beside the front door. "So I go to the thing and push the button—tell the guy to stop buzzing, and he doesn't say anything. All I hear is that crackle you get because the intercom sucks and's like a hundred years old.

"I pee and then I go back to bed, and he starts fucking buzzing again. Sounds like that noise in the hospital when the patient's heart stops—beep beep beeeeeeeeeeeeeeeeeeeeep. Annoying!"

"Would you mind putting your gun down?" inquired Bettinger, leaning out of the way of the raised firearm.

"Sorry." Kimmy set the revolver on the couch, directly between the stuffed creature and the armrest upon which she leaned. "So it's beeping—he's just holding it down—and I go to the door and tell the guy to stop pressing the fuck-ing button, I'm not gonna let him in no matter what.

"I was fucking angry."

"I presumed."

"So now I'm shaking—keyed up the way you are when you've had too much coffee or done some—" The young woman decided to omit the second mind-altering substance from her narrative. "And so I do a couple of shots to calm me down, 'cause that can help, you know?"

"Of course I do."

"So I lay in bed, try to fall back asleep, and I put on some music—some reg-gae, which is the best for going unconscious.

"I'm right at the edge, about to drift off—sort of dreaming about this guy I used to date at Oakfield who was kinda dumb, but really nice and always wrapped everything with Christmas paper—even in the summer when it was like a thousand degrees—and the doorbell rings, scaring the fuck out of me. This door right here—" Kimmy pointed across the room. "Not from the inter-com downstairs.

"There's this moment where I'm not sure if it's real—the doorbell—or part of the dream with Stevie and the Christmas wrapping paper. And then it rings again, and I almost fall out of bed.

"I know for sure—

"He's here.

"So I come in the living room and look at the door, which is totally locked and has the chain on and everything. And the bell rings again, and I'm like, 'Go away,' and he's like, 'I found a cat outside. It got hit by a car and was trying to get into the building, and a guy I buzzed told me you take care of them,' which is true. There're a bunch of strays me and Melissa feed, and when it gets cold like this, they sleep in the lobby or the basement so they won't freeze.

"So the guy's like, 'I'm gonna put her in front of your door,' and I hear a meow."

Kimmy shook her head. "So now I feel bad for yelling at the guy—since he was just trying to help—I thought—and I go over to the door and look through the peephole and see a big guy wearing a dark blue jogging outfit, walking away, and I'm like, 'Wait!'—mainly 'cause I can't afford to pay for a vet—but he just leaves.

"So I open the door and look at the cat, a big orange one—one of the ones that stays here I named Janet. She's crying the way cats do, but's just lying there, shaking, not going anywhere, and I see a piece of white sticking out of her back and realize it's her spine. That's when the big guy grabs me by the neck and throws me inside. He shuts the door and says right in my face, 'Scream and I'll kill you.'"

Tears filled the young woman's eyes.

"I was so scared. He looked like he would do it—he was huge. And he had on gloves and a ski mask like killers do."

A suspicion surfaced within the detective. "Could you tell what color he was?"

"African American."

"Anything else you remember about him?" Bettinger inquired as he turned the page in his notepad, wondering if Dominic was the assailant.

"Had gold teeth." Kimmy tapped her upper incisors. "These."

The detective's partner had no such hardware, though it was possible that he had installed some superficial metal in his mouth as a misdirection.

Bettinger said, "So he's inside . . ."

"Yeah. And he pulls out a gun that has one of those silencers on it and locks the door and's like, 'Where's Melissa?' and I tell him she isn't here, but he doesn't believe me. So we go look in all of the rooms and by the end, when he knows for sure she's not here, he's quiet. And I'm like, 'I told you,' and he hits me with the gun so hard I fall on my ass. There—" The young woman gestured at the paisley rug that was in front of the kitchen. "I've got bruises all over."

"Please let me take you to a hospital after this. You should—"

"No thanks."

Bettinger did not want to pester the woman, and as he stifled another yawn, he wondered exactly how safe it was for him to be on the road at all, much less act as a chauffeur. The middle-aged man had slept eighty minutes in the last thirty-one hours, and his collapse was imminent.

"So then he asks where she is," Kimmy continued, "and I tell him the same thing I told you—'She's been gone since Monday, I don't know, I haven't heard from her.' So then he's quiet, thinking, and I can hear Janet crying outside—it's fucking awful—sounds like a baby—and somebody says, 'You get her?' and he's like, 'Go downstairs and wait. Take the cat.' So I know he has a partner outside helping him.

"Then he gets an idea or something and goes in the bathroom and turns on the light. He puts the stopper in the bathtub and starts running the water—the hot water—and he looks over at me and's like, 'Where's your cell phone?' And I point to my bedroom and am like, 'In there,' and he's like, 'Let's get it.'

"So we go into my room and there it is—on my nightstand—and he's like, 'You're gonna send a text message to Melissa,' and that's when I remember that I forgot to plug it in last night. I open it up, and it's totally dead—no juice at all.

"I tell him I need to charge it, and he's like, 'Go ahead,' and as soon as I plug it in the wall, he smacks me across the face."

The detective frowned, looking at the swollen skin around the young woman's right eye. "I don't like this guy at all."

"Me neither! I thought he broke my whole head, it hurt so bad. And so I'm on the carpet—dizzy, seeing lights—and all I can hear is the water running in the bathtub.

"He grabs me by the hair, stands me up, looks at me, and's like, 'Take off your clothes.' And I get numb. Cold. This guy's a rhinoceros—he rapes me, he'll turn my insides into pesto.

"So I just stand there, shaking—in shock, I guess—and he slaps me and's like, 'Do it now,' and while I'm taking off my socks and nightshirt, I'm thinking of that cat with the broken back and the jewelry store I work at and that Christmas wrapping paper. I don't have a bra on, so I cover my boobs—which aren't that great anyways—and he points his gun at my thong and's like, 'That too.'

"I take it off, but keep my legs pressed together—I'm totally sure he's gonna rape me." Kimmy shook her head. "But then he's like, 'Sit on the bed.' And I do.

"I just sit there, naked, watching the phone charge like it's a rock concert or something.

"It feels like forever.

"One of those little black bars appears, and I tell him I have some power. He nods his head and's like, 'Let's take it to the bathroom.'

"The water's still running in there, and he shuts it off, puts the toilet lid down, and's like, 'Sit.' So I sit on the toilet, and I'm naked and shaking hard. 'Text Melissa,' he tells me. 'Get her to come home right now.'

"So I ask him what I should say to get her to come home.

"And he leans over to the bathtub, puts down a razor blade, and's like, 'Think of something good.'

"It isn't easy to think of something good when you're like that—naked with a stranger in your own fucking bathroom, and he's telling you that. So I start crying—really crying—hard—and he's like, 'You've got forty-five minutes to get her here. Probably shouldn't waste too much time blubbering.' He's calm like my driver's ed teacher was. Or like guys who play bass guitar.

"It takes me about five minutes to think of something, and I'm like, 'I have something,' and he's like, 'What is it?' and I'm like, 'I'll tell her that her mother's here and wants to see her about something.'

"So he asks me if Melissa likes her mother, and I say, 'Like the way most people do—not really, but you sort of owe her everything, so you do your best.' And he's like, 'What if she calls her mother?' and I'm like, 'Why would she do that if she's right here?'"

Kimmy gestured at Bettinger. "Right?"

The detective nodded his head.

"But then he was like, 'Is there a chance that her mother will call her in the next forty minutes?' and I was like, 'Not much.' So then he was like, 'You'd better hope not' and points at the razor blade in case I'd forgotten about it. In case it'd fucking slipped my mind.

"Asshole.

"So I text Melissa and tell her that her mother came over, wants to see her about something private—and the guy takes my phone and tells me to sit in the bathtub. I almost scream when my fruit touches the water—it's fucking hot.

"My skin's still red from that.

"The phone beeps, and he shows it to me. Melissa had texted back, 'I'll be there soon,' and he's like, 'Should I reply, "See you?"' and I nod, and he asks, 'You do it with two letters—*C* and *U*?' and I'm like, 'How else?'

"So he sends her the text, and I know Melissa's on her way here—where a giant scary African-American guy in a ski mask and gloves has got me naked in the bathtub, and who knows what he's gonna do.

"So I start to feel guilty.

"I tell myself all of what's happening—all this crazy fucking shit—has to do with her boyfriend Sebastian, and I don't have anything to do with him except sometimes watching cable when he's over . . . but still, I feel like shit. 'Cause who knows what he's gonna do to her if she doesn't know what he wants her to know.

"And I'm right here too—a witness—and maybe he's gonna kill us both.

"I was thinking this kind of stuff for a while—it felt like a week, but was probably like twenty minutes—when the phone beeps. He reads it and doesn't look happy.

"I ask if it's Melissa, and he says it isn't, so I ask who it is, and he's like, 'Says anonymous.' He's tells me to get out of the tub and walk into the living room, and I do. I'm shaking and have no idea what the fuck's going on, and I ask him, but he just tells me to go to the door.

"So I go to the door and he gets over there—" Kimmy pointed at the closet beside the entrance. "And he aims his gun at me and's like, 'Put the chain on the door,' and I'm like, 'How's Melissa gonna get in if I put the chain on?' and he tells me, 'Ask another question and we're going back to the bathroom,' and I knew what he meant.

"So I put the chain on the door.

"And then he tells me to look through the peephole, and I do. He's like 'Anybody out there?' and I'm like, 'No, there isn't,' and there isn't.

"So then he says, 'Leave the chain on, but undo the other locks and open it—see if there's something on the ground,' and I figure this is what that anonymous text was about.

"I'm soaking wet and shaking, and the places where he hit me feel like they're filled with fire ants, but I do the locks and crack the door and look in the hall and there's a pile of clothes laying there. Sweatpants and a sweatshirt, underwear and some socks. There's a ski mask too—like his. And I tell him what's there, and he's like, 'Get it.'

"My arm's real skinny so I can without undoing the chain. After I get it all in, he has me close the door and lock it.

"He takes the sweatshirt out of the pile, and there's blood on it, and when he picks up the ski mask, he feels something inside. He puts his fingers in the eyeholes and pulls out some dark things that look like cat turds.

"They're toes—from an African American."

Bettinger guessed that the young woman employed the cumbersome (and often erroneous) politically correct term for his benefit . . . and possibly whenever she was in the company of other people whose toes resembled cat turds.

"My cell phone dings, and he pulls it out and looks at it. I know better than to ask who it's from.

"The guy looks at me and's like, 'Get a trash bag and a baggie with ice,' and I go to the kitchen and get them. He puts the toes in the ice, shoves the baggie in the sweatshirt, and stuffs that and all his partner's clothes in the trash bag.

"He looks at me and's like, 'You have one minute to get dressed.'

"We go to my bedroom, where I pull on some jeans and a sweater and boots, and he hands me the trash bag and slides his gun in his pocket, but keeps holding it tight. He grabs my arm with his other hand and's like, 'We're going to the lobby.'

"So then he asks me to look outside and make sure nobody's there. I don't see anybody, and we go to the elevator. It comes and has this old woman who's on her way down, but the guy's standing off to the side so he won't be seen or anything. And he's still got the mask on.

"So we get in the next time it comes, and he presses the lobby, and I tell him I want my phone back. For a second, I think he's gonna punch me like the good old days, but instead, he just gives it over and's like, 'I wasn't gonna kill you. I just had to scare you.'

"I'm pretty sure he's telling the truth.

"Then the elevator stops, and he's like, 'Sorry.'

"I say 'Fuck you,' to him 'cause . . . well . . . I'm still pissed, and he killed that cat for real, which was fucking hateful.

"The door opens, and I can't see much. The lobby's dark—somebody turned off the lights—and there're four guys standing there. Waiting for us."

"Did you know any of these men?" the detective inquired as he rubbed a cramp in his right hand.

"I don't think so—but it was dark, and they were wearing hoodies and had scarves over their faces like old-fashioned bank robbers or something. Seemed like white guys or Hispanics." Kimmy wrinkled her face. "Maybe some of both."

"So one of them points a long knife at the African American and's like, 'The keys are in the ignition and your friend's in the trunk. Take him to the hospital.'

"So the African American gets the trash bag from me and walks out of the building. Three guys follow him, and they've got their hands in their pockets, just like him, but the one with the knife stays behind. I ask him if he's with Sebastian, and he's like, 'Who's he?' and I'm like, 'Sebastian Ramirez,' and he's like, 'Who's he?' playing dumb, since everybody in Victory knows the name—but I get that he's not gonna say anything incriminating or whatever.

"So then he's like, 'Come with me,' and I'm like, 'No,' and he's like, 'You shouldn't stay here,' and I tell him, 'I'm fucking staying.' I wasn't really scared of the African American anymore, and I was sick of guys telling me what to do. Right?

"So then he opens our mailbox—Melissa must've gave him the key—and puts the gun in and some bullets." Kimmy motioned to the large firearm that lay upon the couch. "And he's like, 'You know how to use one?' and I'm like, 'Theoretically?' and he's like, 'Have you ever fired a gun before?' and I'm like, 'I can learn.' So he's like, 'How?' and I'm like, 'Watch a video online.' So the guy's then, 'Okay. Go online,' and walks away.

"So I bring the gun here, lock everything, drink some whiskey, and watch some gun videos."

"I'm glad you're okay," said the detective. "A lot of people don't survive an experience like that."

"It fucking sucked. Want a beer?"

"No, thank you."

"Well I'm having some."

# XXIV

# Diminished by Small Sips

Bettinger massaged his overtaxed right hand as Kimmy returned from the kitchen, drinking from a can of light beer.

"I want to ask you a question," the detective said, "and I promise that your answer will remain off the record."

"Okay." The young woman sat on the couch, adjusted her robe, and pressed the cylinder of cold aluminum to her bruised right eye.

"Have you taken any controlled substances today? Pills? Some weed?"

"What's weed?" Curvature appeared on the young woman's chin.

The detective closed his notepad. "Something that would discredit your testimony if this ever became a court case."

"I didn't call the police," defended Kimmy.

"I know you didn't. And thanks for telling me what happened."

Although the young woman's story might not result in an arrest, it had confirmed that Sebastian Ramirez was in hiding.

"You done?" asked Kimmy. It was clear that she wanted to proceed to her itinerary of weed, alcohol, and gunplay.

"You're gonna need to give me that—" Bettinger pointed at the revolver.

"But what if the African American comes back?"

"First off, you shouldn't stay here. Is there someplace else where you can—"

"Unless you put me in cuffs and drag me out of here, I'm fucking staying."

"I'm not going to put you in cuffs."

"Then I'm fucking staying."

"Okay. I understand. And I have a pretty good idea what'll happen after I leave—" Bettinger motioned to the bottle of whiskey that was on the counter and the bong that lay underneath the recliner. "It's normal after what you've been through. And I think you're right: It's not very likely that this guy will return. You didn't see his face, you're an unreliable witness, and you don't know where Melissa Spring and Sebastian Ramirez are.

"But we might be wrong.

"He—or an associate of his—might come back. If that happens, what're the chances that a drunk girl firing a gun for the first time in her life will beat an armed professional?"

"One out of three?" Kimmy looked hopeful.

"Change that first number to a zero."

The young woman wrinkled her face. "You don't know that."

"I absolutely do know that. Yet the chances that you shoot yourself in the leg or blow off some fingers or kill a neighbor while playing around with it are good. Something I'd put money on."

"You're kind of an asshole."

"There's been talk."

"Fine." Kimmy finished off her light beer and reached for the revolver.

"Wait."

The young woman paused. "Yeah?"

"Can you get me a baggie for that?"

"If you go."

"Deal."


Afternoon had begun while Bettinger was inside of Kimmy's apartment. Walking along the stone path, he shivered, exhaled steam, and adjusted the handle of the bagged revolver that jutted out of his parka like a threat.

The detective soon reached the parking lot within which he had deposited his yellow hatchback.

"Christ's uncle."

Upon the windshield of the car was a splatter of broken eggs that resembled iced phlegm.

Bettinger entered his vehicle, slammed the door, and twisted the ignition, containing his irritation over the prank, which was at least less hazardous than a bear trap. Irked, he thumbed a preset number on his cell phone and put the receiver to his ear.

The big fellow's prerecorded voice said, "Dominic Williams," and a binary entity beeped.

"It's Bettinger. I'm leaving Melissa Spring's apartment right now—after a fairly interesting conversation with her roommate—and heading back to the precinct."

The detective disconnected the call, adjusted the heating vents (which currently blew cool air), and yawned for no fewer than ten seconds. Sunlight shone into the car through the prismatic splatter of frozen eggs and became a dismal rainbow.

Upon his left thigh, the cell phone buzzed.

Bettinger stretched his arms, opened the device, and put the receiver to his right ear. "Yeah?"

"I got your message." Dominic did not sound happy.

"I really appreciate you getting back to me."

"You've got somethin' you wanna say?"

"Do you? I'm starting to think you might have a whole lot on your mind. A heap of preoccupations."

Silence sat between their ears for a slice of a minute.

"You wanna talk?" asked Dominic.

"I want to listen. I want to hear the story of some miserable pricks who keep secrets that get good cops killed. Know any stories like that?"

There was a period of silence during which the big fellow either managed his anger or consulted another person.

Eventually, Dominic said, "I might."

"So it's not just oatmeal in that skull."

"You gonna keep givin' me elbows?"

"Until the day I buy a pair of boots that're made out of rock."

The big fellow snorted into the phone. "We should sit down—do this in person."

"Yeah. You and your short blotchy pal."

"He'll be there."

"I don't mean your dick."

"I fuckin' know who you mean." Dominic was unable to keep the venom out of his reply. "So . . . where?"

"Sichuan Dragon. Be there in twenty minutes."

"Give us thirty."

"You have twenty."

Bettinger killed the connection and pocketed his cell phone. Sometimes he wondered if the real reason that he had become a policeman was so that he could berate idiots.

Soon, he was on the road, driving east. People, cars, and buildings shattered and reassembled as they slid through the icy egg lacquer, but the weary driver could see well enough to safely navigate the terrain. Halfway through his journey, a yawn exploded on his face and lasted for the duration of a red light.

Battling the fatigue that sought to close his eyes, the detective accelerated through the intersection. The street lengthened and grew dark, and a corpse fell from the clouds. It was female and nude and looked like Alyssa.

Startled, Bettinger woke up, sitting inside his hatchback while stopped at a red light. His heart pounded inside his skull, throat, and chest.

"Christ's uncle."

The detective rolled down the windows, inserted an earplug, and called his wife, hoping that the cold air and pleasant conversation would keep him awake for the remainder of his short drive. As he accelerated through the intersection, Alyssa's voice appeared inside of his head.

"You must be exhausted."

Bettinger grunted an affirmation. "Any news on the show in Chicago?"

"I'm talking to Rubinstein at two thirty."

"Great. I hope it goes well."

"Thanks."

"As soon as you have a date for the opening, let me know so I can put in for a couple of days off."

"I will. I think it'll be late March."

"Good. The weather should be better by then."

"Should be. How's work?"

"Busy. I may not be able to come home tonight." Unless the detective took a long nap in the near future, he would be too tired to endeavor the drive back to Stonesburg.

"Something serious is going on?"

"There's something." Bettinger hoped that whenever Alyssa first learned about Stanley and Gianetto, the news item she saw would also contain photographs of the apprehended murderers.

"Be safe." The painter knew better than to ask after details that were not freely offered. "Please don't make this a habit—not coming home."

"I won't."

"You're getting congested."

The detective inhaled through his nose and felt the presence of phlegm. "You're right."

"Of course I am. Pick something up—one of those vitamin supplements. Maybe a decongestant."

"I'll get a decongestant." Bettinger guided his hatchback onto a four-lane street. "Those supplements don't do anything except put vitamins in the sewer."

"There's no harm in extra vitamins."

"The vermin in Victory are healthy enough."

"Be sure to get non-drowsy."

"Okay." The sign for Sichuan Dragon appeared on the right side of the road, and the detective toggled his turn signal. "I'm about to meet some idiots."

"If they don't tell you what you want to know, you have my permission to get rough."

"Thanks."

"Same thing if I'm asleep when you get home . . ." A dirty chuckle emerged from the old man who lived inside of Alyssa's chest. "You have my permission to get rough."

"Expect it."

"For orgasmic purposes," clarified the woman.

"Assignment accepted."

The oldster cackled.

Bettinger secreted Kimmy's gun underneath the passenger seat and changed lanes. "I love you."

"You too. Bye."

"Bye."

Braking, the detective dialed the wheel and entered the lot of the restaurant, where he saw his partner, dressed in gray, leaning against his silver luxury car while drinking from a cup. The big fellow looked up, noticed the hatchback, and tossed his beverage into the trash. Hot coffee splashed upon a cube of frozen lo mein, cracking it in half.

The rear door of the silver vehicle opened, and Tackley stepped outside, buttoning the jacket of his sharp blue suit. As he and his former partner entered the restaurant, the hatchback landed in a parking space.

Thinking about dead policemen and roasted duck, Bettinger left his car and entered Sichuan Dragon. Warm air that smelled like garlic, vinegar, and peanuts enveloped him as he looked around the establishment, which had fewer than a dozen diners. Sitting beside each other at the corner table in which Elaine James had eaten her final meal were Dominic and Tackley.

Harold Zhang materialized. "You're with them?"

"Sort of."

Bettinger strode to the seated duo and dragged the chair that opposed them from the table. Calmly, he sat down and reached for the teapot.

"We don't need to turn this into a meal," said Dominic.

"I'm eating." The detective filled a cup, raised it to his lips, and blew vapors across the table.

Tackley stared. Vitiligo had turned his face into a map of pink oceans and milk-white islands. Lying in the middle of this porous geography were two cold blue pools.

"While I'm eating," Bettinger said, "you guys are talking. Keeping me entertained."

The mottled man gestured with his left hand. Shadows stretched across the table as Perry and Huan materialized.

Bettinger looked at the new arrivals. "Glad you could make it."

"It's New Year's in China." The doughy redhead claimed a chair and looked at his partner. "Right?"

The pockmarked Asian took a seat. "Year of the monkey."

Tackley took the teapot, filled his cup, and eyed Bettinger. "You shouldn't fuck with us." His voice was soft and betrayed no emotion whatsoever.

"I'm looking for cop killers, and I'm fucking with everyone." The detective from Arizona sipped his tea. "If you have good posture, you won't fall over."

Perry looked at Huan. "This guy's like that dog I read about."

"Which?"

"The one that could smell things from real far away—ten miles, maybe even more. Was a show dog, actually."

"Did tricks?"

"When he was a kid. Anyways, the feds were doing a manhunt in West Virginia, looking for one of those crazy survivalist types, and they read about this dog and put him on a plane."

"First class?"

"I'll have to look that up. Remind me. But they get him out there, let him sniff the fugitive's socks, and right away, he bolts into the woods, running after the guy so fast nobody can keep up."

"He's determined."

"Even by canine standards. Next day, they catch up with the dog. He's got one of the fugitive's fingers in his mouth, and he's got a stick in his neck, going all the way through."

"Dead?"

"Yeah." Perry shook his head. "And people like dogs."

"Even more than black detectives who know everything?"

"There's just no comparison."

"Hmmm." Huan contemplated his chopsticks.

Bettinger refilled his teacup and looked at Tackley. "Start with your pal Sebastian Ramirez."

The mottled man's blue eyes betrayed nothing. "What're you trying to do here?"

"Get the cop killers before they strike again."

Tackley contemplated his tea. "What do you think we're doing?"

"Keeping secrets and covering your asses." Bettinger decided to go all the way. "Terrorizing Melissa Spring's roommate."

"I don't know what you're talking about." The mottled man's face was stone. None of the other cops said or did anything.

"Bullshit. Start with what you said to Sebastian in ICU so he'd drop the charges. I'm gonna wager it wasn't 'Gosh, we're sorry,' or 'Your next wheelchair's on us.'"

A heavy silence descended upon the table. Steam rose from the placid surfaces of teacups, but nothing else moved.

"You have history with Sebastian," Bettinger continued, "and I'm guessing it precedes crippling him. If you share data with me, we can work together to find him."

"You're looking for him?" asked Tackley.

"Yes. So tell me a story where you and he are the protagonists. Maybe it's called 'The Crooks.'"

"Fuck you," said Dominic.

Bettinger drank from his teacup and set it down. "I'm not here to make friends."

Huan exhaled smoke. "Understatement of the century."

A shadow that belonged to Harold Zhang slid across the table. "Are you ready to order?"

"Yes," said the detective from Arizona. "I'd like dandan noodles, roast duck, and braised snow pea shoots."

Scratching ideograms upon his notepad, the proprietor looked at the mottled man. "And for you, sir?"

"Nobody else's eating."

"Are you sure? Our food is very, very good."

"Nobody else's eating."

Irked, Harold Zhang departed.

Tackley rose from the table and donned his sunglasses. "Good luck with that investigation, Detective Bettinger."

Dominic, Huan, and Perry rose from the table and followed the mottled man toward the exit. As they departed, one of them said, "Don't get a stick in the neck."

Sitting alone at the corner table where Elaine James had eaten her final meal, the tired, fifty-year-old detective raised his porcelain cup to his lips and discovered that it was empty.

# XXV

# Moving Fulcrums

The roasted duck had more fat than was desirable, but the noodle and vegetable dishes were quite flavorful. Under most circumstances, this array would have provided Bettinger with a very satisfying meal, but today, as he chewed, weary and confused, an emptiness sat in his belly.

He had believed that he could manipulate Tackley and his crew, but whatever concerns had compelled them to converge at Sichuan Dragon had been dispelled by their conversation with him.

As the detective picked at the pickled remnants of his dandan noodles, he contemplated his brief phone conversation with Dominic, the one that had precipitated the meeting. In it, he had mentioned his interview with Kimmy, but not its outcome or much else.

Suddenly, the answer was obvious.

Prior to the meeting, Tackley and his associates had suspected that Bettinger knew the whereabouts of Sebastian Ramirez. This motivation for the quartet agreed with how the mottled man had concluded the conversation only moments after the detective had stated that he wanted to locate the disabled drug dealer. The crew's concerns had been allayed: Bettinger had not found the enemy.

Defeated, the man from Arizona sipped tea. He currently had no leverage and did not even know the location of the fulcrum.

"How was it today?" asked Harold Zhang.

"The noodles and pea shoots were good, but your ducks should go on a diet."

After putting a few bills on the table, Bettinger soaked a urinal cake, washed his hands, and exited the restaurant. The cold attacked.

"Christ's uncle."

As he proceeded toward his yellow hatchback, he noticed something peculiar. The car seemed to be leaning to its right.

A few more strides brought the detective to the driver's side of his automobile, and there, he saw two swollen puddles that were the front and rear tires.

"Fuck."

Upon each sidewall was a five-inch incision through which the air had escaped, and coating the rubber and the asphalt was an icy varnish that Bettinger recognized as urine. He looked around for witnesses who might have seen the crime take place, but saw nobody.

The detective knew who had vandalized his car, and he knew that he was supposed to know. This affront was a postcard that had four signatures.

Carrying teapots that were filled with hot water, Bettinger and Harold Zhang exited Sichuan Dragon and walked toward the lopsided egg- and urine-stained hatchback.

"People like you," remarked the proprietor.

"I'm charismatic."

Harold Zhang frowned as he examined the frozen yolks. "These chickens died for nothing."

The two men removed the frozen eggs and urine from the hatchback and soon returned to the restaurant. There, Bettinger and Harold Zhang washed their hands, the former thanking and ordering a bowl of hot-and-sour soup from the latter.

The detective claimed a table by the window (where he could watch for the tow truck), called the pillbox, and asked Sharon to put him through to Zwolinski.

"You've got me for ten seconds," said the inspector.

"I think Sebastian Ramirez is behind this."

"He's in the hospital."

"He isn't."

There was a moment of silence.

"You just earned yourself two minutes. When'd he leave?"

"Yesterday morning. When I saw that—"

"How come you're not sayin' 'we'? Where's Williams?"

"Somewhere."

"That'll change," promised Zwolinski. "Keep talkin'."

"When I saw that Sebastian was gone, I went to his home."

"He's not home."

"He isn't," said Bettinger. "Nor is his sister, who's his only family in Missouri. I go to his girlfriend's place after, and she's gone too. But her roommate's there, and she's got a story."

"Give it to me in pill form."

"A guy wearing a ski mask comes looking for Sebastian's girlfriend—her name's Melissa Spring—but only finds her roommate. He does some dinner theater with her, makes her send a text message to Melissa, asking her to come home so he can ambush her."

"It's not a physicist under that mask."

"It isn't," agreed the detective. "So four guys turn up—Sebastian's men, I'm assuming—and send the guy in the mask and his buddy somewhere else."

"Heaven?"

"No. But one of them lost some toes."

"Nobody got killed?" asked Zwolinski, surprised.

"A cat did."

"I'm more of a dog person."

The proprietor set a dark bowl of hot-and-sour soup upon the table, and the detective mouthed his gratitude.

"So you think it's Sebastian?" asked the inspector. "The executions?"

"I do . . . though the evidence right now is circumstantial at best."

"I wouldn't call what you've got evidence."

"It surpasses coincidence."

"It does . . . though if Sebastian's behind these executions, Stanley and Gianetto might just be the beginnin'." A sound that was either firecrackers or the inspector cracking his knuckles overloaded the connection. "A preview."

"Any ideas where he'd hide?"

"Not specific—Sebastian's spread out all over the city—but I'll detain his associates. Remove 'em from the street so he's just a cripple in a wheelchair in some shitty room somewhere."

"Be sure to get pictures of him to the airport, bus depots, and train stations. State patrol as well."

"I did all that fifteen seconds ago."

"Have somebody find Sebastian's car and see if Melissa Spring or Margarita Ramirez bought new wheels in the last two months."

"I'll put Miss Bell on that," said Zwolinski. "Where're you now?"

"Leonard and Fourth."

"Sichuan Dragon?"

Bettinger swallowed soup. "Yeah."

"Like it spicy?"

"Keeps me awake."

"I ate there once. Tasted real good, but my ass said, 'Never again.'"

The detective tried not to imagine the bathroom tableau as he raised another spoonful of dark, clumpy broth to his mouth.

"I'm calling Dominic now," announced the inspector. "If he's not there by one, he's suspended. If he's not there by quarter after, he's fired."

The line went dead.

The tow truck departed, pulling the yellow hatchback, and at 12:54, the big fellow's silver car drifted into the lot. It was hard for Bettinger to see his partner through the vehicle's tinted windows, but it was easy for him to imagine what sort of expression sat upon the man's bandaged face.

The detective put down a bill that was three times the cost of the soup, thanked the proprietor, and met his adversary, the pernicious cold. A dozen quick strides brought him to the silver automobile.

Bettinger seated himself, and Dominic silently accelerated toward the adjoining four-lane road.

"My hatchback's in the garage."

The big fellow said nothing.

"You aren't curious what happened?"

No reply emerged from Dominic's mouth.

"Okay." Bettinger buckled his seat belt. "But when this whole thing's over, you'll reimburse me for what you did."

"I don't know what you're talkin' about, and I certainly ain't payin' for anythin' that happened to that piece of shit."

"You will . . . though you may not be conscious when you remit payment."

"You threatenin' me?" Dialing the wheel clockwise, the big fellow glanced at his partner. "I got eighty pounds on you."

"Eighty pounds of stupid."

"We'll see just what it is I got."

The detective adjusted his seat. "I just want you to know it's coming."

"Whatever."

Bettinger was uncertain whether or not his fighting skills would give him enough of an advantage to whip the brute, who was younger and far bigger, but he was certain that he could hurt him badly, which would serve the same purpose. The physical line had been crossed, and the detective had no choice but to respond in kind.

Dominic turned off of Fourth.

"Where're we going?" asked Bettinger.

"You don't know? I thought you knew everythin' since the day you was born."

The car sped past a female vagrant who was yelling at a dog that had usurped her cardboard box.

Again, the detective inquired, "Where're we going?"

"To the fringe. Sebastian's got some buildings down there and we're rounding up his guys."

"Sounds like a good idea."

Dominic snorted. "None of these guys're gonna know where he's at."

"Make that one hundred pounds of stupid."

"Keep that up, and we can go right now."

"Do you think that a guy fresh out of ICU—an incontinent cripple in a wheelchair with one lung—do you think a guy like that executed Stanley and Gianetto himself? Or was even at the scene?"

"I doubt it," said the big fellow, rolling over a dead pigeon that resembled a women's hat from the 1930s.

"So when we detain his associates, we might get the gunmen or some information about Sebastian or both."

"Whatever." The facial muscles that were a part of Dominic's thought process relaxed.

"You've got a better plan, then share it."

The big fellow shouted at a pedestrian (who had the right of way), braked, and turned onto Summer Drive. "There're some things you should know before we get to the fringe."

"Divulge."

Dominic withdrew his cell phone, scrolled down the menu, and handed the device to Bettinger. An unidentified number had been highlighted.

"Call that," said the big fellow. "Let him tell you."

# XXVI

# The Story of Fuckface

The detective thumbed the connect button and pressed the receiver to his ear. After two rings, a person picked up and said, "Don't say my name and don't say yours."

Bettinger recognized Tackley's crisp voice. "Understood."

"I'm easy to imitate, so there's always a chance I'm not who you think I am."

"There's always a chance." It was now clear to the detective why the mottled man wanted to talk on the phone rather than meet in person.

"There's stuff you need to know, and there's other stuff—irrelevancies I'll omit. Don't get nosy."

"I won't."

"If you say my name or the names of my associates, I'll hang up. If you get churlish, I'll hang up. You have the wrong idea about certain individuals, and I need to give you some history."

"Did somebody compel you to make this call?" inquired Bettinger. "A guy who eats kielbasa with his eggs and likes to box?"

"I'll classify that as an irrelevancy."

"Fine."

Dominic cut off a lime green vehicle and gave his victim the finger.

Tackley cleared his throat. "There's a certain individual who you and I and many other people are looking for right now. For the sake of this conversation, I'll refer to him as Fuckface.

"The story with him starts a little over four years ago. I'll use fun names for everyone, so you won't get mixed up."

"Thanks. I'm pretty thick."

"We agree on something," Dominic muttered as he changed lanes.

"A bad batch of skag lands in Victory," began the mottled man. "An addict turns up dead, and a few days later, another one croaks. Black bums, so it's not in the papers or anything, and nobody cares. The dealer—I'll call him

Lethal—realizes what he's got, and instead of flushing his deadly stash or returning it to his source, he sells it at a discount to some high school kids."

"Christ's uncle," said Bettinger.

"I'll call these young entrepreneurs Turd and Dung."

"Sounds accurate."

"So Turd and Dung do what any bright-eyed young drug dealers would do: They step on their skag with quinine. Unfortunately, they don't seem to understand the difference between a gram and a milligram, and soon, their tainted skag has a deadly amount of quinine in every single dose."

"God bless the Internet," said the detective.

"So it's graduation day. Only about one in four Victory kids completes high school, so graduation is a big deal for them. Each year, the police put extra guys out to deal with disturbances and DUIs, but in general, it's just good kids getting rambunctious.

"Turd and Dung are looking to establish their clientele, so they hand out their skag as party favors to their friends—honor roll students who have scholarships and futures."

Bettinger felt ill.

"The first one arrives at St. John's at about one in the morning—an eighteen-year-old girl who's never done drugs before that night. Her lips and fingernails are blue, and her dress is covered with diarrhea. She doesn't even make it to the operating room.

"In the next hour, five more kids turn up in the same condition. Three die, and two are stabilized. One of their friends tells somebody what happened, and as the police hunt down Turd and Dung, eight more kids land in the emergency room.

"Eleven kids die that night.

"Next day, the newspapers go out, and they have the ugliest headlines ever printed in the history of this country.

"The police department isn't complimented.

"A big guy in the precinct who likes to box confers with five detectives—you might've met four of them—and tells them to do whatever's necessary to prevent something like this from ever happening again.

"The big guy is realistic, and so are these five detectives. They're not going to solve the drug problem in Victory. The drug problem can't be solved anywhere in this country, even in cities that have low crime rates, lots of money, and Jewish mayors. As long as there are unhappy people, there will be drug users, and as long as there are drug users, there will be drug dealers.

"The police decide that they need somebody on the other side who can monitor things—an established criminal who can make sure nobody's selling drugs to children or dealing poison. One of the detectives mentions a guy he knows—

"Fuckface."

Bettinger suddenly understood several things about Sebastian Ramirez.

"Fuckface is a capitalist who specializes in ventures such as prostitution and gambling—the kinds of things that Victory police rarely have time to focus on—but also drugs, which he handles through a complex relay system that the cops have never been able to stop. He's ambitious, opportunistic, and morally flexible.

"So he's perfect for what the cops need."

The detective recalled a photograph of the hospitalized drug dealer in which the man resembled an exsanguinated corpse.

"The police offer Fuckface a deal, and he accepts it. It takes him four minutes to find out where Lethal lives, and he gives the address to the detectives, who go right over. The idiot sees the cops at his door and goes through the window, even though there's no fire escape, and he's on the fourth floor."

Bettinger assumed that Lethal had been given some assistance by the police in his act of defenestration.

"For some reason," the mottled man said, "it takes the ambulance more than an hour to show up. By the time it does, Lethal's a cold red pile, and the detectives are all eating sandwiches.

"I heard that those sandwiches tasted great.

"That's the beginning of the relationship between Fuckface and the five detectives.

"Several times a month, he gives them information about his competitors, and in exchange, the police leave him alone. He doesn't go straight, but he makes sure whatever illicit shit he has going on is as safe as can be. He knows that he'll lose his deal with the police if people die from his skag or get robbed in his casinos or get AIDS from his girls."

Bettinger surmised that Tackley and his crew had purchased their luxury cars and tailored suits with a hunk of Sebastian's profits.

"As soon as the next quarter," the mottled man continued, "the statistics show fewer overdoses and drug-related homicides in Victory. Things go from abysmal to just plain terrible.

"The big guy in the police precinct is intuitive and vaguely suspects the nature of the deal between the five detectives and Fuckface, but he doesn't ask for details, and so none are provided.

"The arrangement is condoned, but off the record.

"It works for years.

"Unfortunately, Fuckface is a morally flexible capitalist, and eventually, he gets some new ideas. He does the math and decides to play both sides, even though he makes more money than all five detectives put together.

"It's disappointing, though it's not a big surprise:

"Your hopes aren't very high when you count on a guy named Fuckface.

"For a while, it's small offenses. Fuckface feeds the detectives some bad information—tip-offs with the wrong times or locations—and he apologizes. Fuckface says that mistakes happen, and the detectives tell him not to worry about it, they trust him.

"They say this, but they don't mean it. They know that he's playing both sides, wasting their time, and this makes them frown.

"So there's one more character who's important to this story. His name's Fat Asshole.

"Fuckface wants to make a deal with Fat Asshole, but Fat Asshole has heard some worrisome talk. He's heard that Fuckface is a part-time confidential informant, and it's an established fact that a starving dog in heat on the streets of war-torn El Salvador is more trustworthy than a goddamn CI.

"So Fuckface says he'll prove where his loyalties lie. He knows that Fat Asshole was shot and put in jail a couple of years earlier by a certain detective, and he will deliver this detective to Fat Asshole as a token of goodwill.

"This detective is the fifth one—the guy you didn't meet."

Everything clicked into place for Bettinger, and he felt the weight of the story's imminent conclusion.

"The fifth detective has been looking for a serial rapist, and Fuckface gives him a lead. The location is deep in Shitopia, and when the detective gets there, some guys grab him, take him to a room, and tie him up so that Fat Asshole can have some fun with him.

"Fat Asshole is a sociopath.

"A week later, the four detectives find their missing peer. He's naked. His eyes are gouged out, and his larynx is crushed. His liver is inside his stomach, cut into hunks, chewed up, partially digested. It's been there since he was forced to eat it for his final meal.

"There aren't any words in the English language that can convey what the four detectives felt when they saw their peer—their friend—like that."

"I'm sorry," said Bettinger.

Tackley cleared his throat. "The detectives know that Fuckface was the one who set up their friend. Fuckface is terrified, and he should be.

"He goes into hiding, calls one of the detectives, and gives up Fat Asshole, claiming that Fat Asshole promised not to kill the detective, only give him a beating.

"The four detectives go after Fat Asshole, who pulls out a gun and receives so many bullets that his head looks like tomato puree by the time the smoke clears.

"But there's still Fuckface, the lying fuck who handed the detective over to the sociopath. The piece of rat shit who sold a good man's life like it was a whore's pussy.

"The airports and highways are monitored, and the four detectives search Victory for three days. On the third night, they find a bum named Doggie, ask him some questions, feed him a pigeon or two, and all of a sudden, Fuckface's crew ambushes them. One detective gets a bullet in the arm, and another gets some buckshot across the face."

Bettinger knew that these two men were Perry and Dominic.

"The detectives catch a member of Fuckface's crew and ask him questions in the least gentle way you could ever imagine. So he tells them where Fuckface is hiding.

"The detectives descend upon that location, which is a second-floor apartment in an area that's far nicer than where any of the detectives live.

"As soon as Fuckface hears the thunder, he escapes, runs into a crowded supermarket, and surrenders.

"The detectives put the cuffs on him and are inspired by the various jars and heavy cans and frozen foods that they see. With a great amount of zeal, they use these hard things to crush and reorganize Fuckface's insides.

"The rest is in the papers."

The line went dead.

Bettinger gave the cell phone to Dominic, who then replaced it on his hip.

"Lawrence Wilson was a great detective and the best fuckin' guy I ever knew," said the big fellow, dialing the wheel clockwise. "I don't know what you would've done after seein' your friend like that, but that's what we did."

"How come Perry and Huan weren't demoted?"

"Me and Tackley went a little more overboard."

Bettinger did not find that difficult to imagine. "I understand what you guys did. It's not right . . . but I might've done the same."

Dominic nodded his head. It was clear that his thoughts were with a person who no longer existed.

# XXVII

# Collecting Idiots

Silence returned to the silver vehicle as it sped south.

Shortly after it traversed a phalanx of tenement buildings that were either partially demolished or partially constructed, Bettinger asked, "How long 'til we get there?"

"Ten minutes."

"You know who we're looking for?"

Dominic snorted. "I know 'em."

"Okay."

The detective reclined his seat and shut his eyes. Although he had heard a skewed history of the events, he believed that all of the essential facts were true, especially since most of them could be verified with one call to the inspector. Tackley, Dominic, Perry, Huan, and Lawrence Wilson had probably skimmed from their contact—money or pills or favors from prostitutes—but their agreement with Sebastian had been sanctioned by Zwolinski and resulted in years of solid busts. It seemed as if the bandaged, buckshot thug behind the steering wheel was a little dirty, but not entirely rotten.

"If you didn't fuck up my car," Bettinger said, "I'd apologize for saying that you and your pals were crooks."

"Whatever."

"But you did fuck it up." The reclining detective yawned. "So it's still coming. You and me."

"Make sure you have some vacation days for your recovery."

"You too." Another yawn exploded across Bettinger's face. "Wake me when we get there."

"I'll fire a gun next to your ear."

"Be sure to take off the silencer."

Something replaced reality.

In that thing, Bettinger was sitting next to Alyssa on an airplane in which people smoked crooked cigarettes. The cabin shuddered, and a weird, cold shadow rippled across the seats. Concerned, the detective looked out through his window. Bright fire consumed an aileron, two engines, and the wing.

He wondered if he should tell his wife what was happening.

The airplane rumbled, and a voice in the sky said, "We're here."

Bettinger opened his eyes, and saw the chipped, gray façade of the five-story building that was expanding across the windshield of the silver car. Dominic applied the brakes, and the moving image became a photograph.

The silver car expelled two policemen into the cold. Together, they hastened across the street and up the stone stoop.

The big fellow kicked the front door like it was a broken lawnmower. "Police! Open up!"

"Open up!" echoed the bleary-eyed detective. Scanning the windows of the opposite building, he saw a few curious onlookers. None of them were childhood friends, dead relatives, or giant insects, and thus, he concluded that he was no longer dreaming.

Again, the big fellow kicked the door. "Open this now!"

"Who is it?" asked a man on the far side of the wood.

"The police. Open right now, L-Dog, and don't have no fuckin' gun in your hand neither."

"Dominic?"

"Detective Williams to you." Dominic pounded a fist against the door, and wood cracked.

"Hold up, hold up," implored the fellow inside.

"Now!"

"I'm gettin' it, nigga."

A couple of footfalls echoed, and two bolts snapped. The door withdrew, revealing a tall white guy who had blond dreadlocks, gold teeth, and a black denim suit. "What you—"

The big fellow shoved the sentry aside and entered the pink front hall, trailing the detective.

"Wait a sec," pleaded L-Dog.

The door shut, and Dominic eyed Bettinger. "Get the wigger."

The detective withdrew plastic handcuffs, said "Turn around," and fastened the white man's wrists behind his back. "Face the wall and drop to your knees."

L-Dog sank.

Dominic walked to a paisley recliner chair that had five Chinese food containers upon its armrests. Leaning over, he reached underneath the seat cushion and withdrew a semiautomatic pistol, which he then pressed against an intercom button.

The speaker crackled, and a woman inquired, "Yes?"

"This is Detective Williams."

"Dominic?"

"Send down Izzy, Lester, and Kitty. Right fuckin' now."

The speaker crackled. "What do you want them for?" The woman's voice had an anxious quaver.

"Send them down or me and my partner'll come up there, open a window, and toss them in the invisible elevator."

"I'll tell them."

"They got two minutes." Dominic stole an egg roll, ate it in two bites, and frowned at L-Dog. "How old's this shit?"

"When's today?"

"Fuckin' nasty."

Bettinger cracked the door, looked outside, and saw that the street was empty. "Clear," he said, resealing the entrance.

Dominic put three plastic handcuffs on the recliner and eyed his partner. "The bald white guy's the one to watch—name's Lester. Izzy and the girl ain't stupid enough to get feisty."

"Got it."

The big fellow thumbed the intercom button and said, "Got ninety seconds." Leaning back, he surveyed the Chinese food containers that sat upon the armrest and poked one with his gun. "The hell's this?"

"Spicy tuna roll," said L-Dog. "Probably still good."

"You got sushi from a Chinese place?" Dominic was disgusted. "Musta been high when you ordered."

The wigger shrugged.

Footfalls sounded inside the stairwell at the far end of the hall, and the policemen exchanged a glance that meant "Get ready."

Bettinger cracked the front door again and looked outside. Feigning nonchalance on the far side of the street was a skinny white man who wore sunglasses, work boots, and a giant overcoat.

"The police are conducting an investigation in this area," announced the detective, displaying his badge. "If you stay here, the best thing that'll happen to you is a full-body search." An assortment of soft and hard shoes tattooed the indoor steps, growing louder as they neared the ground floor. "So either put your hands on your head or leave."

The skinny fellow bolted, his overcoat ruffling like a cape.

Bettinger shut the door, turned around, and raised his gun.

Emerging from the stairwell were an austere biracial madam who wore a heavy overcoat, a bald white guy in a green jogging outfit who had wild eyes, and a light-skinned black man in a blue suit who had intricate facial hair and precise three-sixty waves.

"Hands up and kiss the fuckin' wall," barked Dominic.

"Why're you here?" inquired Izzy, the stylish black man.

"Shut up."

The trio raised their hands, and a blond Asian woman who was holding a cell phone as if it were a gun appeared on the stairwell and announced, "I'm recording this."

Bettinger wondered if the Victory police should join an actors' union.

The suspects faced the wall, and Dominic snatched the plastic handcuffs from the recliner.

"You gonna take us to the grocery store?" asked Lester, the bald white guy. "The one by Sebastian's place? Show us some groceries?"

"Shut the fuck up."

The big fellow yanked the white guy's arms behind his back and bound his hairy wrists with a zip tie.

"Aren't you going to read me my rights?"

"Nah."

Lester turned to the Asian videographer. "Detective Williams is violating the law."

"He isn't," Bettinger said as he cracked the door. "You'll hear your rights before you're questioned." Outside, the street was empty.

"That's at the station." Dominic handcuffed Izzy. "When we've separated you."

"What're we being charged with?" Kitty inquired as her wrists were bound.

"Somethin' or other."

"You have to tell us," stated Lester. "You're required to."

Bettinger glanced at Dominic. "He watches a lot of movies."

"Black-and-whites." The big fellow motioned to the pile of blond dreadlocks. "Grab the wigger."

The detective helped the prone man to his feet, looked outside, and saw the families that had emerged from the opposite building. To this gathering, he announced, "Anybody who steps within twenty-five feet of us or the silver car will be arrested for interfering with police business." As his words ricocheted, he nodded at his partner.

Dominic thumbed the intercom. "Izzy, Kitty, Lester, and the wigger are goin' to jail—this place is now closed. The police'll be back in a hour and grab any retards who're still here."

Gun in hand, Bettinger led the shackled quartet from the building. His partner trailed behind the prisoners, followed by the Asian videographer and the eyes of the group that stood on the opposite side of the street. Several of the spectators were smiling.

The criminals were stuffed into the back of Dominic's car, and an old woman yelled, "Put them in the incinerator!"

Her recommendation received a smattering of applause.

"Felons!" decried her husband, shaking a fist that looked like a crumpled grocery bag. "Racketeers!"


Bettinger was sporadically conscious during the cramped thirty-five-minute drive back to the pillbox. Inside the holding area, the big fellow and the detective read the prisoners their rights, charged them with a vast assortment of crimes, and installed them in two unconnected jail cells, the drunk tank, and an interrogation room.

The partners soon returned to the main area, where they saw Perry and Huan arrive, escorting five handcuffed and unhappy Hispanics who were somehow connected to Sebastian.

"Somebody open up the goddamn windows!" Zwolinski bellowed from behind his desk. "Goddamn crooks smell like possum."

Two hasty cadets retrieved a stepladder that would enable them to perform the task.

"Get some coffee," Dominic said to Bettinger, "I'm gonna talk to Izzy."

"I want to be in that room."

"I ain't arguing with you in front of him."

"We won't argue."

Doubt played across the big fellow's bandaged face. "I say, 'Leave,' you heed me. This ain't time for regulations."

"I'll give you room." The detective would not allow his partner to physically coerce the prisoner, but he understood that there were already illicit connections in place and that any deal offered would remain off the record. "I know there's a relationship here."

"Good."

The door that led to the receiving room opened, and in walked five bloodied toughs who looked like they had just finished playing the version of dodgeball that used a cinder block rather than a rubber projectile. Succeeding the line of prisoners and drinking coffee from his antiaircraft shell was Tackley. As he traversed the main area, he lowered his beverage, looked at Bettinger, and nodded.

The detective returned the mottled man's salutation, aware that their tacit exchange was as meaningful as a handshake.

# XXVIII

# Poof

"Sebastian owns that buildin', but the girls, the casinos, the furniture, the dope—all that's Izzy's," said Dominic, leading Bettinger into the rear hall of the pillbox. "He pays Sebastian rent—legal, on the books—and a percentage of his take off the books. That's how a lot of Sebastian's operations go."

The policemen neared the gray door of the interrogation room in which they had earlier deposited the racketeer.

"Did Izzy continue to pay while Sebastian was in the hospital?" asked the detective.

"The rent, probably. But it'd be hard for Sebastian to know if he's gettin' his fair share of the rest."

"That might be something to exploit."

"Yeah. And he doesn't like bein' called 'faggot,' which he is."

A few more strides brought the policemen to the door. There, the big fellow said, "Don't give me elbows."

"I won't."

"I got a direct way to do this if he's churlish."

Bettinger motioned for Dominic to precede him, and in tandem, they entered the interrogation room—a windowless enclosure that had cinder-block walls, four overhead lights, and two wooden chairs, one of which upheld Izzy. The racketeer's wrinkled blue jacket and unbound hands rested upon the only table, which was metal and bolted to the floor.

"If your ass comes one millimeter outta that seat," the big fellow stated, "you get cuffs."

The prisoner fingered his elaborate facial hair, which resembled filigree. "Why am I here?"

"Should I repeat the list?"

"Why am I here now? Today?"

Bettinger slid a red file across the table until it touched the prisoner's manicured fingers. "Peruse."

Izzy lowered his gaze and lifted the cover. Inside was a photograph of Officer Dave Stanley, lying dead and mutilated on the pavement beside the blackened remains of his partner. "I heard about these guys," said the racketeer, grimacing as he examined the picture. "You don't think I had anything to do with this, do you?"

Dominic shrugged. "Their dicks were stolen."

"I don't know anything about this." Izzy closed the file and surveyed the hard faces that loomed on the opposite side of the table. "I'll call my lawyer if you try to push this on me."

"If you call your lawyer, I'll go back to where you work, get five floors of evidence, and turn your charges into a real court case."

"You're not so clean yourself."

"I ain't worried. You want a lawyer or you want to talk to us?"

"You know I didn't have anything to do with last night."

"Your landlord did." The big fellow put his hands on the table. "And we're lookin' for him."

"He's in the hospital. Where you put him."

"He checked out."

Izzy seemed to be genuinely surprised by the news. "I saw him Sunday."

"He left yesterday." Dominic reopened the file and tapped the image of the executed officers. "Same day as this."

A chuckle emerged from the racketeer.

The big fellow closed his fists, and the bandages on his face drew together. "You don't want to laugh anywhere near this picture."

The threat hung in the air, and Bettinger prepared to interpose himself.

"You think Sebastian did this?" asked Izzy. "He's a cripple."

"He had it done, and we're lookin' for him."

"Try ringing his doorbell."

"Ain't home. Vanished with his sister and his girlfriend."

"Is that what innocent people usually do?" inquired Bettinger. "Hide?"

"What does that mean?" Izzy shook his head. "He probably thinks you guys want to finish what you started in that grocery. Throw another frozen turkey."

The big fellow shrugged.

"I'd hide too," said the racketeer.

"Is he in your building somewhere?"

"No. It's a walk-up."

"Where else would he go? The place on Darren Street? Eve's? A flophouse in the perimeter? The Toilet? Out of town?"

"Follow the tracks of his wheelchair."

Dominic straightened his jacket. "I know you're a entrepreneur—"

"An."

"I know you're a entrepreneur," the big fellow resumed, uncorrected, "so I gotta wonder why you're standin' up for a guy who charges you too much rent, takes a slice of your bank, and makes you lick his asshole. Seems like you'd benefit if Sebastian wheelchaired off a cliff."

"I don't know where he is. I swear to God—on my mother's life—on that. I thought he was still in the hospital until you said he wasn't. But if I did know where he was, I wouldn't turn him over. I'm loyal." Izzy tented his manicured fingers and leaned back in his chair. "Though I realize that the concept of loyalty might be hard for you to understand."

"You got it backward, poof—who turned on who. That cockroach Sebastian earned his wheelchair and the bag he shits in." Dominic spun the free chair around and sat on it so that he was at eye level with the prisoner. "But never mind what you think, 'cause here's the deal—here's reality:

"Help me find Sebastian or I'll burn down your operations."

The racketeer was stunned.

"The building's already evacuated," the big fellow continued, "and I got a pickup truck with oily rags and ten gas cans parked a few blocks away. All your casinos. All your herbs. All your beds and fancy linens." He flashed his palms. "Poof."

Izzy looked at Bettinger. "You hear this fucking maniac? You hear—"

"What was that?" asked the detective.

"Did you hear what he said to me? How he—"

"Sorry." Bettinger jogged the side of his head as if it were a jukebox. "My ears are sporadic."

"Goddamn Victory police." Izzy massaged his temples with shaking hands. "Isn't somebody here supposed to be the good cop?"

"He was fired in the seventies."

"Make me happy," said Dominic. "I don't burn down buildings when I'm happy."

Fearful tears glimmered in the racketeer's eyes. "You wouldn't really do it, would you?"

"That's the dumbest question I've ever heard. And I've got a ex-wife who asked, 'Will we still be friends?'"

"I don't know where he is. I told you."

Bettinger placed the plastic bag that contained Izzy's cell phone upon the table. "Send him a text message."

"He won't answer if he's hiding."

"Maybe not." The detective circled the table and landed beside the racketeer's left shoulder. "But plan B comes after plan A."

Izzy withdrew his cell phone from the baggie. "What should I put?"

"He probably knows you got picked up," Bettinger said, "so tell him that we let you go, but confiscated all of your cash. Tell him you won't be able to pay him for a while."

"Type that." Dominic pointed at the cell phone and rose from his chair. "Just like he told you."

"And let me see it before you press send," added the detective.

"Fine."

Izzy typed out a text message and showed it to his editor.

Bettinger read.

*Hey. Fucking pigs raided my plce and took evryting, so there'll be a delay w the rent.*

"Add the word 'Sorry' at the end," said the detective. "So it seems like you're trying to keep things friendly."

With shaking thumbs, the racketeer typed the letters *S-o-r-r-y* and a period. "Send."

Izzy pressed a tiny arrow. A moment later, he said, "It went through."

"Put that thing down," ordered Dominic.

The racketeer set the cell phone upon the table. "The number he gives people doesn't even go to him directly. And even if he gets it, I don't know why he'd bother to respond."

"If he thinks you're trying to use the situation to your advantage—to cheat him of his percentage—he might reach out," replied Bettinger.

Izzy looked uncomfortable.

The detective withdrew a sheet of paper from his pocket. "We got a list of the meds he's on from the hospital. Painkillers, mostly."

"That's surprising." The racketeer's sarcasm was as dry as a Nevada road.

Bettinger set the document upon the table. "Who can he get this stuff from when his supply runs out?"

"Prescription painkillers?" Izzy smirked. "Get me a phone book, and I'll cross off the names of the ten people who can't get him that."

The prisoner's reply was what Bettinger had expected, and his real question was already on its way to his mouth. "Where would Melissa Spring or Margarita Ramirez get a clean vehicle on short notice?"

Something flickered in the racketeer's eyes.

The detective said, "Margarita's car is still in the parking lot of her building, Melissa doesn't own a vehicle, and Sebastian's is impounded. Neither of the women bought one from an authorized dealer, but obviously, they need something—a truck, a van, a big car—to drive Sebastian around in. Who would they get it from?"

"I don't know."

Disbelief shone upon Bettinger's face. "You don't know who Sebastian would go to for clean wheels?"

"I don't."

Dominic kicked the empty chair across the floor. Wood smacked Izzy's right kneecap, and he howled.

"Oops."

Bettinger looked at his partner. "Watch where you step."

"I forget to look sometimes."

This bit of violence might prove useful, but the detective would not tolerate any more such infractions. He mouthed the word "Don't" to the big fellow as the racketeer massaged his hurt knee.

"You fucking broke it," said Izzy, looking up at Dominic.

"Nah—there would've been a snap. Even soft faggot bones."

"It's real hard to imagine why your wife left you."

Bettinger withdrew the unoccupied chair, unbuttoned his jacket, and sat down. "Who would Melissa and Margarita get a clean vehicle from? The purchase was probably made this month."

Sniffing, Izzy wiped his eyes. "I'll give you this if you let me go."

"Nah," replied Dominic. "You give us this and your place won't get torched at midnight. Nobody goes anywhere 'til we have Sebastian."

"What if you can't find him?"

"We'll find him," Bettinger stated as he withdrew his notepad and mechanical pencil. "Who would Melissa Spring and Margarita Ramirez get a clean automobile from?"

Izzy wiped his sweat-glazed face. "Slick Sam."

"Know his last name?"

"No."

"Never heard of him," said Dominic, shaking his head.

"Right," replied Izzy. "That's why people go to him."

"Where's his shop?" asked the detective.

"Shitopia."

"What street?"

"You know that elementary school where those kids were killed in the eighties?"

"I know it," replied the big fellow.

"Across the street from there."

Bettinger asked, "You've got his cell?"

"No." Izzy looked like he was about to vomit.

"Do you know when he's in?"

"You're asking me for his itinerary? I met the guy once."

"Then you shouldn't feel so bad—he's practically a stranger."

Ashamed, the racketeer looked away.

The big fellow placed the cell phone in the baggie, buttoned his jacket, and handed the red file to his partner. "Poofs feel bad about everything. It's just how they are."

"We'll send in a sketch guy," the detective told the prisoner, "and you two can make some art."

No response emerged from Izzy, who sat slumped in his seat, looking at his hands. The policemen exchanged a nod and strode toward the exit.

"Don't get executed," advised the racketeer.

Unkind laughter resonated within Dominic.

A yawn swallowed Bettinger's face as he and his partner returned to the frigid main area and climbed onto the dais.

"You look terrible," Zwolinski said from behind his desk. "Was it the Chinese food? I warned you about that place."

"I'm just tired." The shivering detective zipped up his parka.

"What did Isaac Johnson give you?"

"The address of a chop shop that might've sold a vehicle to Melissa Spring or Margarita Ramirez."

The inspector scratched the thick silver pelt that was atop his skull. "Izzy gave you that?"

"Bettinger pulled it from the ether," remarked Dominic. "Nigga's a asshole, but he's got ideas."

"I theorize."

"Looks that way," observed Zwolinski.

Bettinger motioned to the door. "We need to get to the chop shop bef—"

"Williams will take care of that. I want you to go rest that brain before it has a heart attack."

"I'm capable of—"

"Quiet. The Sunflower Motel gives us a deal." The inspector aimed his mouth at the ceiling and bellowed, "Molloy! Crater Face!"

Perry and Huan looked over from the far side of the pillbox.

"When you leave in twenty minutes," the pugilist commanded, "drop Bettinger off at the Sunflower."

The redheaded fellow and the pockmarked Asian gave thumbs-up signs and returned their attention to the phlegmatic printer.

Zwolinski looked at Dominic. "Go to that chop shop. If it's quiet, get a cadet to do surveillance."

"Okay."

The big fellow walked off of the dais.

"Don't cripple anybody," said the inspector.

Dominic shrugged.

"You do," Zwolinski warned, "and we're in the ring."

"Whatever."

"You didn't do too good last time," added the inspector. "By round six, you were beyond uncomfortable."

Again, the big fellow shrugged.

"Is something wrong with his neck?" Zwolinski asked Bettinger.

"It doesn't seem to let oxygen into the top floor."

"I've suspected that. Tackley gave you some history?"

"He gave me some."

"So that's it. It was an ugly situation, and I was just barely able to keep 'em on. Somethin' like that happens again, they'll be fired—probably go to jail." The inspector rubbed a lump that had an eyebrow. "Make sure it doesn't go that far."

"I've had experience handling pit bulls . . . though usually I put them in the back of the cruiser."

"In Victory, pit bulls ride up front."

# XXIX

# Officer Nancy Blockman
# Observes Other People

Officer Nancy Blockman frowned as she located another piece of eggshell in her hair. The stocky, bulldog-faced, thirty-eight-year-old brunette had showered twice since the embryonic bombs had fallen, but a group of tenacious white flecks still clung to ground zero. Lowering the driver's side window of the stopped patrol car, she jettisoned the shard onto a twilit Victory street, where it skipped twice and disappeared inside a crack that looked like a mouth.

"Did you use cream rinse?" Officer Abe Lott inquired from the passenger seat.

"Cream rinse? You sure you're not gay?"

"Cream rinse's gay?"

Accelerating through the intersection, the policewoman observed her pudgy partner.

"What?" asked Abe, defensively. "Lots of people use it. I use it."

Nancy's former husband, Steven, was a homosexual (regardless of the fact that he had been in a sexually fulfilling marriage with a woman for five years), and ever since he had revealed himself, the policewoman looked for the warning signs in all men. There was no real reason for her to suspect that Abe was gay—he was married, went to strip clubs, and had dirty fingernails—but it was her duty to let him know if he exhibited any of the most common gay traits or affinities.

"I don't want to offend you," the pudgy officer said, "but I think you're a little paranoid about that stuff."

"I'm vigilant, not paranoid. And there's a reason."

"Your husband?"

"No—it's because of scientists," said Nancy, turning off of Summer Drive. "They say that the body is rebuilt from scratch every seven years. Completely. Down to the cellular level. All of it."

"All of it?"

"According to scientists."

"Then what about tattoos? How come they last more than seven years?"

"Because it's ink. It doesn't do anything but just sit there while the cells all around it are having kids and dying. A tattoo's just subcutaneous jewelry."

"Hmmm." Abe played with his revolver as if it were an action figure.

"But my point is," Nancy resumed, "you never know how all this cellular activity might affect you . . . how you might change as the body—and the brain and everything—rebuilds itself. The man you were seven years ago no longer exists."

The pudgy officer looked at his hands. "Seems the same."

"On the outside. But maybe some of your brain cells are different. Mutated. Maybe the next time you go to a strip club, some—"

"Gentlemen's lounge," corrected Abe.

"Maybe the next time you go to a gentleman's lounge, some girl will take off her top, show you her double Ds, and you'll be like, 'So what?' "

"Never." The pudgy officer was steadfast. "Tits are the greatest."

"But why do you think that?"

" 'Cause I'm a man, and because they are."

"It's because you're a man who has a certain biological reaction to tits, and that reaction is because of your programming—your cells. All of that can change when you're being rebuilt. And you're always being rebuilt."

"Man . . ." Abe was exasperated. "This conversation's depressing."

"I'm just saying that you change over time—everyone does. Molecule by molecule. Be vigilant. Watch out for things like 'cream rinse.' "

"But I really like tits." There was a note of desperation in this statement.

"I don't think you need to worry."

"Good." The pudgy officer resumed playing with his gun as if it were an action figure.

"That Langford's another story."

"Langford's a fag?"

"I really don't like that word—I have nothing against homosexuals—but yes." Nancy imagined the officer's handsome face, neat blond hair, and chiseled physique. "If not, his cells are on the brink."

"You see that blonde he brought to the Christmas party? With that amazing rack?" Abe swallowed saliva. "I'd like to see her at the gentleman's lounge." Again, he ingested his own secretions.

"Is that what you fantasize about when you see a woman like that? Seeing her strip?"

"I'm a married man." The pudgy officer tapped his gold wedding band. "Even in my fantasies, I'm faithful."

"That's sweet."

"I take my vows very seriously." Abe ruminated for a moment. "But Langford's girl . . . it was like she was made out of frozen custard." Again, he swallowed saliva. "Wanna get some custard?"

Nancy had long ago realized that her partner's mind was a linear machine. "After we check on this motorcycle."

"Yeah. Of course, of course. Y'know, I've heard it's a lot better for you than ice cream—frozen custard."

"Could be."

The policewoman knew that frozen custard had a high concentration of egg yolks and was very unhealthful, but she decided against correcting her partner. Continuous cellular upheaval and the deaths of Anthony Gianetto and Dave Stanley were as much bad news as the pudgy officer could possibly handle.

At present, Nancy turned onto 178th Street and drove west, toward the part of the Toilet in which the motorcycle had been stolen. The sun was sinking, and the buildings on the horizon were nothing more than dark, silhouetted blocks.

The policewoman turned on her headlights. Bicycle reflectors, watchful eyes, and an array of discarded beer cans emerged from the dark gray swath. Dialing the wheel counterclockwise, she circumvented a sleeping terrier.

"He's cute," remarked Abe.

Nancy did not ask if he had a special affinity for small dogs.

The patrol car rolled through an area of partially inhabited apartment buildings and banked onto a northbound street that was named Luther. Ten minutes later, the cruiser entered the southernmost part of the Toilet. Nailed to a telephone pole by its head was the top half of a dead cat.

Nancy looked away, disgusted. "Who would do something like that?"

"Democrats."

The policewoman rarely discussed politics with her partner. "What's the street number?"

Abe looked at the Biggman's Burger napkin upon which he had scribbled the information. "Eighteen fifty-three Luther."

"Keep an eye out."

"I saw a seventeen sixty-seven on that last block."

"Okay." Nancy slowed the vehicle. "Then we're close."

Because the majority of buildings in the Toilet were unnumbered, any would-be navigator had to be observant and do some math.

In the passenger seat, Abe fondled his gun.

"Stay alert."

The pudgy officer looked confused. "For the stolen motorcycle?"

"For an ambush. Like Zwolinski told us to look for."

"Because of what happened to Dave and Gianetto?"

"Because of them."

The patrol car rolled past a group of black teenagers, compressed a beer can, and crushed a dead pigeon.

"Those things are annoying," remarked Abe. "Why do they keep dying?"

"The air makes them suicidal."

"You always say that."

Nancy slowed the cruiser and surveyed a three-story building that wore no less than five hundred pounds of graffiti. Amidst tags, names, and genitals was a square sign that had been painted black.

"Can you read that?" asked the policewoman.

Abe looked through the driver's window, squinted, and nodded his head. " 'Suck my big fat d—' "

"Not that. By the door." Nancy pointed at the sign. "Can you read it?"

"Looks like a four and a nine at the end."

"So it's two down."

The policewoman tapped the accelerator, and the cruiser rolled past a similar building and arrived at a three-story edifice, which was covered with a large, weathered mural that prophesized some sort of breakdancing utopia.

Nancy stopped the car. "Look around."

"For the ambush?" Abe liked for things to be clear.

"Yes."

The officers surveyed the area, looking for people who might do them harm. Several kids on dirt bikes buzzed past, and a pair of oldsters appeared at a window across the way.

None of these individuals seemed at all threatening.

"I'll go knock," said Abe.

"I'll keep the engine going."

"Good idea." The pudgy officer holstered his revolver, looked at the Biggman's Burger napkin, said, "Garret Oakwell, Garret Oakwell," stuffed the information into his chest pocket, and repeated the name twice more as if he were preparing for a recital. "Sounds kinda fake, doesn't it?"

"He's a taxpayer. Dispatch checked on him before they sent us."

Abe pulled the handle to no avail. Embarrassed, he undid the lock, and jerked the latch a second time, opening the door. Cold spilled into the heated vehicle as he climbed outside.

"Something happens to me," the pudgy officer said, "don't tell my wife about the gentlemen's lounge."

"Okay. Be careful."

Exhaling steam, Abe nodded his head, patted his gun, and closed the door.

Nancy was not especially concerned about her partner's safety. Her experiences on the streets of Victory and as a soldier in Haiti told her that bullets favored people of intelligence.

A heavy white man with silver hair, a long beard, and abraded denim appeared in the doorway of the mural-adorned building. Standing directly behind him was a brunette woman in ancient leather who was either his sister or his wife. No less than one third of her body mass was stored in her rump.

Abe waved as he approached the couple, and Nancy cracked her window.

"'Bout time you got out here," said the bearded biker. "My motorcycle might already be a Canadian."

The pudgy officer continued up the stone walkway. "Are you Mr. Garrett Oakwell?"

"Exactly how many people 'round here got their motorcycles took that you need to ask me that?"

"Sir, please." Abe reached the stoop. "I'm required to follow official police procedures when res—"

"Eat at Biggman's, did you?" Oakwell pointed an index finger. "I see the napkin right there."

"Sir. Please—"

"Maybe you had lunch with the guy who took my motorcycle?" posited the biker. "Maybe he was right next to you, and when he said, 'Pass the ketchup,' you went and passed him the ketchup. A brand-new bottle—still vacuum sealed so it clicked when he opened it."

"Sir. Pl—"

"Maybe the guy who took it used the bathroom same time as you. Maybe his stall ran out of toilet paper, and he asked you for more, and you got it for him. The soft stuff you can wipe with all day."

"We did drive-through."

In the cruiser, Nancy sighed.

"When you were in line at the drive-through," Oakwell continued, "was the one ahead of you a stolen motorcycle?"

"I don't remember." Abe looked over his shoulder and rolled his eyes at his partner.

"What're you looking back there for?"

The pudgy officer returned his attention to the biker. "Is your name Garrett Oakwell?"

"Still haven't figured that out?"

Something entered Nancy's rearview mirror, and she adjusted the angle of the glass for a better view. Two blocks away was a moving object that looked like a van.

Its headlights were off.

Calmly, the policewoman removed her pump-action shotgun from the rack.

"Please just answer the question," said Abe.

"I am now, always have been, and always will be Garrett Oakwell."

Nancy faced her partner and the bikers. "Everyone go inside right now."

"The law isn't welcome in my house."

"Get inside!" snapped the policewoman. "You're in danger." Her eyes returned to the rearview mirror.

The approaching vehicle was one block away. It was a brown cargo van that exactly matched the description of the one that had been spotted the previous night at the crime scene.

"Inside!" Abe shouted as he guided the couple (or siblings) into the building. "Move it!"

Nancy aimed the pump-action shotgun through her rear windshield.

Tires screeched, and the brown van shot forward. The policewoman panned her weapon, tracking the vehicle as it rumbled past the patrol car and crossed the intersection at the end of the block. No license plate sat upon its rear bumper.

Nancy knew that she could not let the cop killers get away. Shouting "Call for backup!" to Abe, she set the shotgun on the passenger seat, shifted gears, and stomped the accelerator.

The patrol car roared.

Tires skirled, and the Toilet turned into a blur as Nancy rocketed toward the brown cargo van.

The patrol car shook as it thundered up the road. Flying stones dented the frame, and the engine wailed, but the policewoman did not raise her foot from the gas. The distance between the speeding vehicles soon narrowed to half a block.

Nancy reached for her shotgun, and a black square appeared at the back of the van.

It was a window.

White fire exploded from the opening. The patrol car's headlights shattered, and a front tire burst, jerking the steering wheel to the left. Metal screeched.

The cruiser fishtailed, its blasted wheel flapping.

Nancy lifted her foot from the gas and turned directly into the skid. The remaining tires caught, and soon, she regained control of her car. Stomping the accelerator, she continued her pursuit.

The distance between the vehicles closed, and again, the policewoman reached for her shotgun.

Fire boomed.

The windshield exploded, and a score of pellets seared Nancy's neck and chest.

Tires thudded. The vehicle leapt the curb, and a telephone pole slammed into the grille. Nancy's forehead pounded against the steering wheel.

Dizzy and bloodied, the policewoman leaned over, located her shotgun, and pointed it forward, through the broken windshield. The brown cargo van was no bigger than a matchbook, and soon, it was a memory.

"Come back here, you faggots! Fucking faggot cocksuckers!"

Officer Nancy Blockman was surprised by her own vocabulary.

# XXX

# Bettinger Versus Sleep

"Wake up."

Bettinger opened his eyes. His bedroom had become a cold white enclosure, and for no reason that he could possibly apprehend, Alyssa was a gaunt, pockmarked Asian guy who had close-cropped black-and-silver hair. Reality rearranged tired thoughts, and murkily, the detective recalled two acts: Sitting at his desk and leaning backward. It had not taken very long for the lurking predator known as sleep to capture its prey.

Huan helped Bettinger to his feet.

"It's from Hawaii," said Perry, extending a thermos of coffee to the arisen detective.

Nodding his thanks, Bettinger received the vessel.

"Huan's got an uncle who sends it for the holidays," said the redhead. "Their soil's way better than all this shit on the mainland."

"It's an amazing place to get buried," added the pockmarked Asian.

"Concentrate real hard and you'll taste hints of cinnamon and almonds."

"Possibly bikinis."

Bettinger tipped some of the odiferous coffee into his mouth. Even in his sleep-deprived condition, he recognized that the beverage was an extraordinary achievement. "This is—"

"You've got two minutes!" Zwolinski shouted from behind his desk.

"We'll drop you at the Sunflower," Perry said as he and the other two detectives proceeded toward the door. "Your car will be in the lot when you wake up—we're covering the repair bill and'll put the keys under your door."

Bettinger had no interest in thanking the redhead for these services. "Fine."

"Don't worry though—Dominic isn't going to walk away from your challenge."

"I wouldn't allow him to."

Perry glanced at his partner and then eyed the contender. "Ever fight an elephant that's made out of angry gorillas?"

"Not since I was a kid."

"Get ready."

"Zwolinski handled him."

"Zwolinski's a titan, and a scientific fighter. Even still, that was in a ring, with gloves, and you don't get dirty with the boss. You, on the other hand, will get the full arsenal."

"I'm ready."

"Want that on your tombstone? 'He was ready.'"

"Put an ellipsis," suggested Bettinger.

"'He was ready . . .'"

Huan considered the revision. "It just became art."

"Make sure it's cursive," added the detective from Arizona.

Grinning, the redhead patted his charge's back and motioned him forward. "I will."

Bettinger strode through the doorway and across the receiving area, where the bereaved receptionist at the front desk did not once lift her gaze from her big white telephone. It looked as if she was expecting a direct call from Heaven.

Something tapped Bettinger's right shoulder, rousing him, and his stinging eyes told him that he was in the back of a parked sedan. Huan sat behind the steering wheel, and Perry slouched in the passenger's seat, eating a candy bar. Magenta twilight painted the detectives' faces, the windshield, and the façade of the Sunflower Motel, which was twenty feet away.

"Show them your badge," said the redhead. "You'll get half off."

"Got it."

Bettinger reached for the door.

"Hold up," said Perry.

"Yeah?"

The redhead finished his candy bar, glanced at his partner, and returned his attention to the backseat. "You could've snitched on Dominic for what he did to that lady yesterday—the child abuser—and you could've told the boss about what happened to your car, but you didn't. You just kept working, pushing the case, coming up with ideas."

"Good ones." Huan held up a folded square of paper.

"Our information," said Perry. "Cells, private e-mails."

Bettinger claimed the data.

"Put them in your phone and flush the list."

"I will. You guys have my info?"

"We do," said the redhead. "If you think of something . . . or if something happens . . . call us."

The pockmarked Asian nodded. "Whenever."

"Thanks."

Bettinger knew that Dominic was a brute and that Tackley was mean, but Huan and Perry both seemed like pretty decent guys, especially considering the environment in which they worked.

The redhead motioned to the motel. "Get a room on the second floor, away from the street and the other guests. Bolt the door, put the chain on, shove a couch in the way. Close the curtains and put your mattress on the ground so you won't get hit if somebody fires a gun through your window."

"That's happened?"

"Some guys in a brown cargo van just took a shot at Nancy Blockman. She's okay, but the guys're still out there."

"I'll be careful," said the detective, disturbed by the news.

Huan extricated a cigarette and blew smoke. "Pleasant dreams."

Bettinger left the car, shut the door, and dragged his elongated shadow into the lobby, where he received a set of keys from the bald fellow who sat behind the front desk.

"Enjoy your stay."

"Mmph."

The bleary-eyed detective returned to the cold, circumnavigated the yellow motel, and climbed up to his second-floor room, which faced the rear parking lot. Listening for noises, he opened the door and made a quick survey of the (well-heated) yellow-and-green interior, unsure if such precautions were paranoiac. His brief but thorough search revealed no clandestine enemies.

Following Perry's advice, Bettinger shut the door, twisted the bolt, drew the chain, pushed a couch in front of the entrance, closed the curtains, and slid the bed's queen-sized mattress off of the elevated box springs. This last endeavor revealed two condoms, a withered joint, and a Mexican scatological fetish magazine.

The detective had never imbibed urine for erotic purposes (or any other), but if he had, he doubted that the taste in his mouth would have been any worse than it was right now. Although he would have paid twenty-five dollars for a toothbrush and a squirt of paste, he was too tired to involve the front desk or return to the oppressive Victory cold to acquire a mint amenity.

Bettinger gargled hot water, spat, gargled hotter water, spat again, and rinsed. Returning to the bedroom, he withdrew his cell phone and highlighted his wife's number. This call would be his final act before relinquishing consciousness.

"Hi," said Alyssa. "How are you?"

The detective discerned a well-concealed note of anxiety in the woman's voice. "You heard."

"Did you know them?"

"I met one of them." Bettinger sat on the edge of the box spring.

"Are you working on it?"

"The whole department is . . . though right now, I'm about to get some sleep."

"Where are you?"

"Sunflower Motel." The detective discarded his boots. "In downtown Victory."

"So you're definitely not coming home tonight."

"I'm not. I'll start the day early tomorrow—pick up fresh underwear and a shirt out here—and try to be home by dinner."

"That would be nice."

A belt fell to the floor. "How was your talk with Rubinstein?"

"Really good. I'll tell you about it when I see you."

"Great. How're the kids?"

There was a pause, which the detective knew was meaningful. "What happened?"

"I don't need to give you something else to—"

"Alyssa . . . what happened? Did Gordon—"

"It's Karen. Those boys were teasing her again—saying racist shit and some sexual things. She walked away, but they followed her. She told them to stop, and they started throwing things at her."

Fury filled Bettinger, but his voice was even when he inquired, "What'd they throw?"

"Potato chips at first. Then milk cartons and taco meat."

"Taco meat." The detective pictured his beautiful little girl spattered with wet ground beef. His heart hammered against his ribs, and his vision narrowed. "And while this was happening, what were the adults doing? Heating up tar? Gathering goddamn feathers?"

"This is why I didn't want to tell you right now."

Drawing a deep breath, Bettinger calmed himself. "Darling . . . what's happening here in Victory is serious—as serious as it gets—but it's my job. I like being a detective—locking up idiots, solving puzzles, helping people—it's the most satisfying thing I could ever do . . . but it's my job. You and Karen are my life. Something bad happens to either one of you, I want to know right away, no matter what. Okay?"

"You forgot Gordon."

"I didn't. I'm sure he'll return to my top tier of loved ones when he goes to college, but right now, he's on tier two."

The old man who lived inside of Alyssa's chest chuckled. "I won't tell him you said that."

"He knows." Bettinger tossed his jacket onto a nearby chair, where it lingered for a moment before falling to the rug. "Can I talk to Karen?"

"She's asleep. Want me to wake her?"

"Let her sleep. What happened to the rednecks?"

"They're in trouble. The main boy's gonna get suspended. Brian Callagan."

"Can you get in touch with his parents?"

After a ponderous moment of silence, Alyssa inquired, "Is that a good idea?"

"I don't think racism spontaneously occurs in twelve-year-olds, so I'd like to talk to the source."

"And say what? Your kid's shitty?"

"I'd like for Mr. and Mrs. Callagan to know that an unpleasant and very black policeman will be directly involved with anything that happens to Karen Bettinger."

"You'll bring extra guns when you meet them?" asked Alyssa.

"At least eight."

"I'll get their number." The oldster chuckled. "You get some sleep."

"I will. And I'll try hard to be home by dinner tomorrow."

"Okay. Touch base in the afternoon and be careful."

"I will and I will."

"I love you," the husband and wife said at the exact same time.

"Good night," added Alyssa.

"Bye."

Bettinger thumbed the disconnect button and placed his cell phone upon the nightstand. Yawning enormously, he undressed, turned on the ceiling fan, and cast his body to the mattress.

Sleep finally won the long-fought battle.

Nightmares bubbled up from the depths of the detective's subconscious mind, but even the worst of them were mild compared to what he would soon see.

# XXXI

# New Uses for an Old Car

A huge palm slapped the glass, startling Bradley Janeski. The hand reconfigured, and a dark finger that could break a sternum pointed at the dirt.

"Roll it down."

The cadet cranked the knob, lowering the driver's side window of the two-seater that had once belonged to his older brother, and prior to that, his oldest brother. Standing in the parking lot of the long-closed elementary school was a big black man whose silhouette resembled the front of a warship. Steam rose from the two dark turrets that were his nostrils.

Like most people, Bradley Janeski was intimidated by Corporal Dominic Williams.

"Park under there—" The big fellow pointed to the partially collapsed overhang that shielded the front entrance of the school. "Stay in the shadows. When you see Slick Sam, you call me or you call Tackley. If you don't get us, try Huan or Perry Molloy. Here—"

A balled-up piece of paper bounced off of the cadet's freckled face and landed in his lap. Rubbing his right eye, the young fellow retrieved the crumpled sphere of data.

"If he bolts before we get here . . ." Dominic unbuttoned his black overcoat and produced a snub-nosed revolver that was covered with cellophane. "Ever shoot one?"

"I scored in the top two percent on the range and grew up hunting with my dad and brothers."

"Take this out of the wrapper." The big fellow tossed the laminated weapon onto the dashboard. "If Slick Sam tries to run off, point it at him—tell him to stop, say you're a cop. Fire a warnin' shot in the air if you have to."

"Yes, sir." Bradley Janeski claimed the revolver from the dashboard and started to peel off the cellophane.

Dominic threw plastic handcuffs onto the sketch of Slick Sam's face, which was lying upon the passenger seat. "Tie him up and keep him in the trunk 'til one of us gets here."

"Yes, sir."

"If he scampers," the big fellow added, "I want you to hit him with your car. Run over his foot, break a leg. Don't go too fast and don't run over his vitals. If he gets in a car, smash into that."

"Shouldn't I just shoot him?"

"We need him alive no matter what."

"I know how to shoot."

"Maybe . . . but even a shot in the leg can kill a nigga. And if Slick Sam pulls a gun on you, you won't be thinkin' 'I need to wound him.' You'll shit your pants and shoot 'til you're empty." Dominic slapped the hood of the car. "This's your gun."

The cadet disagreed with the corporal's insulting appraisal, but was smart enough not to verbalize his opinion. "I'll hit him."

"But first thing you do when you see him is call those numbers for us to come over."

"Yes, sir."

Exhaling steam, the big fellow turned around and walked toward his silver luxury car.

Bradley Janeski closed his window, put the gun on top of the sketch, and raised the binoculars that he had received last month for his twenty-second birthday. Across the street was the unremarkable concrete façade of the building that was said to contain Slick Sam's chop shop.

The cadet's first stakeout had begun.

# XXXII

# E.V.K.

The elevator door opened, and the handsome blond policeman who resembled an actor entered the empty, brightly illuminated sixth-floor hallway of his apartment building, carrying a bag of Thai food and several laundered shirts. Nine athletic strides brought Jerry Langford to his door, where he stopped, set his dinner on the carpet, and withdrew his keys. Metal jingled.

A pale and wiry Czech fellow who wore a black jogging outfit, a ballistic vest, latex gloves, a mask, and a tattoo of the letters *E.V.K.* watched the officer through a peephole.

Langford unlocked the final bolt, and as he seized his takeout bags, his observer opened the door of the unrented apartment that was across the way. The hinges and the Czech's footfalls were quiet, but not silent, and the officer looked over his shoulder. Standing behind him and pointing a silencer-fitted gun at his face was a man who wore a black devil mask.

"Don't make any noise," E.V.K. said through his fangs. "Go inside."

Fear shone upon Langford's face as he complied, backing into his apartment. The officer was a bachelor, and things would be simple unless he had a visitor.

E.V.K. kicked the bag of Thai food into the white apartment, proceeded inside, shut the door, scanned the area, and turned the bolts. Not for one millisecond did his gun point at anything other than the officer's skull.

Stepping over a heap of spilled noodles that looked like rat entrails, the Czech advanced until only three feet remained between the weapon and its target.

"Don't talk," whispered E.V.K. "Just nod. Understand?"

Langford nodded.

The Czech pointed an index finger at a black leather sofa, and the wide-eyed officer seated himself, setting his laundry upon an adjacent cushion.

"Is anybody else here?" E.V.K. quietly inquired as he taped a clear plastic baggie to the side of his gun.

Tears sparkled in Langford's eyes.

It was not difficult for the Czech to interpret the officer's reaction. "Is that person a policeman?"

Langford shook his head, wiped the moisture from his eyes, and set his damp hand upon the laundered shirts. Paper crinkled.

"Jerry?"

The voice came from the adjacent room and belonged to a Southern woman. E.V.K. thought that she sounded pretty.

The policeman lunged at the Czech.

Bright fire emerged from the silencer, and a hollow-point bullet severed Langford's throat, turning his cry into a squeak. The plastic bag that was taped to the side of the semiautomatic gun caught the ejected shell.

Again, E.V.K. fired. Langford's left eye disappeared, and his brains slapped the sofa. As the second shell clinked against its forerunner inside the plastic bag, the lobotomized body reseated itself.

The killer believed that a proper murder should not make any more noise than would the act of putting on a winter coat, and so he was fully satisfied with the volume of his recent enterprise.

He proceeded across the apartment and stationed himself beside the closed bedroom door. Underneath his sneakers, the floorboards creaked.

"Jerry?" inquired the Southern woman.

E.V.K. aimed his gun at the unseen speaker who stood on the far side of the wood.

"Did you remember hot sauce?"

The brass handle turned, and the door opened, revealing the soft face of a voluptuous blonde who had a cute mole on her left cheek, a pair of dimples, and sheer rose lingerie that concealed only the pinkest parts of her anatomy.

Lightning flashed.

A hollow-point bullet tore out a chunk of the woman's throat and slammed her skull against the jamb. Wheezing, she stumbled back.

E.V.K. grabbed the woman's ponytail, yanked her sideways, and flung her onto the bed. Clear fluid that smelled like pinot grigio spewed from her esophagus, and the killer leveled his gun. White fire flashed, lancing her terrified mind.

The fourth empty shell kissed its peers inside the plastic bag.

Blood pooled.

E.V.K. turned to a dresser and opened the top drawer, revealing women's panties, which he then balled up and stuffed inside the blonde's punctured throat and forehead until the wounds were clogged. The killer did not consider himself a perfectionist, but he was neat.

E.V.K. rolled up the woman in the wine- and gore-stained sheets, set her on the ground, and slid her underneath the bed. He then returned to the living room, where he holstered his gun and shoved women's underwear into Langford's wounds. Fortunately for the killer (who did not have time to properly clean the scene), the rug and couch were black and would hide most of the officer's blood from a casual observer.

The Czech searched the dead man, located his police badge, and dropped it inside the baggie that contained the four spent cartridges.

There was only one more thing that E.V.K. needed from Jerry Langford.

The killer unzipped the policeman's jeans and pulled down his boxer shorts, revealing a shaved pubic region, a tattoo of a heart, and a rose-hued phallus, which was wet with urine. Pinching the glans between his thumb and forefinger, he stretched the shaft like a piece of taffy.

A disposable box cutter clicked in E.V.K.'s other hand.

Steel cut a dark line across the taut member, and the tension ripped the outer skin, revealing the pale urethra and the dark purplish-red meat of the corpus cavernosa. A quick, sharp gesture severed these tubes, removing the phallus from its owner.

The killer placed his dripping prize into the bag that contained the badge and spent shells. All of these things were going to the same exact place.

E.V.K. added Langford's bundled body to the mausoleum below the bed, turned out the lights, peered into the hallway, saw that it was empty, removed his mask, exited the apartment, and rode the elevator down to the sky blue lobby.

At the building entrance, the killer held the door for an elderly couple who were having an argument about somebody named Gertrude. As he waited for them to pass, he glanced at his diver's watch, which he felt was the single finest machine in existence. Its platinum hands told him that it was eleven minutes after eight.

Langford's unexpected visit to the launderer had wasted some time, as had the dispensation of the blond houseguest. E.V.K. did not get upset about things that were beyond his control, and he was not upset now, but he knew that he had to alter his dense itinerary.

The killer left the apartment building and walked north, toward the charcoal-colored pickup truck that he had acquired the previous morning.

It was the kind of vehicle that nobody would notice.

# XXXIII

# The Crushing Depths

An aimless guitar solo leaked from the speakers of a jukebox that yielded insect noises rather than bass frequencies. Sitting under a dim blue light in a corner booth, Perry waved his hand in front of his face, dispersing Huan's smoke. The redhead usually tolerated his partner's filthy habit without complaint, but on overlong days such as today, he found it difficult to ignore the surfeit of carcinogens in the air.

"If I get cancer and you don't, I'll put a melanoma in your rice."

"I might notice a lump."

"I'll tell you it's tofu."

The pockmarked Asian turned his head, exhaled filth, and created a flower of sparks, dashing his cigarette inside a flattened beer can. "You just had to ask."

"Didn't want to be rude."

Perry's left shoulder still ached from the bullet that he had taken in November, and the pain reminded him of the day when he, Huan, Dominic, and Tackley had caught up with the lying scumbag who had gotten Detective Lawrence Wilson killed. Although Sebastian had some legitimate grievances from that event (and others), his recent retaliations seemed random . . . if not evidence of outright madness. Gianetto and Dave Stanley were good, honest policemen (almost to the point of inefficacy), and had never even met the Hispanic, nor had Nancy Blockman and Abe Lott, whose lives had been threatened earlier this evening.

"It's tragic." Perry raised a mug of dark stout. "To Gianetto and Dave."

Huan hoisted an iced ginger ale. "To Gianetto and Dave."

Glasses clinked, and the men drank.

"I'm not looking forward to that funeral," the redhead remarked as he wiped foam off of his upper lip. "Italians don't hold it together."

"Understatement of the millennium."

"The food'll be good, I guess . . . and plenty of it. His daughter's sweet six-teen had enough fried ravioli to make a bivouac." Perry sucked down another mouthful of beer. "You gonna bring Heather?"

"Police funerals give her nightmares," said Huan, setting down his ginger ale. "This whole situation's got her worried enough."

"Makes sense."

As was the case whenever Perry grew morbid, he thought of his two sons in California, their mother, and her husband, the man with whom his progeny shared everything except for 50 percent of their genetic code and the first two years of their lives.

"Thinking about your boys?" asked Huan.

"Maybe." The redhead had not seen his sons since the Christmas before the previous one, when he had flown out to visit them in San Francisco. During that trip, he had gotten into an argument that almost turned into a brawl with Dan, the Ivy League lawyer whom his wife had married. "It's all fucked to shit."

"You should see your boys."

"You know what's the worst thing about it? When things were getting hot between me and that prick Dan? My kids—my sons—sided with him—with their stepfather—a fucking lawyer—and I could tell if things got physical, they'd help him out."

"You should see your boys."

"That event doesn't need a sequel. Or a retarded remake in 3-D."

"Don't go to San Francisco. That's Jill and Dan's territory, and you don't fit in with them. Take your sons to a fishing town or a beach resort—someplace new that can be yours together."

Perry considered the suggestion. "Maybe."

"You aren't their father in any traditional sense, so don't pretend like you are. You're a good guy, a smart cop, and a great friend. Show them that guy and they'll want to have some kind of relationship with you."

"I'll think about it."

"See them."

Perry pulled the half-used cigarette from the ashtray and stuck it in Huan's mouth.

A respectful silence sat between the partners who had been best friends since their first year at the police academy.

The pockmarked Asian thumbed his lighter. Firelight shone upon the un-even surface of his face, illuminating all but the deepest pits. Hirsute tobacco glowed.

The song with the desultory guitar solo was replaced by a cut of soul from the seventies. Black men sang in precisely harmonized falsetto about an ice-cream sundae, which Perry concluded was a metaphor for a woman or the most delicious parts of a woman.

"Listen to these dudes," remarked the redhead. "Black guys used to be so cool . . . so much cooler than a white guy could ever hope to be. Man—what the hell happened to them?"

"They became African Americans."

"What a waste." Perry drank an amount and adjusted his sling. "That Bettinger's pretty grumpy."

"Intellectuals are usually grumpy."

"Why?"

"Dumb guys always asking them, 'Why?'"

"Minute ago you said I was smart."

"Things change."

Perry drank another lump of stout. "You think we'll find Sebastian?"

"We'll find him." Huan sucked on his cigarette. "Though right now, something far more important is going on . . ."

"What?"

"Who."

"Who?"

The pockmarked Asian exhaled smoke, and the redhead watched it float toward the bar, where a robust woman with platinum hair had put herself on display. A purple sweater and black slacks affectionately clung to her equipment.

"That's a specimen," remarked Perry. "She's thrown a look?"

"Twice."

"That's four eyeballs."

"Plus mascara."

Perry scrutinized the drink that traveled to the woman's painted lips. "That's an olive in there?"

"Probably not a miniature avocado."

"She looks kinda lonely . . . forlorn, maybe." The redhead gave some beer a tour of his mouth and sent it to the basement. "Might need some cheering up."

"People say you're laughable."

"I try."

The woman pulled a lock of platinum hair behind her left ear and dabbed the corner of her mouth with a napkin. Her movements were sensual and very self-conscious.

"I didn't even say 'Action.'"

"I'm gonna play cards." Huan turned his cigarette into a miniature hearth and rose from the table. "Have fun."

"When you get home, give Heather my warmest and most invasive regards."

Everybody who met the pockmarked Asian's adorable Thai wife had a crush on her.

"Probably not."

"Don't make me steal her away from you," warned Perry.

"You're not exactly her type."

"What kind does she go for?"

"Deloused."

"This from a guy who recycles."

"That's just for pretend."

"Like church?"

"Just like." Huan pulled on his coat. "See you tomorrow."

"Be safe."

The pockmarked Asian shrugged.

"Don't be flip. It's dangerous out there, and you'd better be careful."

"I'll be careful. Good luck with that olive."

"You're talking to a pimento." Perry ruffled his red hair.

Curvature appeared on Huan's chin, which was a very rare occurrence. Departing, he patted his partner's back.

Perry tilted his mug until it became a transparent vessel, set it down, and rose from the booth. Something with dripping church organs and a singer who had the pipes for gospel replaced the soul song about ice cream.

Stretching, the redheaded detective surveyed the bar. The seat to the right of the woman who had platinum hair was occupied by a guy that did not have a chance, and the one to her left was wide open.

"I noticed a vacancy," said Perry, landing upon the latter stool.

The platinum specimen set down her drink, adjusted her tight purple sweater, and pulled a wisp from her face, which was a sharp and striking one that seemed to be of German origin. Although the dim blue lighting made it hard to tell if she employed a significant amount of makeup, the detective was not overly concerned—all of the lamps in his apartment had dimmers.

"I haven't seen you here before," remarked Perry.

"I usually have better ideas." The woman's voice was smooth, and her breasts were things of great interest.

"My name's Perry."

Preoccupied by troublesome thoughts, the platinum specimen watched her olive.

"You can use a pseudonym if you'd like," suggested the detective. "Or I can give you a name that's commonly used in limericks."

The woman continued her ruminations.

"Look," Perry said, "you were sitting here, giving me looks—as noticeable as neon—so I came over. But I'm polite. If you want to be alone, I'll go away."

"You don't need to go."

The drink levitated to the platinum specimen's mouth, and the olive disappeared. Chewing, she set down her martini glass.

Perry observed the machinations of her Teutonic jaw. "I bet your teeth are real soft."

A tiny smile crept underneath the woman's nose. "Soft and sharp."

"Perry."

The chewed olive was sent to the dungeon. "I'm Kristie."

With a raised finger, the detective garnered the attention of the bartender, who was a tacit, dumpy, and dour iteration of his species. "A thing with an olive for the lady, and a stout for me."

"Mm." The creature in the apron faced his bottles and extended appendages.

Perry returned his attention to Kristie. "That's your real name?"

"I respond to it."

"I like responsiveness. You live in this area?"

The platinum specimen frowned. "Do I look like I live in this area?"

The detective knew then that he was talking to a person who had some baggage. "You look like you could live anywhere you wanted."

"Was that a compliment?"

"I'm hoping."

"Seems like an insinuation."

The baggage was turning into freightage.

"Cute girls have options," Perry defended, "and beautiful women have them to the tenth power."

"So that's what women are? Things to look at?"

"No, no, no—of course not. I'm in it for the smell."

"I thought you said you were polite."

"Within reason."

"So you like to objectify women?"

The detective knew then that Kristie liked to go to marches and rallies. "Any person you don't know is an object. Having an interaction like this— talking—gives you some idea what's inside that object."

"But it's mostly about looks for you."

"No. It starts with looks, 'cause that's how attraction works in the part of the brain we can't control." An idea occurred to Perry. "Show me a picture of the last guy you dated."

"I deleted him."

The detective pulled out his cell phone, which had Internet capabilities. "Tell me his name."

"No."

"I'll bet he's handsome," said Perry, pocketing his device. "I'll bet one thousand bucks that you did not rise above the crude impulses of physical attraction and date a bald, zitty midget just because he had a great-ass personality."

"You're not that handsome," said the platinum specimen, grinning.

The detective relaxed, pleased that he had successfully navigated the first minefield. "I've been told I'm pretty damn okay."

A mug of beer bumped Perry's elbow, and as the empty martini glass changed into one that was full, he withdrew a twenty and put it on the bar. Claiming the bill, the creature in the apron returned to its lair.

Kristie nodded appreciatively. "Thank you."

"My pleasure." Perry guided his cylinder of stout toward the woman's glass. "To pretty objects."

"And those less fortunate."

Two distinct pitches rang.

A bathroom door opened, and white light spilled into the bar, brightly illuminating the pair as if they were the stars of an impromptu musical. Perry got a very good look at Kristie, whose face evinced some wear, but was still very pretty overall. If he had to guess, he would have said that she was a youthful and healthy forty-two-year-old woman.

"I'm forty-two," said Kristie, setting down her martini.

"Never would've guessed."

The bathroom door closed, and the spotlight was gone. Troubling thoughts returned to the platinum specimen.

"What is it?" asked the detective.

Kristie sighed. Perry hated this sound, which had been his ex-wife's primary manner of communication during the last miserable year of their marriage, but today in the bar, he let it sail.

"I was supposed to meet somebody here tonight," said the woman.

"You're in luck."

"A guy."

"Still lucky."

"We went out last week—had a really good time—and were supposed to meet up here." Kristie glanced at her watch. "More than an hour ago."

"And then things changed for the better."

The expression on the platinum specimen's face did not affirm the detective's statement, and he knew instantly that his efforts had been wasted. Sipping from his stout, he searched the establishment for new prospects.

Kristie set down her drink. "I think I should call a cab."

A lone star twinkled in the black vacuum of space.

"You don't have a car?" asked Perry.

"My friend dropped me off. Jordan—that's the guy I was supposed to meet—has a car, and . . . well . . ."

"Again, you're in luck."

"No, thank you." The woman shook her head. "Sorry, but I'll just call a cab."

"I'm a cop."

Doubt wrinkled the platinum specimen's brow.

The detective set down his beer and displayed his badge.

"You really are one," said Kristie, relieved. "If it's okay . . . I'd like to go now."

"Sure. Where are you?"

"On Fourth, off Summer."

Perry ingested the remaining stout. "That'll give you plenty of time to make up a phone number."

Kristie drank the triangle of fluid from her martini glass and set it down. "I won't make one up."

The detective helped the woman into her coat and escorted her into the parking lot, where his dark blue luxury car sat beside a neon four-leaf clover that looked like it had been twice picked. Exhaling steam, he opened the passenger door for his guest.

"Thank you," said Kristie, climbing inside. Her words sat in the air—a visible puff lighted green by buzzing neon.

Perry closed the door and circumvented the vehicle, thinking about his children out West (who were always older in reality than they were in his mind) and also of Huan's advice, and soon, he made a decision. After he dropped off the platinum specimen, he would call his boys and see if they wanted to go hiking— maybe in the Cascades or a Carolina. It was eight o'clock in San Francisco, and both of them should be home and awake.

The detective entered his car, shut the door, and turned the key. A basso purr came from the hood, and the driver glanced at his passenger.

The woman was shivering.

"Only takes a second to get warm."

Kristie nodded. Again, she seemed preoccupied by her problems.

"Everything okay?" Perry dialed the heater to its highest setting.

"Just cold."

The detective let the comment sail. Toggling the gear with his bad hand, he backed out of the parking space, found an empty street, and drove.

Warmth and silence filled the plush interior.

"What do you like to do besides hit on Irish cops?"

"I like to read."

"Books? Periodicals? That blog about dogs that can sort of say the *F*-word?"

"Books."

"Thrillers? Romance novels?"

"Romance novels?" A light chuckle emerged from the woman. "Not since I was fourteen."

"You didn't read *Our Eternal Summer*?"

Kristie looked surprised. "You read that?"

"I did. I thought it was pretty good." The detective refrained from revealing that he had cried at the end.

"I'll take your word for it." This was said ironically, but not unpleasantly.

Dialing the wheel counterclockwise, Perry turned onto Summer Drive. No pedestrians were visible anywhere, and in the distance, a pair of triangular tail-lights veered onto a side street.

"So what kind of stuff do you read?" asked the detective.

"History, mostly. Some spy stuff."

"You'll have to give me some recommendations."

"Sure."

A yawn that seemed less than genuine emerged from Kristie, and Perry interpreted it as a cue. The air grew warm, and for several miles, the two of them shared silence and bumps in the road. It was a surprisingly comfortable experience.

The car purred, and outside, the city was dark and empty. Passing by a record store that had been closed since the eighties, Perry turned on his radio and selected an oldies station. A gang of vociferous women were singing about a boy named Billy Jim, whom they had just decided was no darn good.

"I like this one," said Kristie. "Reminds me of being little."

"Grew up in Victory?"

"Unfortunately."

Perry circumvented a dead pigeon and resumed the conversation. "What else do you do for fun?"

"Rent movies."

"What kind? I won't think less of you if they're fetishistic."

"Foreign films. I really like to see other places, other cultures."

Perry brightened at her response. "Did you see *The Crushing Depths?*"

"I don't think so."

"It's Japanese, black and white—takes place in a submarine."

"I'm not into war movies."

"This will be the exception, since it's the single best movie ever made."

"What's it about?"

Although the detective suspected that the platinum specimen just wanted to kill time until they arrived at her home, he decided to oblige her request. "I don't want to tell you too much," he said, "but I'll set it up . . ."

Perry cleared his throat as if he were about to give an acceptance speech.

"Japan's about to lose the biggest sequel ever made—World War II.

"The main guy in the movie's a guy named Taisho. He's a captain in the Japanese navy. Taisho's got a girl he's engaged to named Yuki, and she's a pretty little doll who works in a factory, on an assembly line making torpedoes for submarines. Times are bad, and the factory's behind schedule—even though everybody's working eighteen-hour shifts, seven days a week. Yuki's lost three fingers in the machines and has a terrible cough.

"Taisho loves her anyways.

"So he gets his mission direct from the Japanese Imperial Commander. His orders are to take one midget submarine to a critical point in the Pacific and sink all of the enemy ships that're there—including a fully loaded aircraft carrier.

"There isn't a chance this is gonna work—not one—but Taisho is a soldier, a warrior, and this is what he does. It's his mission, and it's an honorable death.

"If there's one thing the Japanese like more than raw fish and robots, it's honor.

"Taisho spends one last night with Yuki, having dinner, talking, making love—it's an old movie, so the sex is implied with silhouettes and flowers and stuff. Real classy and romantic. He doesn't tell her about the kind of mission he's going on. He just tells her to be happy—no matter what happens."

Perry felt his eyes tingle.

"At dawn, Taisho puts all of his money under Yuki's pillow and writes a note telling her to leave the factory and move someplace with clean air.

"Then he goes and gets his crew together.

"There's Taisho's best friend Goro, who's a big beefy guy, simple and fun-loving, the kind of guy everybody likes, and there's an old drunk guy with gray hair who's missing an arm, and there's a skinny kid with pimples and glasses—lots of scrubs were being used at this point in the war.

"The four of them go to the midget submarine, and it's banged up like a car you'd see in Shitopia. It's made for two people at most, but all of them need to get in there.

"They load it up with torpedoes, and Taisho has them throw out the bed so that they can fit even more. The ship's called C Seventy-three."

"They didn't name it?" asked Kristie.

"Not the Japanese.

"So C Seventy-three leaves the harbor. The special effects look pretty good for the time, but it's an old movie and you can't be too picky about that sort of stuff."

The headlights shone upon the bent sign for Tenth Street, and Perry glanced at his passenger. "You said Fourth, right?"

"Right."

"On their way to the enemy fleet, Goro and the kid with glasses play cards and talk about having kids, and the old guy with one arm goes on and on about his granddaughter, and how he's gonna take her to the hot springs in Kyoto when the war's over.

"Taisho listens to this talk—even joins in a couple of times, playing along, talking about what he's gonna do after the war. He doesn't tell them they're on a suicide mission so that they can enjoy their last day."

Perry turned onto Fourth Street. "Let me know where."

"Okay. What happens to them?"

"You should see it. Maybe we could watch it one day?"

"Maybe." Kristie pointed at a gray building. "Right here."

The detective braked and dialed the wheel clockwise. "Can I use your bathroom? I've got a long drive ahead of me."

The platinum specimen appraised the driver as he parked along the curb, behind a navy blue sports utility vehicle that had tinted windows.

"I'm not gonna make a move or anything," defended Perry, aware that his request had seemed premeditated. "But if you're uncomfortable, don't worry about it—I'll just make some ice in an alley."

Kristie raised an index finger. "Just the bathroom."

"Just the bathroom."

"Will you tell me what happens to C Seventy-three?"

"I don't want to ruin it," said Perry, shifting into park and killing the engine. The tense sequence where the crewmates discovered that they were on a suicide mission was one of the detective's favorites, as was the mutiny, during which Goro died defending Taisho's life. "You really need to watch it."

"Okay." There was something sad in Kristie's voice.

Perry climbed out of the car. Steam wreathed his head, and he shut the door.

"Dropped my purse," said the woman, leaning forward in her seat.

Suddenly, the detective understood.

Three long black barrels emerged from the windows of the navy blue SUV.

Perry reached for his semiautomatic pistol.

Crackling white fire burst from the machine guns. Bullets burned holes into the detective's face, arms, and chest.

His gun clattered against the pavement.

Darkness returned to the street.

Asphalt smacked Perry's face. His insides gurgled and clicked, transformed into a wet jigsaw puzzle.

An engine rumbled to life, and a man said, "Get in."

Kristie's high-heeled boots tattooed the pavement.

Blood sputtered out of the detective's mouth as he said, "I knew . . . that you were . . . f-forty-two."

A car door slammed.

Red life drained out of Perry, and his pierced body grew numb. Using all of his strength, he shifted onto his side and looked at the navy blue SUV. From the back of the vehicle emerged two dark figures who wore stockings over their pale faces, leather gloves, and black coats. Each man carried an assault rifle that had been built for war.

Perry closed his eyes and retreated into his favorite movie.

Shortly after the mutiny, an enemy submarine attacked C-73, engaging Taisho and his men in a long battle at various depths. The one-armed oldster and the pimply kid soon joined Goro in death.

Water leaked into the damaged midget submarine, and the three dead men stared at the lone survivor with wide, unblinking eyes. Near death and wondering at the pointlessness of existence, Taisho crawled across the floor, retrieved the last remaining torpedo, and slotted it inside of the firing tube. His brow wrinkled when he noticed an anomaly—something small and pale that was caught inside the rotor. The bloodied captain carefully extricated the obstruction and gasped upon seeing what it was that he held. Lying in his hands was an index finger that had once belonged to his fiancée Yuki. Fate had given him a piece of his beloved so that he could face his death with honor.

Resolved, the soldier fired the last torpedo. The weapon shot through the water, and the American aircraft carrier exploded in a sunburst that looked like a Japanese flag. As the debris fell, Taisho sank into the dark abyss, the crushing depths, clutching his fiancée's finger in his right hand.

The warrior was content.

"Get him inside," said a man.

Indelicate paws seized Perry's arms and dragged him across the asphalt. A mechanical bolt clicked.

"Toss him in back."

The detective was airborne. A moment later, he slammed against a hard surface. His new environment smelled like garbage bags and blood. The hatch slammed shut, and the entire world turned black.

Pretending that he possessed Yuki's finger, Perry Molloy clenched his right hand and died.

# XXXIV

# A Very Impressive Policeman

Abe Lott patted Nancy Blockman's shoulder. "The doctor says you're gonna be okay."

"I was here—and awake—when he said it."

"You need to convalesce. That's the most important thing."

"Can't do much else."

Abe often forgot that Nancy was a woman—she was neither pretty nor especially feminine (and she wore the same police uniform that he put on five days a week)—but lying there on her back, draped in a hospital gown and half covered with bandages, she looked pretty decent. If he were a single man, he might have enjoyed a little off-duty time with his partner.

"Stop looking at my tits."

"I'm not." Abe redirected his eyes to a tube that connected Nancy and a bag of plasma. "I was just checking the ivy."

"It's two letters—*i* and *v*. Stands for 'intravenous.'" (The woman was like an instruction manual.)

"Right. Ivy."

"Any luck with the van?"

"No. Nothing yet. But they're looking."

"Let me know if you hear anything."

"You're supposed to convalesce. It's important to convalesce." The pudgy officer really liked this word.

"If you hear anything, let me know."

"I'll tell you. And if you need anything, call me."

"I think I'll let the doctors handle the rest." It was clear that Nancy was about to become irritable.

"I'm glad you're okay."

Earlier that day, Abe had borrowed a ten-speed bike from a kid who lived next door to the Oakwells and ridden it to the place where his partner had crashed the patrol car. When he had first seen her—bloody and unconscious inside of the smashed vehicle—he had suffered a panic attack.

"I like working with you," said the pudgy officer. "I care about you."

"Get out of here." Nancy pivoted upon the mattress so that she faced the television.

"*Attack of the Rattlesnakes* is on channel four."

"Put it on and go."


Sitting behind the wheel of his station wagon and wearing regular civilian clothes, Abe steadily consumed banana-flavored frozen custard until his little white spoon scratched the bottom of the empty cup. Something moved on the far side of the parking lot, and when he looked over, he saw Detective Tom Ryder emerging from the tan apartment building that he had lived in since he was a cadet. The handsome fellow wore a slick Italian suit, and his dark hair was feathered—the sort of job that required a blow-dryer, certain chemical compounds, and no small amount of vanity. Most of the girls at the gentlemen's lounge liked him, and it was not just because he had good outfits.

The two fellows waved at each other, and as Tom Ryder approached the station wagon, Abe undid the locks, tossed his empty cup toward a trash basket, and shut the door. From his wallet, he withdrew two gold cards, which were the passes that he had received on New Year's Eve from Wendy. She had told him that VIP stood for Very Impressive Policeman, and all of the guys had laughed really hard at that one. Although she was not the prettiest exotic dancer at Pink Roses, she was the friendliest by far.

Nancy's ordeal and the deaths of Gianetto and Dave Stanley had rattled Abe, and the thought that he might die without ever entering the fabled VIP room of Pink Roses depressed him. It was a place that every man needed to see.

Setting the pair of golden cards upon the dashboard of his station wagon, the pudgy officer raised his gaze.

Tom Ryder was gone.

Abe was surprised by the detective's absence, but assumed that the fellow had returned to his apartment to fetch something that he had forgotten. The guy had separate nail clippers for his fingers and toes, three different hairbrushes, and a piece of grooming equipment that looked like a dentist's tool. (Nancy might have something to say about Tom Ryder's affinities.)

Abe surveyed the parking lot, which was full of automobiles, including a taco truck that was probably being operated without a license. Backing out of

the space directly opposite his station wagon was a navy blue sports utility vehicle that had tinted windows.

The pudgy officer looked at his dashboard clock and saw that it was ten after eleven. If Tom Ryder did not soon reappear, Abe would give him a call. The
brown cargo van was still on the loose, and things were pretty dangerous in
Victory.

Thinking of Wendy's smile, silver fingernails, and bare breasts, the pudgy
officer said, "Hurry up."

The blue SUV continued to withdraw from its space. Less than ten feet
separated its back bumper from the front of the station wagon.

"Hey." Abe tooted his horn. "Watch it!"

The space between the vehicles diminished, and something dark leaked out
of the SUV's rear door.

Again, the officer tooted his horn. "Look where you're going, you stupid—"

A man leapt into the station wagon. The stranger had a stocking over his
pale head, a black overcoat, and an assault rifle.

"Wait! I ha—"

White fire flashed.

Bullets lanced Abe's chest and slammed his head against the window.

Coughing up blood, the pudgy officer raised his hands. "W-w-wait!" He
seized the passes from the dashboard and offered them to the masked gunman.
"They're VIP!"

The next bullet cracked the golden cards and the skull of the Very Impressive Policeman.

# XXXV

# Rita's Bench

Teddy extracted a bottle of vodka from a gutter drain, and two dead rats tumbled onto the pavement. It seemed like one had eaten the other's innards, though perhaps there was a third creature that was alive and plump. The vagrant was not really sure what had happened with these guys.

A police siren whined, startling Teddy. Nobody in the world liked this sound, and an old black resident of the Toilet who had been incarcerated multiple times was no exception.

"Pull over," ordered an amplified voice that sounded like it belonged to a hostile alien.

The vagrant faced Malcolm Avenue. There, a small green sports car veered toward the curb, followed at a distance by a police vehicle that turned the front of the long-closed shopping center into a red-and-blue disco.

Teddy exited the alley, walked in front of Victory's Best Pawnshop (which had been closed since the eighties), and landed upon his favorite bench. Four years ago, he had discovered Rita's frozen body upon its weathered planks, and it held a lot of sentimental value for him. That woman had been a good friend and the very best of her kind.

Unscrewing the cap from the vodka bottle, Teddy remarked, "We've got the grand tier." Only 150 feet separated him and his spectral companion from the curb.

A broad-shouldered Hispanic officer who had a thick mustache and a clipboard emerged from the cruiser, shut the door, and walked toward the green two-seater, which was about a dozen strides off.

Bright, cold vodka filled Teddy's mouth.

"Roll down your window," said the policeman, drawing a circle in the air with his finger as he reached the halfway point between the vehicles.

The driver's window sank. Sitting inside the green sports car was a man who had no head.

Teddy suddenly wondered if the vodka that he had pulled from the gutter pipe had gone bad.

The policeman continued forward. Something glimmered inside the sports car, and the headless driver twisted his shoulders.

The officer reached the rear bumper.

A gun flashed.

The policeman staggered backward, reaching for his pistol, and the headless driver's weapon glared twice more.

Groaning, the officer dropped to his knees, wobbled, and fell forward. His face smacked the concrete, eliciting a wince from the vagrant.

A moment later, the shooter emerged from the green sports car.

Teddy saw that the fellow was wearing a black hood, and thus possessed a head. Relieved that the vodka had not destroyed his mind, the vagrant returned the bottle to his lips.

The shooter kneeled, took something shiny from the dead man's pocket, and unfastened the fellow's belt. Teddy did not think that he should witness what was occurring, but the alcohol that he had consumed did not contain a propellant.

Steel scissors flashed. The shooter took a pink worm from the dead officer's groin and shoved it into a water bottle.

"Gross," muttered Teddy as he swallowed his medicine.

The shooter returned to his green sports car, backed the vehicle over the corpse until it was concealed, and walked over to the police cruiser. There, he climbed into the backseat, prostrated himself, and shut the door.

The tableau was serene. Nothing moved except the spinning lights atop the patrol car.

Silent and unseen, the shooter waited.

Teddy knew that he was going to watch more policemen die tonight. It was a good thing that he had brought refreshments.

# XXXVI

# This Is Where the Titan Dwells

Scratching himself through a brown wool robe and carrying a bottle of red wine, Inspector Zwolinski walked out of his kitchen into the living room, where the shag rug cushioned the pachydermatous soles of his feet. His apartment was very orderly—there was no dust, and his 578 boxing videocassettes were alphabetized, as were his 422 books on the same subject. There was plenty to watch and read, but to its lone occupant, the place felt like a warehouse rather than a home.

Years ago, Zwolinski's honor-roll daughter had tried heroin at her graduation party, and shortly after her demise in the emergency room (the first of eleven deaths that night), the inspector's marriage had disintegrated. The Polish pugilist still loved his ex-wife, Vanessa, and she still cared for him, but they could not live together any longer. The terrible tragedy that they shared was too much for them to look at on a daily basis.

Zwolinski retrieved a corkscrew from the drawer of his lacquered wet bar and opened the bottle of red wine for Vanessa, who worked as a radiologist on the second shift (and would arrive in twenty or thirty minutes). The Malbec yielded a pleasant smell, and after the inspector set it down, he lighted two candles.

Despite their burdened history and official status as a divorced couple, Mr. and Miss Zwolinski spent the night together two or three times a month. The sexual aspect of these rendezvous was intensely pleasurable and far more exciting than it had been during the major part of their marriage. It soon became clear to the inspector that the true enemy of romance was neither the presence of a child nor a heavy workload, but simply overfamiliarity.

There were few things that Zwolinski enjoyed as much as boxing and pepperoni pizza, and when he had reclaimed his bachelorhood at the age of forty-nine, he had spent most of his nights eating slices and watching fights. Eventually, the pizza did not taste as good as it once had (even though it came from the exact same place) and the matches grew predictable.

A relationship was no different.

Zwolinski did not know what Vanessa was going to wear tonight nor what interesting things had happened to her since their last rendezvous, and he looked forward to making these discoveries. He had been in the pillbox for more than fifteen hours (after only three hours of sleep), and this tryst with his lovely ex-wife would help restore him for the coming day.

The aged hands of a ticking grandfather clock told him that it was twelve after one. Thinking about a fight that he had time to watch before his guest arrived, Zwolinski walked toward his videocassettes, all of which had blue plastic labels that he had made with a little typing machine.

The intercom buzzed.

Vanessa was early. Usually, she arrived at half past one, though sometimes—if she was running late—she skipped her trip home, came over directly, and used his shower.

Zwolinski scratched his silver pelt as he strode toward the door.

Again, the intercom buzzed.

The inspector paused.

One of the many admirable traits that his ex-wife possessed was patience, and like most radiologists, she was very deliberate in her actions. Unless Vanessa needed to use the toilet or thought that the resident had fallen asleep (which did happen on occasion), she would not press the buzzer a second time so shortly after the first.

Dark suspicions filled Zwolinski, who had been a detective until his ascendancy to the pillbox dais.

He claimed his revolver from the holster on the wall, shut off the lights, and proceeded to the intercom. Candles flickered, stirring long shadows.

Applying a thumb that resembled a deli pickle to the door button, the inspector leaned toward the panel. "Come in."

Nobody answered.

The speaker transmitted the sounds of hinges squeaking and quiet footfalls. It was either Vanessa or Vanessa and her captors, and the pugilist intended to face whomsoever approached.

Outside on the stairwell, wooden steps groaned.

Zwolinski discarded his robe and raised his revolver. Except for his polka-dotted boxer shorts, he was naked.

Quiet footfalls resounded outside, and the inspector put his eye to the peephole. A shadow moved across the hallway floor.

It had more than one head.

Filling his lungs with air, Zwolinski prepared to engage his enemy. There was no way that he would lose Vanessa, the woman whom he loved, an amazing person who had as many precious memories as did he of the buried eighteen-year-old treasure named Patricia.

Setting his feet as if he were about to throw a right jab, the inspector thought of Gianetto and Dave Stanley, and also of Nancy Blockman, who had been better prepared and was still alive. As he reached for the ballistic vest that he kept on his coatrack, the cold barrels of a shotgun pressed into his neck.

A chill flooded his insides.

"Drop the gun."

Zwolinski released his revolver, which clattered on the floor.

The intruder said, "Nice underwear, gramps."

Another guy snickered.

# XXXVII

# A Wasted Bouquet

Carrying a bouquet of flowers and a smirk, Huan shut the door of his luxury car and walked toward the brown house that he and his wife shared at the eastern edge of the city. The pockmarked Asian was in a good mood.

E.V.K. emerged from the bushes and pointed his gun at Huan's larynx. "Don't make any noise," the killer said through the fangs of his devil mask.

The detective shrugged.

With his free hand, E.V.K. claimed Huan's firearm and tossed it inside a mint green garbage pail.

The detective extended the bouquet. "For you."

E.V.K. pistol-whipped Huan. The flowers struck the ground, and the killer kicked them into the bushes.

"Unlock your car," ordered the Czech, whose English had become fluent during the decade that he had lived in America. "All the doors."

Blood strolled down Huan's left cheek as he slotted a key. Four locks clicked, sounding like jackboots.

E.V.K. walked to the rear driver's side door of the luxury car. Not once did his gun waver from his target's neck.

"Get in slow. If you misbehave—" The killer pointed at the bedroom window that he had earlier visited. Behind the luminous curtain was the detective's wife, an adorable Thai woman who liked candles, silk nightgowns, and mystery novels.

Fear glimmered in Huan's eyes.

E.V.K. motioned to the car. "Slow."

The detective opened the driver's door, and the killer flung the one behind it. Together, they climbed into the car and sat upon its luxurious (and still warm) upholstery.

E.V.K. thought that the vehicle seemed a little bit too nice for an honest policeman. "Do not slam your door," he said as he leveled his weapon.

Huan and E.V.K. reached out, clasped leather handles, and pulled. The
doors swung toward the body of the car, slowly, until they were nearly flush.
Then, the men yanked hard.

Latches clicked.

"Lock it."

Synchronized jackboots stomped.

E.V.K. surveyed the brown home and the unlighted houses on either side
of it. The area was as still as a photograph.

"Back out of here," ordered the killer. "Slow and quiet. Don't turn on the
lights. If your wife comes outside, she's joining us."

Eyes fixed on the front door, Huan started the engine, shifted into reverse,
and backed up until he reached the street.

Nobody emerged from the house.

"There's a construction site on the next block," said E.V.K.

"I've seen it."

"Go there. Do not exceed fifteen miles an hour."

The detective toggled the gear, drove down the block, and dialed the wheel
clockwise. Purring like a feline, the black luxury car crept through suburbia.

E.V.K. recalled the discarded bouquet, the acquisition of which had almost
certainly delayed Huan's return home. "Were you fucking another woman?"

"Playing poker."

"With policemen?"

"Just some guys I know. I won big." Huan turned onto a cross street. "Let
me buy your mother a fur coat."

"Shhh."

"How about a bazooka? Czechs love those."

"Shhh." E.V.K. knew that the fellow was trying to distract him.

The black luxury car arrived at the weedy, one-acre lot upon which a new
home was being built. Moonlight turned the unfinished structure into a pale
arachnid.

"Pull in."

The pockmarked Asian glanced at the devil who inhabited his rearview
mirror. "Where?"

"All the way back."

Huan drove onto the grass. Dead vegetation crackled as the luxury car
drifted past the arachnid and entered the rear lot. Parked near a ziggurat of
cinder blocks was the killer's charcoal gray pickup truck.

The pockmarked Asian stomped the brakes, and the car lurched. Twisting
in his seat, he lunged at his captor.

E.V.K. hammered his gun against Huan's mouth. Incisors cracked like candy.

The detective's back thudded against the dashboard. His lips were purplish-red pulp.

The killer pressed the barrel of his gun into the pockmarked Asian's right eye. At a speed of less than five miles an hour, the driverless car rolled toward a hickory tree.

"You will tell me what I want to know or I will kill your wife."

Huan spat out white splinters that had once been teeth. "What do you want to know?" His words were slurred.

"An address where I can find another policeman."

The pockmarked Asian was stunned. A low branch that looked like a talon harassed the windshield of the rolling sedan and scraped across the roof.

"Give me an address or I'll kill Heather." The multiple executions might soon be discovered, and E.V.K. felt that he only had time for one more.

Tears shimmered in Huan's eyes.

"If you give me a fake address," the killer warned, "I'll come back and take my time with her."

The drifting car impacted the tree. Branches rattled, and tears spilled down the detective's cheeks.

The world was still.

"There's a cop," said Huan, lowering his gaze and swallowing gore. "A detective. Staying at the Sunflower Motel."

"What room?"

"I don't know. He drives a bright yellow hatchback and is blacker than a car tire."

"What's his name?"

Huan's pockmarked cheeks reddened with shame as he said, "Jules Bettinger."

The gun flashed.

# XXXVIII

# More Important than Eggs

A headache that felt like a palpitating creature filled Bettinger's skull. Reluctantly, he opened his eyes.

The motel room in which the detective lay was black, excepting an isosceles triangle of sodium light and the digital clock that told him with bright green numbers that it was half past two in the morning. He had deposited coffee in his stomach throughout the long day, and minutes ago, the surfeit of caffeine had finally overpowered his physical exhaustion and pulled him from the land of dreams.

"Junk."

Bettinger knew his fifty-year-old body very well, and he was certain that he would not be able to fall back asleep until he had eaten a meal and flushed the remaining coffee from his system with water.

The detective yawned, and suddenly, the bright green numbers disappeared. Something had moved between him and the clock.

Bettinger seized his pistol.

The luminous display reappeared, accompanied by the sound of something flapping.

Embarrassed, the detective lowered his gun, cursing the newspaper that lay on the nightstand and the ceiling fan that had given it life.

He switched on the table lamp, and soft amber light filled the room. The barricade in front of the door appeared to be undisturbed.

Bettinger rose from the mattress, stretched, and grabbed his cell phone. Its display told him that he had no messages. An inspection of the carpet revealed his car keys, which had been slid under the door as promised.

He decided then that he would drive over to Claude's Hash House, get some eggs, and return for a little more sleep. Even one additional hour of shut-eye would help him survive the coming day.

The detective walked to the bathroom doorway, stabbed his hand into the dark, and felt along the wall, looking for the light switch. It clicked, and an overheard bulb glared.

Squinting, Bettinger entered the room, urinated, and washed his hands. He gargled hot water several times, but was unable to remove from his mouth a terrible taste that reminded him of a car battery.

"Junk."

While the detective dressed, he happily remembered that Claude's Hash House had a big bowl of complimentary breath mints on its front counter. Even if they had been there since the seventies, he would eat a handful.

Bettinger put on his boots, pocketed his keys, holstered his handgun, zipped up his parka, turned off the lamp, and slid the couch away from the door. His eyes adjusted to the darkness, and he listened to his surroundings. The room was silent, as was the world outside.

Quietly, the detective undid the bolts, turned the knob, and cracked the door. The steel chain grew taut, and as he looked through the opening, a cold wind chilled his right eye. Nobody inhabited the second-floor walkway, and the rear parking lot was empty, excepting his hatchback, which sat in a puddle of sodium light that painted its windows an even uglier yellow hue than the one that covered its body.

Bettinger's exposed eye began to freeze, and soon, he stepped back from the opening.

Gripping his gun, the detective unfastened the chain and walked into the night. Winter attacked him like a thing that hated the main ingredient of every human being.

As he locked the door to his room, he monitored the passageway and the darker environs. It seemed as if he was the only person stupid enough to be outside at this time of night so far north of the equator.

Bettinger hid his firearm, entered the stairwell, and descended to the ground level. There, he traversed a dark and empty passage that led into the parking lot.

A light flashed in front of his face.

The detective withdrew his gun and then realized that what had startled him was his own breath, brightly illuminated by a sodium lamp.

"Christ's uncle."

Embarrassed by his edginess, Bettinger strode across the rear lot to his hatchback, which had two new tires. He opened the driver's door and found a sheet of paper lying on the seat.

*B.*

*It's suposed to snow alot late tonite or early tommorrow so I put a ice scraper in
you're trunk.*

*D.*

The detective sat down, shut the door, and started the engine. As the car
awakened, he withdrew his cell phone and went online. Nine hours ago, Slick
Sam had been the police department's best connection to Sebastian, and Bettinger wanted to find out if the crook had been apprehended.

Cogitating, the cell phone grabbed a signal. The detective opened his account, where the lack of work-related e-mails in his inbox did not say anything
good about the progress of the case. Sitting at the top of the screen beside a
subject line that read "Call" was the name "Jacques Bettinger."

"Junk."

The detective opened the e-mail that his father had sent.

*I'll be up late.*

The rattling heater attempted to make the freezer in which Bettinger sat as
warm as a refrigerator. Toggling the gear, he pressed the accelerator. While the
yellow hatchback crossed the rear parking lot, the detective highlighted the word
"Father," stuck an earplug in the side of his head, and pressed the connect button,
knowing that there was no point in delaying the dialogue.

The car circumnavigated the body of the motel, and in the driver's ear, a
phone rang.

Headlights glared upon the windshield.

Squinting, Bettinger flashed his high beams at the oncoming vehicle. Again,
the phone rang.

The blazing headlights dimmed, and the detective saw the other automobile—a charcoal gray pickup truck, which was currently pulling into the far
side of the parking lot. He looked at the person behind the wheel, but the man's
face was obscured by the tilted brim of a black baseball hat and the tinting that
Missourians were allowed to have on the uppermost part of their windshields.

For the third time, the phone rang. The pickup truck turned into a parking
space, and the hatchback exited the lot.

"It appears as if you've chosen a very exciting place in which to live," said
a deep, creaky voice through the earplug. "A real jewel."

Bettinger glanced in his rearview mirror, but was unable to see through the driver's side window of the pickup truck, which was darkly tinted. Perhaps the fellow had just spent the night with a prostitute or currently had one crouching in the passenger seat so that she (or he) would not be descried. To the hungry detective, none of these transgressions mattered as much as eggs.

"What did you want to discuss?" Bettinger asked Jacques.

"Do you intend to dodge bullets for the next five years?"

"You'd prefer I didn't dodge them? Got you some souvenirs?" The detective checked his mirrors, signaled, and switched lanes.

"I know you think you're clever, but you're just a watered-down version of the man with whom you are speaking."

"So Mom's contribution to my DNA was water?"

"There are some deficiencies."

"Your reverence for the deceased is touching."

"And that sarcasm of yours is what landed you in nigger Siberia."

Bettinger passed a pea green sedan. "Does that mean you aren't going to visit? 'Cause I'd consider that a perk."

"Afraid to face your old man on the checkered battlefield?"

Chess was one of the only activities that the two Bettingers could enjoy together . . . probably because it confined most of their fighting to a two-dimensional rectilinear surface.

"You've been slipping these last few years," added Jacques. "I think your mind is starting to go."

"It happens."

The eighty-six-year-old grew irascible if he lost more than two games in a row, and so the detective occasionally threw a match to keep him happy.

"We don't have to talk about it if it makes you uncomfortable."

"What did you want to discuss?" asked Bettinger, applying the brakes as he turned onto Summer Drive.

"Do you intend to stay in Victory?"

The detective glanced in his rearview mirror, which showed only a dark and empty road. "You're asking me this because of the homicides?"

"Of course not. It's because an astrologer doesn't like where Saturn is going." The oldster's sarcasm was as thick as honey.

"It's possible that I'll be relocated at some point, but I'm going to finish out my term of service no matter where I am." Bettinger switched lanes to avoid a dead pigeon. "I don't like Victory, but I know that I can do some good here."

"Most martyrs don't get hemorrhoids."

"I wasn't aware."

"And they tend not to be bald."

"Balding," corrected the detective. "Haven't caught up to you yet."

"Stay in Victory and you never will."

"So that's your advice? Leave?"

"Or get an A-bomb."

"I really hear the Georgia accent coming out on that one." Although Bettinger did not at all wonder from whom he had received the major part of his personality, he hoped that he was less unpleasant than his progenitor. "So that's it then?"

"I know that you find me irritating—"

"Not at all."

"Quiet. I know that you find me irritating, but what happened to those policemen is national news, and when I heard about it, I went online and read some articles." Jacques whistled. "Twenty-eight newspapers referred to Victory as the single worst city in this entire country." He paused, letting his words resonate. "I know you'll do whatever you want—and that you're long past taking advice from me—but the sooner you get transferred out of that sewer, the better."

"That's beyond my control."

"Alyssa and the kids are far away?"

"More than an hour."

"How are they?"

"Good. Alyssa just got a show at a big Chicago gallery."

"What gallery?"

The detective did not want to hear a diatribe about Zionism, and thus, he withheld the name David Rubinstein from his father. "I forgot."

"If it's not a memorable name, it's not a good name for a place of commerce."

The hatchback's headlights shone upon the sign for Fifty-sixth Street. "I need to go."

"Why're you up so late? Are you playing around?"

This proclivity was one that Bettinger had not inherited from his father. "Bye."

"Get a bulletproof vest."

The line went dead.

Annoyed, the detective took the cork from his ear and turned onto Fifty-sixth Street. The area was very dark, and he feared that Claude's Hash House might be closed, despite the sign on its front door that proclaimed such an event never occurred. If he had been a little more alert, he would have called the establishment before leaving the motel.

Four luminious rectangles that were the front windows of the diner soon appeared on the north side of the street. The detective put on his blinker, slowed his car, and landed in the lot.

There, he surveyed the interior of Claude's Hash House. A trio of bearded truckers sat in a booth near the entrance, and an unhappy, light-skinned Latina occupied a corner table, smoking a cigarette while chastising a man who slouched. Sitting on a stool at the counter and reading a newspaper was a lank black guy who wore kitchen whites, an apron, and a hairnet.

Bettinger exited the hatchback, locked the door, and strode into the diner, which was warm and smelled like hash browns. Rap music issued from the overhead speakers like boisterous precipitation.

"Here." The cook launched a menu down the counter. "Fryer's off, so nothin' deep-fried."

"I'd like eggs."

"How many and how?"

"Four." The detective tossed a handful of mints into his mouth. "Over easy."

"Potatoes?" inquired the cook as he folded his newspaper.

"Hash browns."

The fellow rose from his stool. He was exactly halfway between six and seven feet tall. "Toast?"

"Whole wheat."

"Pumpernickel close enough?"

"I like pumpernickel."

"Coffee?"

"Decaf. And a pitcher of water."

"Got it. Sit wherever you want."

"Thanks."

Bettinger walked toward the window booths and took the one that was farthest from the truckers. On the opposite side of the diner, the Latina dashed her cigarette in an extravagant manner and threw a well-rehearsed look.

"I'm Buford if you need me," said the cook, opening the double door that led to the kitchen.

The detective nodded his thanks, surveyed the parking lot, and looked across the street. There, a sodium streetlamp threw ochre light upon a used car lot that had been closed for years, though the cracked windows of its office still advertised an "Amazing Bargain Bonanza!"

Bettinger wondered if the people who contrived such phrases were actually human beings.

The man who had been slouching beside the light-skinned Latina exited the diner, and as the door closed, the detective returned his gaze to the corner table. Two dark eyes and a pair of freshly painted red lips were waiting for him.

Bettinger gestured to the empty bench at his booth, and the woman nodded her head. Although she probably did not know anything of value about Sebastian or the executions, she may have been an associate of Elaine James's or heard something about her murder. At the very least, a conversation with her would cover up the rap music.

Rings of smooth skin showed between the bottom of her short lavender dress and the tops of her black thigh-high boots as she stalked across the establishment, cradling a white fur coat in her right arm. Her clicking heels stopped the truckers' conversation like a high command.

"Want me to sit here?"

The Latina's mouth worked in a lopsided way, and she had a small lisp. Although she was probably twenty-five years old, these qualities made her seem far younger.

"Please do."

The woman rested her rump upon the bench and arranged her half-exposed breasts, which were large, but believable. "You're not a cop, are you?"

"No."

One of the most helpful misconceptions held by criminals was their belief that this question had to be answered truthfully.

"You still got your jacket on," observed the Latina. "You in a rush or something?"

"I'm not a fan of cold weather."

The woman adjusted the hem of her lavender dress. "Where're you from?"

"Georgia."

"A businessman?" This was said hopefully.

"Sure."

"What kind of business?"

"I sell airplanes."

"That's a good business, no?" Excitement had thickened the woman's accent, which sounded like it was Venezuelan.

"It is. Though you need a lot of storage space."

"For the airplanes?"

"For the airplanes."

"My name is Daniela."

"Nice to meet you, Daniela. I'm Jacques."

"Are you looking for a little company tonight?"

Something crept into the parking lot and slid behind one of the trucks. Bettinger could not see what kind of vehicle had landed, but he knew that its headlights had been off when it pulled in. Within his parka, he gripped his gun.

"You waiting for somebody?" inquired Daniela.

The kitchen door opened, and Buford emerged, carrying a plate, a cup of coffee, and a pitcher of water.

Bettinger rose from the booth. "Go back to your table."

Confusion and irritation shone upon the Latina's face. "Why'd you invite me over?"

The detective turned around, passed the cook, and walked to the back of the restaurant, where he entered the bathroom and cracked the door. Putting his eye to the opening, he observed.

Daniela returned to her table, and Buford set down his burden. Outside in the parking lot, a dark reflection spilled like oil across the steel grille of a truck.

Bettinger strongly doubted that he would be approached by a killer in such a public place, but he was cautious by nature and felt an obligation to isolate himself from civilians . . . even if it meant that he had to eat room-temperature eggs. His phone buzzed, but he did not answer it or remove his eye from the front windows.

Outside, the moving thing entered the light and became two blurry figures.

The detective clasped his gun, and again, his cell phone buzzed.

He waited.

The front door opened, and into the diner walked a good-looking young black couple who wore formal attire. The woman carried a swaddled and cooing infant, and the fellow rolled a plush stroller. They seemed happy, and thus, Bettinger concluded that they were from out of town.

The detective's cell phone buzzed for the third time. A glance at its display told him that the caller was his partner.

Bettinger placed the receiver to his ear. "Yeah?"

"Where are you?" asked Dominic.

"Claude's."

"Make sure nobody's watching you and get away from the windows."

"What's—"

"More cops are dead—executed, had their dicks cut off—and most of the others are missing. It's cop genocide, and you need to get yourself hid."

Bettinger suddenly felt like a ghost. "What do you know?"

"Looks like a coordinated effort all over town. Some niggas in a SUV took a shot at me and Tackley, but blew it, and then we started checkin' up on everyone.

Perry's missing, and Huan never got home. We're at Zwolinski's place now and there's blood fuckin' everywhere."

Needles climbed up the detective's nape. "They went to the inspector's home?"

"Yeah."

A terrible thought occurred to Bettinger. He bolted from the bathroom and slammed into the young black father.

"Excuse you!" chastised the staggered man.

Running across the linoleum, the detective pocketed his cell phone and withdrew his semiautomatic, ready to knock down or shoot anybody who got in his way.

The Latina screamed, "He's got a gun!" as he stormed past her.

Thinking of his family in Stonesburg, Bettinger careened toward the front door. His mind was a hard and narrow place.

# XXXIX

# Vehicular Abuse

Bettinger exited Claude's Hash House, flung himself into his hatchback, and started the engine. Tossing his gun onto the passenger seat, he stomped the accelerator.

The car flew backward and thudded over the curb. On Fifty-sixth Street, the detective cut the wheel, shifted gears, and dropped his boot. Tires shrieked like dying eagles.

Speeding toward Summer Drive, Bettinger clapped his cell phone to his skull. "Still there?"

"Yeah," said Dominic. "You goin' home?"

"Yes." The detective tried not to imagine terrible things.

"Why don't you call—see if they're okay?"

"If somebody's with them—holding them—I don't want him to know I'm coming. And if they're already . . ." This was not a sentence that Bettinger could complete. "If something bad's already happened, I want to surprise whoever's waiting for me."

Tires screeched as the hatchback seized Summer Drive.

"A'ight. Me and Tackley're gonna get Nancy out of the hospital, put her someplace safe, and go look for Perry and Huan. Call when you know the situation with your family. You need backup, we're there instantly."

"Thanks."

The hatchback overrode its headlights, and Bettinger clicked on the high beams.

"Watch yourself," cautioned Dominic. "We just became a endangered species."

"You be careful too."

The detective disconnected the call and flew past a motorcycle that was driven by a hunched biker who wore a petite woman as if she were a backpack.

Monitoring his rearview mirror, he watched the interwoven duo diminish until they resembled mating insects.

The engine roared.

Bettinger sped past a flashing yellow orb and glanced at the dashboard, where a white needle wavered fearfully on the right side of the dial, indicating a speed of ninety-three miles an hour. If a vagrant stepped into the road or a significant pothole appeared or a car ran an opposing light, the detective knew that he would have a serious or fatal accident.

He raised his boot, slowing down the hatchback. It was not easy for him to drive at a safer pace, but he had to be sure that he made it home to his family.

Bettinger honked as he approached every major intersection, and in fifteen minutes, he reached the southern fringe of Victory, where the roads were in even worse shape. The hatchback rumbled like an earthquake, and yet again, the detective was forced to retard his progress.

Rolling toward the black tunnel mouth at a speed of fifty-five miles per hour, he leaned on his horn. A troll waggled appendages and disappeared into a crevice.

The hatchback zipped through the passageway and back outside, where its tires crushed a pigeon, struck the ramp, pulled the vehicle up an incline, grabbed the interstate, and shrieked.

Leaning on the accelerator, the detective sped south. His headlights inhaled the lines in the road as if they were illicit substances. The engine roared.

At a speed of ninety-five miles an hour, Bettinger flew toward the three people who were his entire world. Rocks turned into a wake of red hail in the glow of the hatchback's taillights.

The detective checked to see if someone was trailing him, even though it would be impossible for another car to match his speed in an inconspicuous manner. At present, he saw no followers.

The distance between the two cities was rapidly devoured.

Traffic was thin, and whenever he saw another vehicle, he overtook it. No automobiles remained in his rearview mirror for more than fifteen seconds during his roaring, thirty-minute tear down the interstate, and it was not until he saw the sign for Stonesburg that he remembered to turn on the heater. Vents blasted exhaust onto the stones that were fists.

Dialing the wheel clockwise and applying the brakes, the detective caught the off-ramp and entered the suburbs, where he proceeded at a moderate speed until he was five blocks from his house. There, he slowed the vehicle to a quiet speed and killed the headlights.

Darkness fell.

Bettinger's eyes dilated, adjusting to the night.

Thick clouds diffused the lunar chunk that hung in the sky, and the weak light that the cataract emanated varnished small houses and a variety of four-wheeled pets. Surrounding these man-made artifacts were carpets of dead grass that looked like sandpaper.

Quietly, the hatchback drifted through the suburbs. A glance at the clock on the dashboard informed the detective that it was seventeen minutes after four in the morning. Passing through an intersection, he checked the side streets and saw only darkness and incomplete gray shapes.

Bettinger continued west, crossing lifeless roads at a speed of less than fifteen miles an hour. His journey was almost over.

Moonlight illuminated the sign for Douglas Avenue, the street upon which he and his family lived, and his chest constricted, smothering his ugly little heart. Although the detective had been in numerous physical altercations and three gunfights, a direct threat to his family frightened him far more than anything that he had ever before experienced.

Dialing the wheel clockwise, Bettinger turned the hatchback.

He lowered his window, seized his gun, and fixed his gaze on the tall wooden fence that hid the major part of his little salmon house from its northern neighbor.

The hatchback crept down the street. Freezing winter flooded through the open window, stinging the detective's eyes as the distance between the front of his car and the edge of his property diminished to ten feet.

Gripping his pistol, Bettinger passed the wooden fence and saw his house. Its salmon-colored paint was gray in the moonlight, and all of its windows were dark. The garage door was closed, and there were no cars in the driveway.

Everything looked normal.

Relief tingled the detective's skull, nape, and shoulders, but he was cautious by nature and suspicious by trade and thus did not apply the brakes.

The yellow hatchback continued south, and behind the wheel, Bettinger ruminated. It was conceivable that a killer's vehicle was hidden inside of the garage, though unlikely, since any reasonably intelligent bad guy would avoid using a noisy, unreliable device like an automatic door. A smarter way for the gunman to accomplish an ambush was for him to leave his vehicle someplace nearby and walk over.

Rolling south, Bettinger surveyed the area. All of the cars that he saw were familiar, and every single home was dark.

The detective reached the end of the block, turned east, and drove along the intersecting street, which was the one that he used whenever he went to downtown Stonesburg. Most of the vehicles that he saw were recognizable, and nothing seemed out of place to him.

Dialing the wheel counterclockwise, Bettinger landed on the avenue that ran parallel to the one upon which he lived. He had not been on this street very often, and he doubted that he would notice any anomalies.

The hatchback rolled north. Something caught the detective's eye, and a moment later, his stomach sank.

Parked in the driveway of an unlighted house was a charcoal gray pickup truck.

Bettinger was certain that this was the vehicle that had entered the parking lot of the Sunflower Motel just as he had been leaving.

A murderer was in Stonesburg with his family.

# XL

# Things Fall

The detective drove across the lot of dead grass until his car blocked off the driveway. Two inches separated his door from the back bumper of the charcoal gray pickup truck, which appeared to be uninhabited.

Bettinger silenced his cell phone, slid it into his parka, and clambered out of the passenger's door. Moonlit mist rose from his mouth as he stalked toward the suspect vehicle, his gun pointing at the driver's side window. A thin, balding black man who was three shades darker than the night sky appeared on the glass, but nothing of note lay beyond this reflection.

The killer was somewhere else.

Exhaling steam, Bettinger proceeded toward the east side of the house. His body functioned mechanically as he considered the situation.

The detective knew that he had to approach this tableau as he would any other. He was a professional law enforcer, a decorated bloodhound, and he could not abandon his intellect and observational skills because of his deep emotional investment in the situation. The hostages were not his beloved wife Alyssa, and his two children, Gordon and Karen, but three dead people whom he was trying to bring back to life.

Bettinger reached the side of the house and saw a square hole in the dirt that had probably held a For Sale sign up until very recently, when the vacant home was chosen as a parking space by the killer.

The detective crept toward the fence that divided the front and back portions of the half-acre lot. Cautiously, he opened the gate, passed through, and surveyed the backyard.

A tire hung from a nearby tree, and a mat covered an aboveground swimming pool that was attended by a score of pale lawn chairs. Nothing moved.

Bettinger hastened across the grass toward the familiar copse that divided the block. Cold winds blew as he proceeded, and somewhere, a dog barked.

The detective soon entered the wooded area. Bobbing and weaving like a boxer, he navigated leafless branches until he reached the far side of the copse, where he stopped and looked east. Lighted by the veiled moon were a swing set, a covered grill, and a hitch trailer, all of which Bettinger recognized. This was the backyard of the house that was just south of his own home.

Staying within the trees, he proceeded north. His footfalls were quiet but not silent.

An anomaly garnered his attention as he walked, and he paused. Amidst the dark limbs and four feet off of the ground was a pale swath—the raw wood of a broken tree branch. Somebody had recently passed through the copse.

The crumb of hope that was in the detective's back pocket disappeared. A killer was with his family.

Bettinger continued through the wooded area until he was hidden behind his own backyard. Carefully, he approached the edge of the shadows and appraised his property.

Dull moonlight shone upon dead grass, a bench, a cylindrical grill, nine pine trees, and a hammock, which was stretched between two bald oaks. Behind all of this was the small, salmon-colored house that the night had turned gray. All of the windows were dark.

The tableau told Bettinger nothing, but he knew that he had to act quickly. A passive approach would ensure the deaths of all three captives.

For three seconds, the detective considered the layout of the little salmon house. The bedroom that he shared with Alyssa was the only place that had windows facing the front and back halves of the property, and so it was the most likely spot for a bad guy to position himself. (This conclusion followed his presumptions that the killer was both alone and intelligent.)

Staying within the copse, Bettinger walked north until the larger of the two distant oak trees blocked his view of the rear bedroom window. Concealed by its knobby trunk, he hastened onto the lot, holding his breath as he ran so that no drifting steam would betray his movements. (There were a lot of reasons to hate the cold.)

Bettinger reached the tree, pressed his shoulder to the wood, and glanced at the bedroom window, which was just over thirty feet away. Its curtains were completely closed—an anomaly that all but confirmed the location of the killer.

The detective exhaled steam into his parka, painfully aware that at any moment, a gunshot might ring out and ruin his life.

Every second mattered.

Bettinger crawled toward a pine tree that stood less than ten feet from the back of his house. Blades of gray grass whispered underneath his hands and knees as he progressed, and he hoped that the quiet susurrations were not audible through the pane of glass.

The detective reached his destination, collected a few white stones, and rose to his feet, keeping the pine tree between him and the three-by-four bedroom window that was now less than eight feet away.

His heart pounded inside his temples and fingertips. The worst gamble that any loving husband or father could ever be asked to make was immediately before him, and he had to roll the dice. Hesitation or passivity would yield one dead wife and two dead children.

Bettinger brushed pine needles from his gun, exhaled into his jacket, and drew a deep breath. Pressing his chest against the tree, he tilted his head sideways.

The floral curtains that covered the bedroom window were dark and still. Everything was quiet.

The detective slid his left hand into his parka and withdrew one of the small white stones. A second later, he flung it into the air.

The pebble was inhaled by the dark sky, and for a moment, the world was the same.

Bettinger pointed his gun at the window.

The stone reappeared, falling, and cracked against the roof.

Something thudded against a wall inside of the dark bedroom. A deep voice that belonged to an adult man muttered a couple of unintelligible words.

The curtains wavered. A shadow appeared on the fabric, and the detective tilted the barrel of his firearm down a fraction of an inch to center his target.

Two yards from the nose of his gun was a battered, bloody face that belonged to Alyssa. Panties filled her gory mouth and dangled out of a swollen hole that had once contained her left eyeball.

Horrified, Bettinger surveyed the room. Floating behind his wife's right shoulder was the face of the devil.

It took the detective a second to realize that he was not dreaming or insane, but looking at a mask.

Neither Alyssa nor the killer had seen him, and he knew that he had to act now. Even though the window would shatter in his wife's face—and possibly pierce her remaining eye—he had to shoot. This might be the only chance that he ever got to save the people whom he loved.

Aiming at the space between the devil's horns, Bettinger steadied his hand and squeezed the trigger.

White fire boomed.

The window shattered.

Glass covered Alyssa's face, and the killer's head snapped back on his neck. Together, they fell from view.

The mattress squeaked, and a body thudded against the floor as Bettinger charged the window.

He arrived, stabbing his gun through the opening. Ten feet away and facedown upon the bed were his children, bound, gagged, and naked, looking at the killer who had fallen across their legs. The man's hands were empty.

Bettinger scanned the room for other bad guys, saw none, and pointed his semiautomatic at the killer. A white indentation sat between the devil's horns rather than a hole.

The mask was bulletproof.

Aiming at the killer's heart, the detective fired twice. Lead slammed into a ballistic vest, cracking ribs.

The devil groaned.

Bettinger trained his firearm on the killer's exposed neck, but Karen's spine was right next to the target.

A gun materialized in the devil's right hand and touched the girl's head.

Bettinger's stomach dropped.

The world shrank.

Gordon slammed his face into the killer's arm, and the semiautomatic flashed. The shot punctured the bed directly beside Karen's ear.

Twisting around, the devil pointed his gun at the teenager.

Bettinger fired.

Bullets cracked the killer's sacrum, knocking him to the far side of the mattress, where he grabbed Gordon by the neck and pulled him over the edge. Bodies thudded.

Unable to see his son or the devil, the detective lunged. Glass bit into his hands and face and tore up his parka as he passed through the window. The floor pounded his chest, emptying his lungs.

Bettinger saw Alyssa—nude and mutilated, but still breathing—as he staggered to his feet.

Gordon yelled into his gag on the far side of the bed.

The detective ran.

A gun flashed.

Bettinger's stomach lurched, and an instant later, he saw the awful tableau. The devil was bent over the naked teenager's twitching body. Smoke was in the air.

Instantly, the detective put his gun to the back of the killer's head and squeezed the trigger.

White fire boomed. The devil mask flew into the air, smacked against the wall, and ricocheted.

Gurgling posthumously, the killer collapsed. Next to him lay Gordon Bettinger, whose thoughts were spread across the carpet in dark red clumps.

Karen screamed.

"Don't look," said the detective.

The girl's white eyes turned into black creases.

Slotting fresh cartridges into his clip, Bettinger asked, "Is there anybody else here?"

Karen mumbled the word "No" into her gag.

The detective set a pillow atop his son's blasted head, but the soft white rectangle was not quite big enough to conceal the mess.

An avalanche of despair threatened to overwhelm Bettinger, and thus, he focused his thoughts on the well-being of his wife and daughter. He locked the bedroom door, checked the bathroom, put a trash basket over the killer's ruined face, grabbed a pair of scissors, sat on the bed, and cut the plastic ties from his daughter's mouth, wrists, and ankles. The girl spat out a ball of underwear as the detective covered her shivering shoulders with a blanket.

They hugged.

Bettinger looked toward Alyssa, who lay unconscious upon the bedroom floor. "Let me go help Mommy."

Karen did not let go.

Sitting between his battered wife and his dead son, the fifty-year-old man from Arizona held his daughter. He felt as insignificant as a flea.

"I need to help Mommy."

"Is Gordon gonna be okay?"

"He'll be okay."

"Really?" The girl was smart enough to know that her brother was dead, but old enough to deceive herself. "He'll be okay?"

Bettinger squeezed his daughter and rubbed her back rather than maintain the sad charade. "Let me go help Mommy so we can go."

The girl nodded her head against her father's parka. "Okay."

The detective wrapped up his daughter as if she were an infant, walked into the bathroom, and retrieved some medical supplies. His hands were shaking, and when he closed the cabinet mirror, he avoided his own reflection.

Bettinger approached Alyssa. The nude woman's nose and lips were smashed, and shards of glass protruded from her face. Panties dangled from her mouth and left eye socket.

Food raced up the detective's throat.

Leaning through the window, he launched his insides at Missouri. Putrid steam rose from the puddle, and soon, the fellow withdrew his head, taking a deep breath.

Bettinger kneeled beside Alyssa, pulled the underwear from her mouth, and cut through her plastic cuffs. Gently, he removed pieces of glass from her caramel face and applied butterfly bandages to the wounds, none of which appeared to be especially deep. The detective then laid a throw blanket over the woman's shivering body and felt her wrist. Her pulse was slow, but steady.

Leaning close, Bettinger examined the underwear that depended from Alyssa's left eye socket. Fury claimed his senses, and for a moment, he was paralyzed.

"Is she okay?" asked Karen.

The detective cleared his throat. "She's gonna be fine."

"Can I help?"

"Just stay over there and keep warm." His words were steam.

Bettinger pinched the loose end of the underwear and held his breath. Slowly and gently, he pulled.

The fabric tautened, and Alyssa's head titled forward. Clear fluid trickled down her cheek, but the fabric did not come loose.

The injured woman groaned.

Bettinger cradled Alyssa's head and laid it back down upon the carpet. Trembling, he reclaimed his scissors.

The detective cut the underwear so that only the portion inside his wife's eye socket remained. Her ripped eyelid flickered, trying to close over the fabric, and he had to look away.

Bettinger then dressed Alyssa in underwear, a sweat suit, a wool jacket, socks, and sneakers. Afterward, he took Karen up the hall into her room, where she put on so many layers of clothing that she looked like a miniature football player.

The two of them returned to the corridor, and there, he opened the linen closet, grabbed the darkest blanket that he could find, and looked at his daughter.

"You need to close your eyes."

Terror shone upon the girl's face. "Don't leave me alone."

"I won't. I promise. But there are some things you aren't allowed to see." Bettinger lifted the hem of his parka. "Grab my belt."

Two little hands clutched the band.

It was already clear to the detective that this terrible night had changed his daughter. "Close your eyes, and keep them closed until I say."

"I will. I promise."

Worried eyes became horizontal creases, and Bettinger towed Karen into his bedroom. There, he removed the pillow from atop Gordon's head, took a breath, and unfurled the dark brown blanket. The shroud drifted down and covered the corpse.

Fighting the avalanche of despair, the detective kneeled on the carpet, exhaled steam, and wrapped up his son's body. His daughter never let go of his belt.

"We're going to the car."

"Okay."

Bettinger carried Gordon into the garage. There, he rested the body in the trunk of Alyssa's blue compact, which he then closed.

The detective looked over his shoulder. "You can open your eyes."

Dark creases were replaced by white ovals. The girl looked around the garage, disoriented and shivering.

"Let's get Mommy," suggested Bettinger.

Karen nodded.

Together, they returned to the bedroom.

Snowflakes drifted through the broken window and landed on the floor, the bed, and the dandelion array of short curls that sprouted from Alyssa's head.

Bettinger pocketed his wife's neon green cell phone and scooped her off of the floor. A weak moan issued from her mouth, and he cradled her to his chest, hoping that she would not regain consciousness before she was in a place where a doctor could provide both assistance and medication.

The detective carried his wife to the garage and laid her across the rear bench of the compact.

"I'm in," announced Karen, buckling her seat belt in the front.

The detective closed both doors, walked around the small blue car, and climbed behind the steering wheel. Exhaling steam, he looked at his daughter and said, "It's all gonna be okay."

Karen nodded her head, desperately wanting to believe her father. Her eyes were wide, and her skin was beaded with sweat.

Bettinger thumbed the garage opener. Chains rattled, and the automatic door rose from the ground, revealing the outermost edge of night. Flakes that looked like ashes fell toward the pavement.

The detective shifted into reverse and pressed the gas, taking the dead and abused members of his family away from the little salmon house.

# XLI

# Ammonia


Headlights turned falling snowflakes into bright white fireflies. Speeding toward the Stonesburg freeway, Bettinger glanced at his hatchback and the charcoal gray pickup truck, both of which were still sitting in front of the empty house. Orchestral hold music sounded in his earplug, clashing with the pop station that he had put on the car stereo to distract his daughter from his conversation.

The symphony stopped.

"Mr. Bettinger?" asked a man who had an especially clear tenor voice.

"Yes. Is this the ophthalmologist?"

"Optometrist. My name's Dr. Edwards."

"Is there an ophthalmologist?"

"I'm sorry, but Dr. Singh's away on vacation. I promise I'll consult her if I have any questions, but I've dealt with such things before."

This was said without resentment, displaying a level of professionalism that gave Bettinger more confidence in the eye specialist. "That's fair."

"What happened?"

"She's unconscious, so I don't know the exact details, but some fabric—underwear—is stuck in her left eye. Deep. Jammed in like a cork."

Snowflakes accumulated upon the windshield.

"You can't see the eye itself?" asked Dr. Edwards.

"No."

The wiper cleared the glass.

"What happened before the underwear was put in?"

"Let me ask." The detective drove onto the freeway and lowered the volume of the stereo. "Karen?"

The girl flinched. "What?"

"Did you see the man in the mask do something to Mommy's eye?"

Karen nodded.

"What happened?"

"When he told us to get naked, Mommy screamed at him, and he took out one of those clicky things they use at the post office."

Bettinger's stomach sank. "A box cutter?"

Karen nodded. "He went like this—" The girl stabbed the air with her right fist.

The detective felt a phantom pain inside of his eye. "Okay, sweetie," he said, raising the volume of the stereo. "Listen to the music."

Karen returned her gaze to the windshield wipers, which were busy erasing snow.

"She was stabbed in the eye with a box cutter," Bettinger told Dr. Edwards.

There was a moment of silence.

"How far from the hospital are you?" asked the optometrist.

The detective glanced at the upcoming exit sign and made a calculation. "Less than fifteen minutes."

"I'm heading to the emergency room now. Is th—"

"What're the chances that you can save it? Her eye?"

"I need to see her first."

The detective decided not to press the doctor for a bad prognosis. "Okay."

"Is there anything else that requires immediate attention?"

"She's lost some blood," said Bettinger, glancing in the rearview mirror at Alyssa, whose chest continually rose and fell. "Her pulse is steady, but weak."

"Do you know what ty—"

"O positive."

"You're certain?"

"I am."

"Good. Is she allergic to antibiotics?"

"No."

"Good. Please drive carefully in that snow—a few minutes probably won't make any difference."

"I'll drive safely," the detective said as he switched lanes.

"I'll have a gurney ready—I'm an African American, shaved head, goatee."

"You sound white."

"Then the lessons paid off."

"I'm in a blue compact."

"I'll look for you."

"Thanks." The detective killed the connection and again lowered the volume of the radio. "Sweetie?"

Karen looked over.

Bettinger stomped on his terrible imaginings and forced himself to ask his daughter one of the most loathsome questions in existence. "What did the man do to you?"

The girl looked down at her little fingers.

"Karen?" prompted the detective, unable to breathe.

"He told me to take off my clothes and get on the bed or he'd make Mommy go blind."

"Did he do anything else to you?"

"He tied me up and put undies in my mouth."

"Anything else?"

The girl shook her head. "No."

Relieved, Bettinger leaned over and put a kiss upon his precious daughter's forehead. "You're being very brave."

Karen watched snow gather on the windshield.

A new song that sounded exactly like the previous cut began, and the detective raised the volume. "Do you like this one?"

The excitable little girl who loved or hated most things shrugged.


Twelve minutes later, the blue compact landed in front of a big tan building that was the Salvation Hospital of Stonesburg. Bettinger killed the engine, and twenty feet away, the doors of the emergency room slid apart, admitting a white male nurse and a man who fit the description of Dr. Edwards. Directly between the hastening fellows was a steel gurney.

"Stay here," the detective said to his daughter as he stepped outside. "I'll be close."

"Okay."

Bettinger walked to the back of the vehicle, scooped up his wife, and set her on the gurney. The optometrist glanced at the girl in the passenger seat.

"She was there?"

"Yeah. And my son is—"

Bettinger's throat constricted. Tears filled his eyes as everything that he had suppressed for the last thirty minutes rushed to the surface. Silently, he pointed a trembling finger at the trunk.

"Your son . . . ?" asked Dr. Edwards.

The detective nodded his head.

"I'm sorry," said the optometrist, whose sympathy seemed genuine.

Bettinger knew that he could not break down in front of his daughter, and so he dammed the powerful flood of emotions. "Can . . . I . . . leave my car here?" he asked, wiping his eyes with a fist.

"It's fine."

The detective retrieved his girl, and together, they followed the rolling gurney past the sliding doors into a bright beige waiting room that had five vinyl couches, some magazines, and a high-definition television.

"Stay here for now," Dr. Edwards said without slowing his progress toward the emergency-care area. "The receptionist has your paperwork."

Bettinger nodded his head.

"He'll send for the diener when you're ready."

"Fine." The detective was not yet ready to deal with a morgue attendant.

"We'll get you when we know something," the optometrist added as he and the nurse rolled Alyssa Bright through a double door.

"Thank you."

Bettinger took Karen's right hand and walked her toward the couches, where a Mexican woman who looked like a tall midget mopped the linoleum.

"Smells like pee," the girl said to her father.

"It's ammonia. Keeps things sanitary."

Karen avoided a collection of wet tiles and covered her nose. "Smells like pee."

"Agreed."

The girl sat on the couch that faced the television, which was showing a replay of the local news broadcast from the previous night. Suddenly, the anchorwoman's solemn face was replaced by an obese cartoon cat who had an impressive mustache and a very snug vest.

"Thank you," Bettinger said to the janitor, who was holding a remote control in her right hand.

"The news isn't for kids."

"It isn't."

The tiny woman employed her mop as if it were an oar and rowed herself to port.

Bettinger faced Karen. "Want me to take off your jacket?"

Staring at the television screen, the girl shook her head.

"Need to go to the bathroom? It's right here."

Again, his daughter declined his offer.

"Do you want something to drink?"

Karen shrugged.

"Apple?" suggested Bettinger. "Cranberry?"

"Cranberry."

"I'm going right there—" The detective pointed at the vending machine that was located on the other side of the waiting area. "Okay?"

The obese cat fell off of his tricycle in an extraordinarily complicated manner, but Karen did not in any way respond to his antics. It looked like her trauma was turning into psychological shock.

"I'll be right back."

Bettinger kissed the top of his daughter's head and proceeded toward the vending machine. On his way over, he withdrew his cell phone, highlighted the name of his partner (who had called him four times during the last hour), and thumbed the connect button.

Dominic picked up on the first ring. "You okay?"

"Somebody was waiting for me at my house. I killed him, but my son's dead and my wife's in bad shape."

"Motherfucker." The big fellow broke something. "How's the little one?"

"In shock, but physically okay."

Bettinger arrived at the vending machine.

"You at the hospital?"

"Yeah. What's the situation in Victory?"

"Bodies turnin' up all over—missin' cops and some people who're probably witnesses."

"Perry and Huan?"

"Executed. Badges and dicks gone like the rest."

The detective felt empty. "I'm praying all this is a fucking nightmare."

"The dude who works the front desk at the Sunflower is missin'."

Bettinger remembered writing his address on the form that he had given to the clerk, and it was suddenly obvious how the killer had discovered the little salmon house in Stonesburg.

"Then he's dead," stated the detective. "That killer didn't have compunctions."

"Learn anythin' from him?"

"No, but he left behind a pickup truck I'll search when I can."

"Those homo faggots in Stonesburg P.D. get involved?"

"Nope. The tableau was quick and quiet."

"Don't call them."

"I didn't intend to." There was a dark implication in Bettinger's reply.

"So then you know how this needs to go?"

"I know."

"You won't get squeamish?"

"My daughter's traumatized, my wife's gonna lose an eye, and my son's in the trunk of a fucking car," hissed the detective. "I'm not gonna get squeamish."

"Neither are me and Tackley."

Bettinger slid a dollar bill into the vending machine and typed in the number of the prison cell that contained cranberry juice. "Got anything new on Sebastian?"

"Me and Tackley been leanin' on people since we left Zwolinski's, but nobody knows nothin'."

"Zwolinski turn up?"

"Still missin'."

The crimson bottle was taken from its cell by a whirring robotic claw.

"Anything with Slick Sam?" asked Bettinger.

"The cadet's still at the chop shop—I just talked to him—but Slick Sam ain't showed yet."

The robot flung the bottle into the nether chamber.

"I'll get to the killer's pickup as soon as I can." The detective bent over, slid aside a clear panel, and claimed the beverage. "But I'm not leaving until I talk to my wife."

"A'ight. Call when there's somethin'. Even one of your maybes."

"You do the same."

"I will."

The line went dead.

Bettinger traversed the waiting room, gave the bottle of juice to Karen, and approached the front desk, behind which sat the receptionist, a young fellow who had glasses, acne, and short blond hair. Near a half-eaten muffin on the table lay a big art book that was open to a painting of a rotund fellow in fancy dress who gripped a yellow parakeet in his right hand as if it were a bonbon. The bird looked worried.

"Pardon me."

The receptionist slid a black clipboard across the table.

"Thanks," said Bettinger, claiming the paperwork. "Do you have on-site day care?"

The young man looked at Karen. "For her?" A dislodged crumb bounced upon the fancy fellow's ascot.

"Yes."

A blue clipboard slid across the desk.

Bettinger claimed the second collection of papers and cleared his throat. "I need to see the diener."

"You have a body?"

The detective nodded his head and received a white clipboard.

Somebody said, "Jules Bettinger," and he looked over. Standing at the doorway that led to the emergency-care area was the male nurse who had been with Dr. Edwards.

"Please come with me."

"One sec."

Bettinger hastened across the waiting room and placed the black, blue, and white clipboards on the sofa beside Karen. "I'll be gone for a couple of minutes."

The girl did not respond.

"I'll keep her company," said the little janitor.

"Talk to the nice woman or the man at the desk if you need me."

"Okay."

The detective hugged his daughter and jogged across the waiting area. As he neared the portal, the nurse flung the door.

"She's awake."

A sickness spread throughout Bettinger's guts. Inhaling deeply, he proceeded through the doorway, toward his single favorite person in the world, whom he would soon tell the worst news that she would ever hear.

# XLII

# Alyssa and Jules Talk

The nurse escorted Bettinger along a narrow hall, past several computers, and into a bright white room that had numerous partitioned areas and a vaguely floral smell. As the pair strode across the linoleum, they passed an obese redneck, a girl in a wheelchair, and a supine old man who was attached to a turquoise machine that beeped and hissed like a mechanical snake. Manic laughter emanated from behind one of the closed curtains, and it was unclear to the detective if the person was insane or the victim of a malicious tickler.

The nurse guided Bettinger to Dr. Edwards, who was currently washing his hands inside a stainless-steel sink. A grim expression sat upon his face.

"She's gonna lose the eye?" asked the detective.

"Yes. Most of the retina's destroyed." The optometrist shook excess water from his hands and pulled a paper towel from a dispenser. "Right now, she's getting antibiotics and plasma—I want her as healthy as possible before the anesthesiologist arrives."

Bettinger was confused. "Why's she going under?"

Dr. Edwards tossed the crumpled towel into a bin. "I need to remove the eye and clean out the area."

The detective felt queasy. "That can't be done on a local?"

"I want to be thorough. We can't risk an infection in a place like that."

"What kind of infection?"

"MRSA. Can be fatal if it enters the brain."

The room tilted, and Bettinger grabbed the nurse's arm, steadying himself. Cold sweat poured down his face.

Dr. Edwards gestured to an empty bed. "Maybe you should lie down for a—"

"No." The detective released the nurse's bicep. "Let me talk to her so you can do what you need to do."

"She's on a very strong painkiller, but still lucid. I told her about the surgery, though not anything else that transpired . . ." The optometrist motioned to a beige curtain in the far corner. "Over there. You've got a few minutes."

"I put a chair," added the nurse.

Bettinger walked to the curtain, pulled it aside, and saw Alyssa. Intravenous tubes sprouted from her arms, connecting her to suspended plasma, and the bandages that covered her caramel skin looked like bright white parasites. Next to the thick gauze that covered the left side of her face was a red and staring eye.

"Jules?"

The detective entered the room, closed the curtain, and hugged his wife. Plastic tubes slithered across his face.

"The kids?"

Bettinger pulled Alyssa firmly to his chest. "Gordon was killed. Karen is safe."

"Gordon was killed?"

"Yes. He was protecting Karen when it happened. He saved her life." The detective clenched his jaw in order to maintain his composure.

"Gordon's dead?"

"Yes."

A terrible silence sucked the air from the room, and the detective could not do anything but hold his wife. It felt like they were plummeting through the dark toward the bottom of an impossibly deep canyon.

Alyssa cleared her throat. "But Karen's safe . . . ?" Her voice was tiny.

"She's watching cartoons right now."

"Okay."

Bettinger relaxed his embrace, kissed Alyssa on the mouth, and took each of her hands. Navigating tubes and machinery, he sat on the small plastic chair that the nurse had provided for him and looked at his wife. Tears sparkled in her good eye, and the gauze on the left side of her face was damp.

Again, Alyssa cleared her throat. "Does Karen know?"

"About Gordon?"

The woman nodded her head.

"She does, but she's pretending not to."

"Like the tooth fairy?"

A tidal wave of sadness hit the detective. "Yeah." Clearing his throat, he motioned to the curtain. "The doctor said that—"

"That was you outside?"

Bettinger was confused.

"Who shot the window?"

"Yeah . . . it was. Sorry about the glass."

"You had to—that psycho was gonna kill us all."

The detective squeezed his wife's hands.

"You killed him?"

"Yes."

"He deserved it."

"He deserved much worse."

Alyssa nodded her head.

Again, Bettinger motioned to the curtain. "The doctor said—"

"Why did he want to kill you? You're . . . you're from Arizona. We're all—" The woman's voice cracked. Shaking her head, she fought back tears. "We're all from Arizona."

"He was working for someone in Victory who doesn't like cops."

"Did you get him too?"

"That's what we're working on right now."

Alyssa lowered her eye. "Do you need to go back to work?" There was fear in her voice.

Bettinger squeezed his wife's hands. "I want to get this guy—the boss—badly. Desperately. But if you tell me to flush my badge down the toilet, and forget about it, I will. You've suffered too much—for no goddamn reason—and the decision's yours to make."

A sad smile appeared on the painter's bandaged face.

"I'm serious," said the detective.

"I know you are." Alyssa took a deep breath and shook her head. "I don't want you to go to Victory. I'm scared . . . and . . . and I don't want something to happen to you. But I can't ask you to walk away from this. For . . . for you to just sit around and hope that somebody else gets the man who did this to us."

Bettinger kissed his wife's hands, certain that he had married the single most thoughtful woman in the world. "I'll put Karen in the hospital day care, and we'll move back to Arizona when this is over. I'll get some kind of desk job."

"I look forward to buying you paperweights."

"And we'll fly up to Chicago for your show at the gallery."

Tears filled the woman's eye.

Bettinger knew that Alyssa was thinking about how proud Gordon had been of her upcoming exhibit.

Tubes stirred as the woman wiped her right cheek.

Leaning forward, the detective hugged his wife. "I love you."

"I love you."

"Mr. and Mrs. Bettinger?" Dr. Edwards inquired from the other side of the curtain.

"Do I need to go?" asked the detective.

"Please. The anesthesiologist's here."

"Okay."

Bettinger kissed Alyssa once more, and as he stood up, the woman wiped her eye.

A lean white fellow with sunken cheeks and short silver hair shuffled into the room, rolling an instrument that looked like a Russian satellite.

The detective placed his wife's neon green cell phone upon the gurney. "Call me when you get out of surgery."

"Okay. Be careful."

"I will."

Bettinger departed before he or his wife had time to crumble.

# XLIII

# Snow from a Violescent Sky

After the detective had completed his paperwork, he deposited his daughter in the day-care facility and his son in the morgue. Each child received a kiss and an apology.

Bettinger left the building and entered a world that was veiled in snow. Violet flakes fell from a sky of the same color as he walked toward his wife's blue compact (which was still illegally parked in the emergency lane). Compressed by the rubber soles of his boots, the inch-thick blanket of petrified precipitation squeaked.

The detective entered the car and drove onto the freeway. Emanating from the speakers was a cloying pop song that seemed morbidly ironic to a man who had just turned his son's body over to a diener.

Bettinger shut off the radio and drove in silence.

The compact rolled east. Although it was half past six, the violescent sky was not any brighter than it had been at five in the morning.

The detective told his partner that he was returning to the suburbs to examine the killer's possessions, but both policemen knew that the real point of the phone call was to prove that they were both still alive. Changing lanes, he heard several shouts through the earplug and concluded that the pained individual was being interrogated by Tackley.

"Getting anything from that one?"

"Some blood, couple teeth."

"Good luck."

Bettinger killed the connection. Cars draped in violet blankets drifted along the freeway, and white headlights glared.

The detective thought about his son, whose final act had been a heroic display of love and courage. Gordon had saved Karen's life, and this selfless sacrifice was a sad glimpse of the man who he would have become as an adult. His death was terrible, and Bettinger was further pained by the fact that he would never be able to convey his gratitude to the young hero.

If there were a pill that instilled a belief in Heaven, the bereaved father would have put it in his mouth and swallowed.

The exit sign appeared, and the detective steered onto the snowy off-ramp, where his tires slipped, flung slush, and squeaked. Applying the brakes, he reduced his speed until it compared to that of a bicyclist. The man from Arizona knew that he needed to be careful—he had very little experience driving in the snow, and he did not want a thoughtless accident to get between his hands and Sebastian's throat.

Bettinger entered the suburbs of Stonesburg, drove onto the most familiar street, and slowed the compact. The windshield wipers shoved powder across the glass, revealing the little salmon house. It was an unwelcome sight.

The detective cut the wheel, landed, and exited. Gun in hand, he surveyed the area, which was still, except for the snow that landed upon roofs, lawns, and roads.

Bettinger entered the little salmon house, a place of violence that was no longer his home . . . if it ever had been.

Exhaling a flower of steam, he strode into the master bedroom. Snow covered the mattress, the carpet, and the legs of the killer.

The detective kicked the upended trash basket from the dead man's head. Two frozen eyes stared up at him from the ground.

Bettinger searched the corpse and found the box cutter, two additional clips of ammunition, and a set of keys, which he pocketed. He discarded the loathsome tool and put the killer's other possessions—including the pair of semi-automatic handguns—into a plastic bag. It was extraordinarily unlikely that a professional hit man would have any traceable hardware, but the weapons might have some other use.

Bettinger stripped the corpse. Nothing remarkable was revealed, except for a tattoo of the letters *E*, *V*, and *K* on the dead man's left shoulder blade.

The detective snagged the charger for his wife's cell phone and some extra clothes for her and his daughter. Carrying these possessions as well as the plastic bag, he returned to the cold.

Bettinger drove the blue compact to the end of the street, around two corners, and onto the parallel avenue. There, his headlights illuminated the lot where his yellow hatchback sat behind the charcoal gray pickup truck.

The detective parked his wife's car. Surveying the immediate area and the violet environs, he stepped outside and walked across the powder. At the killer's truck, he stopped and examined the flatbed. The only thing that lay inside of it was a corrugated sheet of snow.

Observing a passing (and obviously masochistic) jogger, Bettinger withdrew the killer's keys, slotted the most likely candidate into the driver's side door, and turned his hand.

The lock shot up.

Flinging the door, the detective climbed into the truck, which smelled strongly of lemons. The snow-covered windshield was an opaque swath of dull violet, but the rear glass was clear and allowed a view of the street.

Bettinger slid across the bench and opened the glove compartment, which contained a vehicle registration. Attached to this by a paper clip was a driver's license that had a picture of E.V.K.'s aquiline face. There was no chance that these documents were legitimate, but still, the detective pocketed them. It was possible that the forger was a local person who knew something about the killer or Sebastian or the other hired guns.

Bettinger slid his fingertips along the ceiling (which was made of plush black upholstery) and discovered the edge of a nearly invisible flap, which he then carefully opened. A silencer-equipped semiautomatic handgun like the one that had killed his son lay inside the hidden compartment. The detective removed the weapon and inspected the rest of the shallow enclosure, but found nothing else.

Frustrated, Bettinger snorted steam.

All of this stuff was useless.

The detective climbed out of the truck, looked at the bench seat, and dug his hands into its rear crevice as if he were fishing for lost quarters. His thumb landed upon a metal latch, and he pressed it down.

Something clicked.

Bettinger grabbed the bottom cushion and raised it like the top of a chest. Between the steel supports that held the seat in place was a hollow compartment that housed a red, white, and blue cooler.

Ice rattled as the detective removed the heavy container from the nook. Straining, he lowered the seat cushion and set down his burden.

Bettinger lifted the lid, revealing a pool of ice and water that contained eight six-packs of beer. He dumped this collection of cold, frozen, and canned fluids onto the snow and quickly realized that the cooler weighed far too much for an empty piece of plastic.

Something had been hidden inside of it.

The detective put the container down, opened his utility knife, and stabbed an inner wall. Ghostly vapors leaked from the hole.

Bettinger held his breath, adjusted the angle of his blade, and applied more force. Plastic cracked, and a false bottom popped loose.

The detective discarded the partition and looked into the cooler. Chilled by the frigid emanations of dry ice were six plastic baggies. Each one contained a bloodstained police badge, a few spent cartridges, and a severed penis, though in one collection, there was no male member, but instead, two spotted opalescent masses that resembled oysters.

It took Bettinger a moment to realize that he was looking at a pair of ovaries.

Sickened by the sight, he turned his head. Mist poured from the cooler, making the frigid interior of the truck even colder.

Grimacing, the detective put on a glove, seized the pieces of dry ice, and tossed them into the snow, where they crackled and hissed like firecrackers in reverse.

The mist in the cab dissipated, and Bettinger returned his attention to the cooler. Lying underneath the frozen and excised genitalia was a laminated envelope.

A dog barked, startling the detective.

"Christ's uncle."

Bettinger stepped out of the truck, surveyed his violet environs, and saw some activity at the far end of the block. There, an unfortunate oldster tugged on a leash, waging a war against his pet, which was either a mastiff or a horse that had learned how to bark.

The detective reentered the truck, withdrew a piece of paper from the envelope, and read.

*Dear Sir,*

*My identity is unimportant.*

*I am an anonymous agent who has been hired by a go-between to enlist your services. I do not know and will not ever know the identity of the unknown third party who is funding this enterprise.*

*Enclosed in this package you will find $50,000. These bills are unmarked and numerically unrelated.*

*This stipend of $50,000 is an advance payment for the executions of two (2) police officers in the city of Victory, Missouri, next month on the exact day of Wednesday, January 30. No lethal action should occur in this location before the stipulated date.*

*If you decide not to render these services, you are required to return this payment to the address below.*

Bettinger looked down and saw that the address had been removed from the bottom of the letter. He then continued reading from where he had left off.

> *(If you neither return the money, nor fulfill your obligations, you will be executed.)*
>
> *It is the sincerest hope of the unknown third party that you will kill more than two police officers on the day of the event.*
>
> *For each and every Victory policeman that you kill, you will earn an additional sum of $25,000. The women officers are also targets, but at a discounted rate of $18,500 (for obvious reasons).*
>
> *The unknown third party wishes to eliminate the entire police force of Victory, though an elimination of the majority of officers is also a satisfactory end result.*
>
> *No less than fifteen of your peers have been contacted and offered the same exact terms, and thus, in order to keep things simple and honest, each of you must be able to prove your murderous achievements.*
>
> *The unknown third party has stipulated that the proof must be the penis and badge of each executed policeman, and in the case of a slain female, her badge and ovaries. These excised bits of anatomy should be frozen in order to prevent their decomposition during the long period of silence that will follow the day of executions. (Formaldehyde—though permissible—is not recommended.)*
>
> *You will be contacted six to twelve months after January 30 and asked to exhibit proofs of any and all killings that you committed so that the unknown third party might properly remit payment.*
>
> *Best wishes to you and good luck!*

Trembling with anger, Bettinger returned the letter to the envelope and stuffed it in the back pocket of his corduroy pants.

It was time for him to drive north.

# XLIV

# Idling in Shitopia

Snow fell from the violescent sky onto the eyes of a dying pigeon.

Sitting inside the black two-seater that was parked underneath the over-hang of the abandoned school, Bradley Janeski watched the inclement weather bury the bird, which was the fourth one that he had seen collapse during his eleven-hour surveillance mission. Frozen talons were all that remained of the other feathered corpses.

The blizzard was supposed to land at nine o'clock (according to the news), and the weary cadet feared that he might be stranded in Shitopia if he did not soon depart. Slick Sam had not visited the concrete building that was pur-ported to be his chop shop, nor had anybody else, and the twenty-two-year-old doubted that his first stakeout would yield anything but stoppered sinuses and a cough.

Bradley Janeski thumbed a preset number on his cell phone and pressed the receiver to his ear.

"You see him?" asked Corporal Dominic Williams.

"I don't think he's gonna show. The blizzard's on its way and—"

"Shut up."

The cadet closed his mouth.

"I know you're uncomfortable," the big fellow continued, "but you're stayin' there 'til you see him. When you do, call me or Tackley."

"How about Detective Huan and Detective Molloy?"

There was no response to this question, and Bradley Janeski wondered if the line had been disconnected.

"Corporal Williams?"

"Just me and Tackley." The big fellow cleared his throat. "Huan and Mol-loy are workin' on somethin' else right now."

"Okay, though I'm gonna need to get some more food if—"

"Have a snow cone and stay put."

The line went dead.

Bradley Janeski folded his cell phone and reclaimed his binoculars from beside the sketch of Slick Sam, whose lupine features, thin mustache, and oiled hair were so burned into his retinas that he saw them superimposed over everything—even when he closed his eyes. Except for the level of the snow and the amount of neural activity in the fourth pigeon's brain, nothing in the area had changed since his last survey.

The cadet donned his cap, exited the car, urinated, zipped up his pants, brushed flakes from his clothes, returned to the hidden two-seater, twisted the ignition, and cranked the heat. This cycle of activities had been repeated no less than eighteen times since he had begun his stakeout.

Bored, Bradley Janeski stuck an earbud into the right side of his head and thumbed his media player.

A man with a rich baritone voice read from the text of a book.

"—and shut the door. His training had not prepared him for this.

"Outside in the hall was a cacophony of metallic sounds. Grinding and whirring. Clanks. Hank knew the thing was getting closer. It smelled them."

A blue luxury car appeared at the south end of the block.

Bradley Janeski stopped the audio book and raised his binoculars. The traffic on this road during the last ten hours had consisted of seven cars, and thus, each automobile was an event.

Focusing the conjoined antireflective lenses, the cadet monitored the blue luxury vehicle. Snow crackled underneath its tires as it rolled up the street toward the hidden observer.

Taillights flashed, and the vehicle stopped.

Bradley Janeski's stomach lurched.

The blue luxury car had landed directly in front of the concrete building. A collapsed fence, some snow, and a distance of three hundred feet were all that lay between the hidden two-seater and the new arrival.

Without taking his eyes from his binoculars, the cadet reclaimed his cell phone. His superior's number had already been highlighted, and all that he had to do was press the connect button if he saw Slick Sam.

The blue car's taillights were dark, but the plume of exhaust that rose from its rear end told the young man that the vehicle was idling. Behind the tinted glass, somebody moved.

Bradley Janeski's heart pounded.

The window flashed, and the driver's door opened. From the interior of the vehicle emerged a white fellow in dark blue who had smooth tan skin, a mane of well-oiled black hair, and a lupine face.

Bradley Janeski thumbed the connect button. As the phone rang, he descried a passenger inside of the blue car—a woman who had red hair, a brown fur coat, and a magazine.

"Yeah?" said Corporal Dominic Williams.

"Slick Sam's here."

"Alone?"

"There's a chick."

The car dealer said something to the woman and closed the door, shutting her inside.

"We'll be there in fifteen," said the big fellow.

"The chick didn't get out, and the car's in idle."

"The car's in idle?"

"Yeah."

"Go arrest him. Do just like we talked about with the car."

The cadet buckled his seat belt and lowered his window. "What about the chick?"

"She's whatever. It's him we need. Go."

The line went dead.

Across the street, Slick Sam walked toward the front door of the concrete building. A key ring that had numerous occupants glimmered in his left hand.

Bradley Janeski knew that he should not let the suspect go indoors.

He tossed his cell phone and binoculars onto the sketch, shifted gears, and stomped the accelerator. The two-seater surged forward, shedding the shadow of the overhang.

Slick Sam looked over his shoulder.

Roaring across the lot, the black car flung snow. "Police!" the cadet yelled through his open window. His bumper clanked against a fence post, scattering sparks.

The suspect darted for the blue vehicle.

"Hands in the air!" shouted Bradley Janeski, firing his snub-nosed revolver at the sky. The shot boomed like an exclamation point.

Slick Sam reached the door of his blue sedan.

The two-seater thudded onto the sidewalk. Thirty feet separated the car dealer and the careening automobile that sped toward him.

Slick Sam dove out of the way and belly-flopped on the powder.

Bradley Janeski steered for the suspect's legs.

"Stop!" yelled Slick Sam.

Shins cracked underneath the two left tires, and the cadet stomped the brakes. A concrete wall pounded the grille, catapulting the young man forward until his seat belt snapped taut. His revolver flew out of his hand, ricocheted off of the windshield, and tumbled underneath the passenger seat.

Dazed, the cadet shifted into park—an act that he realized was somewhat redundant. He did not know if he should be proud or ashamed of his actions.

"Fuck!" yelled Slick Sam. "You broke my fucking legs!"

Bradley Janeski prostrated himself, slid his left hand under the passenger seat, and felt around for the revolver, hoping that it had not fallen through the hole in the floor that his older brother had not yet fixed. A window exploded, accompanied by the sound of a gunshot.

Glass covered the prone cadet's back, and he shouted, "You're under arrest! Put down your—"

Gunfire boomed, and a round piece of sky appeared in the car's ceiling.

Cursing himself for letting his car get so messy, the cadet dug through the soda cans, magazines, and crumpled bags that were underneath the passenger's seat. Cold air blew through the hole in the floor, freezing his fingertips as he searched for the snub-nosed revolver.

Bradley Janeski heard something, and he paused to listen to it more closely. It was a quiet and steady crunching sound. Somebody was walking through the snow.

"Ma'am," the cadet said, "get back to your vehicle right now or I will shoot you." He slid his hand through the hole in the bottom of his car and felt around for the gun. "I have permission."

"You . . . have permission?" repeated Slick Sam, who sounded equally pained and incredulous.

"Yeah," said Bradley Janeski, patting the snow underneath the two-seater. "Completely." His pinkie landed upon notched metal.

"To shoot an unarmed woman?" asked the car dealer.

"The chick can just go home or whatever," the cadet said as he seized the fallen revolver and raised it through the hole in the floor. "All I want's you."

"Why?"

Bradley Janeski adjusted his rearview mirror until he could see Slick Sam. A gun was in the fellow's right hand, and the area around his crooked legs looked like a cherry snow cone. Kneeling beside him was the redhead in the brown fur coat. It did not look like she had a weapon, but there was no way for the cadet to be certain.

"Ma'am!" shouted Bradley Janeski. "Get back in that car and drive away."

"I'm not leaving him like this," protested the woman, who had a sour New Jersey accent. "In the snow with his legs all—"

"You're not taking him anywhere," said the cadet, pointing his revolver at the sky. "Now get back in that car of yours and drive off or I'll shoot you to death. You've got ten seconds."

"What kind of cop are you?"

"This kind!" The gun boomed. "Ten. Nine. Eight."

"Those aren't seconds!" protested Slick Sam.

"Seven. Six. Five."

"Go!"

"Four. Three."

The redheaded woman bolted across the snow, fell on her face, rose to her feet, clambered into the vehicle, changed gears, and sped off.

"You're a real gentleman," remarked Slick Sam, whose voice had become slurred. "Tip top."

"Throw your gun against the wall or I'll back over your legs."

The groggy car dealer stared at the black two-seater. "You'll . . . what?"

"Ten. Nine. Eight. Seven."

The pistol clattered against the side of the concrete building.

"Cocksucker."

# XLV

# A Talk with Shitdick

Bettinger drove the charcoal gray pickup truck toward Victory. The vehicle was a better choice than his bright yellow hatchback, since it had elevation and snow tires, and was as inconspicuous as it was disposable.

Although the detective had very few experiences driving in the snow, he knew that automobiles like this one had better traction whenever they carried cargo, and so he wrapped the killer's corpse in a blanket and dumped it into the flatbed. This contribution of pounds was likely the most beneficent act ever committed by the vile sociopath who had murdered Gordon.

Despite the additional weight, the pickup truck fishtailed thrice during the trip north. These jarring events occurred when Bettinger changed lanes, and mostly because he found it hard to maintain a safe speed. Whenever he thought of his son or his wife or his daughter or Sebastian or the killer or the things that he had found in the cooler, his right boot grew heavy.

The windshield wipers shoved powder across the glass, and through the opening, Bettinger saw Victory. Covered with snow and viewed from a distance, the city resembled a mildewed autopsy.

The detective's cell phone buzzed, and he took the call. "Yes?"

"Where are you?" asked Dominic.

"The exit."

"We got Slick Sam."

Bettinger was surprised by the news. "He say anything useful?"

"He's still unconscious."

"What happened to him?"

"Some of his legs broke. Go to four twenty-eight Orchid Terrace, off of Thirtieth, and call when you're near."

"Four twenty-eight Orchid."

"Mm."

The line went dead.

---

Bettinger parked the charcoal gray pickup truck on Orchid Terrace, directly behind Dominic's silver car, which now had chains on its tires. Beside the two vehicles was a brownstone that had boarded-up windows, barbed-wire fences, and three ancient missing-person notices where the subjects' faces looked septic.

The detective drew his gun and stepped outside, scanning the area. Something clanked.

Bettinger turned around. A flap that was a cellar door scattered snow as it swung open, and Dominic rose from the ground, wearing a black overcoat and matching gloves. Dangling from his right hand was a gun.

The detective locked the pickup truck and walked toward his partner.

"Close it behind you," the big fellow said as he descended concrete steps.

Bettinger entered the stairwell, pulled the cellar door shut, and slid the iron bolt. Smelling dust, he followed the big fellow into the earth. Below them shone a dim yellow light.

"Here—" Dominic proffered a piece of black cloth.

Bettinger claimed the fabric, which was a ski mask.

The policemen entered a dank storeroom where a dirty hanging lightbulb illuminated rotten cardboard boxes and a stained twin mattress that was covered with cat skeletons. Saprogenic growth covered the small bones like kitten fur.

"Put yours on," said the big fellow, donning his black ski mask. Between his lips were fake gold teeth.

Bettinger then knew for certain that Dominic was the man who had terrorized Kimmy, the stoner who lived with Sebastian's girlfriend. The big fellow's crime was not a true surprise to the detective, nor was the fact that he no longer cared about an intimidation tactic and a dead feline. Much worse things had occurred since that time.

Bettinger pulled the ski mask over his head and followed Dominic to a closed door. There, the big fellow knocked in three groups of two.

An old bolt clacked, and the door retreated into an unlighted room. A crisp, soft voice said, "Come in."

The detective followed his partner into the darkness, which smelled like urine and feces. Plastic crinkled underfoot.

Hinges squeaked, and a bolt clicked. A lightbulb appeared overhead, glaring, and its radiance illuminated the third masked policeman, a stack of cinder blocks, four stone walls, a corroded boiler, three boarded-up vents, and the pale flesh of the naked and unconscious white fellow who was lying handcuffed and fettered atop the clear tarpaulin that covered the floor. Cellophane wrapped the man's legs, which were bloody and swollen, and a piece of his right shin-bone had cut through the plastic. The captive's lupine physiognomy, oiled hair, and thin mustache exactly matched the sketch that Bettinger had seen at the pillbox.

"I just gave Shitdick a little morphine," remarked Tackley.

"How're his vitals?"

"Sufficient." The mottled man gestured at the captive. "I'll lead this, though grab the reins if you see something."

"I will."

Dominic snorted steam. "Let's."

Tackley kneeled on the tarpaulin, raised his left hand, and slapped Slick Sam. The car dealer shuddered, but did not awaken.

"I can do it." Dominic put the heel of his enormous boot over Slick Sam's shaved testicles.

"Don't," said Tackley. "This needs to be gentle." The mottled man elbowed the captive's larynx.

Slick Sam yelped, and urine arced into the air.

"Watch it." Dominic pointed at the activated phallus. "He isn't empty."

The captive opened his eyes, which were red and dilated. "Where the fuck . . . ?" Confused by the narcotic, he appraised the boiler room, its masked occupants, and finally himself. The color drained from his face when he saw his own legs. "Get me to a hospital. I need—"

"Shut up." Tackley withdrew a photograph of Melissa Spring, the attractive young woman who was Sebastian's girlfriend. Holding up the image, the mottled man said, "You sold a vehicle to—"

"Take me to the hospital right now."

"You sold a vehicle to this woman." Tackley shook the photograph. "What kind—"

"I won't say anything until I get some medical—"

An open hand slapped the captive's face, and again, the mottled man shook the picture.

"What kind of—"

"Until you get me a doctor, 'Fuck you' is my all-purpose answer."

Tackley pounded Slick Sam's nose, snapping the cartilage.

"Fuck!"

Bettinger drew closer. "If you want some medical attention, you'd better answer him."

The captive spat blood. "Not until I see a doctor."

"That's not the order of things," replied the detective.

"My legs look like fucking headcheese!"

"How about lasagna?"

Tackley motioned to Dominic, who claimed a cinder block from the stack, balanced it on the palm of his right hand, and held it out. Pieces of grit fell upon the cellophane that wrapped Slick Sam's broken legs.

The captive was terrified. "Don't," he said, "I j—"

"What kind of car did you sell her?" The mottled man raised the photograph.

"You'll—you'll kill me once I tell you."

"Why do you think we're wearing masks?" asked Bettinger.

Slick Sam had no answer to this question.

"It's so we can let you go after you help us," stated the detective. "You're not who we're after—so don't get in the way."

"Get me a doctor, and we'll—"

Dominic heaved the cinder block at the ceiling. The slab hung in the air for a moment and then plummeted toward Slick Sam's legs. Terrified, he shut his eyes.

The big fellow caught the block in his left hand, and loose grit bounced off of the cellophane.

"He's a below-average juggler," remarked Tackley.

"But I hope to improve."

Slick Sam opened his eyes. His entire body was shaking.

The mottled man raised the photograph of Melissa Spring. "What kind of vehicle did you sell her?"

"A blue jeep."

Bettinger took out his mechanical pencil and leaned forward. "Manufacturer?"

"Stallion Star."

"What hue?"

"Cobalt."

"You give her a license plate?"

"No."

"She had her own?"

"Probably, but I never saw it."

"V-six?"

"Eight."

The detective scratched the information onto his notepad as quickly as it was uttered. "What kind of tires?"

"Mud terrain."

"For off-road?"

"Yeah."

Tackley and Dominic exchanged a meaningful glance, and Bettinger motioned for them to take the reins.

The mottled man leaned forward. "Did she mention the Heaps?"

"We didn't hang out." Slick Sam spat bloody mucus. "She just told me what she needed. Paid cash."

"When was that?" asked Bettinger.

"Five, six weeks ago."

"Anything else customized?"

The car dealer ruminated for a moment. "She had me put straps in the back."

"For what? A wheelchair?"

"Dogs."

"You see these dogs?"

"When she came over."

"What kind are they?"

"Dobermans."

"The best," remarked Dominic. "How many she got?"

"Four."

"Anything else?" asked Bettinger.

"No. Nothing."

Dominic hurled the cinder block across the room, and Slick Sam flinched when it shattered against the wall.

"Now g-get me to a doctor."

Tackley rose to his feet. "You'll go when everything's resolved."

"But what if something happens to you?"

"Pray that it doesn't."

"You can't just—"

The mottled man kicked the captive's jaw, knocking him unconscious. He then rolled the man onto his stomach, withdrew a half-filled syringe, and stuck it in an exposed buttock so that its plunger was within reach of the fellow's bound hands.

"How much morphine's that?" asked Bettinger, pocketing his notepad.

Dominic frowned. "Does it matter?"

"Yes. Especially if he gave us bad info."

"He didn't."

"In case."

"There's not enough to kill him," said Tackley.

"Okay."

The policemen departed from the boiler room, and the mottled man switched off the light, closed the door, and turned the lock.

"What're the Heaps?" asked Bettinger, pocketing his ski mask.

Dominic peeled the fabric from his face and removed his gold teeth. "What's north of Shitopia."

"Didn't know there was more city past that."

"It's not city." Tackley wiped sweat from his white-and-pink face with his mask. "It's decades of disaster piled on top of itself—a wasteland."

"You think Sebastian's there?" inquired the detective.

"It's the only place in Victory that requires off-road tires." The mottled man seized a cardboard box that was labeled KITCHEN and carried it toward the stairwell.

"Ain't those tires good for the snow?" posited Dominic. "Maybe he knew 'bout the blizzard?"

"Not five or six weeks ago," said Bettinger.

"All this shit sounds like guesses."

"It's what we have."

"Wait here."

Dominic climbed the steps, undid the bolt, and opened the cellar door. For the better part of a minute, he scanned the outside area for assassins. "It's clear."

Bettinger walked toward the stairwell and the falling snow. Tackley followed, carrying his cardboard box, the contents of which clanked with his footfalls.

# XLVI

# Canine Itinerary

Ice crunched underneath the falling boots of the policemen as they strode toward their vehicles. Held in Bettinger's right hand was one of the killer's silencer-equipped semiautomatic guns. Its safety was off.

"Sorry 'bout your wife and son," said Dominic, dusting snow from his shoulders. "I can't even imagine how that must feel." He exhaled steam through his nostrils as he walked. "My ex had a miscarriage when we was together, and that was rough. Pretty much the beginnin' of the end for us."

"I'm sorry about Perry and Huan," said the detective. "They seemed like good guys."

"They were."

"Better than us," remarked Tackley. His little blue eyes were hard.

Bettinger reached the charcoal gray truck, withdrew the note from his pocket, and held it out. "Wanna go over it?"

The mottled man set the cardboard box on the hood of the silver car and took the letter. His eyes flickered left to right for the duration of a minute.

"Seems like the killers aren't local," said Tackley, handing the note to Dominic.

"I inferred that as well."

"We'll need to get their names from Sebastian before we kill him."

"I'm not sure he'll know who they are," said Bettinger. "It looks like he used a couple of middlemen to keep things anonymous."

"That's fiction. Too many variables could go wrong in a setup like that. And if he really doesn't know, we'll make him find out."

The detective thought of the box of kitchen supplies. "Okay."

Dominic looked up from the letter. "Gianetto and Stanley got killed the day before it was supposed to happen."

"It was after midnight," Bettinger said, "so technically it was the right day."

"I guess." The big fellow took an ice scraper from his car. "We better find that fuckin' Sebastian."

The detective considered the situation. "How big are the Heaps?"

"Big."

"Do we have some kind of canine division?"

Dominic scraped chunks from his windshield. "A dude named Wendell works freelance with the department."

"Dogs won't help us," said Tackley, putting his cardboard box into the car. "They make too much noise for something like this, and the blizzard's almost here."

Bettinger shook his head. "I don't want dogs—I want their whistles."

"Why?" asked Dominic.

"The Dobermans."

Tackley grinned, revealing two rows of small yellow teeth. "Four of them."

The big fellow heaved a slab of ice as if he were a giant. "But don't whistles make them sit? Or do tricks?"

"Only if they're trained that way," said the detective, clearing the powder from the truck's windshield with his right arm. "Most dogs bark when they hear one."

A grin of comprehension illuminated Dominic's face. "Nigga's got ideas."

Tackley flung the passenger door. "We'll swing by Wendell's place, get some whistles on the way up."

"Good."

The big fellow circumvented the silver car and opened the driver's door. "You can ride with us if you want."

"We should have more than one vehicle," Bettinger said as he entered the pickup truck, brushing powder from his scalp. "I'll follow."

"Good thing you ain't driving the mustard."


Dominic slammed a battering ram against the back door of a two-story brownstone. Wood buckled, and canines barked.

"Sounds like a dog army in there."

Bettinger flanked his partner, holding a plastic bag, which was one of a dozen that he had retrieved from the grocer down the street. Wendell was not home, nor was he answering his phone, and the closest pet store was thirty-five minutes out of the way (and possibly out of business). Breaking into the dog handler's home was the quickest and surest way for the policemen to acquire an ultrasonic whistle.

Again, the big fellow raised the battering ram.

"Don't let it fly open," advised the detective. "We don't want them getting out."

"I'm bein' delicate."

Dominic swung. Wood cracked, and the canine clamor crescendoed. The big fellow set down the siege device, tore off the doorknob, and tossed it into the bushes.

"You ready?"

Bettinger nodded, kneeling.

Dominic poked the door with an index finger. A barking head launched through the opening, teeth gnashing, and the detective covered it with the shopping bag. The hood was then attached to the confused beast's collar by a piece of duct tape.

Blinded by cheap plastic, the bewildered animal attacked a receipt.

"That's ridiculous," said the big fellow.

"Definitely."

"Ain't gonna suffocate, is it?"

"No." Bettinger walked the animal into the yard. "Plenty of air."

A barking head that belonged to a German shepherd appeared in the opening and received two shopping bags. As the detective guided the hooded beast from the brownstone, the big fellow looked inside.

"The others are in the detention center."

The policemen walked through the doorway, entering a turquoise kitchen that smelled like wet hay. On the far side of the room, three mutts barked from the insides of large wire cages.

Dominic shook his head. "Doin' time."

"There's a main kennel area?"

"He converted the garage."

"Let's."

The big fellow led his partner across the kitchen and down a hall to a reinforced metal door. Paws scratched the other side of the barrier as if it were an instrument in a jug band.

Bettinger undid the locks, turned the handle, and pushed. Warm air and dog smells spilled into the hallway.

The detective looked through the opening. Inside the garage was a large stainless-steel kennel that had four compartments. Sleepy German shepherds sat in two of the cells, while a pair of beagles and something fluffy that looked like a four-legged monkey patrolled the grounds.

Bettinger walked into the warm enclosure and started to sweat. It seemed as if the most comfortable room in the entire state of Missouri was inhabited by dogs.

"My ex-wife got one." Dominic pointed at a Teutonic prisoner. "But bigger."

The detective approached a metal supply cabinet that was big enough to be a fat man's coffin and opened its door. Inside were bottles, jars, and a series of posts from which depended various clippers, scissors, collars, chains, and dog whistles.

Bettinger took all of the lattermost instruments.

The policemen departed the room and retraced their steps up the hallway. As they neared the kitchen, the detective handed half of the whistles to his partner.

"We only want the ones that're completely ultrasonic."

"Ain't they all?"

"Some produce noises people can hear."

"Sure as fuck don't wanna be blowin' those in the Heaps." The big fellow waved at the caged animals as he passed through the kitchen. "Good luck gettin' parole."

The policemen returned to the snow and blew whistles as they circumnavigated the building. Wendell's dogs and others that were much farther away responded with a chorus of barks and woofs. Seven tests identified three entirely ultrasonic instruments.

Bettinger and Dominic approached Tackley, who was inside the silver car listening to local talk radio. A gun sat in his left hand, and his window was ajar.

"Here—" The detective handed one of the selected whistles through the opening. "Anything on the news?"

"The roads will be impassable in about an hour." The mottled man pointed to the backseat. "There's an extra ballistic vest."

"I've got one. And a mask."

Dominic raised an eyebrow. "A ballistic mask?"

Bettinger nodded, thinking, *If it were a regular mask, Gordon would still be alive.* His eyes began to sting.

"Remember that grocery where they found Elaine James's body?" the big fellow asked as he circumvented the front of his car. "In Shitopia?"

"On Ganson Street."

"Yeah." Dominic opened his door. "That road goes all the way to the Heaps."

"Got it."

Bettinger walked to the charcoal gray pickup truck and climbed inside. The ballistic devil mask, bulletproof vest, and additional silencer-equipped semiautomatic that he had taken from the killer were all on the bench cushion, bundled up in a blue towel. Atop these items, the detective set his whistle, which was made of stainless steel and surmounted by a morose English bulldog.

The silver car rumbled, exhaling steam, and rolled forward. Bettinger started his engine, shifted into gear, and followed Dominic and Tackley into the blizzard.

# XLVII

# Dark Gray

Nature assaulted the city of Victory. Snow covered exposed surfaces, and for most of the detective's journey through the downtown area, he saw very little except the red taillights of the silver car that he followed. Both vehicles were able to traverse the five inches that had fallen (the sedan had chained tires, and the pickup truck had deep treads and helpful elevation), but the blizzard had arrived in full and would continue to roar until the roads were impassable.

The policemen knew that they had to beat the weather, and thus, they drove at a speed of fifty miles an hour across the frozen accumulation. Any car that got in the way of the two-vehicle convoy received high beams and honks.

Driving east on Fifty-sixth Street, Bettinger saw Claude's Hash House, Baptist Bingo, and the pillbox, which looked like a Siberian outpost. Windshield wipers shoveled powder across the glass, and overhead, the violescent sky glowered, exhaling snow.

The silver car's taillights grew larger and slid together, which was what happened whenever Dominic slowed down and turned. Bettinger braked and dialed his wheel clockwise, following his partner north.

As the convoy progressed up the avenue, the violescent sky darkened. It was not quite ten in the morning, but already, it looked like dusk.

The detective traversed five blurry miles on this road, and as he began a sixth, he saw the parking lot of a long-abandoned shopping mall. Beside the curb sat three snow-covered cars that were all the same exact same size and shape. Spinning police lights shone atop the trio of inert lumps, turning the landscape red and blue.

It was not hard for Bettinger to guess the fate of the officers who had driven these vehicles.

He tried not to think about what was inside the cooler.

Fifteen minutes later, the convoy entered the Toilet, where the divine eraser was steadily removing vandals' signatures and advice. Nobody was outside.

Something crackled underneath the truck's left tires, and the detective knew that he had just turned a pigeon into squab tartare.

The taillights of the silver car shone, grew, and slid together. Bettinger braked and dialed the wheel counterclockwise, following Dominic onto a cross street. A couple of blocks later, the convoy navigated another turn and was again proceeding north.

Snow fell.

Shortly after ten thirty, the detective passed the cat that had been nailed by its head to a telephone pole. The creature no longer possessed a body.

"Christ."

The pickup truck lurched, fishtailing, and Bettinger lifted his boot from the gas. Gradually, the truck slid to a stop.

The detective dialed the wheel counterclockwise, hoping that the new angle would put some dry powder underneath the tires. He tapped the accelerator. The engine rumbled, and the truck lurched from the furrow.

Snow covered the windshield and was shoved aside by the wipers as the detective caught up to the silver car.

The convoy sped north. For twenty minutes, Bettinger pondered his wife's surgery, his son's death, and Sebastian Ramirez.

Eight inches of powder were on the ground when the silver car fishtailed.

The vehicle slid across the road, spattering snow, and slammed against an embankment. There, its spinning tires flung slush.

Bettinger braked and rolled down his window as he neared the marooned car.

Taillights flashed, and soon, Dominic emerged from the sedan, holding two big black squares in his right hand. "Floor mats," the big fellow shouted when he made eye contact with the detective.

Bettinger parked the truck, grabbed his rugs, and walked outside. Snow needled his scalp as he walked toward his partner.

"As if things ain't bad enough already." Dominic wiped violet precipitation from his face. "Fuckin' goddamn weather."

The policemen put a floor mat under each of the tires and withdrew from the vehicle, dusting themselves. Inside, Tackley scooted behind the steering wheel, shifted gears, and accelerated. The silver car surged out of the slush, jettisoning rugs and ice.

Bettinger returned to his truck, buckled up, and followed Dominic west until they reached Ganson Street. There, the convoy turned right and headed north.

Dark rectangles that had once held doors or windows gaped on either side of the Shitopia street, and to the detective, the bleak area seemed no more hospitable with its snow makeover. Despair, violence, and defeat permeated northern Victory like nuclear fallout.

The silver car reached an intersection, circumvented an overturned van, and disappeared on its far side.

Seeing the obstacle, Bettinger applied his brakes and turned the wheel. Tires squeaked, and the pickup truck lurched, sliding across the powder directly toward the capsized automobile, which was less than fifty feet away.

The detective righted the wheel, hoping to gain some traction. Tires gripped fresh snow, and the truck shuddered.

Fifteen feet separated the vehicles.

Impact was unavoidable. Tightening his fists, Bettinger braked and cut the wheel.

The truck slammed into the overturned van, and the detective lurched. His seat belt snapped taut, bracing him as his vehicle skidded. The violet world receded.

Trailing slush, the truck slid across the intersection. The front bumper pounded a telephone pole, and the detective flew toward the windshield. His body jerked to a stop, and something cracked. A brush fire of pain flared across his left side, and instantly, he knew that the seat belt had fractured his ribs.

The truck was still.

A rope of snow dropped from a jarred telephone line and bisected the street.

Bettinger exhaled an unconsciously held breath, and pain shot across his damaged ribs.

Grimacing, he shifted into reverse and tapped the accelerator. Wheels flung slush, and the vehicle sank into the snow.

"Christ's—"

Tires screeched, striking pavement, and the truck lurched backward. Relieved, Bettinger slowed down, shifted gears, and drove north on Ganson Street. The silver car was no longer visible.

Snow covered the windshield, and the rubber blades faltered, straining against the thick accumulation.

Suddenly, the detective was driving an igloo.

"Junk."

Bettinger dialed his windshield wipers off and on, and the slumbering blades awakened, clearing paths through the snow. The road ahead of him was empty, except for a falling pigeon that disappeared in a cloud of powder like a feathered meteor.

Leaning on the gas, the detective zoomed through an intersection and up the next street. Little red rubies that were taillights twinkled through the snowfall, and soon, he located the silver car, which was waiting for him at the end of the next block.

When a distance of ninety feet separated the two vehicles, Dominic continued forward.

Hail fell, rattling on the truck's windshield as Bettinger followed his partner north. The speedometer needle returned to the number 50 and did not sink. Slow progress was not an option.

The automobiles passed apartment buildings that lacked façades—a hive of exposed cubicles in which lay ruined toilets, sofas, mattresses, chairs, pipes, and doors. Each edifice was a five- to ten-story diorama of failure.

The convoy rolled through a score of intersections, continuing north across the abandoned terrain.

Thunder boomed, and the silver car's taillights glared.

Suddenly, Bettinger was speeding toward the back of Dominic's sedan, which had come to a complete stop. He raised his foot from the gas and dialed the wheel to the right, hoping to avoid the unseen barrier or pit that had stopped the other vehicle.

Snow peppered the windshield, and the truck swept past the silver car at a speed of forty-two miles an hour.

The path remained clear and solid.

Gently, the detective applied the brakes. The truck slowed and eventually stopped.

Bettinger toggled the gear, opened the door, and climbed outside. Shielding his eyes, he looked down the block.

The front of the silver car was below street level—a gigantic pothole (or something even deeper) had ended its journey—and the windshield was cracked. Doors swung open, releasing Dominic and Tackley.

"Fuckin' Shitopia," exclaimed the big fellow.

Bettinger cupped his hands beside his mouth and called out, "Need some help?"

"Stay there," replied the mottled man.

"Okay."

Dominic retrieved a big green duffel bag from the trunk while Tackley claimed the cardboard box and tactical vests from the backseat. Together, they walked north.

Bettinger returned to the cab of the pickup truck, cleared room for his passengers, and sat back, waiting for them to arrive.

Outside, the winds whistled, and the violet snow turned white. A crosscurrent blew, skirling, and bright motes veered like wary insects.

Crunching footfalls sounded behind the truck. The duffel bag thudded against the bottom of the flatbed, shaking the vehicle, and Dominic appeared outside the passenger window. As he opened the door, the clouds shifted, and the landscape turned gray.

The big fellow slid across the bench into the middle of the cab. Most of his bandages had been removed by the crash and the blizzard, and for the first time, the detective saw the collection of thick stitches, dark scabs, and pale scars that adorned his saturnine face.

Metal clanked as the cardboard box landed in the flatbed, and soon, Tackley climbed into the vehicle, wiping snow from his silver hair, which had acquired a dark red streak above his left eyebrow.

Bettinger shifted into gear. The truck rolled forward, carrying three policemen and a wide assortment of unkind tools.

"How far are the Heaps?"

"Couple of miles." Dominic ripped a stitch from his face and discarded it.

"Leave that alone," remarked Tackley.

"It was buggin' me."

"Leave it alone."

At a speed of fifty miles an hour, the pickup truck continued north. Bettinger hoped to reach the Heaps before the battle against nature was lost.

Trembling wipers shoved snow off of the glass, revealing a series of dead condominiums.

"Remember when they was buildin' those?" Dominic asked Tackley.

"Yeah."

"Like a different world back then."

"It was a different world back then."

An unanswered question returned to Bettinger's mind, and he glanced at his passengers. "How did you get Sebastian to drop the lawsuit?"

Dominic threw a frown. "What the fuck does that matter now?"

"It matters because I want to know." The detective's face and fists hardened. "And if you say it's none of my business, I'll break your fucking teeth."

A heavy silence filled the cab of the truck.

Bettinger circumvented a dip in the road, surprised by the threat that had leapt from his mouth, but also certain that he could and would commit the declared act of violence. An important part of his life was gone, and an angry, grieving entity that could usurp rational thought had filled the void.

The windshield wipers squeaked.

Shifting in his seat, Dominic looked at Tackley, who kept his eyes on the road.

"You care?" inquired the big fellow.

Snow turned the windshield into a pane of glaucoma, and soon, the shuddering wipers swept it clean.

The mottled man shrugged.

"Okay." Dominic glanced at Bettinger and then returned his gaze to the blizzard. "When Sebastian came out of his coma, he filed charges against us. We told him we'd bust up his operations—all of them—unless he dropped the suit, but he didn't care. We closed them down, and Sebastian kept on talkin' with his lawyers. Week after that, we told him we'd go after his associates' operations unless he dropped the suit, but he didn't care 'bout that neither. Nigga just wanted to take us down." The big fellow cracked his thick knuckles and shook his head. "This motherfucker got a cop—our friend—tortured to death, and there was no fuckin' way he was gonna take our badges and win."

Bettinger could not see more than sixty feet ahead of the truck. Anything that appeared in the middle of the road would be narrowly avoided or run over.

Dominic glanced at Tackley and returned his gaze to the storm. "So we kidnapped Sebastian's sister and girlfriend—took them to a place in the fringe. Then we went and visited him—told him the kinds of things that would happen if he took us to court."

Bettinger clenched his fists. "Did you tell him they would be raped?"

"Yeah. And we had some abortion tools—this was before Melissa had her miscarriage. But we wouldn't've done any of that stuff to them—it was just scare tactics."

The detective recognized the strategy. "Like you did with Kimmy?"

"Who?"

"Melissa's roommate."

"Like with her."

"Did Melissa lose her child—Sebastian's, I'm assuming—while you had her?"

"Accidentally."

"Fucking Jesus Christ," exclaimed Bettinger. There was a time—not very long ago—when he would have shot or arrested such men. Now, they seemed to be his allies.

"We didn't do anything but tie her up and scare her," defended Dominic. "It was just talk."

"Talk can be enough." Bettinger tried not to think about how his own poorly chosen words had cost him his job in Arizona and affected his family. "You didn't expect some sort of retaliation after he dropped the suit?"

"Sebastian was scared. He knew what would happen if he tried to hit back."

The detective saw a suspicious lump in the road and dialed the wheel clockwise. Shaking, the weary vehicle fought its way through the elements.

"And what happened," the big fellow added, "all this we're dealing with right now, ain't no 'retaliation.' It's fuckin' insanity."

"Not to Sebastian."

The truck lurched, fishtailing. Dominic and Tackley buckled their seat belts, and Bettinger stomped the gas. Spinning rubber struck dry powder, and the vehicle surged, once again under control.

"It's still fucking insane," added the big fellow. "What he did."

"You crippled him, and while he was in the hospital, adjusting to life with a diaper and a wheelchair and one lung, you killed his unborn child and threatened to rape his loved ones." Bettinger glared at his passengers. "Is there a sane reaction to something like that? When everything you care about is threatened or destroyed by a group of men who are empowered by the state?"

"He should've come at us directly."

"And have the entire precinct pick up where you left off?"

Dominic shrugged, fingering the collection of scars that the shotgun pellets had scored into his left cheek.

"You want to offer us another critique?" Tackley asked Bettinger. "Tell us what a smart guy like you would've done?" The mottled man's voice was even, but his blue eyes were baleful.

Bettinger avoided a shadow in the road that might have been a corneal imperfection. "There's no point. We all want the same thing. Find Sebastian, get the names of the gunmen, kill Sebastian."

"That's it."

"I'll want a confirmation that he's responsible before we kill him."

"You'll get a confession."

"And the women?"

"They facilitated mass murder." Tackley's reply was cold and definitive.

"Accomplices," added Dominic.

Bettinger did not dispute these statements, but he doubted that he could shoot a woman in any situation other than one of self-defense.

It was clear that his associates had no such limitations.

Snow poured down, obscuring the abandoned concrete world as the pickup truck sped north.

Dominic plucked another wire from his face. Blood ran from the wound over sutures and scabs until it reached his chin, where it swelled like a tear.

Tires boomed. The policemen jerked forward, and seat belts snapped taut. A drop of blood spattered the windshield.

The rumbling world scrolled east.

Metal grated against concrete as the vehicle skidded, trailing a wake of slush. Braced, the detective and his associates waited for impact.

A brick wall pounded the hood. Bettinger's fractured ribs cracked, and his forehead bounced off of the steering wheel. Somebody's blood spattered the glass.

Suddenly, the truck was still.

The blizzard rushed in through the shattered windshield, and steam rose from the hood.

Leaning back, the detective looked at his passengers, who were both unbuckling their seat belts.

"We're close to the Heaps," Dominic said as he slid across the bench and followed Tackley outside.

Bettinger shut off the engine, donned his ballistic apparel, holstered his silencer-fitted guns, pocketed his dog whistle, zipped up his parka, opened the door, and entered the blizzard. Hail rattled upon the devil mask that covered his face.

# XLVIII

# The Heaps

Tackley withdrew a couple of shiny items from the cardboard box and deposited them in the duffel bag that was slung over Dominic's right shoulder.

"That mask fits," the big fellow said when he saw the detective.

"Yeah."

The mottled man pulled the zipper to its stop, and soon, he and his former partner donned ski masks and tactical vests.

Snow fell on the policemen as they abandoned the dead pickup truck.

Bettinger trudged north underneath the gray sky, ignoring the pain in his ribs. His boots disappeared in the white blanket, resurfaced, flinging white clumps, and then vanished again. It looked like fourteen inches of snow had fallen during the last two and a half hours.

On either side of the road loomed tall gray buildings that had been eroded by years and weather. The wind that blew through these rounded obelisks sounded resentful, if not hostile.

Bettinger's corduroys were wet and his shins were numb by the time he reached the next intersection. "How many blocks?" he asked his associates.

"Four or five."

The masked policemen kicked furrows up Ganson Street. Upon a rooftop that was once an enclosed penthouse floor, turquoise toilets and matching bathtubs collected snow.

Something crunched, and Bettinger looked toward the noise.

Dominic lifted his left leg from the white blanket. Beige innards, brown ice, and gray-green feathers adhered to the bottom of his boot.

"I'm real fuckin' sick of these things."

The trio reached the next intersection and circumvented a garbage bin that had been relocated by somebody into the middle of the road.

"Glad he didn't drive into that," Dominic said to Tackley.

"Because the building was so soft?"

Bettinger noticed that the mottled man had a busted lip and a missing incisor.

The wind keened as it changed directions, and snow flew horizontally. Ice shot directly into the detective's eyes.

"How long's that been there?" asked Dominic. "Never seen it before."

"I don't know," replied Tackley.

Bettinger cleared the snow from his mask and looked north.

Lying on its side across Ganson Street was half of a high-rise building. Structural beams jutted from the massive, snow-blanketed obstruction like the ribs of a dead animal.

"How'd it get there?" asked the big fellow.

"Explosives." The mottled man pointed at an upright building that had been diminished by half.

"Why? Keep people out?"

"Who knows why Heapers do anything."

Boots sank in the powder and tossed white clumps. It soon became clear to the policemen that the toppled structure would preclude any further progress along Ganson Street.

"There's a way around?" asked Bettinger. His feet were numb, and his skin felt unnaturally tight, as if he were wearing a wetsuit.

Tackley motioned west with his left arm, and all three men trudged in that direction. Ice crunched, and the wind skirled. The weather was not a confluence of elements, but a cognitive and malicious thing that hated humans.

Bettinger's right boot slipped on a buried sheet of metal, and his broken ribs clicked. The pain forced a yell from his mouth and drove him to his knees.

Dominic glanced over. "You okay?"

"Fine," Bettinger said as he rose to his feet.

Inexorably, he trudged.

Numbness overtook sensation in the detective's appendages, and he tried not to think about things like frostbite.

The policemen continued along the side street until they reached the next intersection. There, they turned north.

Bettinger looked ahead, but was unable to see the far end of the block through the dazzling white precipitation. The cold bit his exposed neck, and his numb feet alternately sank in the blanket and flung clumps. He knew for a fact that if Hell existed, it was not a place of warmth.

Winds skirled, sending a barrage of hard pellets directly at the detective. Ice crackled against his ballistic mask.

Reaching the end of the block, Bettinger finally saw the northern horizon. His first impression was that he was looking upon the largest junkyard in the world, a place where all of the buildings had been replaced by massive piles of rubble. The size of each of these cyclopean anthills varied (depending upon the number of bulldozed structures on that block), though the smallest ones were at least a hundred feet tall and half again as wide. Between these mountains of ruin were uneven roads that had leafless trees, automobile shells, and unidentifiable lumps.

Bettinger did not need to ask his associates if they had reached their destination.

Together, the masked policemen proceeded up the street and entered the Heaps.

Tackley motioned to the snow-covered ground. "Watch out for pits."

"And bear traps," added Dominic.

Two very unpleasant denouements occurred to the detective.

A 150-foot pile of rubble loomed on the right side of the street, mirroring its sibling across the way. Cellars, garbage chute receptacles, boiler rooms, laundry areas, and branching brick passageways sat below the ground, exposed to the sky by acts of demolition and the passage of time.

"How big're the Heaps?" asked Bettinger.

"Not sure." Dominic brushed white epaulets from his shoulders. "Never been all the way."

Boots crunched snow as the trio neared the end of the block.

The detective stopped, raised his mask, and withdrew his dog whistle. "Let's try it here."

Pausing, the other men retrieved their instruments.

The policemen filled their lungs, stuck the mouthpieces between their lips, and blew. Jets of steam shot through the apertures, waggling in the cold like translucent tongues.

Bettinger ran out of air and removed the whistle from his mouth, as did Dominic and Tackley. Silently, they awaited a response.

No sounds other than those made by the winds emerged from the Heaps. Snow drifted into a sunken laundry room, filling the gaping mouths of capsized washer and dryers.

The trio continued north. Winds hissed, bitterly cold, and again, the detective shielded his face with the devil mask.

The policemen strode through an intersection and up a street that lay between two more colossal heaps.

Snow drifted into a partially exposed boiler room, and something occurred to Bettinger. "Is there any power out here?" he asked his associates. "Or would you need a generator?"

Tackley wiped snow from his eyes as his small black shoes crushed ice. "People have tapped the grid below Shitopia—some of that still works—but Sebastian would probably bring his own supply."

"If visibility gets better, we should look for exhaust—jeep and generator."

"Fine."

Bettinger circumvented a tree that resembled a hunched crone.

"Maybe we should split up," suggested Dominic.

"No." The detective had already considered and dismissed this idea.

"We'd cover more area."

"And greatly increase the chances of one of us getting stuck alone in a bad situation."

"We're all adults." The big fellow plucked a piece of crimson ice from underneath his ski mask and tossed it aside. "Armed ones."

"We stay together until we know the layout." Tackley's tone did not invite further discussion.

"Whatever."

Footfalls crackled.

Bettinger stopped, raised his mask, and withdrew his dog whistle. "Let's go again."

All three men slotted instruments in their frowns.

"Hard," said the detective.

Abdominal muscles constricted, and six lungs shot carbon dioxide through half as many whistles. The detective and his associates blew until they ran out of air, at which point, they pocketed their instruments and listened.

No response came from the Heaps.

Northward, the policemen trudged.

The level of the snow climbed. Every footstep that Bettinger took was an exertion, eliciting pain in his ribs while taxing his lower back, his groin, and his quadriceps, but he did not slacken his pace.

"Tackley arrested some cannibals up here once," said Dominic, withdrawing a pair of binoculars from his duffel bag. "Some women."

"Should we get back on Ganson Street?"

"It changes directions up here," said Tackley. "We might be on it right now."

"Thought I smelled somethin'. There—" Dominic pointed a gun at the heap on the west side of the next block. "See it?"

Bettinger eyed the indicated pile. "What?"

"Smoke. Comin' from that heap."

The mottled man took the binoculars from the big fellow, made a quick survey, and handed the instrument to the detective, who raised his mask and looked through the eyecups. A thin ribbon of greenish-gray smoke rose from the base of the rubble heap.

"Looks like something toxic is burning," remarked Bettinger. "Doesn't seem like the kind of thing Sebastian would do . . . unless he was trying to attract attention."

"It's Heapers," Tackley said as he walked around a pit.

"The homeless who live up here?"

"Yeah." The mottled man holstered his gun. "Human garbage."

"Should we interrogate them?" asked Dominic.

Bettinger lowered the binoculars and his mask and gestured to the rising snow. "We don't have time to talk to idiots or crazy people."

"So we just keep blowin' these goddamn whistles?"

"We keep our eyes open and blow the whistles."

Dominic snorted a critique.

Bettinger knew that the dog whistle strategy was a long shot (especially in this weather), but it was the itinerary until one of them came up with a better idea.

The white blanket rose like high tide as he trudged over a hill, circumvented a lump of snow that might have contained a refrigerator, and continued onto the next block, where loomed two more colossal piles of rubble. An idea came to him, and he turned to his associates.

"Is the whole area like this? Just heaps?"

"There's a part with a few buildings," said Tackley.

"We should go toward those."

"We are."

The mottled man was not the most forthcoming individual with whom the detective had worked.

Trudging north, Bettinger raised the binoculars and surveyed the inhabited heap. A campfire illuminated an inverted bathroom and the outstretched hands of vagrants who wore clothing that was made out of carpet swaths, duct tape, and garbage bags. One of the individuals yawned, revealing the toothless gums of a crystal meth addict.

The detective returned the binoculars to the big fellow and lowered his mask.

Snow crunched underneath the policemen's heels as they crossed an intersection, proceeded up the block, and traversed yet another.

Bettinger could not feel his legs, but somehow, the insensate limbs continued to function. Something snapped, and he looked down to make sure that it was not a part of his anatomy. All of his extremities appeared to be intact.

"Another Heaper," said Tackley.

Bettinger raised his gaze. Beside the road sat a snow-covered, six-foot-wide cube. A rusty pipe extruded from its eastern face, exhaling smoke.

Dominic produced his semiautomatic pistol and approached the dwelling.

The detective doubted that the Heaper who lived inside the cube would be useful, but he knew that there was no way to stop his partner from making an inquiry.

At present, the big fellow draped his ski mask over the chimney pipe and withdrew.

The line of smoke disappeared.

Bettinger clasped his weapon and prostrated himself, twenty-five feet from the edifice, while Tackley kneeled, taking aim, and Dominic huddled beside a tree.

The policemen waited. Snow fell from the gray sky, growing the blanket that covered everything. The detective tried not to think about his wife's surgery or his son's blasted head.

Someone coughed.

The policemen watched the cube, awaiting its denizen.

Something clanged. A coughing fit followed this noise, and the unseen person muttered something that sounded like a made-up word. Powder scattered when a plywood hatch atop the dwelling swung open.

A filthy head emerged from the roof, and Bettinger was unable to tell if the Heaper was a young black man or an old white woman.

"Put your hands in the air or we'll shoot!" shouted Dominic and Tackley.

The frightened individual raised his or her arms and waggled a filthy stump. "I only got one hand."

Bettinger removed his mask. "Have you seen a blue jeep around here?"

"Are you gonna take my crate?"

"If you tell us the truth, you can keep the crate."

"I always tell the truth. Ask anybody but Willie." The Heaper nodded his or her head. "Now what was your question?"

"Have you seen a blue jeep around here?"

"Can I put my arms down?"

"Sure."

The filthy individual relaxed his or her limbs. "What was your question?"

Doubts multiplied regarding the cerebral competency of the witness. Again, Bettinger inquired, "Have you seen a blue jeep around here?"

"I don't see colors very good."

"Have you seen any jeeps around here?"

"I don't know especially much about automobiles."

"Have you seen any kind of vehicle pass through here in the last two weeks?"

"I heard one last month." The Heaper ruminated. "Maybe that was a dream."

Dominic reclaimed his ski mask.

"Go back in your crate," Bettinger said to the interviewee.

The Heaper retracted, closing the flap over his head like a jack-in-the-box.

Again, the masked policemen continued north.

The snow was an inch above Bettinger's knees and every step that he took was a lurch or a lunge. Dominic was taller and fared better, as did Tackley, even though the powder was not far below his waist.

The trio reached the end of the block and was assaulted by crosswinds.

"We should've taken that guy's fire," mumbled the big fellow. It seemed entirely possible that he was becoming a caveman.

Bettinger stuck the whistle in his mouth and blew. Steam shot from the instrument as well as its two siblings, which sat in the mouths of his associates.

No reply emerged from the Heaps.

Pocketing the gloomy bulldog, the detective lunged north. His front boot shot through snow, a piece of cardboard, and into open space. He fell forward, and the ground pounded his head. Concussed, he slid toward an open manhole.

"Hold on!" shouted Dominic, running over.

Bettinger's hands scored grooves across the snow as he sank into the opening. His legs kicked the open air.

"Grab o—"

Something clanked, and the big fellow yelled, tumbling to the ground.

The manhole swallowed Bettinger.

A hand seized his collar, and the detective dangled above pitch-black oblivion.

"Find the ladder," rasped Dominic.

Bettinger set his foot upon a rung and grabbed the uppermost bar with his hands. "Got it."

The big fellow released him, groaned, and withdrew his hand.

"Thank you," said the detective, whose heart was still racing from his unexpected fall. Carefully, he ascended the ladder and removed himself from the manhole.

Dominic sat in the snow nearby, gritting his teeth as he pulled at the jaws of a rusty bear trap that had bitten into his left leg.

"Christ's un—"

A quiet gunshot flashed, and Bettinger looked over his shoulder.

Tackley was pointing a silencer-fitted assault rifle at the heap that stood on the west side of the road. "A few were coming over to see what they'd caught," he explained, looking through the weapon's telescopic sight. "First-aid kit's in the side pocket."

Bettinger went to the duffel bag and unzipped the indicated compartment.

Dominic raised his ski mask. His lacerated face was glazed with sweat, and his respirations were labored. "Good thing I got my tetanus shot."

"Good thing you happen to be a bear."

The detective found the first-aid kit, kneeled beside his partner, and raised his snow-crusted mask to better see the injury. It looked like boot leather had stopped all but three of the trap's teeth from penetrating flesh.

"Tackley," said Bettinger.

"Yeah?"

Gunpowder glared, and an ejected shell struck the powder.

"I need help getting the trap off."

"Fine."

The mottled man squeezed the trigger, and the barrel of the assault rifle flashed like a strobe light. Something rumbled, and Bettinger looked toward the noise. An avalanche of concrete, glass, and toilets poured down the side of the heap.

Somebody screamed.

"Goddamn Heapers," said Tackley, slinging his assault rifle and walking over.

Bettinger pointed to the right side of the bear trap. "Press that down. Don't let go no matter what."

The mottled man put his shoe on the indicated spring, and the detective set his knee atop the one on the opposite side. Carefully, each of them leaned forward, applying pressure. Snow and metal creaked, and the bear trap relaxed.

Bettinger pulled the jaws in opposite directions, exposing three red teeth. "Take your leg out," he said to his partner. "Carefully."

Dominic removed his boot from the trap, winced, and knocked Tackley's shoe.

Bettinger jerked his hands back as the jaws clanked shut. Stuck between the trap's red teeth was the glove that it had pulled loose.

"Christ."

A pained snicker came from the big fellow. "Close."

The detective reclaimed the stolen glove, pocketed it (and its mate), and opened the first-aid kit. "Take that off."

Dominic winced as he untied his laces and withdrew his foot from the chewed boot. His sock was red.

"And that."

The big fellow removed the fabric, revealing a bloodied lower leg that had three deep, reddish-black grooves just above the ankle. Snow fell on bare toes that looked like potatoes.

"Size eighteen and a half," remarked Dominic.

Bettinger located butterfly stitches, cotton swabs, and a bottle of alcohol, but did not see any saline solution. "Do you have water?"

The mottled man motioned at the sky.

"You know what you're doing?" asked the big fellow.

"Sure," said the detective. "I have kids." A moment later, he felt the undertow of grief. "A kid." His words were tiny.

"We'll get Sebastian," said Dominic. "For yours and ours."

A snowdrop landed on a deep wound and turned red.

Bettinger squashed his despair, raised the bottle of alcohol, and unscrewed its cap. "This won't feel great."

Dominic shrugged. The sweat that dripped down his face belied his nonchalance.

Carefully, the detective poured alcohol onto the bloodied leg. A grunt came from the big fellow's mouth, and geysers of steam shot from his nose.

Using a cotton ball, Bettinger swabbed the wounds. Thick dark fluid was gradually replaced by clean bright blood.

Tackley handed Dominic two blue pills.

"No aspirin," said the detective, unsure what was being given to his patient.

"They aren't aspirin."

The big fellow put the medication into his mouth and swallowed it with snow.

Bettinger donned latex gloves, pinched the largest wound shut, and sealed it with three butterfly stitches. He then repeated this process on the other two gashes.

"Move your foot up and down," advised the detective.

Dominic waggled the extremity, and two butterfly stitches popped loose. Fresh blood colored the snow.

The detective applied more bandages and had his patient test their resiliency. This time, the butterfly stitches held.

"You done?" asked Dominic.

"One more thing."

The detective wound gauze around his partner's ankle until the roll was depleted.

"Done?" asked the big fellow as he shook red crystals from his sock.

"Yeah."

Bettinger stood up and grunted, ambushed by the pains that he had acquired during his car accidents and recent fall. "Are the sewers an option for us?" he asked his associates while massaging his side.

"No." Tackley rolled the assault rifle in a towel and returned it to the duffel bag.

"We don't have a lot more time up here." The detective gestured at the rising snow. "You're sure it's not an option?"

"A lot of those tunnels collapsed." The mottled man pulled the zipper to its stop. "We don't want to stumble around in the dark, hit a dead end, and have to backtrack."

"We don't."

Tackley slung the duffel bag over his left shoulder, and Dominic gritted his teeth as he pulled on his left boot.

"We just keep on goin' 'til it's impossible."

Bettinger picked ice out of the devil's eyes.

# XLIX

# Dominic Knows Something

Aided by his former and current partners, the big fellow rose to his feet. Snow fell on his grimacing face, and he hastily covered up his agony with his ski mask.

"Let's go," announced Dominic, stumbling forward.

"Do you need some——"

"Let's fuckin' go."

Again, the masked policemen proceeded north.

Bettinger discarded his latex gloves and replaced them with their woolen superiors, but the insensate pieces of meat at the ends of his arms did not apprehend any change.

The detective lurched. His progress was slow, and every time his forward foot plunged into the snow, he anticipated it finding a bear trap or the gaping entrance of a sewer.

"We should stay off the road and walk single file," Bettinger suggested to his associates.

"Why?" asked Dominic.

"To keep clear of manholes and reduce the risk of stepping on something bad."

"Nigga's got ideas."

The policemen veered onto the buried sidewalk and became a three-person phalanx. Tackley took the lead, followed by Bettinger, who was succeeded by Dominic.

The winds skirled. Fifteen lurching, churning, frigid minutes later, the mottled vanguard motioned to the west.

The policemen trudged onto a narrower cross street where they were shielded from the wind by an exceptionally wide rubble pile. There, they paused and blew their whistles.

The Heaps offered no reply.

Pocketing the instruments, the trio staggered through the white tide. The winds gentled, and a moment later, the size of the falling snowdrops increased twofold.

Dominic thudded against the powder.

Bettinger faced his partner. "Are you—"

"I'm fuckin' fine." The big fellow rose to his feet, spat out snow, and dusted himself. "Let's keep on."

The trio crossed a lumpy intersection, traversed the following block, and circumvented a snow-covered van that had two trees growing out of its roof. Looking at the impaled vehicle, the detective was reminded of several outsider art shows that he had attended with his wife. Unbidden images of her battered body and ruined eye filled his mind.

It was better for him to focus on his pains, the cold, and Sebastian.

The plump snowdrops grew sparse, and Bettinger looked toward the western horizon, which was much clearer than it had been only seconds earlier. Beyond the heaps stood the tops of two ruined buildings.

"Fuck."

Something thudded.

The detective looked back.

Dominic was lying on his side in the snow. His shoulders shook, and steam burst erratically from his covered head like a series of smoke signals.

Bettinger was not sure how much longer Dominic—or any of them—could continue. As the big fellow rose to his feet, the detective withdrew the steel bulldog from his pocket.

"Let's try again."

"Whatever."

The policemen inhaled deeply, put their whistles to their mouths, and blew.

A dog barked.

Needles danced upon Bettinger's nape. The policemen removed the whistles from their mouths and looked in the direction of the far-off sound.

A second canine launched some woofs, and a moment later, both beasts quietened. It was clear that a person had silenced the animals.

The detective's heart pounded.

Dominic raised the whistle to his mouth, but Tackley caught his wrist and shook his head. "Wait until we're closer."

"It's them," remarked the big fellow. "It's Dobermans."

Bettinger wanted to believe his partner's assertion. "I hope so."

"It is. I grew up with Dobermans and know the bark."

Tackley removed his assault rifle from the duffel bag, an ugly smile sitting in the bottom hole of his ski mask. "They raised him."

"Might explain why he killed Kimmy's cat."

"That first one sounded just like one I used to have named Julia." Dominic withdrew a semiautomatic gun from his clip-on holster. "Someone's probably walkin' them while the storm takes it easy."

"That's a good guess," agreed Bettinger.

"A accolade from the king of guesswork."

"You're our dog expert."

"I understand them."

The detective pointed at the pair of ruined buildings that stood on the horizon. "Sounded like it came from over there."

"A little bit north of that." The mottled man raised his rifle and looked through its telescopic sight. "When we're halfway, we'll blow the whistles."

"Unless the storm picks up before then."

"Unless that."

Spirited, the three-man phalanx lurched toward the buildings. The wind was a distant whisper, and the plump snow fell straight. As quickly as possible, the trio traversed the block and its westward neighbor.

Bettinger wiped ice from his fangs and looked over his shoulder. Five yards behind him staggered Dominic, whose gait was as labored as it was lopsided. Red dots colored the tracks made by his left foot.

"Keep going," said the big fellow.

"I'll look at that again when we get inside."

"Whatever."

The detective returned his attention to the mottled man's back, which vacillated smoothly with each of the fellow's small, quick strides. Of the three policemen, he was in the best condition by far.

"I still got Perry's DVD," said Dominic. "The one with the Japanese guys in the submarine."

Boots compressed snow.

"*The Crushing Depths*," said Tackley. "Did you watch it?"

"It's got subtitles." This seemed to be a complete answer.

The mottled man scanned the area through his telescopic sight. "It's a good movie."

"It is," added Bettinger, who had seen it on late-night television.

"I'll watch it."

The policemen neared a snow-covered object that resembled a gigantic bed. Sitting atop the mass was a hub from which extended a very long pole.

"Is that a tank?" asked Bettinger.

Tackley nodded.

"Then the odds I'm dreaming all this just went way up."

"They didn't." The mottled man paused, pulled a beer can from his right boot, and continued walking. "There used to be a war museum up here."

"Junk."

Passing the tank, the detective looked over the vanguard's head to the northwest. The broken buildings were larger than before.

Tackley proceeded up the sidewalk of a cross street, and Bettinger followed, trudging through the accumulation. His right foot slipped, and his rib cage clicked. Agonized, he dropped to the powder.

"You okay?" asked Dominic.

The detective grunted. It felt like a dagger had pierced his intercostal muscle.

Suddenly, strong hands were under his arms, helping him to his feet.

"You can walk?"

The sharp pain turned into a throbbing ache, and Bettinger nodded, picking snow out of the devil's eyes.

Dominic squeezed his partner's shoulder. "Whenever it hurts, just think about killin' Sebastian."

The phalanx continued north.

Bettinger gripped his side and his gun as he trudged through the white adversary. Every part of his anatomy was pained or numb or a throbbing combination of these two states.

"Huan was really ahead at the game last night," remarked Dominic. "It was like five bills he left with."

"He was a great poker player," said Tackley.

"I wonder if he got a chance to—"

"Save it for the funeral," barked the mottled man. "We don't need this now."

"Sorry."

The phalanx crossed an intersection and landed on the opposite sidewalk.

Tackley stopped. "Let's try here."

The policemen put whistles in their mouths and heaved carbon dioxide. Ribbons of steam shot into the air.

Dogs barked. The bestial remonstrations were far louder than before.

The men stopped blowing.

Bettinger fixed the location of the barking animals, which was a little bit south of the two ruined buildings and directly to the west. "They moved."

"They're gettin' their walk," replied Dominic. "Like I said."

Suddenly, the animals were silent.

"There were three that time," added the big fellow. "Julia, the other one, and a smaller guy."

The policemen replaced the whistles in their pockets and started toward their four-legged quarries. Rather than lurch through the snow, Tackley shuffled his legs, which noticeably reduced the amount of noise that he made. Bettinger and Dominic mimicked his manner, and soon, the phalanx sounded like three mills grinding peppercorns.

Nearing the end of the block, Tackley pointed out the wide heap that lay between the policemen and the animals.

The group shuffled toward the indicated pile. The mills ground peppercorns, and the volume of falling snow increased.

Quietly, Dominic asked, "We blow again? Before they go inside?"

Tackley shook his head. "Those mongrels told us plenty."

"Dobermans."

Shuffling forward, Bettinger surveyed the heap, which was a snow-covered collection of concrete slabs, support beams, and pipes. Atop the mass stood a statue of a gigantic headless man who had skewered two bicycles with a broken sword.

The phalanx reached the base of the rubble pile and began their southwestern circumnavigation. Winds blew, covering up the peppermill noises of their progress.

Tackley maintained the vanguard position, surveying the area through his rifle's telescopic sight. His coat snapped taut, catching upon something in the snow, and he hastily jerked it loose.

Bettinger soon passed the object, which was a cracked tombstone.

The phalanx continued around an overturned school bus into the area beyond the heap, which was an uninhabited clearing of powder. On the far side of this three-block expanse loomed a gray-green four-story building, half of which had been demolished. Several broken pillars jutted from the collapsed façade.

"The old courthouse," whispered Dominic, wiping snow from his mouth. "That's where my mother got sentenced."

"Shoot anything that moves," said Tackley.

The big fellow took the binoculars out of the duffel bag. "What if it's Sebastian?"

"This isn't wheelchair weather."

The mottled man started toward the partially demolished courthouse, leading the phalanx.

Although Bettinger felt like he and his associates were exposed targets, he knew that there was no better alternative. The isolated building was three blocks away from the nearest heap, and to reach it, they had to cross the white plain.

The detective shuffled.

His left side throbbed, and his muscles burned, but the thought of killing the man who had murdered his son, mutilated his wife, terrorized his daughter, and wiped out the major part of the Victory police force was an anesthesia. Proceeding across the plain, he saw a depression in the snow that resembled Gordon.

Tackley lowered the scope from his eye and pointed to the right. There, Bettinger saw nothing.

The mottled man led his associates in the indicated direction, and ten grinding strides later, the detective saw three small dots upon the snow. As he drew nearer, the anomalies grew larger and distinguished themselves as the products of a dog's rear end.

Dominic nodded sagaciously. "Dobermans."

The phalanx reached the droppings, and surveyed the surrounding snow. Paw prints led to the bowel movements and away from them, toward the collapsed courthouse.

The policeman followed the trail. A second set of tracks joined the first and continued in the exact same direction.

The detective eyed the building, which was now four hundred feet away. Its front entrance was a pile of snow-covered rubble, and the windows on its north face were boarded over.

Tackley directed Bettinger's attention to the ground. Joining the dog tracks were some deeper marks that had been made by a pair of women's sneakers. The detective wondered if they belonged to Sebastian's girlfriend, Melissa, or his sister, Margarita.

Fighting the wind, the phalanx shuffled toward the courthouse. A winding set of paw prints crossed through the others, and a sinkhole of yellow powder sat at the intersection. Fifteen more steps brought the policemen to a place where a fourth set of dog tracks joined the pack, and there, the woman's trail veered away from those of the animals.

The phalanx followed the bipedal impressions. Twenty feet east of the building, paw prints rejoined the footprints, and a few yellow exclamation points commemorated the event.

The policemen shuffled west, keeping beside the tracks, which were parallel to the north face of the building.

Bettinger's left foot plunged into something soft, which might have been a garbage bag, and pain shot through his ribs. Grimacing, he extricated his boot, sucked air into his lungs, and continued forward.

Tackley neared the corner of the building and held up his hand.

The phalanx stopped.

Silently, the mottled man prostrated himself and looked around the corner.

Winds skirled, and powder fell. A snowflake entered the devil mask, landing upon the detective's right eyelashes as he and his partner watched the prone fellow.

Tackley nodded his head, rose to his feet, and proceeded south.

Bettinger shuffled around the corner. Ahead of him, the trail continued south, leading toward the dark entrance of a three-level parking garage that was 250 feet away.

The policeman staggered their positions so that each of them had a clear line of fire. Quietly, they progressed toward the opening.

A dog barked, and the trio flattened themselves.

Prone, the detective eyed the parking lot entrance, which was black and revealed nothing. He aimed his tactical light at the ground, switched it on, and waited, lying on the cold blanket between his two prostrated associates. His mistreated, fifty-year-old flesh was numb, excepting the pain caused by his broken ribs as they pressed skin and muscle into his ballistic vest.

The snowfall thickened. A ponderous minute passed, but no sounds or living things emerged from the dark entrance of the parking garage.

Tackley rose from the blanket. His thumb touched the scope of his rifle, and a red dot flew across the ground like an alien insect.

Bettinger and Dominic got to their feet.

Quietly, the masked policemen proceeded south.

Falling snow concealed them within the white landscape, and soon, the distance between them and the garage diminished by half.

One hundred feet away, the dark entrance gaped like a maw.

Tackley panned his assault rifle to the right, and his red dot tripled as it struck a car window, shot through the opposite glass, and landed on a concrete wall.

Bettinger shuffled onward, gun in hand, aware that he might be killed in the very near future. It was especially unpleasant to think about how his death would affect Alyssa and Karen, both of whom were already traumatized.

Ruminating, the detective fixed his objectives. He had to kill Sebastian, and he had to stay alive.

Everything else was irrelevant.

Seventy feet separated Bettinger from the opening of the parking garage.

Shuffling, he swept his tactical beam through the darkness. The circle of light illuminated a hubcap, riven concrete, and a cardboard box. Nothing moved.

The detective proceeded, and soon, less than fifty feet separated him from the entrance.

He pointed his weapon at the right side of the garage, where the circle of light illuminated rusty pipes, a gate, and a pair of staring eyes.

A red dot appeared on the human face, and Tackley's assault rifle flashed.

The head shattered, bursting into hunks of brown, white, and gray ice.

Bettinger tilted his tactical beam, and the circle of light illuminated the garbage bags, duct tape, and carpet swatches that comprised the frozen Heaper's clothing. Sitting in the vagrant's right hand was a beer can from which depended five small icicles.

Although the detective was relieved that the mottled man had not murdered anybody, he was a little unnerved by the fellow's nearly instantaneous dispatch of lethal gunfire. Bettinger had very fast reactions, but Tackley was a cobra.

The policemen entered the parking garage. Layers of snow sloughed from their bodies onto the concrete like old skin.

The detective panned his tactical light in an arc, illuminating rubble, charred automobiles, barbed wire, a rotten cardboard box, pipes, and the ramp that led up to the second level. Excepting the dead vagrant whose head now resembled Neapolitan ice cream, the immediate area appeared to be uninhabited.

Dominic pointed his tactical light at some bits of snow that the dogs and the woman had left behind.

# L

# The Pillars of Justice

The trail of white clumps led Bettinger and his associates past a mattress, an overturned car, a crate, a hole in the floor, and a dented elevator, before it veered to the right and disappeared inside a dark, open doorway.

Shutting off their lights, the policemen put their shoulders to the wall and listened.

No sounds emerged from the portal.

Bettinger wiped powder from his mask, looked into the doorway, and turned on his light. Clumps of snow led across a gray landing to a flight of descending stairs. Affixed to the near wall was a corroded sign that read TO UN-DERGROUND LEVEL.

The detective pivoted, shining his light at the steps that went up to the second floor. Not one snowdrop lay upon them, and it was clear to him that the dogs and their human companion had all gone underground.

Bettinger slid into the stairwell, walked across the landing, and descended. Although he treaded carefully, every sound that he made was amplified into significance by the acoustics.

The detective shut off his light as he neared the intermediate platform.

Something boomed.

A head slammed into Bettinger's back, catapulting him to the far side of the landing. Stone pounded his ballistic mask, pressing it sideways across his face, and something snapped.

The detective soon found his footing and leaned against the wall. "You okay?" he asked the big fellow who had fallen down the steps.

"Mm."

Something warm that tasted like a mixture of copper, dirt, and honey slid into Bettinger's mouth. This fluid and the new fire in the middle of his face told him that he had just broken his nose.

"Junk."

Pressing his shoulder to the corner, the detective shone his tactical light down the nether stairwell, which was uninhabited and ended in a closed gray door. Bits of snow and half as many clear puddles sat on the steps, and the existence of water—as well as the stinging sensations all over his body—told him that the temperature was slightly warmer belowground.

Tackley helped Dominic to his feet. Grunts echoed as the big fellow clasped a rail and wobbled.

"Can you walk?" asked Bettinger, whispering.

Dominic put a fraction of his weight on his hurt foot, and a grimace filled the bottom hole of his mask. "Bind it."

Tackley and Bettinger exchanged a glance. It was obvious to both of them that the big fellow would be more of a liability than an asset in his present condition.

"You're staying here," whispered the mottled man.

"No fuckin' way." Dominic's words resonated throughout the stairwell.

"Keep it down."

"I'm going." (This protest was quieter.)

"You aren't."

"And you can't," added Bettinger.

"Fuck you."

The big fellow took one step, wobbled, and collapsed to his knees. Gritted teeth appeared in the bottom hole of his ski mask.

"Idiot," said his associates.

Clouds of steam burst from Dominic's mouth as he heaved his back against the wall. His eyes glimmered with pain and disappointment.

Tackley withdrew the first-aid kit from the duffel bag and set it beside Dominic. "Guard the rear."

"Whatever."

Bettinger was uncertain whether or not his partner would stay behind. "If you come after us, you might get shot."

"Fuck you."

"Learn some synonyms."

"Fuck you."

"He's right," remarked Tackley, handing four blue pills to the injured man. "Take two more. Don't follow us."

"Whatever." Dominic pocketed the medication and winced as he moved his bad leg. "Duct tape."

The mottled man withdrew a thick gray roll from the duffel bag and gave it to the big fellow.

"Kill your tactical until we're clear," said Bettinger.

Dominic turned off his light. "If you do him without me, do it rough."

"We will," promised Tackley.

Bettinger continued down the stairwell. A few bits of snow and two small puddles sat on the lower landing directly in front of the closed gray door. The mottled man reached the bottom of the steps, and the detective shut off his tactical light.

Darkness filled the stairwell.

The policemen held their breaths as they listened for noises beyond the gray door.

Silence loomed.

Bettinger pressed the push bar, and metal squeaked. Again, he listened for disturbances and heard nothing.

The detective leaned his weight forward, but the door did not move. Gently, he released the push bar.

"Locked."

A zipper was pulled across the darkness. Something clicked, and Tackley's headlamp glared, illuminating the steel pieces of the lock-picking set that he held in his pink and milk-white hands. He kneeled, selected a rod that ended in a right angle, and slid it between the door and the jamb at the exact level of the push bar. Employing an ellipsoidal motion, the mottled man hooked the spring latch.

A click echoed.

Bettinger pushed the door, opening it a fraction of an inch.

Tackley returned to his feet and shut off his headlamp.

Darkness consumed the stairwell.

The detective pushed the door so that it was two inches from the jamb. Through the hooded nostrils of the devil mask, he smelled a rich history of urine and rot.

Everything was quiet.

Bettinger rose to his feet and crept from the stairwell. The subterranean garage in which he found himself was very dark, but not opaque: A small amount of daylight was admitted by two small holes in its ceiling, one of which he recognized as the pit that he had earlier circumvented.

Eyes adjusting to the gloom, the detective surveyed the area. The ramp that led to the upper level had collapsed, and strewn about the large enclosure were hunks of concrete, a score of abandoned vehicles, and half as many cardboard boxes. It seemed very unlikely that a disabled criminal who had the resources to kill off an entire police precinct would hide himself, his loved ones, and a pack of Dobermans in a place like this.

Bettinger crouched beside an overturned station wagon, and the small ugly shape that was Tackley materialized, raising his assault rifle. The luminous red dot flew to the opposite end of the parking garage and sat on a wall.

Behind the car, the policemen awaited a response.

None was offered.

Bettinger pointed his gun at the ground and switched on his tactical light. At the edge of the luminous circle he saw two very faint paw prints.

The policemen followed the trail, but it quickly grew impossible to discern from its surroundings.

Pausing, Bettinger searched the area for more tracks. His tactical beam drifted left and right and back again until it struck a damp stain—a nexus where the animals and their human companion had lingered. Directly behind this mark was the sliding door of an old gray cargo van that was backed up to the garage wall.

The detective shut off his light and aimed his gun at the vehicle's passenger window. Inches below the glass shone the mottled man's prophetic red dot.

The policemen approached the gray cargo van. Except for the sounds of their boots arranging grit, the subterranean area was silent.

Bettinger kneeled beneath the passenger window, adjusted his ballistic mask, and stood.

The devil stared back at him. Beyond his dim reflection loomed pure darkness.

The detective sank below the glass, shook his head, and tapped his weapon.

Ten feet away, the mottled man nodded an affirmative response.

Bettinger stood, aimed his gun at the center of the window, and turned on his tactical light. The beam shot through the glass, illuminating the cargo van's charred interior.

Nothing moved.

Heart pounding, the detective circled to the front of the vehicle, where he pointed his light through the windshield. Behind the molten seats was an empty cargo area, the back of which was concealed by a navy blue tarpaulin.

Bettinger and Tackley tried the doors.

All of them were locked.

The headlamp glared. Kneeling on the driver's side of the van, the mottled man slid two steel tools into a tarnished keyhole. Grinding metal echoed as he rocked the pick across the tumblers, and a rat ran out of a capsized car.

The lock popped.

Tackley replaced his instruments, shouldered his bag, and aimed his assault rifle.

Bettinger opened the door and climbed into the van, which smelled like charcoal. Soot swirled in his tactical beam as he walked into the cargo area, kneeled, and grabbed the edge of the navy blue tarpaulin.

Tackley materialized inside the front of the vehicle.

The associates exchanged a nod, and together, they turned off their lights.

Darkness filled the cargo van, excepting the lone red dot that shone upon the navy blue fabric.

Bettinger pulled the tarpaulin.

Fabric crinkled. The red dot disappeared and blinked back into existence on a remote surface that could not possibly be inside of the van.

Breath held, the detective listened to the darkness. The only thing that he heard was the sound of his own pulse.

"Okay," whispered Bettinger.

Something clicked, and the headlamp glared, illuminating the van and a roughly hewn tunnel that led from the garage through yards of stone and metal into the partially demolished courthouse. The only thing that was visible in the adjacent building was a beige wall, which happened to be the same exact color as the detective's house in Arizona.

Ignoring the pains that filled his body, he climbed into the opening and crawled through layers of concrete, brick, ventilation, wiring, insulation, and metal until he reached the far end of the passage, where he paused. Directly before him was a hallway that had beige wallpaper and brown carpeting.

Bettinger leaned forward and looked around. To the left he saw pure darkness and to the right he saw the glow of incandescent lighting. The radiance spilled from underneath a closed door that stood at the end of the hallway.

Carefully, the detective clambered out of the tunnel. Pain shot down his side and through his face, but he remained silent.

A red dot appeared on the distant door, and suddenly, Tackley was standing beside Bettinger.

The detective checked his ballistic mask, his bulletproof vest, and his silencer-equipped gun. Ready, he nodded.

Bettinger and Tackley stalked forward, abreast, their quick but gentle footfalls muted by the carpet. The light that glowed beneath the closed door at the end of the hallway shone like a beacon.

Soul music sounded from somewhere, and to the detective, it sounded like a memory from another lifetime. Underneath his tactical vest, his heart thudded against his hurt ribs.

The distance between the associates and the sliver of light diminished to ninety feet.

A dog barked.

Bettinger paused, as did Tackley.

The creature did not offer a second complaint.

Cautiously, the policemen resumed their stealthy approach. Eighty feet lay between them and the door.

Again, the animal barked.

The policemen stopped.

A second dog tossed basso woofs, and a third yipped, remonstratively.

The time for stealth had ended.

Bettinger and Tackley bolted toward the door at the end of the hall.

Dogs barked, clamorously.

The detective leveled his gun, and the mottled man put his red dot directly beside the brass handle.

A shadow darkened the line underneath the door.

The assault rifle spat white fire. Bullets chewed up the wood, and a woman shrieked.

Bettinger's blood went cold.

The brass knob flew from its housing, and light spilled through the hole. Dogs barked and growled.

Pain lanced the detective's side as he ran, and the mottled man gained the lead.

"Sebastian!" yelled the woman. *"¡Ayúdame!"*

Tackley slammed his shoulder into the door, knocking it wide.

Toenails clicked across the floorboards of a room that had pine green walls as Dobermans charged the intruder. White fire flashed, pulverizing snouts, tearing off jaws, and severing paws.

Dogs squealed.

*"¡Mis hijos!"* shrieked the woman.

Bettinger reached the doorway of the pine green room, which appeared to be a waiting area. Sebastian's petite sister Margarita was on her back, cradling a gory hand that had only two remaining fingers.

Tackley stepped on the woman's right ear, slammed her head to the ground, and fired shots across her face into the floorboards. Gunpowder scorched her eyes.

Margarita wailed as Bettinger hastened toward the oak door that was the only other way into the waiting area. Knocking over a huge bag of dog food, he slammed his shoulder to the wall.

Something clicked.

Automatic gunfire rattled in the adjacent room. Bullets tore through the oak door, sending splinters everywhere. A brass placard that read JUDGE'S CHAMBER flew into the air like a frightened butterfly.

Bettinger kept his shoulder to the wall, and Tackley crawled behind the front counter, dragging Margarita by her long black hair.

A moment later, the woman shrieked.

The gunfire stopped. A hole that was the size of a long-playing record sat in the middle of the door, surrounded by a constellation of smaller apertures.

"Come out with your hands up," the mottled man yelled, "or your sister gets a makeover."

"Tackley?" There was disbelief in Sebastian's voice.

Tackley wound a thick clump of Margarita's hair around his hand, made a fist, and tore off a patch of her scalp.

The woman's shriek filled the room.

"Here's an answer," said the mottled man, tossing the hirsute clump through the hole in the door.

Bettinger focused his thoughts on his mission and his family. Nearby, a Doberman with two legs stepped on its own entrails as it tried to stand.

"There's some disturbing stuff on the news," Sebastian remarked from the judge's chamber. "Is Dominic okay? How about Perry and Huan? I'm very concerned about you guys."

"Come on out," ordered Bettinger. "Now!"

"Do I know you?"

"One of your guys stabbed my wife and killed my son."

"Oops."

A bright red urge to run through the door and strangle the cripple filled the detective, but he restrained the impulse.

Tackley tore another piece of scalp from Margarita's bleeding skull, and tossed it through the hole.

"¡Ayúdame!" yelled the agonized woman. "¡Por favor!"

"Throw your gun through that hole right now or I'll shoot her in the bladder," said the mottled man.

An assault rifle flew through the opening and clattered across the waiting room floor.

"You've got ten seconds to come out."

"Melissa needs to unlock the gurney," said Sebastian. "Give—"

"Nine seconds."

Tackley rolled something across the floorboards that knocked against Bettinger's left boot. Lying there was an unarmed stun grenade.

"Eight."

The detective picked up the nonlethal explosive, pulled its pin, and held the spoon against the cylinder.

"Seven."

The red dot landed directly beside the doorknob, and unseen gurney wheels squeaked.

"We're coming, little man," said Sebastian.

"Six."

"We're coming, goddammit."

Bettinger let the spoon fall to the ground, extended his arm, and dropped the stun grenade through the hole in the door.

"What the fuck was—"

Light boomed, filling the judge's chamber, and Tackley's assault rifle spat fire.

"Stop!" screamed Sebastian.

Bullets devoured oak, and sparks shot from the doorknob until it flew into the room.

Tackley released his trigger. In the quietude that followed, Bettinger prostrated himself behind the jamb, reached out, and shoved the door. The blasted panel swung away.

Smoke billowed into the waiting area.

The detective adjusted his ballistic mask and peered around the edge. Ten feet from the door and lying on a gurney was Sebastian Ramirez. His gaunt face, narrow chest, and stick-like legs had been seared red by the stun grenade, and his blue satin robe was in pieces. Pressed into the bottom of his chin was the barrel of the huge revolver that he held in his right hand.

A red dot appeared on his elbow.

"I know what you want to know," announced Sebastian. His eyes were watery, their photoreceptors overstimulated by the stun grenade, but his voice was cool and remarkably even. "Let the girls go or I will take my own—"

The assault rifle flashed.

Sebastian's elbow cracked. His revolver tilted forward, and he fired, blasting white fire across his own jaw and nose.

Tackley shouted something that was not a word.

Sebastian's pistol fell to the ground, and quick footfalls sounded deep inside of the judge's chamber.

Bettinger raced through the doorway and kicked aside the gurney. In the far corner of the luxurious chamber stood a ladder that led to a hole in the ceiling. The bare legs of a woman in a rose-colored robe were near the top rung.

Gun raised, the detective fired.

Lead clanked against aluminum, knocking the ladder sideways, and Melissa Spring fell from the ceiling. Her back slammed against the floor.

Bettinger stepped on her hand, which held a snub-nosed pistol, and pointed his semiautomatic at her face. Although the slim and pale brunette was twenty-three years old, she did not even look old enough to drive.

"Drop the gun," said the detective.

The revolver tumbled from young woman's fingers.

"Who the fuck're you?"

The man wearing the devil mask claimed the relinquished weapon, but did not reply to her inquiry.

"FBI?" suggested Melissa. "No way these local idiots could ever find us here."

"You get her?" Tackley asked from the waiting area.

"I did."

A pair of steel handcuffs flew through the air, struck the carpet, and bounced.

"And her legs," the mottled man added as a second set landed beside the first.

Melissa looked toward the door. Her face stiffened, and soon, tears filled her eyes. "Sebastian . . . ?"

Bettinger clapped handcuffs onto the stunned woman's wrists and ankles. Massaging his hurt side, he stood upright and looked toward the door.

A reddish-black crater had replaced the bottom half of Sebastian's face. Three molars sat in the exposed roof of his mouth, directly above a white splinter that was all that remained of his jawbone. His death was imminent.

Tackley dragged his bound and unconscious captive to the door by what remained of her bloody hair.

Bettinger searched the judge's chamber for what he needed, found the object in a plastic container, and carried it toward the gurney. A song that had played at his wedding emanated from the stereo, which was connected to a small solar generator.

The mottled man pocketed his ski mask and looked at the blasted invalid. "So I'll interview the women instead."

Tears sparkled in Sebastian's eyes.

Yellow teeth appeared between Tackley's milk-white lips when he saw what it was that Bettinger held.

"No!" yelled Melissa, struggling against her bonds. "No!"

Tackley handcuffed Sebastian's wrists to the gurney, seized his neck, and held him down.

Bettinger discarded his devil mask and jammed the stoma of a colostomy bag into the disabled man's mouth. "This is for my son and for my wife," said the detective, squeezing the pouch like a bagpipe.

Feces shot down Sebastian's throat.

"Stop!" yelled Melissa.

The disabled man convulsed, shuddered, and vomited. Stool and bile refilled the colostomy bag, and Bettinger squeezed it again, sending the warm excreta back down his victim's throat.

Again, Sebastian retched. Brown fluid sprayed into the bag and squirted from his nostrils.

The detective withdrew the stoma, sprayed vomit and feces into his victim's eyes, and stepped away from the rank mess, discarding the pouch. His heart was pounding.

Blinded by excrement, Sebastian Ramirez lost consciousness. It was clear that he would never again awaken.

"You fucking animals!" yelled Melissa. "You crippled him, you killed our baby, and now—"

Tackley stepped on her mouth, eyed his associate, and motioned to the door. "Go help Dominic."

Bettinger's blood grew cold. "What're you gonna do to her?"

"Go help Dominic." The mottled man pointed to a set of keys that lay atop a television set. "Find that blue jeep."

Melissa turned away from Tackley's heel and gasped. "Don't leave me with him. Please don't—"

The mottled man kicked the young woman in the stomach, knocking the air out of her system.

Bettinger's pulse raced. His voice was hard when he asked, "What're you gonna do to her?"

"Stuff." The mottled man rested his hand upon the grip of his assault rifle. "Take comfort in the fact that you can't stop me."

A red dot landed upon the detective's thigh.

"Go help Dominic."

Earlier that day, the detective had defined his two objectives: Kill Sebastian and stay alive. He could not risk his life—and the future well-being of his wife and daughter—for a woman who had facilitated mass murder.

It was time for him to leave.

Jaw clenched, Bettinger snatched the car keys and walked toward the exit. The smells of blood and excrement filled his head.

"Meet me on the ground floor of the garage," said Tackley. "This shouldn't take more than an hour."

The detective covered his face with the devil mask.

Melissa wept.

Sickened, Bettinger circumvented Sebastian's corpse and Margarita's unconscious body. As he stepped over the duffel bag, he saw the pair of shiny items that the mottled man had taken from the cardboard box of kitchen supplies.

The objects were cheese graters.

Bettinger hastened across the floorboards of the pine green waiting area. Something whimpered behind him, and he could not tell if it was one of the women or one of the dogs.

# LI

# Partners

Suppressing hideous thoughts, the detective walked down the carpeted hallway, crawled through the tunnel, landed in the van, opened its side door, and entered the subterranean level of the parking garage. There, he turned on his tactical light and swung it in an arc. The bright beam divined no inhabitants.

Bettinger walked toward the exit, passing by rotten boxes and dead cars. A rat scurried from one vehicle to another for some purpose that made no more sense than did any of the terrible events that had occurred in Victory during the past twenty-four hours.

Ahead of him stood the entrance to the stairwell. A piece of cardboard that Tackley had wedged between the door and the jamb was still in place, holding it open.

Bettinger pointed his tactical light at the ground directly in front of the portal. Sitting in the luminous circle were familiar paw prints, the tread marks of his boots, and the small footprints of his mottled associate.

The detective killed his beam, approached the door, and put his shoulder to the wall. There, he turned his ear to the narrow opening and listened.

Thick breathing sounded inside of the stairwell. The pitch of these ugly respirations was familiar.

"Dominic?"

"Yeah."

"I'm coming up."

Bettinger turned on his tactical light and entered the stairwell.

Dominic coughed. "What happened?"

"We killed Sebastian."

The detective climbed toward the landing where the big fellow was sitting.

"Where's Tackley?"

"Getting information from Melissa."

"You make Sebastian suffer?"

"Yeah."

"Good."

Bettinger ascended, his footfalls amplified by the acoustics. "Right now, we need to find that blue jeep."

"Okay." Dominic pulled his ski mask over his lacerated face.

The detective reached the landing and helped his partner to his feet. It looked like the big fellow had applied an entire roll of duct tape to his bad ankle.

"You can walk?"

"Yeah." Dominic gripped the rail, hunched forward, and began to climb. "Took more of those painkillers."

"Let's get out on the ground floor and go up the ramps." Bettinger assumed that the doors to the other levels would be locked, and he desperately needed to see some daylight.

"Okay."

The big fellow reached the landing and winced as he leaned against the wall. His shoulders rose and fell like those of a person who had just run a race.

The detective stalked to the door, cracked it open, and listened. Nothing was audible except for his partner's heavy respirations.

Bettinger peered through the opening. Diffused daylight illuminated the ground floor of the garage, which appeared to be uninhabited.

The detective leveled his gun and walked through the doorway. His partner followed after him, limping, but did not greatly inhibit their rate of progress.

"Are the Dobermans okay?"

Bettinger looked back to see if Dominic was joking. Genuine concern showed in his small eyes.

"Tackley shot them."

The big fellow looked down and shook his head. "I guess he had to."

"Watch out," said Bettinger, pointing out a hole in the floor that was a skylight for the nether level. A latticework of rusty pipes covered half of the opening.

Dominic limped around the hole. "Thanks."

"You should stay here." The detective gestured at the inclined ramp that led to the second level. "I'll go up and find the jeep."

"I can make it."

Bettinger shrugged.

The masked policemen continued across the parking garage. As they passed the beheaded vagrant, the detective accidentally kicked a chunk of ice that had some wisdom teeth.

"How'd you do it?" asked Dominic.

"What?"

"How did you kill him? Sebastian?"

"Talk to the little guy."

"Don't want to get into it?"

"I won't get into it."

Together, the partners strode toward the ramp. The sounds of their labored strides bounced in every direction.

"Well I wanna thank you for what you did," said the big fellow. "You figured it all out—with Slick Sam and the whistles—and we never would've found them if it wasn't for you."

Bettinger slammed a fist into Dominic's mouth.

The big fellow staggered backward. "What the fu—"

The detective pounded his partner's nose, snapping the cartilage.

Dominic reeled, stunned by the blow.

Pain shot up Bettinger's knuckles, and as he set his feet apart in a fighting stance, he discarded his ballistic mask and his gun. His eyes were stinging.

Dominic tore off his hood and spat blood. "What the fuck's wrong with you?"

The detective slammed a right hook into his partner's ear, knocking him to one knee.

Bettinger chambered his left leg.

"Stop this shit right now," Dominic warned, "or I'll k—"

The detective's right boot thudded against the big fellow's tactical vest.

Dominic toppled, falling backward onto the homeless man. A frozen arm snapped off and slid across the concrete.

Tears poured down Bettinger's face. Raising his fists, he charged at his partner.

Dominic dove forward, grabbed the detective's legs, and upended him.

Cold concrete slammed against Bettinger's hurt side, and the pain that shot through his body felt like a flamethrower burning raw nerves. Agonized, he yelled.

Dominic slammed a forearm against his partner's vest, forcing the air from his lungs.

Bettinger threw a knee into the big fellow's stomach, and a huge closed fist hammered his right ear. Just as it began to ring, Dominic pounded it again.

Gasping for air, the big fellow said, "Don't make me—"

The detective stomped on his partner's bad ankle.

A yell exploded from Dominic's mouth, filling the garage.

Bettinger got to his knees, made a claw with his right hand, and slashed his fingertips across the big fellow's face, tearing scabs and stitches.

Dominic yelled and slammed on his back, his face bleeding in a dozen places. "That's it!"

Bettinger swung.

The big fellow grabbed his partner's wrist and twisted it around. Bright pain filled the detective's right shoulder and exploded when the bone popped out of its socket.

Shouting, Bettinger collapsed.

Dominic released his partner's dislocated limb, gasped for air, and sat up. "For a smart guy . . . you're a fuckin' idiot."

The detective pushed at the ground with his left hand and rose to his knees. His right shoulder radiated a sharp screaming pain that filled his entire body.

The big fellow wiped loose stitches and bits of skin from his face. "What the fuck's all this?"

Bettinger lunged at Dominic.

The big fellow grabbed his partner's neck and slammed his face into the ground. Cracked concrete was all that the detective could see.

Dominic spat and pressed a knee into the prone man's spine. "I ain't gonna let you up until—"

The detective threw his left elbow, but a big hand slapped it away.

Again, Dominic spat. "I ain't gonna let you up until you're sorted out."

Tears dripped from Bettinger's eyes onto the concrete. His body was a place where assorted mental and physical traumas had gathered.

"You through with this?" inquired Dominic.

The inside of the detective's mouth tasted like blood and stone, and he no longer knew how to talk. Less than an inch away from his eyes, tears pooled.

Again, the big fellow asked, "You through?"

Bettinger thought of Alyssa and Karen, who were waiting for him at the hospital in Stonesburg. Concrete rubbed against his face, scouring it like sandpaper, and he soon realized that he was nodding his head yes. The pressures on his neck and spine disappeared, and big hands rolled him onto his back. Overhead loomed the rotten ceiling of the parking garage and his partner's tattered face.

"Take them." Dominic put two blue pills in Bettinger's left hand.

"What—" The detective coughed. "What are they?" His voice was a harsh croak.

"Painkillers."

"What k-kind?"

The big fellow shrugged. "The kind Tackley's been on since he broke his back."

"When'd that happen?"

"'Ninety-four."

Bettinger sat up. Fires had replaced his insides, and all around him, the garage wobbled. A firm hand landed upon his shoulders, steadying him as he put the blue pills into his mouth and choked them down with blood.

# LII

# Return of the Ugly Men

Every footstep jogged Bettinger's dislocated shoulder and injured ribs, but the narcotic made his pains bearable. Hobbling up the ramp, he felt removed from reality, as if he were walking around in an old movie, and he wondered how Tackley was able to remain quick and sharp while under the influence of such powerful medication.

"That wasn't because of what I did to your car?" asked Dominic. "Back there?"

"I'm gonna pretend that question's rhetorical."

The partners soon reached the second level. Part of the ceiling had collapsed, and a heap of rubble sat directly ahead of them.

Bettinger shone his tactical light toward the left side of the obstruction, illuminating tracks that had been made by a set of off-road tires. The ambling duo followed these around the heap and through a motley collection of cars that were burned or capsized or both.

Dominic's beam landed on a warped shopping cart, and the partners paused. Lying upon the rotten blanket that covered the bottom of the basket was a nude black infant. The frozen baby had died with its eyes and mouth wide open.

"Should we do something?" asked the big fellow.

Bettinger limped away from the tableau and did not stop until he found the blue jeep.


Heat blew from the dashboard vents, warming the battered policemen as they waited for the third member of their group on the ground level of the parking garage.

Dominic lifted a hand from the steering wheel, stabbed an index finger into the radio, and wrenched the dial. Static hissed on every station, and Bettinger wondered if perhaps the civilized world had ended during their absence. Eleven hours had passed since he had awakened in the Sunflower Motel, but the elapsed time felt like a century.

Leaning over, the big fellow opened the glove compartment, looked inside, and withdrew two jewel boxes. "Had pretty good taste in music," he said as he slotted a compact disc into the console. A bass drum thudded in the speakers, jarring the detective's nose, ribs, and dislocated shoulder, and black men who might have been tone deaf filled the air with immodest rhymes.

Bettinger looked through the exit at the Heaps. The blizzard had ended, and the lumpy piles of pure white powder that he saw resembled stratocumulus clouds.

"It's like the shittiest Heaven ever."

Shortly after three o'clock, Tackley emerged from the stairwell, wearing the duffel bag on his left shoulder and the ski mask over his face. A series of quick strides brought him to the driver's side of the jeep, where he opened the rear door.

"You get the names of the killers?" asked Dominic.

"I did." The mottled man climbed into the backseat, closed the door, and thumbed the lock.

Bad smells filled the vehicle.

"The middlemen too?" asked the big fellow.

"Those were just fiction. Melissa and Margarita did everything for Sebastian while he was in ICU—even went to Florida and Illinois to send the letters."

This information did not make Bettinger feel any better about what had happened to the women.

Tackley slapped the wall of the jeep as if he were killing a gnat. "This thing should be able to handle the snow."

"Should."

Dominic shifted gears and accelerated. As the jeep rolled toward the exit, daylight shone upon the swollen, bruised, and bloodied faces of the men who sat up front.

"What the hell happened to you two?" asked Tackley.

Neither Bettinger nor Dominic offered a reply.

"You did that to each other?"

The big fellow shrugged.

A tire shattered the vagrant's hand as the jeep left the parking garage. Sunlight surrounded the vehicle, and three cell phones buzzed.

Bettinger reached his good arm across his body, seized the plaintive device, and tilted his foggy skull. The screen told him that he had thirty-seven missed calls and fourteen messages.

"Hold on," said Tackley. "There's something that we need to discuss right now."

Bettinger and Dominic eyed the mottled man through the rearview mirror.

"The killers are national," Tackley stated, "and we'll need to figure out a credible source for their names before contacting the feds."

Snow squeaked beneath the mud-terrain tires as Bettinger ruminated. "I'll say I found a list in that cooler. It doesn't make complete sense why he'd have it, but he's guilty and dead, and nobody can cross-examine him."

The mottled man considered the proposal for a moment. "That should work."

"You'd better dispose of this jeep too."

"We know guys."

"And leave Slick Sam outside an emergency room."

"Sure we will."

Tackley's sincerity was dubious, but Bettinger had no interest in getting shot over a felon who might already be dead and frozen in a downtown basement.

Nobody asked about the women.

After a brief moment of silence, the policemen raised their cell phones.

Bettinger highlighted his wife's name and pressed the connect button. His right ear was still ringing from the two heavy blows that Dominic had landed there, and thus, he clapped the receiver to the opposite side of his head. The rapper boasted about gangbanging a white bitch, and the detective slammed the heel of his right boot into the console, silencing the misogynist.

Dominic and Tackley exchanged a glance in the rearview mirror.

"Nigga's gone psycho crazy."

Bettinger listened to the phone ring, thinking about botched surgical procedures and MRSA brain infections—terrorized by his own imagination.

Somebody picked up on the other end.

"Jules?"

The voice belonged to Alyssa.

Relief flooded through the detective's body, and a moment later, he relaxed his muscles and remembered how to breathe. "How'd the surgery go?"

"You're okay?"

"Yes. How was the surgery?"

"Fine. Was asleep until an hour ago—they just brought Karen up."

"Dr. Edwards is comfortable with how everything looks?"

"Yeah."

"How's Karen?"

"She's okay. Really quiet."

Bettinger knew that he could not talk about his daughter right now. "You feel okay?"

"Yeah—though pretty numb. Are you hurt? You sound different."

"I'm fine."

"You . . . did what you needed to?"

"I did." There was some satisfaction, yet no pride in this statement.

"So you're done?"

"Completely. As soon as Dr. Edwards says you're okay, we'll pack up and go back to Arizona."

There was a silence on the line, and Bettinger knew that Alyssa was fighting back tears. The two of them were no longer in any immediate danger, and now they had to face life without their son.

Snow crackled underneath the tires of the jeep, and the detective cleared his throat. "I'll call when I'm close."

"Okay."

"Love you."

"I love you too."

Bettinger disconnected the line and pocketed his cell phone. Leaning back in his seat, he observed the mountains of powder that comprised the Heaps.

Dominic eyed his partner. "You leavin' Victory?"

"Instantly."

"Ain't curious 'bout that Elaine James case you started?"

"Not curious enough."

The big fellow shrugged.

Pressing deep furrows into the blanket, the jeep rolled toward the tank.

"Zwolinski is alive," announced Tackley.

"Fuckin' right he is!" Dominic slapped the dashboard. "Like I said when we boxed—the dude's indestructible."

Bettinger was pleased to hear that the inspector was still alive. "Where's he been?"

"I'll play the messages. He's medicated and rambles for a while." The mottled man swallowed some pills and set his cell phone upon the cup holder that divided the front seats.

"Fifth message," announced a female robot. "Twelve thirteen P.M."

"Tackley," barked Zwolinski. "I got your messages.

"I'm in ICU—I don't remember gettin' here, and things are sorta fuzzy, so I want to let you know what happened—all of it—before I go into surgery."

A hospital machine beeped, and somebody muttered something.

"I'll call you back."

The line clicked, and the female robot said, "Sixth message. Twelve thirty-two P.M."

"It's Zwolinski. Here's what happened.

"I was in my apartment, waitin' for Vanessa to come over—got the wine and everythin'—but when she buzzes, I know somethin's wrong—that somebody's taken her hostage. They're all comin' up the hall together, and as I'm gettin' ready for 'em, these two black guys ambush me from behind. One points a scattergun at my head, and the other's got a pistol. They tell me to drop my revolver, and I do. They relax.

"Mistake.

"I duck left and come in with an uppercut. It's like round seven of that rematch of Tyler versus Billings, except when I land my punch, there's no padded glove, and I shatter the guy's jaw—the one who's got the scattergun.

"It's beautiful.

"He drops his weapon, and when I go for it, the other guy shoots. The bullet hits my shoulder, knocks me flat. It stings, but I've been shot before.

"Plenty.

"I grab the scattergun and shoot the guy with the pistol—right in the neck. The other guy's on his knees, holding his face, and his jaw looks about as firm as a tit on a ninety-year-old.

"I'm on my feet, throwin' a hook into the ear of the one I just shotgunned. The pellets had done a number on his neck, and my punch rips his head right off his shoulders.

"Things are lookin' good.

"I turn back to finish off the other one, and I hear Vanessa scream, right outside the door. A guy who's with her says, 'Open up or she's dead.'

"So this's a shitty situation I'm in.

"I tell 'em, 'Hold on,' and look to see how many guys're out there, but it's dark 'cause they covered up the peephole.

"So they're a little smarter than the idiots they sent inside.

"I tell 'em, 'I'll kill both your guys unless you let my wife go right now.' And I say it just like that—I call Vanessa my wife—and decide right then and there that we're married again. If we both die—or if just one of us goes—I want it to be that way.

"'Let my wife go,' I say—this time even louder.

"The guy says, 'You have ten seconds to come out.'

"Nobody gives me the countdown. In the ring or in life—it just doesn't happen.

"He starts countin', and the world goes red.

"I gouge out the eyes of the guy with the smashed jaw—keep him alive in case I need a hostage—and while he's screamin', I put on that bulletproof vest that I keep on the coatrack.

"People always make fun of me for keepin' that there, but here's why I did it.

"I pick up the other guy's head and carry it to the door, though I can't remember exactly what I was gonna do with it.

"Taunt 'em, maybe?

"Throw it?

"I'm not really sure.

"I start to undo the chain, and the door explodes. Splinters and shotgun pellets burst everywhere, into my right hand and arm, though my vest takes most of the impact.

"Knocks me on my ass.

"Through the hole in the door, I hear Vanessa scream and the sound of guys runnin'. They're gettin' away, and I know they've still got her.

"I get up, and I've gotta look worse than Victor did after ten rounds with Upwell. The palm of my right hand is covered with blood and looks like a chew toy, so I squirt it with superglue and make a fist.

"Clench hard.

"The bleeding stops, though now it's like a club or somethin'.

"Since I've only got one workin' hand, I put the keys in my mouth—which'll also keep 'em from jinglin'—and put the glue in a slot on my vest. I grab my gun and run aft—"

A click precluded the rest of the inspector's sentence, and the blue jeep rolled south, compressing powder.

"There's more?" asked Bettinger.

Tackley nodded.

Dominic steered around a crater that looked like it belonged on the surface of the moon, and the phone beeped.

"Seventh message," announced the female robot. "Twelve thirty-six P.M."

"It told me my message exceeded the time limit," said Zwolinski.

"I hope it saved it all.

"So I run up the hall with my keys in my mouth and my gun in my left hand, wearin' my bulletproof vest and boxer shorts like I'm some kinda fugitive stripper.

"I get outside and see a brown cargo van tearin' through the lot—they had a driver waitin'—and I know this's the bunch that killed Gianetto and Stanley and took a shot at Nancy.

"I get in big blue, start the engine, go after 'em.

"Go after Vanessa.

"It's dark, but I keep my lights off.

"When I get to Summer Drive, I see 'em pass through an intersection. They've got their lights off too, and when I see that, I feel this weird calm come over me.

"Victory is my enemy, my archrival. I've spent decades studyin' how he fights, how he moves, how he hits, where he can take a hit, and where he can't. He beat me when he took my daughter, and he beat me when he ended my marriage, but I've beaten him too—hundreds of times—and I never left the ring.

"Not once.

"So whoever's inside that brown cargo van has a major disadvantage. They can't possibly know Victory like I do.

"It's beyond impossible.

"So I follow 'em—two or three blocks behind—givin' 'em plenty of air, stayin' in the shadows. I keep my lights off, and whenever there's a streetlamp, I weave.

"I'm like Lightnin' McDaniels—the Irish Phantom.

"Victory throws some jabs at them—potholes, detours, roadkill—and after they almost lose a tire, they turn on their lights—includin' their hazards for some reason.

"A cadet could follow 'em now.

"I hang back even farther—four blocks between us, sometimes five. It's like steppin' into the ring with a toddler.

"They slow down, and so do I. They pull onto a side street, and I know they're about to do somethin'.

"I reach the corner and see 'em drivin' toward a parkin' garage. I go on past, speed up the next block, circle back.

"By the time I get there, they're gone, but I'm not worried. I know they're in that parking garage—probably switchin' vehicles.

"So they're in the corner—got the turnbuckle at their back. I park outside the garage, put the keys in my mouth, grab my gun, go in.

"The ground floor's empty, so I go up the steps to the next level. They're not there either, but I hear some voices above me and climb up to three.

"I get there, stayin' in the shadows, and I see the brown van and three guys walkin' away from it, toward a white town car.

"I don't see Vanessa. They didn't drop her off anywhere, so I know she's still in that van.

"I want to beat these assholes to death, but she's my priority, and I just let 'em get in their white town car and drive off.

"I run over to the van and try the door, which is locked. I break the window with the handle of my gun, unlock it, climb inside. Vanessa's there, lyin' on her stomach under the bench, not movin', and there's blood all over her. Every muscle in my body goes rigid, and I bite down on the keys in my mouth, and it's like that day in the emergency room with my daughter all over again, and I'm just frozen.

"Paralyzed.

"Then she breathes.

"I spit out the keys, put down the gun, get her on the bench. Her blouse is covered with blood, and as I'm unbuttonin' it to see what the wounds look like, I notice somethin' on the floor in between the front seats, and all of a sudden, I know things are about to get complicated.

"It's a thirty-eight that's lyin' there.

"One of these morons—probably the physicist who put on the hazard lights for no reason—left his goddamn gun in the van, and I know they'll be comin' back to get it.

"Let me call you back before your stupid machine cuts me—"

The line clicked, disconnecting, and a moment later, the female robot said, "Eighth message. Twelve forty-one P.M."

"Your phone's an asshole," declared Zwolinski.

"So we're in the cargo van, and I know the crooks're comin' back soon. I put Vanessa under the bench, shut the passenger door, crouch down, though there's nothin' I can do 'bout that broken window.

"I hear a car.

"Headlights pan across the garage like it's a stalag, throwin' long black shadows all over the place. I look in the side-view mirror and see the white town car pullin' up.

"It stops.

"The back door opens, and a black guy who looks like William Watkins Jr.—the featherweight champ from 'eighty-two—gets out, and the driver, a white guy with curly black hair, says, 'I think I put it in the glove compartment.'

"Obviously, this moron's the one who put the hazards on.

"So the guy who looks like William Watkins Jr. puts a cigarette in his mouth, lights it up, and sucks cancer as he walks toward the van. He looks pissed, which he should be, since he's cleanin' up after Mr. Hazard Lights and is about to get executed.

"I'm crouchin' down, ready to shoot, watchin' the mirror, and the closer he gets, the more he looks like William Watkins Jr., and there's a moment where I think, 'Am I about to shoot the featherweight champion of 'eighty-two?

"Obviously, I'm a little out of it—this guy looks how William Watkins Jr. looked over thirty years ago. And if it happens to be William Watkins Jr.'s son, then he picked the wrong type of work.

"So he gets close, and when the smoke clears from his face, he sees that the glass is broken, and I shoot him in the head.

"Twice."

"Zwolinski's a good shot," Dominic informed Bettinger. "Got a good percentage."

"I send two through the windshield on the driver's side, and Mr. Hazard Lights is done. The passenger door opens up, and the last guy bolts. I fire at his legs until he drops, and when he starts crawlin', I pick up the thirty-eight and shoot until he stops movin'.

"So that's it for these guys.

"I put Vanessa on the bench, undo her shirt, find the wounds—she was stabbed twice in the stomach—and glue 'em shut. Her vitals are low, and it's clear she's lost a lot of blood.

"I think.

"The hospital's thirty minutes from there—we're in the fringe—and I'm not sure how long she's got or if they even have any blood in the bank.

"I grab the keys and a cell phone from William Watkins Jr. and drive out of the garage, takin' Vanessa with me. I go two blocks over—into what used to be the Fountain Park area—and find a drug house.

"Plenty of choices over there.

"I break down the door, go up a hall, find a den. Addicts are sprawled on the couches like fungus, and they just stare at me, confused. I'm there in my boxer shorts and ballistic vest, have a glued-up club hand, and am covered with blood. They probably think I'm a hallucination, and they're certainly hopin' I am.

"I slap a guy to prove I'm real, and I tell him to get me some syringes—new ones, still in the plastic, a box of 'em.

"He gets me a box, and I take it to the van.

"I sit next to Vanessa, who's still alive, but weaker than before.

"She's on her way out.

"I'm not a handsome man. My back isn't great, and I don't have all the reach a guy my size should have, but there's one physical attribute I'm real proud of.

"My blood's type O negative—the universal donor.

"I fill up a syringe—usin' my good hand to hold the needle and my mouth to draw the plunger—find a vein in her arm, and give her my blood. Not too fast, but not too slow either.

"I do it again, and when the blood clots up the needle, I get a new one.

"Somewhere around the fifth or sixth, I start to get real dizzy. That's when I call the hospital and tell 'em where we are.

"I hang up and fill another syringe, and I keep givin' until things go dark.

"Then I wake up here.

"Vanessa's still unconscious and in ICU. I know she's gonna make it, and the doctors think so too.

"That's my blood in there . . . and it knows how to fight."

Dominic dialed the wheel, circumventing a lump of powder, and the bones of a pigeon snapped underneath the tires.

Zwolinski cleared his throat. "See you tomorrow mornin' at Gianetto's funeral. We go back to work right after, so bring a change of clothes."

The line went dead.

Bettinger shut his eyes. Snow crackled as he relinquished pain, consciousness, and the city of Victory.

# LIII

# Excisions

Bettinger, Alyssa, and Karen returned to Arizona. Very few people attended the short, private funeral service that they held there for Gordon.

No speeches were made at this gathering.

The media celebrated the detective, who was publicly credited with stopping one of the killers, saving (most of) his family, and acquiring a list that identified all of the paid gunmen, the living remainder of which were promptly arrested and returned to Victory.

A lot of these men died in jail.

Bettinger's reward was an office in the exact same precinct that had expelled him approximately two months earlier. There was no small amount of resentment on either side of this reunion, which had been mandated by government officials in both Missouri and Arizona.

Inspector Kerry Ladell rose from his wide wood desk and extended his hand. "Welcome back."

"If you give me your condolences, I'll break your teeth," warned Bettinger.

"That's how it's gonna be with us?"

"People shouldn't live in the cold."

The inspector returned to his leather seat, which sighed as if it were exasperated. "Five years is a long time to be an asshole . . . though I suppose you're an expert."

"I know upon whom to shit."

"It's like you never left."

"My family might disagree with that. Those that can."

A poisonous silence hung between Bettinger and the man who had sent him north.

Nobody apologized to anybody, and the detective returned to work, ignoring his boss and his peers. Some people were transformed by tragedy, and others were gentled by such experiences, but the main difference between the old Bettinger and the new one was that the new one had a lot more nightmares.

Karen returned to the middle school that she had previously attended, but she did not socialize with the children that had once been her friends nor anybody else. Her grades were still very good, and whenever she was not studying, she did puzzle books (Sudoku and crosswords) or watched game shows or did both simultaneously, continually filling her mind with numbers, words, and trivia. The reason for this behavior was obvious to the child psychologist whom she visited as well as both of her parents, but they did not discourage her. There were far worse ways of coping with trauma.

In March, Alyssa Bright had her first show at the David Rubinstein Gallery of Chicago.

Although it was a group exhibition, the monocular painter had received a lot more attention than had any of her peers, primarily because of the interviews that she had done for *Bold Canvas*, two national newspapers, and an assortment of periodicals throughout Arizona, Missouri, and Illinois. These articles had focused far more on the woman's personal tragedies than her art and were not added to the family scrapbook.

Bettinger knew that Alyssa was conflicted about the attention that she was receiving. To some degree, the media was exploiting her disfigurement, the Police Murders (as the press had dubbed the event in Victory), and worst of all, Gordon's death. Half of the woman's paintings sold at the exhibition, but this success was small and nearly joyless.

The couple made love on the final night of their stay, but it was a dark and anonymous endeavor. Bettinger's nose had healed badly, and his right ear was a lump, swollen by the abuse that it had received from Dominic. His face had changed and so had Alyssa's ability to look at it.

Once again, the couple returned to Arizona.

In April, the burned bodies of Sebastian Ramirez, Margarita Ramirez, Melissa Spring, and Slick Sam (whose real name was Reginald B. Garrison II) were discovered in a fringe sewer, and several photographs surfaced on the Internet. Bettinger and Alyssa had never discussed what had happened in Victory on the day of the blizzard, and he did not know or ask if she had seen these gruesome images.

The detective did not sleep very well that month. Most of his nightmares were deeds that he could never discuss.

In May, David Rubinstein sent an e-mail to Alyssa in which he requested pieces for an upcoming show that would feature her and only one other artist. The gallery owner stated that he was only interested in new works.

Conflicted by the opportunity, the woman thought upon what she should paint, if anything. Two weeks of desultory efforts resulted in a pile of abandoned canvases, several of which she had ripped apart in fits of anger.

Lying abed in the room where Karen had been conceived, the couple conversed. Bettinger raised the subject of paintings and listened to Alyssa talk about how hard it was to create art when their son was dead and their daughter was a stranger.

"Have you tried to put some of what happened in your work?" the detective asked the pile of curls that pressed against his bare chest.

"I don't want to do pieces like that—be identified as a victim. I can't stand that 'poor me' shit."

"You're not that kind of artist—or person—but you're angry. Maybe you should put that on the canvas."

"Anger?"

"About what happened to our kids. To you. The way some critics talk about your eye and Gordon like they're your gimmicks."

"Fuck them."

"Say that with your brush."

"Like art therapy?"

"Like that. Don't come up with a concept, just trust in your techniques, which are fantastic, and let it out."

Bettinger wanted—and perhaps needed—to see paintings like these.

Alyssa kissed his left pectoral muscle. "I'll try."

A few minutes later, the painter returned to her workshop.

Bettinger opened up a novel, reclined, and read about some cowboys who were far less intelligent than the horses upon which they sat. A couple of chapters galloped him to the edge of consciousness, where he slotted a bookmark, yawned, and switched off the light.

At three in the morning, the detective was drawn from his nightmare by warm kisses upon his neck and the caress of fingertips along his engorged phallus. Alyssa turned on the bedside lamp, and in its amber radiance, the couple made love.


Discrete track lighting shone upon the twenty-two new paintings that adorned the exposed brick walls of the David Rubinstein Gallery of Chicago. Admiring these works, Bettinger buttoned the jacket of his brown suit and walked toward the bar. Tonight was the public opening of Alyssa Bright's third exhibition, and her very first as a solo artist. The new series of oil paintings, entitled *Excisions,* was dark, but not as oppressive as its predecessor, *Exsanguination,* which the detective appreciated, but had been unable to look at without feeling ill.

"Three glasses of champagne, please."

"Certainly, Mr. Bright," said the narrow white woman who was the bartender. She was not the first person to give Bettinger his wife's last name, and the proud husband offered the server a grin rather than a correction.

Three crystal flutes were expertly arranged on the silver linen and filled with champagne.

"Thank you," remarked the detective, setting a bill upon the table.

"Sir . . . you don't need to tip."

"Mr. Bright's a big spender."

Bettinger claimed the celebratory fluids and turned away from the table. The monetary yield from the second exhibition greatly exceeded what the detective made in a year, and although he and his wife did not consider themselves wealthy, they could now afford luxuries that had previously been out of their reach.

Carrying the bubbling flutes, Bettinger neared David Rubinstein and Alyssa. The forty-seven-year-old woman wore a green, single-strap dress, a sparkling smile, and glasses that had one black lens. Behind her bare left shoulder was a painting of a vaguely demonic face that had been rendered in iridescent oils and slashed with a box cutter.

The detective handed drinks to his wife and the pristine gallery owner. "I look forward to another very successful show."

"Hopefully," said the painter.

"Definitely."

"Listen to your husband, my dear, or I'll have him muzzle you," remarked David Rubinstein, whose social manner and sexual preference could be described with the same three-letter word. "Unless he does that already . . . ?"

"I'm an authority figure," said Bettinger.

The rheumy old man who lived inside of Alyssa's chest snickered.

There was no sound in the world that the detective enjoyed as much as his wife's hideous laughter.

Raising a glass, Bettinger said, "To Alyssa Bright's third and most successful exhibition."

The painter nodded. "Deal."

Crystal clinked, and soon, the trio rolled champagne into their curved mouths.

A cell phone buzzed inside of the detective's pocket, but he ignored the interruption and let the call go to voice mail.

Two Asian women who were either journalists or admirers or both approached Alyssa, and Bettinger took his wife's glass and departed so that the coming conversation would not be altered by his presence. Tonight was her night.

People with loud voices, louder perfume, and very expensive sweaters came through the front door as Bettinger returned the flutes to the bar and found a quiet corner. There, he removed his cell phone and looked at the display, which showed the name "Williams, Dominic." The detective had not spoken to the big fellow since the day of the blizzard.

Irked, Bettinger put the receiver to his ear and listened to the message.

"It's Dominic. Solved the Elaine James case if you wanna hear."

The line went dead.

On more than a few occasions, the detective had pondered the abandoned case, and although he was loath to speak to his former partner, it seemed that one quick phone call would allow him to forever excise the odious matter from his mind.

"Christ's uncle."

Bettinger returned to Alyssa, placed a kiss upon her cheek, turned away, opened the front door, and entered the air-conditioned walkway of the luxury mall that housed the gallery. Sitting on a bench, he thumbed a connection and put the receiver to his ear.

"Hey," said Dominic.

"What happened?"

"Me and Brian—my new partner—started with them files you pulled—the ones for the other dead hookers. We went to the scenes, checked 'em out, and found tripod marks like you did on Ganson. But when we pulled samples from the bodies, there was different DNA in each of 'em.

"So it's multiple niggas killin' hookers and fuckin' them in front of cameras—like a new trend or somethin'." It sounded like the big fellow was grinning. "You wanna take a guess what's goin' on here?"

All of the anger that Bettinger had felt toward his partner and Tackley and the city of Victory and himself resurfaced. "I want this conversation to end as quickly as possible and have no sequel."

"Grouchy-ass nigga. Sure don't sound like that Arizona air's doin' you any good."

"I don't have long."

"So there's a gang called the Angels—they've been around a long, long time, runnin' operations. Stealthy. They used to have initiations like liftin' a car or takin' a dealer's stash or killin' a guy in another gang, but this here's what they got now."

Bettinger was confused. "What is?"

"This Elaine James situation. It's what a young nigga's gotta do to get in with the Angels and prove his loyalty. Grab a hooker from a rival operation, kill her, and videotape himself fuckin' the body—showin' his face and sayin' his name to the camera while he's doin' it. Once he makes this tape, he gives it to the head guy in the Angels, and that movie's like collateral—insurance that'll guarantee the young guy stays loyal for life."

The detective felt ill. "Fucking Christ."

"Yeah."

A slim and pretty redhead who looked like a fashion model walked past the bench, holding an infant inside of a thickly padded harness.

"Victory isn't a place for women," said Bettinger.

"It ain't."

"You get the guys?"

"Indelicately."

The Elaine James case was closed, and this call had served its purpose. "Thanks for letting me know."

"You was involved—started the whole thing off. Who knows what you could do if you was still here . . . ?"

"I'll pretend that question's rhetorical."

"How's that desk job treatin' you?" Dominic's voice had a mocking tone. "Got all them pencils lined up nice and correct?"

"I'm with my wife right now, and she's happy."

Bettinger thumbed the disconnect button.